THE SPHINX SCROLLS

A BALLASHIELS MYSTERY

Stewart Ferris

Published by Accent Press Ltd 2016

ISBN 9781910939383

For Colin

Acknowledgements

When a novel gestates for twenty years between the initial spark of inspiration and its eventual publication, inevitably many people will have contributed towards the help, advice, feedback, ideas, nagging, sympathy, moral support, encouragement and cups of tea required to complete the project. So, with apologies to those left out simply because two decades is too long to remember everyone who may have played a part in this process, I wish to thank: Amanda Byfield for providing the glass of port that fuelled the first page of the first draft; Alastair Williams and Tim Bates for invaluable advice and feedback; Christophe Helmke for giving me first-hand experience of a Mayan archaeological dig; Dorie Simmonds for her infinite patience in waiting ten years for a first draft; Lynn Picknett for the priceless edits and suggestions without which Ratty would not have been let loose upon the world; my parents, without whom I wouldn't have been let loose upon the world; the staff and postgraduate students at Surrey University's Creative Writing department; and Penny Hunter, Rebecca Lloyd and Hazel Cushion for believing in this book and turning a twenty-year dream into reality. Finally, the biggest thank you goes to my wife Katia, who has done more than anyone to support, aid and inspire me to make this book happen.

'A ... record of the first destruction, and the changes that took place in the land ... falls between the paws of the Sphinx'

– Edgar Cayce, 1933

Abrasive dust filled the rough-hewn tunnel. Dr Ruby Towers called for a vacuum hose and held a protective mask to her mouth. Now she knew why her team members had complained so vehemently about cutting into limestone in that confined space. After each ten minute shift they would come out of the passage shaking and coughing. So she had taken her turn, enduring the same deafening roar, the same choking heat as the rest of them. And she had been the one to break through.

She dropped the drill and wiped the grit from her goggles. Her pulse raced. After months of planning and overcoming bureaucratic hurdles, after weeks of scanning, measuring and arguing, and after days of gruelling tunnelling, this was her moment.

She poked her scuffed aluminium Maglite into the opening. Her eyes struggled to focus beyond the whirling particles picked out by the torch. It was frustrating, but the mere presence of airborne dust thrilled her. It signified an end to the section of rock. She ripped off the mask and goggles and waited for the cloud to dissipate. Now she could see her prize.

A chamber.

The space was cramped, smaller in dimension than some of the individual blocks used on the nearby pyramids. Objects were stacked in the centre of this timeless cavity. She counted them. Ten. They were clay tubes, just a few inches in diameter and no more than two feet in length. All were greyed by immense antiquity.

Was this the fabled Hall of Records? Was this the repository of the knowledge of a lost civilisation? Would this discovery finally unravel the mystery of the age and purpose of the Great Sphinx of Giza?

'Can we get the camera in here?' she shouted over her shoulder.

The documentary cameraman and the presenter squeezed alongside her in the narrow shaft. The cameraman pointed the lens at the presenter, former soldier Matt Mountebank.

'So tell us what you've found,' he said, with calm authority in his Manhattan accent.

The camera swung round to Ruby's face, almost pressing against her nose.

'We're directly beneath the flank of the Sphinx,' she announced, her voice excited and high pitched. 'This tunnel was begun a century ago by tomb robbers using explosives. Our scanners revealed a chamber just ahead, so we applied for permission to extend the tunnel to join up with that chamber. That way there will be no external damage to the monument. And now –'

She paused. Matt was pulling faces at her from behind the camera. As usual. She kicked him in the leg with her heavy Altberg boot.

He stopped.

'And now we're through,' she continued. 'This peephole is enough to prove that the Sphinx houses an archaeological treasure. The clay tubes will almost certainly contain scrolls. If they are intact and readable, the ancient riddle of the Sphinx could be solved. We might be about to find out who built it, when they did so, and why.'

'Turn off the camera. Everyone out.'

Ruby turned around. The Head of Antiquities was

silhouetted in the tunnel entrance, flanked by two police officers. Dr Shepsit Ibrahim did not appear to share Ruby's enthusiasm for the discovery.

'Keep rolling,' whispered Matt. 'This could be good.'

'Your licence has been revoked,' shouted Dr Ibrahim. 'This dig is finished.'

'You've got to be kidding, Shepsit!' protested Ruby. 'We've been working towards this for months. I've found the chamber. I can see there are clay tubes in there. I can probably pull them out without even widening the hole. We can't stop now!'

'I'm sorry, Ruby,' Ibrahim replied, her tone softening.

'But you're in charge, Shepsit. You can overrule this and get our licence back.'

'I'm the one stopping it, Ruby. It's over.'

Ruby felt as if she had been punched in the stomach.

'What about Cambridge? All those nights we stayed up, solving the problems of the world, dreaming of making discoveries like this. Doesn't that mean anything to you?'

Passionate tears began carving their way through the dust on Ruby's cheeks. Ibrahim's head bowed and she said nothing.

Ruby resisted the overpowering urge to slap her former college roommate as she stepped outside, police escort or not. In the unforgiving daylight, the two policemen seemed odd. Their uniforms didn't fit, and neither did their features: more Central American than Middle Eastern. She grudgingly acknowledged them in her limited Arabic and received no response. They remained curiously clamped to Ibrahim's side.

'What's got into you, Shepsit?' Ruby pleaded. 'And why are the police involved? This doesn't make any sense.'

Dr Ibrahim rolled her eyes sideways, left and right.

Ruby followed her gaze and looked at the police officers again. They seemed edgy. As they turned she noticed one of them was pressing something firmly into Ibrahim's back beneath a small rag.

A pistol.

Ruby glanced at Matt, fearing that his special forces training might tempt him to play the hero. His Gulf War memoirs were legendary. He was not a man to mess with.

'Don't try anything stupid,' she grunted. 'I don't want Shepsit hurt.'

'Sure,' he replied, surprising her with his willingness to concede defeat. The ex-warrior began to walk away from the site with the rest of her despondent team.

'Is that it, Matt? You're not going to do anything?'

'You just told me not to.'

'I know, but you must have some trick you can use to overpower them?'

'Rubes, those guys have guns. I got a damn microphone.'

Ruby stomped after him. More blatantly fake policemen had gathered at the perimeter, ushering people from the scene and clearing the way for their forthcoming escape. She stopped and glanced back at the Sphinx. It had survived Napoleon's soldiers using it for target practice. It had foiled tomb robbers for millennia. Now, dwarfed by the grandeur of the Pyramid of Khafre behind it, the Sphinx stared forward with serene nobility while thieves dressed in police uniforms plundered priceless secrets from its heart.

FRIDAY 5TH OCTOBER 2012

The turret room. Dark and disorderly. A sanctum of clutter. Nowhere could be better suited to the task of concealment.

The pace at which he scaled the tower's dizzying steps was out of proportion to his paltry level of fitness, all the more so considering the additional effort required to lug the artefact. He stumbled into the room and steadied himself against a cluster of broken Hepplewhite chairs, gulping stale air, scanning his surroundings: above, an ornate ceiling stained by his failure to repair the turret roof; right, Grinling Gibbons wall carvings, home to a colony of unappreciative woodworm; ahead, Regency chests of drawers stacked haphazardly; left, a sofa that reputedly once supported the grateful behind of Edward VII; everywhere else, tea chests, piles of books, papers and paintings, all illuminated by the muddy glow of windows caked with seven centuries of grime. This was the ideal place in which to lose the relic.

He opened a drawer. Too obvious. He looked behind a stack of portraits. Not enough space. Suddenly the suitability of the room was less apparent. Wherever he stashed it, she would stick her nose there sooner or later. He danced in panic, hugging the ancient piece of carved stone to his palpitating ribs. The door at the base of the spiral staircase slammed, sending a sinister echo up the steps to announce her impending arrival. He could now hear her clunky Altberg boots clomping closer to him. It was too much for him to process. The future of his home, his life, and his family tree depended on his ability to hide the stone stele.

The footsteps grew closer. The door handle twisted. The stele was still in his hands, decidedly unhidden. He glanced at the sofa.

'Why didn't you wait for me?' puffed Ruby Towers.

'Wanted to get a head start,' he replied, stretching out his legs and settling into the seat, wondering how he could get rid of his unexpected and unwanted guest. 'Can't find the confounded thing anywhere, though.'

'So rummage. I'm dying to see it. So is everyone at the museum.'

'Bit of trouble in the leg department,' he lied, knowing he needed to come up with something far more convincing. 'You go ahead.'

She sensed an awkward tone in his voice. Almost as if he didn't want her here today. Almost as if there was something more important in his life. There had never been anything in his life, important or otherwise. He was just Ratty being Ratty, she guessed.

'How could you lose it?' she asked him.

He braced himself as the horse-hair cushion beneath him sank lower in the frame under the combined weight of the stele and his backside.

'You said it could be worth a few spondoolies, so I placed it somewhere safe.'

'A few, but not a lot. The museum doesn't have very deep pockets, Ratty. They were thinking more of a token payment to you, that's all. So where did you put it?'

Here was a chance for him to tell her to mind her own business.

'Not sure, my little duck-billed platypus. The old neurons don't seem to want to talk to each other.' He cursed silently at his inability to stem the flow of mindless platitudes.

'You've forgotten? It was only a week ago that you said I could take it to London. I thought you were keen to find out what they would offer.'

'Well it's here somewhere,' he told her in a tone that he considered to be cutting, but which went unnoticed. 'I know it looks a tad harum-scarum, but it has all been organised and cleaned.'

'Organised and cleaned?' questioned Ruby, running a line through a layer of pearly dust with her finger.

'Absolutely. Yes. By the sixth Earl.'

'And which one are you?'

'Eighth.'

'Are we even in the right turret?' Ruby sighed.

'*Certes*, old coco plum,' he babbled, utterly at a loss as to how to extricate his life from her. Rudeness to a house guest was, in his eyes, a crime akin to treason. Telling her to leave and reneging on his offer to let the museum assess the stele was like unravelling a millennium of social breeding. He reverted to his safety net of banality. 'Had to close the other turret. Surveyor said it could fall down. Utter tommyrot, of course. They said that about the gamekeeper's cottage.'

'Part of the gamekeeper's cottage *did* fall down. You told me at Cambridge.'

'Quite, quite. Always wondered where he'd gone.'

Ruby began the task of sorting through the junk, tackling the job slowly and systematically as if it were an archaeological dig. But the joy that she normally experienced in excavating the past was absent today. Ratty was odd. His behaviour was noticeably weirder than usual.

'Awfully sorry about that Sphinx business, by the way,' he added.

'Shepsit thinks the thieves had Spanish accents. But that's all we have to go on. They disappeared before the real police could get there. At least no one was hurt.'

'I always thought they were such good eggs.'

'Eggs?'

'The Spanish.'

'Oh. Tell me more about what I'm looking for,' she said, trying to get him to focus on the immediate problem.

'A queer Mayan wotsit,' he mumbled. 'Part of two doodahs that could be fitted together to reveal some kind of thingummy.'

'And in English, please?'

'One of those intriguing johnnies that look like tombstones but aren't. Mayan stone tablets. Like portable stelae. Half of a pair. But circular, like a giant ha'penny.'

The relic upon which he was so painfully seated was about eighteen inches in diameter, dark greenish-brown, inscribed around its edges with symbols and images. The flat side showed a pattern of seven dots. The other side of the stone – the side upon which he was unwisely perched – featured a fist-sized round protrusion in its centre, plainly intended to slot into something. All such details had been eagerly relayed to Ruby in last week's telephone conversation.

So much had changed in that week.

'I know what it looks like. I want to know its story. How it came into your possession.'

'Great-great Uncle Bilbo –' he began, shifting his position slightly and trying to prevent his eyes from watering.

'Great-great Uncle *who*?'

'Bilbo. Another Lord Ballashiels. Victorian explorer. Source of the Nile and all that. Pockets full of essentials. Quinine. For malaria, you know. It's in tonic water. Good excuse to dilute it with gin. Worked. Didn't get malaria once. Come to think of it, though, dropped dead of cirrhosis.' He was talking drivel. He needed to focus. He needed her out of there.

Ruby sighed again. Ratty was hard work.

'But he did last for a year or so somewhere around Belize, I think,' continued Ratty. 'Maybe Guatemala. Isn't that where you're tootling off to?'

'You mean the UNESCO job? Haven't decided whether to accept it yet.'

'Be careful, old chum. They say there's a civil war brewing.'

'That's why we need to help them protect their heritage. After what happened in Egypt this is more urgent than ever. Emergency archaeology. High-resolution three dimensional scans of every pyramid, statue and stele so we know what's been lost in case the worst happens. Anyway, what did your great-great uncle get up to?'

'Went a bit loopy by all accounts. Some savages … is that what you call them these days, "savages"? It's awfully confusing remembering which words cause offence. Anyway, these savages looked after him in the jungle. Or is it a rainforest? And he wrote about it in his diary, which is in that heap over there.'

Ruby picked up a tattered diary. Scrawled across the front in faded mauve ink were the words: 'Bilbo de St Clair, his Diary. Private. KEEP OUT'.

'How old was he, fourteen?' she asked, flicking through it.

'In some respects, yes. Younger as he got older, if you see what I mean? Quite potty at the end.'

'And he was out there searching for the pair of stelae?'

'The local savages told him not to. Sort of cursed. Something to do with the end of the world. Sounds fun, he thought. Who cares about the end of the world with a liver nine parts hobnail boot?'

'Quite the adventurer, wasn't he? You sure you're descended from him?'

Ratty grinned and ran his bony, freckly hands through his oily hair. He was fully aware of the contrast between this exciting and dynamic ancestor and the pathetic specimen he had become. A trip to the further reaches of his own garden was a major expedition for Ratty – he couldn't even contemplate what it must be like to set off into a real jungle equipped only with a hip flask, a stiff hat and an even stiffer upper lip. It humbled him to think that Bilbo had actually done something with his life.

'Quite, quite. Anyway, he only found the one part of it. When he showed the stone to the natives they covered their faces and chucked him out of their village. A bit inconvenient, actually, as he'd just married one of the ladies and hadn't got round to the interesting bit.'

Her eyes rolled. He sensed her frustration. He had been wittering on in his characteristic style, side-stepping the need to cause offence and send her home. He longed to give her something to make her journey worthwhile; Stiperstones Manor was over a hundred miles from London, and he couldn't bear to be on the receiving end of the acerbic tongue that would inevitably lash in his direction when she realised he had behaved in a fashion unbefitting their long friendship. And yet he was powerless. She could not be permitted to take the stele. He would have to insult her and take the forthcoming verbal abuse on his diminutive chin.

'Bilbo wore many quills down to their stumps in recounting the legends of the indigenous – no, that's the offensive one, isn't it – savages,' he continued, attempting to focus her attention on the diary, still incapable of unleashing any perceptible malevolence. 'The Mayan long count predicts the date the world will end, or be reborn, or wotnot, but it doesn't say how or why or whether you need to hide in the cupboard under the stairs to survive. Bilbo writes about the legends of the stelae, and their power to counteract the doomsday stuff.'

'You don't look very comfy on that sofa.'

Had she said that with a hint of suspicion? He couldn't tell.

'You have no idea,' he replied, wondering if the cold stone beneath him would give him the type of complaint about which he preferred not to complain. 'Listen, old wombat, let's retire to the library for a glass of something civilised. Take the diary to the museum instead.'

'Ratty, I came for the stele, not the diary. Why invite me to take it if you don't know where it is?'

'To be fair, it wasn't a formal solicitation.' A knot tied itself in his stomach.

'Can't a girl surprise an old friend?' She sounded hurt. His ungallant attack was working, although it pained him more than she.

'Like the way you surprised me by running off when we went on that date at uni?' he asked her.

The coldness with which he was compelled to treat her was tearing at his soul, more wounding to him than the limestone protrusion beneath his posterior. Ruby was the only person in the world capable of putting a smile on his gaunt face just by showing up in his life. She did not deserve this.

'Tell me about the inscriptions on the stele,' she said after a pause in the officious tone she normally reserved for addressing unruly students at a dig. 'Are they Mayan glyphs?'

'Yes. Such a limited canon,' said Ratty, permitting himself a few moments of amiability. 'One can't develop much of a library when every syllable needs to be engraved laboriously in obsidian.'

'Was the other part of the stele ever found?'

'Goodness, look at the time,' he spluttered, looking at the part of his arm where his watch would be had he not been forced by his new-found poverty to trade it for a hamper of food. Ruby's stern expression made him fidget. 'How is that charming American gentleman caller of yours?' he squeaked. 'Had an apostle's name, as I recall. Luke? No, Matthew. Matthew Mountebank. Yes, it was Matthew, wasn't it? Not exactly Saint Matthew, as far as one can tell from his broadcasts. Pity your soldier boy couldn't stop those brigands from pilfering those Sphinx scrolls.'

'His name's Matt. And never mind him. You're hiding something, Ratty. I know you too well.'

'Fiddle-faddle and twaddle,' he replied, vainly hoping such a robust rebuttal would be the end of the matter. 'Let's go downstairs. You first. And do take Bilbo's diary.'

'Why are you doing this?' She thrust the diary at his face like an apoplectic lover who had just discovered an affair described within the pages. Then her tone softened, to Ratty's enormous relief, to one of raw disappointment. 'I was really shaken up by what happened in Egypt, Ratty, and I was looking forward to seeing you. I was thinking about how your eyes have shone so brightly whenever I've surprised you over the years. I expected your face to light up as you opened the door, but you're treating me like a stranger. You've wasted my time. I just hope you're not planning to do anything with that stele that I might make you regret.'

The smile with which he attempted to contradict her accusation was unconvincing, merely serving to display his very aristocratic teeth – uneven and slightly yellow. She pocketed the diary and headed for the door with body language that made no secret of her foul mood.

Finally able to relieve himself of the discomfort of sitting on the stele, Ratty stood up and self-consciously peeked inside his blazer wherein sat the letter from Guatemala that was simultaneously the solution to his problems and their inception.

MONDAY 19TH NOVEMBER 2012

The airport terminal felt like a refuge from the fighting and destruction in the city – which had sometimes skirted close enough to Ruby's hotel for staccato gunfire to be audible from her room. The consequences of the battle were visible everywhere today: closed shops, cabs not running, empty streets.

She collected the ticket left for her at the airline desk by her new UNESCO boss – a curiously annoying and frequently absent man called Paulo Souza, who in Ruby's opinion had so far displayed remarkably little competence for his role heading up the protection of Guatemala's heritage. The agent at the ticket desk informed her that her flight was delayed by three hours. She slumped onto a steel bench, pulled out a map of her destination and spread it over her knees, noting the positions of many unexcavated Mayan pyramids that could be at risk of looting if the country's political instability deepened. With the meagre resources of her department – Paulo Souza hadn't yet allocated her an office and none of the vital scanning equipment had so far arrived – the treasures of the Mayan world faced a desperate future. She bowed her head in frustration.

It was then that a shadow fell over the map. She looked up.

He was a slender man of indeterminate age: thinning white hair, safari jacket, beige slacks. He held a panama hat while mopping his brow. His pale, colourless eyes looked at her shrewdly.

'The map looks old,' he remarked.

'Um, er, hello,' said Ruby, thinking how odd it was that a stranger should engage her in her own language. 'Do I look so English, or have we met before?'

'You have a slight look of Marks and Spencer's about you,' her new companion murmured. 'But perhaps the superior Marble Arch branch, not some provincial outlet.' He spoke perfect English, but with a very slight foreign inflection that owed little, or nothing, to Central America. For the moment, Ruby couldn't place it.

Don't speak to strangers, Ruby told herself. Especially strange men. And yet there was something about him that had already won her confidence. Perhaps it stemmed from the simple context of a friendly approach against the background of a locked-down city at war with itself.

She stood up.

'And you are?'

'My name is Otto,' he stated. '*Doctor* Otto.' He straightened his jacket, then pulled out his sleeves, and then straightened his jacket again.

'I'm Ruby. Ruby *Towers*,' she said, holding out her hand. '*Doctor* Ruby Towers.' She added, 'Of archaeology, that is. Nothing useful like medicine.' She waited for him to shake her hand, but his was not forthcoming. She retracted hers. Dr Otto laughed briefly, a tiny, rusty sound as if it was a rare occurrence.

'You would be surprised how useful archaeology can be, right now, even here,' he said. 'Doctor Towers –'

'Ruby, please. I always think it's best to be informal when one's been dodging bullets all morning.'

'Quite. Ruby, then. Actually, I have been waiting for you. I hope you will not be offended if I comment that you are younger than I expected.'

'Younger? I'm the wrong side of, ahem, thirty. How

did you know I was here?'

'Señor Souza told me you would be here this morning.'

'Paulo Souza? From the UN?'

Otto appeared thrown by the second part of her question. He adjusted his sleeves again.

'Er, yes, Paulo Souza.'

'Are you with the UN too?'

'I have an, er, affiliation. Listen, your flight is delayed considerably. Perhaps that is to our mutual advantage as there is someone I wish you to meet concerning Mayan antiquities. Would you mind coming with me for an hour?'

She didn't need to think about it. If she could make one small contribution towards the conservation of Mayan relics rather than sitting uselessly in an airport, she had to do it.

He held out his hand, but when he recoiled as she moved hers towards him, she realised that he was only pointing the way. He seemed asexual, a dry academic, perhaps more comfortable with a book than with a companion. Without wasting breath on more words, he led her at a brisk trot out of the airport entrance directly to the parking lot.

The grey S-class Mercedes was too wide for the faded markings that defined its parking space, and the proximity of the adjacent cars made impossible the kind of elegant ingress that such a vehicle deserved. Ruby hugged the door as she squeezed clumsily around it to get in. As she did so she noticed that the window glass was at least an inch thick.

'It is the S Guard model,' explained Otto as he slid himself into the driving seat. 'Bullet-proof glass, armoured body panels. I have no reason to fear guns, grenades or bombs.'

'Any other day I'd have said you're paranoid. Today it makes perfect sense.'

She closed the door and felt secure, cocooned from the turbulent city. From within the protective shell of this car, the towers of smoke that indicated ongoing skirmishes between the army and the guerrilla fighters seemed unreal. With little traffic on the streets Otto reached his destination in minutes. He stopped the car, pulling backwards and forwards several times until it was parked perfectly parallel to the kerb. He climbed out and walked round to open Ruby's door. As she stood up he held out his hand once again, but she knew by now that it was not for her to hold.

'Follow me.' He tipped his head towards the grand entrance of a detached colonial building. Two short, bulky men in black suits leaned against the pillars on either side of the door, one fiddling with his headset like a bouncer outside a nightclub, the other impatiently looking at his watch. Ruby was not disturbed by the presence of these men, but she was terrified by what was adjacent to the house. Or, rather, what was no longer adjacent. The almost perfectly circular sinkhole was eerily tubular with vertical sides. The neighbouring colonial villa had simply vanished, sucked deep into the earth, but miraculously most of Otto's property was unaffected. A section of his garden wall protruded over the edge, suspended on air. A length of concrete sidewalk also appeared to have nothing supporting it. Severed cables dangled downwards, and water dribbled from a snapped pipe. There was no sign of the bottom of this pit; the sun's angle was not yet high enough to illuminate its nadir.

'Sorry, Otto,' she said, clinging to the car. 'I don't think it's safe to go near a sinkhole.'

The air above them whistled, ripped apart by a high velocity round. The two men in black winced, and then tried to pretend they hadn't. A window on a distant office building disintegrated, glass tinkling to the street.

'Please, Ruby, it is perfectly safe,' explained Otto, staring at her with unblinking eyes. 'This city is built upon soft volcanic soils. Sometimes underground rivers create chambers that collapse and cause sinkholes. This one appeared yesterday. No one was hurt.' He put his hand over his mouth as he continued, 'A structural engineer has already surveyed my home. There is nothing to worry about.' He returned his hand to his side and led the way into the tenebrous cool of the building, nodding respectfully to the two men as they opened the door for him.

There was a jug of iced water. There were cakes. There was an electric fan whirring above them. Hardback volumes lined three of the walls from floor to ceiling, extensive collections arranged by genre: History, Cultural Arts, Modern and Ancient Languages, Medicine, Science and – most significantly – an entire wall dedicated to the writings of humanity's greatest philosophers. Here, Aristotle and Plato dominated the shelf space over lesser thinkers. There were also deep luxurious cushions, tapestries, and ornate but clearly tasteful furniture. And there, in the middle of this room, was a man, sitting rather melodramatically in deep shadow behind a weighty Victorian desk on which an object the size of a small bicycle wheel sat beneath a loose shroud.

Otto poured a glass of water and handed it to Ruby, then straightened the jug so that its handle lined up with the edge of the table. While she downed the water in one great grateful gulp, the man in the olive green leather captain's chair on the other side of the desk wriggled out of the shadows into the light, an expression of utter terror upon his face.

'Ruby? What on earth are you doing here, old fruit bat?'

'I'd ask the same, but something tells me I already know the answer, Ratty.'

Otto raised an exceptionally pale eyebrow. Ratty, indeed. These Brits were sometimes unfathomable. He dragged a chair over for her, aligning it carefully with the desk. Ruby sat down, unconsciously nudging the chair away from its perpendicular alignment. Otto grimaced as if hearing fingernails on a blackboard. He slid the cakes into neat rows as if to compensate for the chair. Ruby was momentarily distracted by his little habits, but her mind swiftly returned to this unexpected encounter with an old friend.

'It seems you're making a habit of visiting me unannounced,' declared Ratty with a voice from which all confidence had been stripped.

'Don't you start that,' she countered firmly. 'I had no idea you'd be here. Doctor Otto invited me on an archaeological matter.'

'You said you'd bring your government's top scientific expert chappy to carry out the verification, Otto,' whispered Ratty, even though the Doctor was further away than Ruby. 'You never mentioned it was a chap-ess.'

'Verification?' she echoed.

Ratty slowly pulled the shroud away from the object it had been covering on the desk, watching her eyes as he did so for any warning signs of an imminent explosive outburst.

'I believe you were hoping to see this spiffing little how's-your-father before, Ruby.'

'Doctor Towers, I have brought you here today to verify that this stele is of genuine Mayan antiquity,' declared Otto, stepping forward and picking up a bundle of papers from the desk. 'I wish to purchase it from Lord Ballashiels on behalf of my client. Please take a close look at it. In order to release the funds, and for insurance purposes, I need your verification of these importation documents to prove that it is not a fake.'

She said nothing during the full minute that she glared at Ratty. Otto cleared his throat in frustration at Ruby's uncharacteristic silence.

'Don't you have anything to say, old wingding?' Ratty asked. Ruby was staring intently into Ratty's eyes, her expression fixed in unyielding disapproval. He squirmed uncomfortably – only slightly more than he squirmed when he was comfortable. 'Jolly good. Well, no hurry.'

'What do you already know about it?' Ruby eventually asked, turning to Otto.

Otto appeared affronted at this question. The mild contortion of his facial muscles suggested that whatever he knew about the stele was not her concern.

'I have considerable knowledge,' he whispered.

'Such as?' she pushed.

'It is one of a pair of stelae.'

'And?'

'Their glyphs must be read together.'

'What happened to the other part?'

Otto's patience was stretched further with every impertinent question.

'The other was discovered by a German archaeologist in eighteen eighty-nine.'

'Do you have it?'

'It is in the possession of my client, yes. He would like to reunite the pair.'

'And your client is?'

'My client is anonymous.'

'And rich?'

'He is a man of means.'

'So this is nothing to do with the UN?'

He stepped towards her, holding out the documents.

'Enough. I asked you a simple question, Doctor Towers. Is this stele a genuine Mayan artefact? If so, please sign this certification form.'

Ignoring him, Ruby threw a vicious stare at Ratty. This was precisely the scenario she feared. Countless Mayan sites and relics had already been devastated by looting. With thousands of unexcavated temples still lost in the rainforests of Central America there was no way to stop the ongoing desecration, but the thought of losing something of potentially global significance to a faceless black market collector made her livid.

'Could Ratty and I have a minute in private, please, Otto?' she asked, secretly almost enjoying the dread creeping across Ratty's face at the prospect of being left to face her wrath alone.

Otto bowed his head in frustrated subservience and exited the room.

'It takes a lot to keep a home like mine from falling down,' confessed Ratty in a voice that seemed to beg for mercy. 'One does what one can with the resources one has, but there isn't much lolly left in the old coffers. The casinos have not been kind to my forebears.'

'I know times are hard, but you told me you were selling some antiques. And I offered to help you sell the stele to the British Museum. I never thought you'd sink this low.'

'You said the museum couldn't pay much. And then the bank started repossession thingies. They said if I don't repay my debts by the end of the month I'll lose the manor. And then Doctor Otto came forward with an offer that was too good to resist. Actually he rather made it clear that resistance was not an option, in any case. He appears to have friends in low places.'

'What about the report I e-mailed you about my research into Bilbo's diary?'

'Ah, yes, the old electro mail service. Thing is, couldn't pay the bills. So I, er, didn't get it.'

'How could you afford to fly here if you can't even pay for your broadband?'

'In anticipation of a hefty wedge from Doctor Otto I took out a loan against the manor.'

'I thought you were mortgaged to the hilt already.'

'With one institution, yes, but I found another. Private bank. Happy to take my word as a gentleman. Lent me enough for first class flights, top hotel and all the gin and tonic I can eat.'

'Isn't that fraud?'

'Is it? I wouldn't know. With Otto's dosh I'll pay it all back before anyone notices.'

She exhaled slowly. The report on the diary had taken her many hours to prepare. Her motivation hadn't been historical curiosity, it was merely to demonstrate to Ratty the importance of keeping the stele in responsible hands. She had learned of Bilbo's insatiable pursuits of female Mayan descendants, his casual dismissal of the local legends regarding the cursed pair of stelae, and his xenophobic rivalry with a young German engineer and amateur archaeologist named Karl M. – there was no reference in the notes to this person's actual surname. It seemed they were both aware of the stories surrounding the pair of stelae: Karl M. was desperate to obtain them in the name of von Bismarck and the German Empire; Bilbo was equally keen to dig them up in the name of Her Majesty's Britannic Empire. Archaeology driven purely by jingoistic pomposity, Ruby had thought as she decoded the drunken, smudged Victorian handwriting and typed it into her laptop.

Further research had revealed that Bilbo's nemesis,

Karl M., eventually located the other half of the stele – some years after Bilbo's liver had given up the struggle – and brought it back to his homeland. Brief years of Teutonic pride and excitement then dissipated amid the distraction of the Great War.

If the mythologies concerning the pair of stelae were to be believed, then the unification of the stones could lead archaeologists to an as yet unknown site of major importance somewhere in Central America. No complete sense could be made of the inscription on Ratty's piece without the other half, however. Its display in a Berlin museum was documented until the time when the Nazis came to power, but in the mid-1930s the museum had been closed and the trail went cold.

'Ratty, my e-mail was trying to tell you that the inscriptions and the legends indicate that when the two stelae are aligned correctly they reveal a series of place names. Your section reveals half of the information. If it's placed together with the other half, we would have a set of four locations. The point where lines between all of the places intersect is the key. With both pieces of the stele you have the precise location of something that was of value to people thousands of years ago.'

'Treasure?' he asked, eyes suddenly widening.

The door began to open again.

'Listen,' she continued sotto voce, 'if this stone ends up on the black market along with its other section then the most significant Mayan site yet to be discovered will be raided for profit and lost to the world. I would never forgive you for that.'

Before Otto could reach for the verification document, Ruby blurted out, 'I refuse to sign anything.'

'Doctor Towers, enough. By your attitude I am now convinced that the item is genuine. His Lordship *will* sell this artefact to me today. Please wait outside whilst we conclude our business. If you then sign this form, I will return you to the airport.'

She counted a few beats in her head, then made her final comment to Ratty.

'Time has transfigured them into Untruth,' she said, without the sense of poetry that the phrase deserved. Ratty looked up at her, his expression one of bemusement. 'Time has transfigured them into Untruth,' she repeated as she walked out of the room and the villa.

The Mayan tablet remained in the centre of the ornate desk, stared at by two equidistant men. Outside, the sinkhole widened. The foundations of the villa juddered. A piece of the ceiling fell to the floor and the ceiling fan sprayed plaster dust throughout the room, causing the stele's usual dark greenish-brown surface to take on a white hue. Ratty hoped the dust would not harm the object, though if anything it made the enigmatic glyphs easier to see. Frankly, the dust – and the possibility of the whole building toppling into a bottomless pit – was the least of his worries because at the moment he was feeling an utter chump.

'Lord Ballashiels, I do hope you are not considering wasting my time.'

'Good Lord, of course not. Wouldn't dream of it.' The fresh sweat oozing onto Ratty's brow made it amply clear that he was thinking of doing exactly that.

'It is vital, Lord Ballashiels,' continued Otto, retaining the utmost formality, 'that the stele comes with me at the conclusion of our meeting. We must reach an agreement.'

'Absolutely, old boy.'

'So if you do not consider my offer to be acceptable, it would be appropriate for you to suggest a deal that would satisfy your needs.'

'Couldn't agree more, old fruit.'

25

But Ratty was deeply troubled. He had arrived in the country determined to give in to Otto's threats and offload this useless piece of stone he had inherited. Selling this stone, or 'repatriating' it, as Otto preferred to call it, would resolve his current pecuniary embarrassment, extricate him from any fraud charges that would ensue once the two lenders realised they'd secured their cash against the same property, and keep the banks from throwing him out of the home that had been in his family for centuries. He had been perfectly single-minded about carrying out his plan. Nothing could derail it.

That had remained true until Ruby's visit, and now he didn't know what to think. Somehow the few words she had spoken drove a wedge between Ratty's fears and his conscience.

A thought was forming in Ratty's mind that history would not look kindly on him should he part company with the stele. Ruby's simple quotation from a Philip Larkin poem had burrowed deep into his psyche, profoundly disturbing him. He didn't consciously know why it was having such an effect; he felt it more than he understood it. And what he felt was that his actions in this room would be remembered for a long time. Future generations would talk about how close he had come to making an irrevocably bad decision. Losing the Ballashiels stately home and a short spell in an open prison would be a mere blip in the family's history compared with shouldering the responsibility for the loss of an archaeological treasure which for all he knew could turn out to be as valuable as the missing Sphinx scrolls. He had to make the correct moral decision.

The danger to his life that would accompany such a decision was something for which he was completely ill-equipped, however. Otto had made clear from the outset that a fair price would be paid for the stele, but that generosity was edged with an unequivocal reference to the powerful men at Otto's disposal who would think nothing of separating the blue blood from Ratty's aristocratic body. He was on the precipice and needed to step back.

'Your price, Lord Ballashiels?'

Ratty wrapped his arms around the stele and dragged it closer to him. Otto was visibly fighting with himself to maintain self-control, endlessly adjusting and readjusting his sleeves.

'Listen, old boy, I've been giving it some thought, and, well, perhaps it's best if the stele stays –'

Otto stood up and held out his hand, signalling that Ratty should cease talking.

'I don't know how I can put this any clearer, Lord Ballashiels. You will sell me the stele today. There is no alternative.'

Ratty pulled the stele still closer, stiffening up inside in preparation for the anger this would trigger. He was fully aware that Otto had two gorillas in suits at his disposal. Feeling irremediably out of his depth, Ratty picked up the stele and hugged it to his chest.

Otto could no longer maintain his composure. He stormed out of the room and called for the men he believed were guarding the door. Ratty stood up, still hugging the stele, and paced around. He could hear Otto in the corridor dialling on his phone and screaming for assistance. Why did he need to phone for help? It could only mean one thing: that those security men had gone.

Ratty was torn between his fear of physical violence and the unforgiving sternness of Ruby's – and perhaps the world's – eternal disapprobation. Otto might have his toughies back here within a few minutes. It had not escaped Ratty's notice that the city was virtually deserted today, and there was no functioning police force that would come to his aid should things turn ugly in this room. If Ratty was going to get away from this situation with his body unblemished and his stele in his possession, he would have to make a move that was both brave and smart.

He froze. He had never done anything either brave or smart in his entire life.

He tried spreading his legs apart in what he hoped might look like an aggressive stance, but with the stele still cradled in his arms he was in danger of losing his balance. So the legs came back together again. He tried puffing out his chest, but the difference was imperceptible.

Otto turned the door handle to come back in. Ratty was going to have to do his valiant and ingenious thing, whatever that was, right away. He took a deep breath and hurled himself backwards at the closed window, intending to make a fast and dramatic escape of the type he had seen performed by well-paid actors in the picture houses. When he bounced back onto the floor, curtains swishing behind him, stele still tightly clasped in front of him, he was more than a little surprised. Looking up, he was further astonished to note that Otto was approaching him with a large loaded syringe in his hand.

Have courage, Ratty told himself, before realising the sight of the needle was making him feel faint. He looked away and his strength returned. When he glanced back the needle was out of sight. Otto had been distracted by the dishevelled drapes and was fussily straightening them with his left hand, holding the needle at his side with the other. From his prostrate position on the floor, Ratty took the opportunity to flick a ladylike kick at the newly-aligned curtain, causing the frustrated doctor to start again. By the time the curtains were hanging to Otto's satisfaction, Ratty had scrambled to his feet, temporarily abandoning the stele in order to put some distance between himself and the needle that once more threatened to enter his personal space.

'I say, old chap, had all the inoculations before I came out here. Jolly kind of you and all that, but really no need.'

'This won't hurt you,' said Otto in a doctorly tone. 'My serum has proven completely harmless in tests.'

'*Your* serum? Jolly impressive. Didn't know you were into the old medical research malarkey.' Ratty was aware that by reversing slowly around the room, keeping out of Otto's reach, he was leaving the stele unguarded on the floor, but Otto wasn't paying it any attention just yet. 'Personally,' continued Ratty, trying to keep a dialogue going for long enough for him to complete a circuit of the room and get back within reach of the stele, 'I've never been keen on mice.'

'Mice? I never said anything about mice,' declared Otto.

'Don't approve of bow-wows and little monkey fellows getting roped into all that testing, either. Not my cup of tea at all.'

'Nor mine. Animal testing is a waste of time. You cannot beat the real thing. Now be still.'

'Look, it's getting awfully late. If you wouldn't mind putting that disagreeable pointy thing away?'

Ratty was now back where he had left the stele and picked it up with a rapid swoop. The needle rushed towards him as he did so, bending uselessly as it hit the stone.

'The stele remains with me, Your Lordship. Please put it down.'

'I'm terribly sorry, but I really ought to point out that a contractual sale has not actually taken place and therefore the item remains my property, and furthermore … ouch!' Otto had slapped him across the face as if demanding a duel. 'I say, that brought tears to the old mince pies, what, what. Almost gave me a shiner. Ho-hum. Look, I don't want to appear rude but I really ought to be going. It's been jolly nice meeting you and thank you so much for the fondant fancies.'

He reversed towards the corridor.

'My assistants will be here very soon,' declared Otto, pointing at the front door. 'Put the stele down and we can resolve this like the gentlemen that we are. My assistants, however, are not gentlemen and I cannot be responsible for their actions.'

Ratty continued edging backwards along the corridor, avoiding the steps down to the basement, towards the rear of the building where he hoped there might be another exit.

'I say, old boy, what's that behind you?'

'Your simple trickery will not work with me,' responded Otto.

'Delectable gilt frame on that painting. Fits awfully well in this colonial villa. Just a mite wonky, though.'

Otto resisted the burning temptation to turn around.

'I can assure you, Lord Ballashiels, that every painting in this villa has been hung with a spirit level to ensure absolute accuracy. Put the stele down, Your Lordship. Allow it to be repatriated. It is the honourable course.'

'Quite, quite. Sort of stuck to the old digits, though. Can't seem to let go. Oh well, perhaps another time?'

Otto began to reach out to try to grab the stele, easily matching Ratty's pace as he reversed along the corridor towards the back door.

'That picture really doesn't look awfully level to me,' said Ratty, looking once again over Otto's shoulder. 'It seems frightfully skew-whiff.'

The Doctor gave in to the temptation to look back, overwhelmed and distressed to note that Ratty was correct about the angle. Now that the imperfection had been brought to his attention its adjustment could not be delayed. The picture had to be straightened. As immutable forces started to take control of Otto, he sought the strength to resist from the rational side of his mind, but even here, his command was weakening. He scrambled to recall a useful epithet of advice from Aristotle, reassuring himself that it was up to him whether or not to act in any particular way. He carried his own moral responsibility for his actions, Aristotle told him, and therefore he possessed the power of decision, of choice, of control. The philosopher, however, could not prevent him from losing that control. A mountain of instinct finally crushed his rationality. Unable to restrain himself, he returned to the painting and straightened it, almost weeping in frustration as he stood back to check that it no longer offended the aesthetic sensibilities that ruled his life.

In so far as the word meant anything in this city, Ratty was safe. He escaped through Otto's garden, climbed over a half-collapsed brick wall into what remained of the neighbouring property, skirted dangerously close to the edge of the almost bottomless sinkhole, and then opened a gate on to a backstreet. Not only had he eluded the Doctor, he had been both brave and smart. Ratty glowed with pride. All he had to contend with now was the sickening prospect of the bankruptcy, homelessness and disgrace that would be his reward should he manage to flee the country in one piece.

Ruby landed at Flores Airport, in the heart of northern Guatemala's rainforest. Paulo Souza wasn't there to meet her, but, given her unpreventable late arrival, it was not surprising that he hadn't stuck around. This was just as well since she had fallen into a deep sleep moments after take-off and hadn't even glanced at his site report. She climbed into a waiting tuk-tuk, pulled out the laser printed pages and held them tight in the breezy open cab, but with exhaust fumes and grit spitting at her face she soon gave up trying to read.

Before the cell phone coverage ceased entirely she sent a text to Matt. He would be landing in the capital any minute now, expecting her to be waiting dutifully. Fat chance. She had briefly considered not telling him where she had gone, motivated by her ongoing resentment at his inability to overcome the thieves at the Sphinx, but it was only fair to give him the option of following her to Flores and on to the jungle site where he could tag along until she had finished for the day. The whole trip including flight and tuk-tuk ride would only take him an hour or two.

The entrance to the jungle clearing was marked by a scattering of vehicles and a man in a white suit who smoked a dusky, oily-looking cigar without the use of his hands. The Oscuro Presidente was clamped ferociously, yet somehow stylishly, between his lips. His eyes squinted as the rising smoke caused sunbeams to flash across his face. The cigar wiggled up and down in acknowledgement of Ruby's arrival.

Like most Guatemalan men of Mayan descent, Paulo Souza was shorter than Ruby. His stocky frame and strong, square features would have suited a wrestler. At forty-eight, the majority of his life had been spent against a background of either all-out civil war or very fragile peace frequently punctuated by clashes fought in the name of ideology, greed or hunger. It had instilled in him a somewhat blasé indifference to danger. Despite his often desperate experiences, his eyes still danced with a youthful energy. His roguish half smile – a magnet for Guatemalan women – did nothing for Ruby. Like it or not, though, he was her new boss and she had to exude a degree of civility in his presence.

Paulo paid Ruby's tuk-tuk driver and walked immediately along a dirt track into the gloomy forest. Ruby followed some paces behind like a petulant child. Sweat ran down her back, soaking into her belt. Her shirt clung to her skin, sodden pores deprived of air. A simple 'Hello, how was your trip?' from Paulo would have helped her mood. A waggling cigar just didn't do it for her.

'You should not have left your hotel today,' he mumbled from the side of his mouth.

'What are you talking about?'

'It is too dangerous for a lady.'

Somehow in that one sentence he had managed to hit her with everything she disliked about so many of the men she seemed to encounter in this country.

'Oh for God's sake!' she snapped. '*You* told me to come.'

Paulo made a sort of shrugging 'hmm' sound as if weighing up an argument, then added, 'You are late.'

'You're lucky I made it at all after you sent that creepy doctor to find me at the airport.'

'Did you read the report I sent you, my dear?'

'I am *not* your dear.'

'The artefact we found has been made from a significant quantity of gold. I have submitted a request for military protection for the site due to its value. Do not be alarmed if soldiers arrive today.'

Unable to summon a coherent response to this revelation she grumbled to herself and tried her best to catch up with Paulo over the uneven ground.

The clearing was no larger than a couple of tennis courts, and the hole was about the right size and depth to swallow a family car. Trees had been felled to make space for a Faun ATF-60 mobile crane, a JCB excavator with tracked wheels, and an elongated flatbed truck. But no one was there. Ruby wondered if the workers had returned to Flores for lunch and a siesta. Paulo looked at the deserted equipment and tapped his watch impatiently, sighing at Ruby. The site was not far from the ancient Mayan jungle city of Tikal, but at a kilometre outside of the protected Maya Biosphere there was no evidence of any temples here. Unexcavated temple mounds were easy to spot, appearing as small hills, usually grouped together, protruding from relatively flat land like turtles on a beach. There was no such evidence of previous habitation around this clearing; the only mound in the vicinity was a fresh pile of soil.

She approached the muddy edge of the hole and peered down, holding on to the top of the aluminium ladder that had been placed there. The sides of the pit had been mechanically scooped to create a sheer cut through the clay soil. About ten feet below ground level was a thin stratum of crystals that sparkled in an almost perfect ring. Immediately beneath the crystal layer was the object that Paulo had been so keen for Ruby to investigate.

It was a convex metallic shape, badly dented by time, nature and the teeth of the mechanical digger that had uncovered it. Parts of it had been polished clean of mud to reveal that gold was its principal constituent. The object filled the pit entirely and appeared to continue further underground in all directions. Ruby had never seen a Mayan artefact on this scale before. She didn't know what it was, or how far it extended under her feet. The only thing she was sure of was that they were going to need a bigger pit.

'Have you ever seen an object so beautiful without looking in a mirror?' Paulo asked, snapping Ruby back from her reverie.

'What do we know about it?' she asked, ignoring his sledgehammer charm.

'Only what we see. Just some gold sheeting. We don't know what is beneath it.'

'How was it found?'

Paulo seemed uncomfortable at being asked this question. He waggled his cigar in his mouth, mumbling something which sounded to Ruby like 'I'm not at liberty to say'.

'But it was found accidentally, right? I mean, those teeth marks from the digger must have been accidental? From now on we're going to be digging by hand with trowels, obviously. I'll need a university team as soon as we can get one over here. At least eight people, given the size of the hole. And the project could last several weeks so we're going to need a toilet and cooking facilities. Could do with a Bimini cover to keep the sun and rain off. I'll work out a budget tonight.'

Paulo puffed on his cigar, saying nothing.

'Why have you got a crane here already?' she asked, suddenly aware of the collection of specialist vehicles. 'And the flatbed truck? Those things are normally rented on a daily basis, but not until you need them. We're weeks away from being able to lift this thing out. Do you want me to budget for them standing idle all that time? This could waste the funding we need for other projects. And while I'm on the subject of funding, when are we going to get a proper office? I've been working from my hotel room since I arrived in this country, and you keep saying we'll be getting offices soon. You haven't even introduced me to the other people in the department yet. And in any case, the whole department is useless until our scanning gear arrives, and what are you doing about that? Paulo? Are you listening?'

She walked over to the crane. The window was

smashed on the driver's door. She looked in and saw an ugly crimson stain on the seat. She turned to the adjacent JCB excavator. The door to its cab showed signs of forced entry. Next, she examined the cab of the flatbed truck. Its door was missing altogether. Things were sometimes rough and ready in this country, but these vehicles were worth over a million dollars between them and a rental company would normally take far better care of them.

'Where did you rent this equipment, Paulo? A scrap yard?'

Paulo checked his watch again.

'Ruby, my dear, some resources I requested have not arrived. Time is short today. I need to make some calls, but there's no signal here so I'll try from the road. Why don't you have a dig around? I won't be long.'

She put her bag back over her shoulder and climbed down the ladder, descending deeper into history with every rung. The gold surface held her weight. She crouched down and flicked away some soil with her trowel, exposing more seamless flat gold to the sunlight. There was, as yet, no hint that she was anywhere close to the edge of this object, this structure, this enigma. No hint as to its overall size or shape or purpose.

The brightness dimmed. She looked up and saw the silhouette of an unshaven man peering into the hole. He had a rifle slung over his shoulder and was wearing a tatty uniform, but it was not that of the Guatemalan army. More men joined him, similarly dressed. Ruby climbed out and squinted. Through narrowed eyes she could see a familiar, worrying logo on their arms. These men were part of the guerrilla forces that had caused such mayhem in Guatemala City that morning. They were the men with whom she thought she would never have to come face-to-face. These can't be the soldiers Paulo requested, she decided. They were from the wrong army. A responsible

United Nations official like Paulo wouldn't hire rebel fighters or mercenaries.

A loud diesel engine thudded to life. The business end of the mechanical digger squelched as it cut mercilessly through the soil, enlarging the pit one scoop at a time. This was a rough, mindless desecration of an important archaeological site, and it was her job to stop it.

She strode boldly up to one of the soldiers and shouted in Spanish that the excavations must cease. The man shoved her aside and briefly pointed his rifle at her. She scurried away and thought of Matt. For the first time in weeks she wished he was with her. For all his faults, he could make her feel safe. She waited at the edge of the clearing for Paulo to return, sickened by what these men were doing. She was only in Guatemala for one reason: to make detailed three-dimensional records of Mayan archaeological sites that could be used to reconstruct or repair them in case of war damage. It was a role in which she was failing utterly.

In the southern district of Guatemala City, a man in a striped blazer was marching conspicuously along an avenue, carrying a heavy stone tablet under his scrawny arm. He repeatedly looked back over his shoulder as he strode purposefully – yet nervously – towards the airport. He seemed to flinch frequently as if he thought each passing car would deliver a hail of bullets into his back.

His stately pile would have to be saved some other way. And if he couldn't save it, well, he would just have to take whatever the courts threw at him. He was beaten. It would be enough just to escape this mess with his life. Ruby had implied that to sell his stele would have been wrong. Extraordinarily wrong. Three hours drinking gin and tonic in an underground bar had given him the clarity to see that she was right. He now needed to get on a flight.

Any destination would do.

Ratty recoiled again as a car sped past, followed by another. His nervous system was on full alert, exhausting him physically and mentally. He paused in the shade of a ceiba tree next to a public fountain in one of Guatemala City's more attractive avenues and looked up and down the road. It was time to ditch the striped blazer. He would never look entirely indigenous, no matter what his apparel, but resembling a lost extra from *Brideshead Revisited* would only hinder his chances.

Moving on again, now less encumbered by unnecessary attire, he would have covered the distance with relative ease had it not been for the dead weight of the stele. He switched it from one arm to the other as he walked, but it was undeniably tough going. How he was going to get on to a flight with this relic he wasn't sure. The importation paperwork was still in Otto's villa. Normally customs men were awfully strict about undocumented Mayan items leaving their country. It was all so much easier in great-great Uncle Bilbo's day.

An ash grey Mercedes S Class motored almost silently from the north, and it seemed to be slowing down. Probably not a taxi offering him a lift to the terminal, he figured. Probably not a chauffeur asking for directions. Probably not good news at all. It stopped beside him and the rear door began to open. The omens were grim. He should have listened to his inner Eurylochus, warning him of unpropitious gods that whip up trouble from nowhere. He resigned himself to the idea that his personal odyssey was about to be forcibly and prematurely terminated.

As two burly men advanced towards him from the Mercedes, followed by a relieved-looking Otto, Ratty came to an unanticipated realisation. This did not have to be the end of his odyssey. He could choose to continue.

He could refuse to be bullied. He could avenge the objectionable manner in which he was being treated. He could fight back.

But not immediately. This battle was lost, but he convinced himself that the loss was a strategic move that would ultimately win him the war. He would not let the stele out of his possession for long.

'Time has transfigured them into Untruth,' he told himself. He still didn't know what it meant, but he now knew that it was the engine that powered his determination. As the stone was grappled from his hands, and into his empty palm an envelope was unexpectedly shoved, he made the decision not only to bring his stele home again, one day, but also to gain possession of the other half. He would live a life worthy of great-great Uncle Bilbo, worthy of the descendants he was yet to spawn. He would be admired and respected by the as yet unborn ninth Earl, and the tenth and the eleventh. His place in his family's history would be a talking point, rather than an uneventful and mostly unsuccessful caretaking of the stately home. It was as if the sun had punctured an overcast afternoon. His whole being lit up with a positive energy that he had never before experienced. As the stele was bundled into the back seat of the Mercedes and driven away at a speed that would have raised the eyebrows of a police officer – had there been any on the streets today to witness such an affront to the traffic laws – Ratty knew that his life finally had a goal, a purpose, a new odyssey.

He returned to the cooling generous shade of the ceiba tree and played with the envelope in his hand. It was a standard little envelope for letters. Nothing was written on the outside. It didn't feel as if there was much inside, either. He carefully tore it open along the top and removed the single piece of paper. There was writing on one side of it only, partly printed text and partly handwritten.

He realised he was looking at the short contract of sale that Otto had drawn up in anticipation of a legitimate transfer of the stele that morning. Where the sum of money was meant to be entered he had inserted a zero by hand in scarlet ink. Down the bottom of the page was a paragraph written in the same scarlet script.

'Lord Ballashiels,' it said, 'it is with regret that I obtain this artefact in circumstances that are an affront to the sense of propriety and dignity with which I normally conduct my affairs. Be assured that the use to which the stele is to be put is of significance to the state of Guatemala and to history. To that end, I understand that you may have family documents that can illuminate the context in which this stele was originally located, documents for which I am prepared to pay a fair price. I hope you can overlook the unseemly manner in which I behaved today and see fit to meet with me for a more civilised discussion tomorrow. You have my number. Otto M.'

That Otto chap was certainly pushing his luck, thought Ratty. There was no reason to believe him after what had transpired today. Ratty was always happy to trust a true gentleman: anyone born into sufficient means to be able to avoid the degradation of having a proper job, coupled with an expensive upbringing that valued culture and refinement, would automatically earn his complete confidence. For all his superficial formality and politeness, however, Otto was no gentleman.

Ratty drank some water from the fountain and considered the horror of a second meeting with Otto. There might be more needles, more ruffians. It was not an appealing prospect, but perhaps it could be turned to

Ratty's advantage. It could give him a chance to get close to the stele, a chance to recover his property and fulfil his personal quest. A plan began to form.

By the time Paulo returned to the clearing, the pit was fast approaching twice its original size. One side of the golden artefact had been revealed, though its overall shape was still unclear. The rebel soldier operating the yellow JCB excavator was doing his best to avoid causing damage, but every now and then the awful sound of metal scraping against metal made everyone cringe.

'Paulo, make them stop!' Ruby shouted as soon as she saw him, all her pent-up fury released in a single eruption. 'This isn't archaeology – this is vandalism!'

'These are exceptional times,' mumbled Paulo. 'Things will become clear to you, but I cannot explain right now.'

'Explain what?'

'It is a kind of emergency situation.'

'You're not making any sense. And you said soldiers were coming to protect the site – these are guerrilla fighters. Are you crazy?'

Paulo replied only with an infuriatingly incomprehensible waggle of his cigar.

Down in the rapidly expanding pit the outer edges of the golden object had been located. End to end it was almost thirty feet and was roughly triangular in shape – though with all of the damage caused by the digger and the natural distortion that came with years spent beneath tons of soil it was difficult to be sure of its intended outline.

A soldier jumped down onto the top of the artefact with a thud that was muted by surrounding mud. He was holding a portable oxyacetylene cutter which he ignited and began searing a rough line through the gold and whatever lay beneath, tracing the outline of a trap door.

Paulo marched around the clearing, observing everything, looking satisfied, unaware of Ruby's concerns that this mockery of an archaeological dig would result in endless paperwork, committee hearings, disciplinary action and possibly the end of her promising career. She followed him to the edge of the now gargantuan pit. Inside it was an object larger than any she had uncovered on previous digs, unlike any Mayan relic she had seen before. Unlike *any* relic she had seen *anywhere* before.

Two soldiers stood on top of it. They wrapped cloths around their hands and gripped the edges of the hatch that had been cut into the gold.

'We're ready for your input now, Ruby,' said Paulo. 'Would you mind giving us an assessment of what you see when they lift up that hatch?'

'The UN will fire you, Paulo. And me. Just tell me why this has to happen.'

Paulo shook his head and pointed down into the pit. She gingerly positioned herself close to the unstable edge of the pit and watched the two soldiers lift up the golden square, leaving a hole large enough to climb into. But Ruby couldn't see a thing: it was too bright outside and too dark in the hole.

'Perhaps, my dear, it is better if you climb down to take a closer look?'

'For the last time, Paulo, I am not your sodding dear. Shut it.' Boss or not, she didn't care. Their professional relationship would inevitably end today. His actions had proved to her that he was not worthy of his position. She couldn't go on working for someone she didn't respect. But she climbed down the ladder. However legally and morally and scientifically wrong this dig was, she could never resist the chance to see into a space that had been lost for millennia.

She knelt down at the edge of the jagged opening. It was still hard to see inside. Her hands shielded the glare of the sunlight reflecting off the surrounding gold surfaces. Slowly her eyes adjusted. The inky nothing took on shapes, tones and shadows. There was depth. Colours emerged. Finally, the items beneath her took on meaning.

The void into which Ruby was peering comprised only a fraction of the total size of the artefact. Either the soldiers knew exactly where to cut the opening, or, more likely in Ruby's opinion, this artefact contained dozens of chambers of similar size and they could have cut the opening anywhere with the same result. This thought gave her comfort; the sparks from the torch and the lumps of molten metal had speckled the chamber with contaminants and damaged its delicate and precious contents. If there were as yet undamaged sections inside the artefact she might later get the chance to open them up under controlled conditions. Thoughts of her forthcoming resignation began to dissolve.

She looked up into the brightness once again. Paulo was standing at the edge of the pit, steadied by the ladder.

'Would you like to tell me what you make of that, Ruby?'

'Paulo, it's incredible. It looks like some kind of gold sarcophagus. There are two sets of bones in this section. The skeletons are not in good condition, but that's possibly due to the way you let these thugs rip it all open.'

'How old would you say those bones are?' He was toying with her. He already knew the answer, but he wanted to test her.

'From the decomposition I would guess we're talking Pre-classic Maya at the latest, possibly even from the Archaic period. If it wasn't for the metal construction I'm standing on I'd even say they were from the Lithic period, but I know that's impossible.'

Ruby was thrown on to her back by a sudden strong vibration, narrowly missing the ragged metal hatch next to her. Concerned that this was the start of an earthquake, she spread her weight and tried to cling on. Several voices, heavy with ridicule, suggested that she was over-reacting.

'They are just tensioning the lifting cables, my dear. Do not alarm yourself. Perhaps it is time to come back up.'

Was he enjoying winding her up? She was convinced he took masochistic pleasure in the double whammy of his sexist patronisation and his nonchalant lack of concern at yet another affront to archaeological integrity. It was way too soon to think about lifting the artefact out of the ground. No assessment had been made as to its ability to withstand the stresses caused by the lifting points. A steel cradle would need to be built underneath and around it in order to spread the load evenly. Yanking it out with straps at either end could result in the whole thing buckling in the centre under its own unsupported weight. Besides, not enough time had been spent examining the two skeletons she had found lying inside it. Moving this enormous find with a crane, and then on a truck across pot-holed roads, would disturb any other bones or pottery it was hiding, reducing the potential mine of information to be gathered about the positioning of items with regard to the dead and the beliefs of those who had created this metal tomb. She climbed out again, flabbergasted that an attempt to lift the artefact was to begin immediately, barely minutes after the excavations had revealed its full shape and depth.

The arrival of an old stately Mercedes bearing a tattered flag in place of its three-pointed star seemed utterly incongruous to Ruby. The flag was red and white with two yellow stars, indicating that the car was carrying the Inspector General of the Guatemalan army. Ruby could see an important-looking military official driving, but which side was he on? The soldiers around her stood to attention. The Mercedes pulled up and a peroxide blond man climbed out.

Lorenzo Luz was just thirty-five, but a combination of sharp intelligence and dogged loyalty, coupled with an exceptionally high death rate among the rebels, had enabled him to rise quickly through the ranks. His dyed hair made him instantly identifiable among the Guatemalan fighting men.

He patted the roof of his newly and savagely acquired vehicle while his men saluted him. He then surveyed the messy scene with a disapproving expression. The artefact was suspended inches from the base of the pit by wide straps. Duckboards under the wheels of the mobile crane prevented it from sinking into the soil under the weight of its load. Lorenzo shook Paulo's hand and signalled that the extraction should continue. Each man resumed his duty. The engine of the crane revved loudly and the artefact began to rise. The flatbed truck reversed along two more rows of duckboards, close enough to the pit to be able to receive its priceless load.

The artefact was lifted clear of the pit and the crane swung it round to the waiting truck. It appeared to be massively heavy, but was clearly well within the sixty-ton capacity of the Faun crane. The truck sank a few noticeable inches as the tension was released from the straps. The boards under its wheels bent with the strain. The extraction from the pit was complete.

As soldiers climbed over the truck, covering the strange cargo with tarpaulins and attaching it securely with ropes, a volley of angry shouts made them reach for their weapons. Three civilian men ran into the clearing. They wore polo shirts in the colours of the rental company that owned the crane, excavator and truck. The massive golden artefact was still half exposed, but their focus was elsewhere.

Ruby glared at Paulo. He avoided her gaze.

'An administrative oversight,' he mumbled. 'This equipment wasn't rented. There wasn't time. It was, I believe, kind of borrowed.'

The sleazy situation in which Ruby found herself seemed a world away from the respectable image of the organisation for which she was working. She wondered if archaeologists in other remote places were subjected to the same degree of compromise, surrounded by such blatant criminality. Adapting to local culture was one thing, but stealing equipment and using guerrilla fighters to do the job of trained historians and technical specialists had turned this dig into a pillaging raid.

Lorenzo appeared to be mediating a heated discussion between the owners of the vehicles and the soldiers who had apparently taken them some time before dawn. Ruby edged closer so she could listen.

'Look at this. And this. And this!' One of the men in polo shirts was pointing at the damaged parts of his excavator. 'You are going to pay for this!'

Any remaining veneer of patience upon Lorenzo's face was fading fast, but he made one final attempt at conciliation.

'What is your name?' he asked, with ill-disguised indifference to whatever the answer may be.

'Anibal,' replied the head of the rental company.

'Anibal, look, some cock-ups were made by failing to sign the right paperwork for these vehicles, I admit. We were up against a strict time limit and couldn't wait for your office to open.'

'You bastards stole them!' was Anibal's response, inflaming Lorenzo's now transparent annoyance.

'Look, we have already finished with the JCB. You

can collect the crane and the flatbed tomorrow from the old airfield at Tikal. Submit your invoices to the government and it will pay for the rental and for any damage.'

The peal of derisory laughter triggered by Lorenzo's implication that he was legitimately associated with the government reddened his face and caused his fingers to twitch. Anibal carried on regardless, convinced that no invoices would ever be authorised for payment on behalf of scruffy guerrilla fighters who hadn't showered in days and who were the sworn enemies of the state.

'You will never pay! You are guerrillas! You are nothing!' Anibal, high on the euphoria of rage, ran to Lorenzo's Mercedes and kicked a dent in its door.

Lorenzo pulled a pistol from his holster in a smooth movement and fired three shots. Anibal and his colleagues slumped to the mud.

Matt looked out from the tuk-tuk. Here, there were no more huts, no signs of any habitation or human life. Damp, domineering trees cloaked the light from the road. When they were close to Matt's destination – a narrow track between the trees that led to the jungle clearance site – the driver tensed up and stopped as abruptly as his inadequate brakes would allow. Assorted vehicles were pulling out from among the trees on to the road ahead.

'Are we there?' grumbled Matt.

'*Si*, is almost where you want go but I wait for traffic. You pay now.'

Matt leaned forward and handed him a bundle of *quetzales*. He remained at that angle, squinting to see ahead, but the vehicles were obscured by a fog of exhaust and dust. There might have been rifles protruding from the silhouette of a pick-up truck receding into the distance, but he couldn't be sure. It didn't concern him.

Blatantly armed men were not exactly a rarity in this part of the world.

When the last of the vehicles had faded from view the tuk-tuk driver chugged to the gap in the trees from where they had all emerged, then halted, barely allowing Matt enough time to get both feet on the ground before he drove away. Matt banged the bonnet of an old Ford pick-up truck parked on the edge of the track as he walked past, checking the directions Ruby had carefully given him.

A thick and foetid stench began to invade his nostrils as he strode deeper into the ancient forest. With a hand over his mouth, he walked on towards the jungle clearing. Here, a choking black cloud billowed from multiple fires. He coughed, and tried to crouch low enough to get under the pall of smoke emanating from a mechanical excavator, almost every inch of its yellow paintwork firmly ablaze. The flames were erratic, spitting high and low, accompanied by the groaning of stressed steel. He ran cautiously past, wincing as the machine seemed to flex and shake as its superstructure creaked in the extreme heat. His peripheral vision caught the moment it exploded, now just yards behind him, and he registered the danger in his mind before the sound reached his ears. He felt himself ignominiously hurled up into the black air, then flung down hard, face in the dirt. The exploded vehicle was now surrounded by small puddles of burning fuel.

His first thought was of Ruby. Was she here? Was she injured? His heart began hammering and he leapt up, all of his senses buzzing. He checked himself for injuries, but found he was fine other than for the extensive covering of mud.

'Ruby!' He stumbled around the clearing, coughing and shouting through the smoke. No sign of anyone. 'Ruby?'

He tried to call her on his cell: no signal.

He paused to listen. There was nothing but the harsh crackling of the fires. Then he found the excavated pit. And in the pit he found the bodies.

The 'Do Not Disturb' sign still hung from the handle of the penthouse suite. With hindsight Ratty knew this had been an unwise choice of accommodation. Without the means to repay his fraudulent borrowings, the most expensive hotel room in Guatemala City now seemed a ridiculous extravagance. Ruby had a lot to answer for. Life would have been simple without her. He could have sold the stele and lived luxuriously in blissful ignorance of the dire consequences for the world's archaeological heritage. But all his life he had taken the easy option and it had been unremittingly dull. Now he had allowed his friend to push him into the path of danger and he had never felt more alive.

His key card worked at the first attempt, setting the light in the lock to green. He walked in and instantly wished he hadn't. The suite had been ransacked. The television was smashed. The contents of the mini bar were spread all over the floor. The bathroom mirror had been shattered, but the worst damage of all was to Ratty's finery. Shirts, blazers, trousers and shoes lay in shreds on the floor of the walk-in wardrobe. Ratty was aghast that anyone could disrespect a Nutters of Savile Row dress shirt. He tearfully picked up the remains of his favourite clothes and placed them on the bed. Destroying an expensive wardrobe of suits was the classic revenge of an ex-wife, but Ratty had no wife, ex or otherwise.

So much for 'Do Not Disturb', he thought, sitting on the bed at the centre of a scene that was a microcosm of the city today. How had they got in? The door hadn't been forced. Either they'd had a key or they'd come in through the window from the spacious balcony. He stood up and slid open the balcony door, hitting the wall of heat as he stepped outside. He had never thought to lock this door, since he was eight storeys above ground. Looking up, he realised it may be a long way up, but it was only ten feet down from the roof of the hotel. Anyone could have dropped down onto his balcony if they had access to the service staircase to the roof.

Mystery solved. Next he needed to know who. And why. If it had been a random act of vandalism then 'who' didn't matter and 'why' didn't exist, but it was clear to him that someone was trying to scare the heebie-jeebies out of him. It could only be Dr Otto. And yet the case against him wasn't as clear cut as Ratty would have liked. Otto had a vaguely Teutonic twang, which in Ratty's mind would normally be enough to convict anyone, and yet he didn't have an obvious motive to scare Ratty away. Why do this if you wanted someone to stick around for another meeting? Was he trying to instil in Ratty a sense of fear in order to make him co-operate more willingly? Or, Ratty mused, did he just object to his sense of fashion?

Whatever it was, whoever it was, it wouldn't shake him. He would use up what little remained of his ill-gotten funds to buy new outfits as soon as the shops re-opened. Trouble was his tailor was four thousand miles away and the local stores tended not to cater for his peculiar tastes. But the clothes he was wearing were in no condition to be worn again. He paced about the wrecked room, brain turning over fast, allowing himself to consider the wildest thoughts, ripping off his dusty and tattered garments as he did so.

Finally, he stood still, naked. A man stripped of his wealth, his style and his dignity. A bare body. A blank canvas.

He closed his eyes and asked himself if he was ready for this. The crazy ideas in his head had barely stopped spinning when he came to his conclusion.

He was going to embrace change.

In fact, he decided, he would use this incident to try something he had never attempted before: moving his fashion style forward by several decades. He would go even further than that. He would shake off the old Ratty, leave behind the daft clothes and fussy appearance that had made him a laughing stock at Cambridge. He would be reborn for his odyssey, a butterfly emerging from its pupa, unrecognisable to those who knew him. No longer a figure of mockery. No longer the awkward aristocrat. His plan took another step forward.

'Help.' The voice from the base of the pit was weak, straining to push precious air from searing lungs.

Matt wafted smoke away from his face, unnerved that one of the bodies was alive. Just. The man was lying partly on top of one of the other men. His legs were in an unnatural position. Matt's stomach churned. This was not the kind of situation in which he had expected to find himself today. All he was ready for were awkward hugs and kisses with Ruby followed by a candlelit meal with the possibility of a romantic atmosphere if he didn't screw it up and start arguing with a waiter. Carnage in a hole in the ground was an unwelcome diversion.

'You OK down there?' He regretted his question before he had even finished shouting it, uncomfortable at his own crassness. A true hero would get straight down there, no questions asked. Something deep within him tried to convince him that this was someone else's problem, and someone else would fix it. He fought the urge to walk away. But there was no one else who could help; he sensed an unfamiliar moral obligation. No doubt

Richard Dawkins would be able to explain what he was feeling. He had met the famous British biologist at a book signing and had been amazed that the queue for signed copies of a book about whether God existed was longer than the queue for his war memoirs.

He grabbed the ladder that was lying near him and dropped it over the side.

'Hang in there, buddy,' he called as he climbed timidly down the rungs.

'Help me,' groaned the man.

Matt looked at him more closely. He wore the same polo shirt as the two dead men, branded with some kind of company logo. All three shirts were blood-stained. The living man also had a horribly broken leg, his snapped femur bone pressing unsubtly against the inside of his trousers, threatening to tear the fabric open. It was too much for Matt. He felt himself turn green. Deep breath, he told himself. Fight the gag reflex. This was a living person. He had to say something, do something. The Dawkins instinct, whatever it was, somehow gave him the strength to avoid throwing up. He forced himself to communicate with the man.

'What's your name, pal?'

'Anibal.'

'Matt. What the hell happened here?'

Anibal looked at him through fading eyes. A spark of recognition lit them briefly.

'You look like Matt Mountebank.'

'Er, yeah. You're in pretty bad shape. I got no signal on my cell so I can't call –'

'They shot me. Shot all of us. Threw us in here.'

That much Matt had already gathered. What in hell he could actually do about it, however, he had no idea. Anibal, on the other hand, seemed confident in Matt's capabilities.

'Losing blood,' wheezed Anibal, starting to sound weaker.

'I can see. Just don't know what I can do.'

'Like the scene in your book? Guy gets shot and you save his life?'

'You really read it, then, buddy?'

Anibal seemed convinced that his ebbing life was in safe hands. The pain from his stomach and leg wounds subsided as the blood continued to flow out of his body. There was nothing more for him to fear. Matt coughed awkwardly.

'That scene, you know, my, um, editor at the publishing house might have embellished that. You can't always believe what you read.'

'But you saved his life, right?' He spoke slowly now: his body had decided speaking was a lower priority than keeping his heart beating.

'Christ, man, you gotta understand there was a bit of artistic licence there. I was just trying to tell a damn good story.'

Matt tried to recall the scene in *Eye of the Desert Storm*. He hadn't actually read it for a couple of years, and was now sketchy about some of the details, but he remembered something about saving a dying man by tying a tourniquet round his leg for the open fracture and an improvised bandage round his body to seal both entry and exit wounds together.

'Hurry,' whispered Anibal.

In his book Matt had used his clothing as bandages, but the clothes in the anecdote were at least vaguely hygienic. There was nothing on him or the dead guys that was remotely clean. Even if by some miracle Matt succeeded in stemming his patient's blood loss, Anibal would rapidly and inevitably succumb to infection. He took off his belt and wrapped it around Anibal's thigh.

Matt didn't know much first aid, but he had seen enough movies to know that if Anibal survived he would have to lose his leg. The tourniquet would cut off the blood supply to the limb, causing it to die within minutes. He then whipped the pants off one of the bodies and tied them tightly around the stomach wounds, trying not to look too much at the blood.

Anibal appeared comforted by the attention he had received. Matt just wanted to get out of that pit. He wanted fresh air. He wanted to wash his hands of the bodily fluids that didn't belong to him, but first he needed to know what had happened to Ruby.

The late afternoon sunlight reflecting off the medical instruments on the stainless steel trolley sparkled with a brilliance that made the items difficult to see. Three syringes lay in a regimental line, each filled and ready for injection. A small Petri dish of pills sat adjacent, along with a thermometer and a blood pressure monitor. Dr Otto adjusted the blind in the window to reduce the glare, ensuring that the slats lay perfectly horizontally. Now he could see the items clearly. It was important to administer the treatments correctly so that the results would be consistent, measurable and meaningful. The experiment had been running for many years already, sometimes in circumstances that were less than ideal. Otto had faced all of the challenges and changes as they came along, calmly and methodically adjusting to new environments and locations when necessary. The only constant in the experiment was his subject. One man: unwaveringly enthusiastic, always co-operative. The drugs guaranteed it.

He checked his watch. It was time.

He opened the door to the adjoining room and indicated to his subject that he was ready. The man strode confidently towards Otto, head held high, sleeves rolled up in familiar readiness. He sat himself on a metal-framed chair and meditated serenely as one injection after another penetrated his arms, then washed down the pills with a large glass of expensive imported mineral water.

'I made it,' said the man, proudly.

'I congratulate you,' replied Otto. 'But it has taken too long to get here, even with the vast resources I have provided. Time is now extremely short and there is much to do. We are a long way from being ready.'

Otto performed a brief examination of the patient, checking heart rate, blood pressure and body temperature. Most days the examinations were more thorough, but today his subject had other priorities that demanded his attention, and Otto was resigned to a bare bones session.

All of the medical signs were satisfactory. Otto recorded the results on a laptop, pleased to note that there were no mystifying aberrations from the anticipated long term trends. The subject looked healthy, he had to admit. His skin tone, body fat index and natural hair colour would not have shamed a man half his age.

'I won't let you down, Otto. We'll be ready.'

'Good. You can leave, Orlando. Or shall I call you Mr President?'

The man smiled, returned to the adjoining room and closed the door behind him. The Doctor began the rituals of cleaning, disposing and tidying that followed each of these sessions. The services of a nurse could have helped him with the more mundane duties, but he refused to employ an assistant, partly due to the necessity that his work remain strictly confidential, and partly because something deep inside him gained an Aristotelian pleasure from small rituals.

His mind turned to other matters while he cleaned. His encounters with Lord Ballashiels had been most troubling.

He thought about the handwritten message that His Lordship must by now have read and digested. He thought about the two agents he had sent to His Lordship's hotel room. That perturbed him further. He thought about what he would say to His Lordship when and if he called. No response came immediately to mind that would earn back the confidence that had been lost.

It wasn't theft, Matt convinced himself. It was in a good cause. He closed his eyes and screwed up his face in disgust as he reached into the trouser pocket of Anibal's fresh corpse and pulled out a set of keys. He looked at the brand name on the fob: Ford. It matched the truck parked at the entrance to the jungle clearing.

Anibal had managed only a few words before his breath failed to come, and Matt wasn't sure he really understood many of them. The dying man clearly didn't have a clue who Ruby was. Only the words 'Tikal' and '*aeropuerto*' had been communicated clearly. They were all he had to go on.

Tikal. That was some kind of ancient thing in the jungle, he thought as he climbed out of the pit. Ruby had mentioned it before, and Matt had seen signs pointing to it. It was no more than a couple of miles away, but the airport he had landed at was at Flores, not Tikal. The idea of an airport at Tikal just didn't make sense. He couldn't imagine anyone building an international airport next to Stonehenge, or converting the leaning tower of Pisa into a control tower. Ancient monuments and airports just didn't go together. Anibal's mention of an *aeropuerto* could have been a delusional comment. The convoy he'd witnessed leaving here earlier wasn't heading for Flores Airport, however.

He wondered if he ought to chuck some soil onto the bodies below. Maybe say a few words as a mark of respect for three men he knew nothing about. At least show some sympathy for the demise of one of his fans. No, he decided, jingling the keys and running to the road. They were dead and Ruby might still be alive. He had to find her.

He climbed into Anibal's pick-up, slid back the seat to accommodate his longer frame and inserted the key that he had taken from the man's pocket. The rugged six-litre engine roared to life, while the air-conditioning soothed him with fresh, cool air.

He pointed the pick-up along the dirt road towards Tikal.

Within a mile there was another sign, and soon enough the entrance gate to the Tikal National Park loomed large above him, an ominous structure not dissimilar to the gates in *Jurassic Park*. Matt spotted a guidebook seller and pulled over.

'Hey, buddy! There an airport here?'

'Is only one hundred *quetzales*,' said the man, now leaning against the pick-up truck. He was short and stocky, a typical modern Mayan, and wore a green Tikal Park uniform.

'No, I just need to know if there's an airport here.'

'This book contains map of Tikal. Is only one hundred *quetzales*.'

Matt found the exact sum in cash and handed it over. He unfolded the black and white hand-drawn map and scanned it for anything that looked like a runway. The area included the Tikal reserve and some of the surrounding Maya Biosphere, but there were very few place names other than those of the temples and plazas of the old city. Cursing, he jumped out and approached the guidebook seller. By now another driver had pulled up and was demanding the man's attention, so Matt walked over to his hut. Inside was a second stocky man, dressed casually and smoking a cigarette.

'Is there an airport here?' asked Matt.

'*Si*,' replied the man after a cursory glance. '*El aeropuerto*.'

'Speak English?'

'*Si*, is old. The archaeologists build it when they excavate the place, but noise and pollution from the airplanes is damage the old temples so they build a new one at Flores.'

'How do I get there?'

'Just drive into the reserve and turn right before visitor centre. I no think you can get in there. Is closed since forty years.'

Matt drove further into the reserve, but there was no sign of habitation, just a narrow dirt track tunnelling into the suffocating jungle. He drove through it for twenty minutes, totally alone in the interminable greenery, before the track opened out into a parking zone, a visitor centre and undiluted sunshine.

To his right he glimpsed the remains of the airstrip, well on its way towards becoming as ravaged by the ferocious rainforest as the pyramids of Tikal themselves. Nothing would ever land here again. At the far end of the overgrown runway was a large building, an old hangar. The only challenge remaining was working out what to say to people who were sufficiently sadistic to shoot the guys in the matching polo shirts. One thing at a time, he decided. Park the car and watch the scene for a while. See if Ruby was there. Better to make sure than to rush in, all guns blazing. Not that he had any guns.

Before he had a chance to slow down a loud bang coincided with the pick-up lurching violently towards the trees. Compensating hard, he wrenched the steering wheel round with both hands. Loose gravel and ruts in the track resisted his efforts, and the pick-up careered off the road at a tight angle. Matt jammed the brakes and the wheels locked up, embedding themselves in the soft earth as the vehicle stopped, its front tyre blown apart by a shot from an unknown enemy.

Taking off a dead guy's soiled pants was supposed to have been the low point of today, but somehow things had gotten worse. It was like he'd been sucked into the horrible, violent military matrix of his own book. But he knew exactly what to do about it.

He would run away.

He threw himself out of the car in a split second, dashing at full tilt into undergrowth. Another shot sang past his ear. His heart rattled. He stole a peek up over the foliage. The dirty white wall of the aircraft hangar protruded past the tree line. Two soldiers staggered around the edge of the roof, apparently in celebratory mood. Their interest in Matt briefly waned, and their attention turned to hunting any examples of wildlife big enough to take a bullet.

Matt began to wish he had a copy of his war memoirs on him, a quick read of which might instil the sense of heroism that he badly needed. He thought once more of Ruby. Did she need someone to save her? Images flashed through his mind of the kind of peril she might be facing. He blinked hard, trying to block the horrors from his head, but they simply grew more vivid, more terrifying. And as they did so, he felt a strange sensation rushing through his veins. It was not dissimilar to a slug of rum. It was a sense of euphoria: a pain-killing, fear-diminishing wash of adrenaline.

He shook himself to see if it would go away.

It was still there. The courage had come.

He resolved to creep closer to the hangar, slip past those guards and give Ruby the rescue she was probably praying for. Ducking beneath the sea of ferns, he crawled towards the building. Above him was a small window. He stood up and peeked.

The murky interior was alive with the buzzing of a cloud of flies. The blur morphed into a toilet. Matt hauled himself in through the ragged opening and fell inside. A pernicious odour stung the back of his throat. He picked himself up and stepped out into the cavernous body of the hangar. It was empty apart from something monstrous silhouetted in the centre. It seemed exotic, ponderous, an immense mass. It drew him like a magnet. He walked over to it, horribly aware of the echo of his footsteps across the hangar floor.

On closer inspection he saw it was dented and distorted. It couldn't be – but it really was – coated in gold. This object was worth millions. That would explain the guards, then. Might even explain why they were celebrating. For a moment he forgot Operation Ruby. He touched the tattered golden sides, running a hand along the muddy metalwork. It was large enough to accommodate people, but there were no windows, not even a door. At its blunt end there appeared to be a hollow but it was indistinct and full of mud. Maybe it was some kind of sculpture.

A stepladder had been left leaning against the artefact. On one of the steps was a gun-like object, but its casing was of dusty plastic and on closer inspection it looked no more interesting than a hair dryer. Matt pocketed it anyway, and climbed up quickly, telling himself this was no time for sightseeing.

One brief look wouldn't hurt.

He took hold of the jagged metal of the damaged front section and climbed cautiously onto the top, looking for some evidence of a way inside. This was taking too long, he told himself. He should be looking for Ruby, not indulging his curiosity.

Just a few more seconds. He needed to prove to himself that this was just a piece of art.

A piece of art with a crumpled hatch.

With a tug of the roughly cut edges he lifted it a few inches.

Matt heard voices behind him. There was only one thing to do. He pulled harder and opened it wide enough to squeeze inside. The hatch fell closed above him.

He was in a tight, dusty compartment, lying uncomfortably on what felt like sticks and stones. He took hold of the hair dryer-like object from his pocket and pointed it upwards. It would have to do.

The door above began to open. The dim light of the hangar trickled into Matt's chamber, bringing with it the sound of a voice.

'... indentations on the side show this. You see this feature? But where is the corrosion? It's like ore. How is this possible?'

Matt relaxed. This man spoke in English. He didn't sound like a soldier. Matt figured he might be able to bluff his way out of here.

Then a young woman with a British accent spoke up.

'Would you mind not blowing that revolting smoke in my face?'

Matt spluttered. He thought he had heard Ruby, but he wasn't sure. Whoever it was had not yet seen him. They were fiddling with the sharp edges of the hatch, trying to open it wider.

'Anything for you,' said the man's voice. 'Hearing your sweet voice is like being tickled by a flower on my –

'Paulo!'

The door dropped shut again, sealing Matt inside.

'From what I saw earlier I think some of the bones have

been crushed in correspondence to the deformation of the gold outer skin,' Paulo explained. 'They can't have been disturbed since their death.'

'So you think … no, it's impossible. You're saying that these bodies have been lying in this thing for, what, thousands of years?'

Ruby could barely think straight. Her muscles ached. Her head was light. This golden thing in front of her, this beautiful sarcophagus, couldn't possibly have been constructed in an age when humankind was barely out of the trees. The bones looked like they were from the Stone Age. That was Barney Rubble in there. Humankind's only achievement from that period of history was smashing rocks together and painting unconvincing mammoths on cave walls. The ability to work with metals was unheard of back then. No one in their right mind would date this artefact so far back in time.

And yet, there was something about it that didn't belong in any other time. Its shape shared nothing with subsequent cultures. For an object found in the heart of the Maya Biosphere there was nothing in its lines and curves to suggest Mayan origin. She gripped the door at the top of the artefact once more, and Paulo joined the effort.

Matt was now certain it really was Ruby's muffled voice he had heard. When they finally pulled back the hatch, he had composed himself.

'Got your text, Rubes,' he said, coolly, as if he was having lunch and they had just walked into the restaurant. Both Ruby and Paulo jumped several inches in the air, narrowly missing falling off the ladder that they were precariously sharing.

'Matt!' screamed Ruby, shaking from head to toe and gripping the rough edge of the hatch so hard her palms began to bleed.

Paulo, now in control of his reflexes, grabbed her arm to steady her.

A piercing light fell onto the craft and the people on its back as the main hangar doors rumbled open.

'Who are you?' hissed Paulo.

'He's with me,' sighed Ruby.

Paulo could see the silhouette of a man walking towards them. A look was sufficient to tell Ruby to shut the hatch with Matt still inside. The two drunken guards had shimmied down from the roof and now stood, with some difficulty, at the doorway. Lorenzo walked towards the artefact, grinning broadly.

'Keep still,' Ruby whispered as she closed the hatch.

'Come down,' said Lorenzo, stroking back his blond hair.

Smears of her blood marked her short passage down the aluminium rungs. Paulo tried his best not to stain his suit as he followed her, but soon gave in to the inevitable.

'If we are going to be of any use to you, Paulo and I need more time to assess this find.'

'Perhaps. But what we discover is something special. You are probably no aware the President is arrested this morning. Guerrilla forces signed a deal with the army. General Orlando the Indestructible is new President. We have big celebrations. Is General Orlando – President Orlando – who now owns this artefact.'

'Oh no – this is a UN find. Right, Paulo?'

Her boss looked at the floor, saying nothing.

'UN? Hah! No matter, you are both honoured. The President would like to see you. My men will take care of this while you are gone.'

'I can't leave,' objected Ruby, cutting in front of him, hands clasped tightly together to mask the burning pain. 'This find has been disturbed by your soldiers. Parts of it may need to be protected from moisture in the air. There is a radiation risk. You should all keep away from it. I must do a detailed check to see if any permanent damage has been caused.' Her voice had begun to wobble. Matt was in trouble. She had been blabbering on, desperate for a ruse to get everyone out of there long enough for her to guide Matt to safety.

'Of course,' said Lorenzo. 'You start in a few days. Come.'

She considered Matt's chances if these trigger-happy soldiers found him hiding inside the object they were supposed to be guarding. Not good. Should she confess to his presence and try to defuse the inevitably tense stand-off that would result? They might still shoot him, but if she said nothing then at least there was a slim chance that he could get away without being seen. It felt like his life was in her hands and it wasn't a responsibility she appreciated. To tell or not to tell. It tore her up inside.

As Lorenzo shuffled her towards the waiting car, she made her decision.

TUESDAY 20ᵀᴴ NOVEMBER 2012

The random shape was not dissimilar to the coastline of Italy. Monika Loewe almost thought she could see a Venetian lagoon forming around a white button as the still-steaming coffee stain spread unhurriedly across her shirt. It was typical of her to see it as if from an orbiting satellite, she pondered, at once detached from the situation and yet profoundly angry that she had lowered her guard and become a victim. Again. She thought she had made her deficiency in the sense of humour department perfectly clear after the first incident. It was reasonable to expect some form of initiation ceremony for a new employee, but this was just juvenile. She looked around her at the grinning faces of her colleagues. Each possessed a science doctorate. It was pathetic. She put the half-empty cup of coffee on her desk and reset the sabotaged gas lift switch under her chair so that it could now take her weight without plummeting down to the floor.

Monika Loewe had just achieved her dream job with the European Space Agency, and already she loathed it. Her ambitious goal had kept her motivated during the difficult decade she had spent waitressing in seedy Hamburg bars to pay her way through graduate and postgraduate college. She never stopped to count her tips at the end of each shift; her only desire was to rush back to her bedsit and study. The cumulative effect of thousands of hours of lost sleep was etched upon her face. Wrinkles had come early. There was no space for laughter lines.

Beating a hundred other applicants to this job at the Tracking and Imaging Radar at Wachtberg, not far from Bonn, was a significant moment in her life. Her mother would have been proud had she lived to witness it, but the excesses of the student culture in the mid-1970s had finally caught up with her. A degree in Medicine hadn't given her the common sense to look after her own body, and she had slipped away just weeks before her daughter's moment of triumph. Whether there existed a father to make proud, Monika had no idea. Her mother had always forbidden any enquiry into the matter. But as the wretchedness she felt at her mother's passing evolved into a more bearable ache in her soul, she'd begun to wonder.

Monika was now part of ESA's Space Situational Awareness Programme, tracking objects in low Earth orbit and beyond. Satellites, meteorites, and the thousands of pieces of junk that now littered the thermosphere and exosphere, it all had to be tracked and recorded, not only to protect astronauts and spacecraft, but also to be aware of any objects that could fall to Earth. She took her achievement seriously. Unlike the jerks with whom she had the misfortune to share her working environment. Especially unlike Rocco Strauss, the worst of the bunch. She would never have guessed that such a conservative-looking white collar exterior could conceal a mind that was, perhaps appropriately for his job, completely off the planet.

Rocco seemed to believe in every conspiracy theory going. Yesterday he'd bored Monika with evidence of Hitler's retirement years in Patagonia after the war, followed by 'proof' that the twin towers were brought down by an experimental energy field weapon rather than by the planes. His latest hypothesis was that the Chinese didn't have the expertise to send a robotic probe to Mars and to bring it back to Earth with samples of Martian soil, as the world currently believed they were doing. She wondered how he found the time to collect such a vast body of misinformation when he was busy setting up pointless practical jokes. If he wanted a reaction from her, he was going to be disappointed.

She stared intently at her monitor. She had earlier left the computer guiding TIRA's vast radar dish to a section of northern sky. But it had moved.

Someone had pointed it at the planet Mars.

If a city could experience a hangover, Guatemala's capital awoke to a throbbing humdinger of one. Shop and office workers swept broken glass into the street before opening up. They used blankets to cover the bodies on the sidewalk. Some arrived at work to find their premises reduced to steaming rubble. Despite the destruction of the headquarters of a television station, word had reached the entire population via other media about yesterday's coup. The trails of destruction that had been gouged through the city all converged on the government buildings and the presidential palace.

Ruby's overnight journey back into the heart of the revolution had been bumpy and uncomfortable, hours of insomnia exacerbated by uncertainty and self-doubt. Had she done the right thing in keeping silent about the illicit concealment of her soon-to-be-ex lover? Would it have been better to explain Matt's presence in the artefact to the soldiers rather than risk his subsequent discovery? Would he still be waiting in there for her when she returned to Tikal? The many ways in which his presence could contaminate a priceless slice of history appalled her. The manner in which Paulo had orchestrated the violent extraction of the artefact sickened her. And her indecision and hesitancy at whether to confess Matt's presence tormented her. In the grip of oppressive emotional discord, sleep was not an option.

The presidential palace was as ungracious and unsubtle as a motorway bridge, a modern recreation of Spanish colonial architecture in breezeblock and concrete. Its painted exterior, formerly a vibrant and textured jaundice, had been rendered opaque by the effects of cordite, shrapnel and smog. A familiar, but not unpleasant, smell hit Ruby's nostrils as she was led into the President's inner suite, but it wasn't until she saw the swimming pool dominating the floor space that she recognised the odour as chlorine. President Orlando swam towards his guests and walked up tiled steps, out of the water. Nothing about his demeanour remotely suggested he was embarrassed at conducting his business almost naked. An assistant smoothly passed a large, fluffy white towel to him, which he deftly tucked around his waist, the water from his light brown hair and muscular legs leaving rivulets on the marble floor.

Having coolly looked his visitors in the eye, the President said nothing. He breathed deeply, then jogged around the pool towards a lavish Victorian Gillows Serpentine desk. The marble floor was wet and slippery; he skidded for a few feet, but managed to maintain his balance and reach his desk in one piece.

He drank some Evian. A cheerless silence descended while those in the room waited for him to finish.

'It is not easy to achieve perfect physical condition,' Orlando eventually declared.

Tired, cynical eyes widened. Ruby blinked to tame the involuntary response, but she could not disagree with his assessment. His body had a dark, even tan, his muscles were well toned, his posture was straight and his nails were manicured. He was clean-shaven and there was not a single strand of grey on the full head of hair that might have given away his age of forty-five years.

'I am tuned to such a state of health that I haven't had so much as a cold in over a decade. That is remarkable, is it not?'

Heads nodded nervously.

'With the knowledge and technology of cutting edge modern medicine,' he continued, 'I believe something wonderful, something magnificent, is upon us.' Orlando looked at his rather indifferent and perplexed audience. 'Billions of our ancestors have crumbled to dust. Countless generations have perished. They learn and develop as humans all their lives and then – zap. All over. Back to a blank canvas with the next one. That pattern does not have to be repeated for ever. Ah, but I bore you with my dreams.'

'No, not at all,' protested Paulo, unconvincingly. 'Please go on.'

'It is my belief that with the appropriate medical supervision and intervention, our generation could be the first one for which a demise is optional.'

Heads looked blankly at each other.

'Unless you break your skull on a wet marble floor,' quietly uttered the lips on Ruby's face, much to her consternation and frustration.

Paulo shot her a black look, then glanced at the President with eyes that begged for leniency. Orlando wrapped a clean white dressing gown over his shoulders and sashayed towards the source of the errant words.

'It would take significantly more than that to finish me off. I have health care that is, how can I put this, somewhat unique.'

'Either it is unique or it isn't. It can't be "somewhat" unique,' grumbled Ruby.

'Are you hurt?' Orlando asked, ignoring her English lesson and looking at her hands. They were still stained red from the cuts she'd received gripping the rough metal on the top of the artefact the previous day.

'I'm sure I'm not the only one here with blood on their hands,' she replied automatically. There was no measurable gap that Ruby could perceive between those words spilling out and the onset of an all too familiar regret at her inability to keep her thoughts to herself.

'Doctor Ruby Towers, hmm. Welcome. My name is Orlando. What do you think of my new palace? I am lucky that it survived. We did not expect them to put up such a fight, but now this is my home, and I am having it polished and tidied.'

'I noticed them tidying a couple of your victims on the driveway.'

Paulo glanced at her nervously. Ruby found herself actually biting her lip.

'Please excuse her,' offered Paulo, 'it is her hormones talking.'

'You must show respect,' Lorenzo snapped at Ruby.

But she continued to stare directly into the President's face. Paulo looked at his boots. The atmosphere tensed in anticipation of the President's response, which did not come immediately.

He walked away, rubbing his hair with another towel. From his desk he picked up his Omega Seamaster watch and a ring, putting them on as he walked back to Ruby.

With a tight smile, he said to her, 'I have never killed

another man, Ruby. If my soldiers deem it necessary to fire in self-defence then that is their decision, but it has never been my goal to end lives. The opposite, in fact, is true. However, it is worth noting that if no one ever died, you would have no bones to dig up and study in your job.'

'Interesting. Irrelevant, of course, but interesting,' she retorted.

'Ruby, President Orlando is our host and we are his guests,' whispered Paulo, just loudly enough for his President to hear him.

'Of course. I'm just a little unused to the etiquette of this country. Where I come from we don't kidnap our guests.'

'She does not realise her place. Where she comes from women speak their minds in the rudest fashion. I will endeavour to teach her some manners,' Paulo whined.

'I know of your reputation, Ruby,' said the President, ignoring Paulo. 'We are honoured to have you in our country.' He flashed a huge smile, showing almost blindingly white teeth. 'Anyway, to business.' He turned to Paulo and Lorenzo. 'I have been informed of the discovery of the artefact at Tikal. You will organise resources, personnel and equipment to conduct a full examination of it. I want the Tikal hangar equipped within forty-eight hours. Doctor Towers will head the research team, and I will send her there when the hangar is ready. I bid you good day.'

Paulo and Lorenzo bowed awkwardly and clumped out of the room.

'It has taken me longer than planned to gain control of this country,' Orlando said, now addressing Ruby. 'There are now but a few weeks remaining. I must work fast. So must you. These are exceptional times. Much remains to be done before ... well, let me say simply that this is why your project at Tikal must proceed at a pace that may appear unprofessional.'

'A few weeks until what?' Ruby could not help asking.

'Ruby, while I have you here as my guest I would appreciate the chance to discuss archaeology with you,' he said, apparently changing the subject.

'Look, I never agreed to ...' began Ruby before the sound of approaching footsteps climaxed with a bold knock that drew Orlando's attention from her. The doors slid open and a soldier marched in, delivering a couple of pieces of paper to the President.

Orlando gestured to Ruby to take a seat at the far end of the room. From her new position she tried to overhear the hushed conversation between the President and the soldier. Some of the words floated into her ears, but they remained isolated, unconnected with each other and without any kind of significance. The word 'justice' was the only thing she understood with any clarity.

Orlando signed two pieces of paper with his dominant dashing squiggle, handing one copy to the soldier and putting the other on the desk. The man wheeled round before marching out of the room, nodding politely to Ruby.

'Let's get away from my office. There will be too many interruptions.'

He led her through a side door to a small ante-room. There was an uncomfortable-looking chair, a stainless steel trolley with some shiny surgical items laid out neatly and some locked cupboards. This room in turn led through to the magnificent library that the previous President had converted into a centre for emergency planning. A patch of sunshine found its way through the smog, spilling through the open French doors onto the maps, documents, telephones and televisions scattered all over the long desk and on the floor. Clearly the room had been abandoned in a hurry. This mess of papers and technology represented tangible proof to Orlando of his personal triumph. Ruby could see he was thoroughly pleased with himself.

'Your own career I find fascinating, Ruby,' he said, stepping outside and putting on a pair of $4,000 Moss Lipow sunglasses.

'You do?' Ruby was forced to squint, having been separated from her $40 sunglasses the previous day.

'So. I know that you are from England. You have degrees from the University of Cambridge and you recently dug inside the Sphinx and found ten scrolls.'

'I assumed they were scrolls. The clay tubes were stolen, so I'll never know for sure what was inside.'

'They were scrolls.' He looked at her with a certainty that she found curious, but she was too tired to infer any deeper meaning.

'After the Sphinx project was cancelled I returned to England and worked in a museum before coming here at the request of the United Nations. UNESCO.'

'It is my duty to inform you that you are mistaken.'

'I hardly think so. I work for the UN. Paulo is my boss.'

'Paulo Souza?'

'Yes, Paulo Souza.'

Orlando permitted himself a faintly disturbing chuckle.

'It may surprise you to learn that the same Paulo Souza has never had any connection with the United Nations.'

'That's impossible. I've been working with him for weeks.'

'It makes no difference. You now have the privilege of being in my employment. Come, Ruby. There is more to see.'

'No. This is nonsense. I was asked to come to Guatemala by the UN. I have a contract. Signed by Paulo. He's been with them for —'

'He has been working for me for many years,' cut in Orlando. 'He will never be a great actor, but his little deception appears to have been a success.'

'What?'

'Please accept my apologies for misleading you, Ruby, but it was the only way we could get you into our country and under my wing. You will get used to working for me.'

A rare moment of speechlessness came over Ruby. Things began to fall into place. The lack of a permanent office, the excuses she had been given about communication problems when she had wanted to contact New York, the isolation she had endured. The job offer, the interview, the paperwork – all a sham. She felt stupid. Embarrassed. The gentlemanly profession which worked on the trust of decent people had let her down.

Paulo's behaviour now made sense. Her entire Guatemalan experience now made sense. Everything made sense. And yet nothing made sense. Why was she so important to a newly installed Third World dictator? How could someone with such a capacity for evil and brutality even have been aware of her existence?

Ruby's thoughts were distracted by a large, rare orchid in an ostentatious chrome planter. One of the pure white petals of this *Lycaste skinneri* – the national flower of Guatemala – displayed a perfectly circular bullet hole. Another bloom hung by a fibre, its stem half-severed.

'An appropriate symbol for your country,' said Ruby.

Orlando followed her line of sight.

'Mice. Let us walk around to the back. I prefer to conduct my affairs outside. A lifetime of habit, I suppose.'

A scraping noise made Ruby turn. A body dropped from the arm of a mechanical digger into the back of a truck on the main driveway. It landed with an indifferent thump, devoid of dignity. Paying no attention, Orlando walked on along the elegant and mostly undamaged patio that surrounded the palace.

'Don't you have stuff to do?' called Ruby, chasing behind him. 'You know, doing Hitler impressions and killing people?' The turmoil in her stomach caused by the uncertainty as to Matt's fate was making her even snappier than usual.

Orlando laughed and patted her affectionately on the shoulder. Her whole body tensed and she fought the urge to spit at him as he invited her to sit with him at one of the garden tables.

Orlando's comment about the scrolls finally cut through her tiredness.

'You seemed pretty sure that what I found in the Sphinx contained scrolls,' she said, trying to avoid a mildly accusatory tone. 'You can't know that because they are lost to the world.'

'Indeed,' he replied. 'The scrolls are lost to the world.' Before she could push him further on his remarks, he changed the subject. 'You have also worked in Antarctica,' he said. 'Tell me why you went there.'

'It's not something I'm proud of. The science was weak from the start and the whole premise of the dig was dubious.'

'You didn't find Atlantis, then?' mocked Orlando.

'Some members of the team were convinced there were good reasons for believing we might find traces of former habitation. A lost civilisation. Call it Atlantis if you will. I wasn't convinced, but I went along because I wanted to see Antarctica.'

'Why look for Atlantis at Antarctica?'

'I'm sick of defending that dig. Can we talk about something else?'

Orlando said nothing, just relaxed in his chair and waited for her to continue. She sensed he was using subtle control techniques over her, but was too fatigued to put up much of a fight.

'This was not my theory,' she groaned. 'Basically, Plato described Atlantis as an island continent beyond the entrance to the Mediterranean Sea, which has to be in the Atlantic if he was correct. He said the State of Atlantis was an advanced seafaring nation which, according to legend, disappeared under water at what we now know to be the end of the last Ice Age, about twelve thousand years ago. As the polar ice melted, sea levels rose around the world, which is why every society on Earth has a collective memory of a devastating flood, usually passed down through the generations in story form. The Judeo-Christian story of Noah's Ark is very similar to native American legends from long before the two cultures ever met. The global flood was a fact, but it didn't last for just forty days, it was permanent. So it's entirely sensible and logical to deduce that towns or even whole nations might have been lost. But the difficulty with the Atlantis myth is that we know there are no submerged continents in the Atlantic.'

She paused and looked to see if Orlando had become comatose with boredom. He lifted his sunglasses to the top of his head. Surprisingly his eyes were lit with enthusiasm, giving her the confidence to continue.

'All we have is an actual ice-covered continent at the southern end of the ocean. The theory that my colleagues wanted to explore was that rather than flooding, tectonic movement shifted Atlantis south over the pole where it consequently froze over. But we couldn't find any evidence beneath the ice of previous human occupation. Surprise, surprise.'

Orlando leaned even further back in his garden chair, face tight as though he was teasing her, keeping something back.

'Do you believe in the legend of Atlantis at all?' he asked.

'I'm not sure. There's no logical reason why it can't be true, but it might just be a fanciful story. I'm a scientist so I'm open-minded. If we find evidence, then I'll investigate and draw my own conclusions. Nothing has convinced me so far, although the Santorini theory has some merit.'

Ruby was distracted again, this time by distant shouts from soldiers on the other side of the palace and the crashes and bangs of their 'tidying'. Orlando leaned forward, suddenly totally focused.

'And what about the artefact that was found yesterday?' he asked, his own enthusiasm for the subject shining uncontrollably through his body language and tone of voice. 'I understand that the bodies inside may date back to the end of the Ice Age.'

'Subject to confirmation by carbon dating. We can't be sure yet,' she answered, attempting a tone of professional detachment which entirely failed to remain in place long enough to stop her sounding like an excited schoolgirl when she added, 'but the patina of the bones indicates a substantial age.'

Orlando smiled. He let the profundity of her comment sink in, enjoying their momentary connection with a lost antiquity.

'I have some archaeological insights that I may choose to share with you. Join me here in an hour or so.'

'And what if I decline?' she said, trying not to exhibit her tussling feelings of flattery, annoyance, curiosity, and concern.

'That is your choice, Ruby, but I know you will not decline me. You are a guest in my palace, but I have to insist that you do not leave until we are ready to return you to Tikal.'

'Considering your men confiscated my wallet and passport this morning I'm not likely to get very far.'

'Nevertheless, you should remain under my wing. For your own protection.'

'Protection? Who from? You?'

Orlando pulled the sunglasses back over his eyes and looked away.

'Can I help you?'

Ratty spun round, briefly forgetting that his head felt as if it was on fire. The shop assistant was short and curvaceous. Ratty was unsure if her facial expression – eyebrows raised, mouth open wide – was one of sympathy or infuriation. He had been lurking in a corner of her clothes store scratching his head maniacally, desperate for the burning to cease. Somehow his appearance and state of distress were enough for this young lady to be confident in addressing him in English.

'Good afternoon,' he replied.

'Is your hair uncomfortable?' she asked.

It was one of the most intimate questions a female had ever asked him. The condition of a gentleman's thatch was the concern of himself and his barber, no one else. It was certainly not the business of an anonymous shop girl. And, to boot, a shop girl in an establishment where all the garments were already made, hung out on racks like pieces of meat for people to buy regardless of how well they might fit. No samples of raw cloth, no one to measure one's inside leg, not a tailor in sight. He hadn't even been offered a glass of champagne. Then he checked his instinctive reaction. He was in considerable pain. The black dye he had applied to his hair back in the hotel room – the first stage in his reinvention – was killing him. Perhaps there was something she could do. Ho hum, he decided, when in Rome …

'Gosh, well, now you mention it –'

Before he could finish explaining away his state of botheration he found himself being ushered towards the customer toilet at the rear of the shop. She bowed his sticky black head over the sink and began rinsing cold water over it. He stood still, back stiffly arched, unused to such rapid intimacy, unable to deny that the intensity of the burning sensation was decreasing. She started rubbing his head with the hand towel, then stood him up straight to take a look at him. He was not at his most elegant, but his new jet black hair was very imposing.

She rinsed her hands and led him back to the racks of clothes.

'I say, thank you. The old frizzies feel much better now.'

'Was that the first time you changed your hair colour?'

Another intimate question. This was edgy stuff, almost thrilling.

'One is something of a novice in that department,' he mumbled.

'You must shampoo and rinse after a few minutes. Remember next time,' she explained, calmly. 'So what kind of clothes do you want? Looking for a change of image?'

She glanced at his tattered upper class English suit and gesticulated at the clothes on sale in her store. There were denim jeans of various shades of blue and black taking up an entire wall. Combat-style trousers with lots of useful-looking pockets were displayed in tints of green and brown. Leather jackets hung in regimental rows, gradually shrinking in size from one end to the other. Clumpy shoes adorned shelf after shelf. Every item was as far from Ratty's current image as it was possible to be. It was what he knew he wanted, but, overwhelmed by the enormity of the change, Ratty merely nodded to the assistant. She understood and took his hand as she guided him through the metamorphosis that he hoped would fill him with the confidence to continue his odyssey.

Ruby walked down a wide, gaudily-decorated hall that ran along the rear of the palace. The inspiration for its rows of crystal chandeliers hanging from vaulted ceilings painted with Renaissance-style quasi-religious themes appeared to be The Hall of Mirrors at the French Palace of Versailles. Something had been lost in translation, however, as the effect was more Ikea than Louis XIV, and this aesthetic down-sampling was aggravated by the occasional splash of blood on the parquetry.

People worked at improvised desks, and the floor was littered with phone and electricity extension cables. At one end of the corridor, men were carrying television broadcasting equipment into a room, preparing for the presidential address to the part of the nation that could boast television sets or Internet access. In a feverish hothouse atmosphere, people came and went, but no one paid much attention to Ruby.

She considered the option of walking out of the door and seeking refuge at the British Embassy. Orlando's subtle threats were probably meaningless, she convinced herself. She couldn't see why he would bother to initiate reprisals against her if she left the palace. She was just an archaeologist, after all. There was nothing special about her. But then why had he gone to the trouble of luring her to this country with a false employment contract in the first place? There had to be something more profound about his reasoning. Something important for which he needed her. Was it possible that Orlando had had something to do with the theft of the clay tubes from the Sphinx? The more she considered the matter, the less unlikely it seemed. How else could he be certain that the tubes contained scrolls?

The world outside offered freedom, if she could make it to her Embassy, but if she chose that option she would never find out if the Sphinx scrolls were in Orlando's possession. Nor would she get to study that incongruous piece of metalwork at Tikal that seemed to date back to the Stone Age. Working with Paulo Souza these past few weeks had not exactly been a pleasure, but he had never tried to harm her. She felt sure he would look out for her when she was sent back to Tikal. And if Orlando really needed her skills then she was in no real danger, she reassured herself.

She opted to stick around and search the palace for a likely location for the scrolls.

'Excuse me,' she said in her politest Spanish to a random stranger, a carpenter dressed in overalls tied at the middle with a jangling tool belt. He was the third person she'd approached, and so far no one had been able to help. 'I'm an archaeologist working for the President. Can you tell me where I can find his private collection of antiquities?'

The carpenter looked her up and down before replying, 'I saw some guys moving things into a room on this floor yesterday, along the corridor from the office with that dumb pool. Flight cases, books, maps. That sound like what you're looking for?'

She thanked him and tried, unsuccessfully, to find her way back to the area of Orlando's office, but a couple of wrong turns led her to a servants' staircase – an unembellished set of concrete steps down to the basement and up to the other floors. A door opened violently behind her, crashing against the wall and sending echoes ringing up the stairwell. In her panic at being somewhere that perhaps she shouldn't, she scurried up one flight of steps to get out of the way. Looking down she saw six men enter. It appeared that the first two men were being held at gunpoint by the other four.

One of the men at gunpoint had a familiar face with an even more familiar pissed-off expression.

Matt.

She froze, forcing herself, despite a flurry of conflicting emotions – including relief that Matt was alive and sheer annoyance that this situation was interfering with her plan to find out if Orlando was hiding the stolen scrolls at the palace, to listen carefully to what they were saying and doing. The six men clattered downstairs to the basement where they opened and shut another door without any pretence at finesse, and all was silent. Ruby rushed down and waited for the soldiers to return. The men emerged less than a minute later.

'Hi,' said Ruby.

They peered at her suspiciously.

'What?' said one.

'It's very exciting. All this revolutionary … stuff,' she said, wondering if she was overdoing the wide-eyed female.

'Are you lost?' asked another.

'No, just taking a break. Got a cigarette?'

The first soldier produced one from a battered pack and lit it for her. She held it to her lips with no intention of taking a drag. When the soldiers began to walk away, she stood up.

'What goes on in there, then?' She pointed down into the basement.

'The basement.'

'And those men?'

'Criminals.'

'What will happen to them?'

'You ask many questions,' said the first one. He pulled the cigarette from Ruby's mouth and trod on it. 'Smoking is bad for your health.'

The soldiers left her alone on the stairs. She found herself saying the word 'justice' in her head. It was one of the words she had overheard Orlando saying to the soldier who had interrupted their first meeting by the indoor pool. She recalled Orlando signing a document as he said it. She wondered what kind of justice existed here.

Turning swiftly on her heel, Ruby resumed her search for Orlando's office, but now her priorities had shifted. The hunt for the scrolls would have to wait. She finally located the room and knocked on the door, the whiff of chlorine confirming that she was in the right place.

No answer. She pushed open the door. The room was empty. At its far end she could see the little bit of paper on the mahogany desk where the President had left it. She ran around the edge of the swimming pool towards the desk.

Her scream could be heard at the end of the corridor. It terminated only when the slide on the wet marble resulted in her falling beneath the warm, clear water. As she sank below the surface she regained a little self-control and opened her eyes, feeling the sting of the treated water. Instantly she noticed that the pool extended under the floor at the deep end. The small amount of air left in her lungs was enough to enable her to sit for just a few seconds beneath the overhang, from where she could see shadows moving in the room.

Ruby forced herself to control her bursting lungs a little longer.

The shadows disappeared. She hadn't been spotted. She pushed hard to swim out from the sheltered recess and towards the water's surface and took a deep, gargling breath.

Her vision was blurred and she blinked rapidly, scanning her surroundings as if through the shutter of an old cine camera. Orlando's poolside office remained unoccupied. Clearly the staff had better things to do than to worry about wayward archaeologists.

This is an odd design for a pool, she thought. An underwater recess like that would be a nightmare to clean. She ducked below once more to take another look at it out of curiosity. It was almost like a submerged cave, and it continued into blackness. Highly peculiar.

Quietly easing herself out of the water, she helped herself to Orlando's towel and stood dripping by his desk, the oddity of the pool design quickly forgotten. She wiped her wet hands and picked up the document that she had earlier witnessed Orlando signing.

Matt's name was on it. Her knees weakened at the realisation that she held in her hand the authorisation for his execution.

She had made a bad call. She should have owned up to Matt's presence in the artefact when she'd had the chance. No doubt he had managed to wind up his captors and aggravate the situation, knowing him as she did. How many times had she tried to explain to him that the aggressive techniques for getting your own way in New York don't translate to the Third World? His short fuse was his own worst enemy. But this mess was something she could still resolve. She had the ear of the President. If she stayed on and performed well at Tikal, and if she wrote a report that made it clear that Matt had not caused any significant contamination of the artefact in which he was found, Orlando would be sure to grant her the small favour of setting Matt free.

She continued reading the document.

The execution was scheduled for tomorrow morning at ten.

Her eyes began to blur again, but this time it wasn't an effect of the chlorinated water.

It was time to make the call. The mobile phone was almost fully charged, the signal was strong, the number was stored in its memory. The hand that selected the number and hit the dial button was Ratty's, but it was not the same timid Ratty who had considered croquet an extreme sport, or the daft Ratty who thought wild boar was an appropriate dish to serve to a vegetarian friend. This was the hand of New Ratty. Ratty II, the sequel. Ratty Plus. He was Improved Ratty, Recycled Ratty, Ratty Reborn.

Frankly, Ratty didn't know what he was or how to think of himself. As he stood on the street outside the clothes emporium with his phone to his ear, wearing everything he had just bought and with his old suit in a dumpster behind the store, he felt anonymous and mysterious. It was as if he were attending a masquerade ball, hidden behind a disguise. It gave him confidence knowing that he no longer stood out painfully in a crowd. He could move with the shadows, an incognito phantom.

No one passing him by would have thought him anything other than a streetwise, fashionable man. There was a hint of menace in his look, a touch of James Dean in his appearance. Everything he wore was black, from his newly-dyed hair down to his leather boots. The black Levi 501s were held up with a black leather belt secured by a heavy brass buckle. His black T-shirt fitted snugly beneath the black leather biker's jacket, from which dangled some rather unnecessary tassel strips.

As his phone connected with that of Dr Otto, he felt a sense of empowerment, of invincibility.

Beep. Beep. Be –

'Hello, Lord Ballashiels. So you have read my note?'

'I, er, gosh, yes, er, right.' Ratty took a deep breath. The sound of Otto's voice had sent him into an incoherent, palpitating and perspiring mess. His confidence dissolved in the afternoon heat. This new image of his was going to take a little more work than he'd thought.

In the palace garden, carpenters toiled loudly to build a new structure from old timbers. The endless hammering clearly annoyed Orlando, who was unable to hold back from shooting unfriendly glances at the workers as he talked energetically into a cordless phone from his favourite garden chair. Ruby, her hair and outfit failing to dry in the intense subtropical humidity, waited a polite distance away until he finished his conversation, and then boldly pulled up a chair next to him. Orlando's black looks instantly became a warm smile when he saw her. Willing herself to quell the surging crisis adrenaline in her body, she tried to pretend nothing had changed.

'Why does the Tikal artefact fascinate you so much?' she asked him with forced nonchalance.

'Why don't I ask you the same question?'

The hammering stopped, but was soon replaced by a more irritating scraping as the carpenters cleaned the mildew from yet more lengths of damp timber. Ruby glanced at the construction, but so far it didn't resemble anything in particular.

'It's been under the ground a long time,' she said. 'To me, whenever I discover a long-hidden object, it's like looking through a window into a different world. The Tikal artefact is a window that no one has seen before, and I get the feeling that I'm seeing an ancient world that may have been pretty advanced. More so than perhaps we thought possible. And yet those bones inside it looked at least ten thousand years old. They lived and died in a civilisation that had man-made achievements and natural disasters just like our own, and yet utterly unlike our own, if that makes any sense.'

'The mists of time clear when you look into them, Ruby. You sense the thunder of great cataclysm; you hear the screams of ancient people witnessing the end of their brief empire.'

Was now the time to plead for Matt's life? Not yet – she was starting to connect with Orlando. Just a little closer and she'd be able to get what she wanted.

'Tell me what you expected to find out when you were excavating the Sphinx, Ruby.'

'You probably know there's evidence to suggest that the Sphinx might be far older than people originally believed. Its pharaonic head has led Egyptologists to assume it was built by Pharaoh Cheops four thousand years ago, but it's possible that Cheops only discovered the Sphinx with its original head at that time, possibly leonine, and had it re-carved in his own image. It could be that when Cheops found it, the Sphinx was already a decaying ancient monument.'

'So you are saying that rather than the Sphinx marking the beginning of mankind as an advanced, technological race, it may actually mark the end of its first advanced period?'

'The Sphinx was carved out of an outcrop of natural rock, so there's no certain way of dating it, but geologists studying the erosion of the stone noticed that some of the fissures were vertical, caused by rain, rather than horizontal from wind and sand. And yet there hasn't been a rainy climate on the Giza plateau for seven thousand years.'

'Fascinating. Do go on.'

'There are other clues to its age, besides the weathering. If it was built twelve thousand years ago, that was the Age of Leo. The eyes of the Sphinx at that time would have been looking straight at the constellation of

Leo. The constellations have since moved around the sky. It's as if the Sphinx was built as an eternal marker for that point in history.'

'If that is so, what are the builders of the Sphinx trying to say?'

'If I had been able to retrieve those tubes and study their contents, I might know the answer to that.' She looked him in the eye, searching for a reaction to her deliberately provocative statement, but she couldn't read anything in his face. She shook herself. Another layer of reality was shouting in her ear. This cosy chat was all well and good, but meanwhile Matt was still in the condemned cell and the moment of his demise was hurtling towards him.

'Please excuse me, Ruby. There is much I need to do if we are to avoid this month marking the end of mankind's second advanced period.'

'And what does that mean?'

'Simply that the world is going to end. Unless I complete my work, of course.'

Her heart fluttered, not in fear of his banal and unoriginal New Age prediction, but at the thought that she had taken too much of his time and blown her chances of negotiating freedom for Matt. He began dialling a number on his phone.

'Wait, there's something else,' she blurted, holding her hand over his phone so that he couldn't see the buttons. 'A friend of mine has been arrested. I understand he's being held in the palace under a sentence of death. His name's Matt Mountebank.'

'Ah, yes. The spy.'

'He's not a spy!'

'He is a famous American Special Forces soldier. What else would he be doing in my military installations?'

'It wasn't a military installation! It was an archaeological site. He was only there to visit me. You must have seen him interview me on that documentary ...' She almost ground to a halt, wretchedly wringing the words out of the usually well-buried side of herself. 'You ... know we had ... an affair. A relationship. In Egypt.'

'I see. So he's a "special" friend, is he?' Orlando was crowing. She sat on her hands to quell the urge to wipe the smile off his face with a swift slap.

'Yes. Kind of. Well, he was. It's pretty much over now.'

'Of course I have the authority to change his sentence, but men in a position like mine do not change decisions. Especially on my first day in office. It isn't good for the morale of my people. They need to see my strength and commitment to my word. Therefore, it is out of the question.'

'Please, Orlando, this is a man's life we're talking about. He's done nothing to hurt you. I'll do anything. Just don't kill him.'

'Not that it matters, given the fate shortly to befall the world, but have you ever considered, Ruby, that death need not mean the end?'

She looked at him in disgust, appalled that a murderer could now invoke philosophy into his facile argument. An unbearable crescendo of sawing and hammering battered her ears. She was in no mood for discussing the afterlife.

'I'm a scientist,' she grunted, despondently. 'Death is the end.'

'Not necessarily,' he replied, glancing over her head at the almost completed scaffold.

She followed his eye line. Someone was going to be executed. And soon.

Otto was seated in a bar on the ground floor of a nondescript hotel, facing someone who in no way at all resembled the Lord Ballashiels with whom he had clashed the day before. His Lordship had been studying a collection of topographical maps and books about Mayan history and glyphic writings, and the result was a mess that covered most of the circular table between them.

'See those two chaps – guys – at the bar?' Ratty pointed a finger at two burly, pot-bellied local men enjoying beers and watching a chat show on a television in the corner.

'Yes, I see them,' replied Otto.

'I want you to know that they are with me. You start any kind of kerfuffle and they will spring into action. Trained bunny boilers, both of them.' He folded a map on which were many handwritten annotations. Ratty's pattern of folding did not follow the map's original creases, and Otto seemed visibly pained to witness such a desecration.

'Of course. I understand,' pretended Otto. 'Although I thought the colloquial term "bunny boiler" referred to jealous female killers, its etymology being the American movie *Fatal Attraction*.'

'What? Yes, assassins, then. They are assassins. Trained in the ancient art of, er, assassing.'

'Assassing?'

'Yes, so watch your step, Doc.'

'My step? I am seated.'

Ratty sighed. Every attempt at playing the tough guy was deftly deflected by the Doctor. The two 'assassins' at the bar cheered as the presenter of the television show put on a feather hat and performed a little dance. One of them slid off his bar stool, stretched his back and staggered off to the toilets, oblivious to Ratty and Otto's presence. Ratty's face dropped as he watched the man disappear.

'To business,' he declared, regaining focus and putting the maps and books into a small leather satchel at his side. 'Where are the stelae, old, old – just where are the stelae?'

'I do not have them, Your Lordship.'

Ratty felt a squirm coming on, but he suppressed it. He folded back the ends of the sleeves of his leather jacket, revealing a fake gold bracelet on each wrist. He looked around the room, then leaned forward and looked Otto in the eye.

'Look, if you don't co-operate I'll give my boys the nod.'

'The nod? What is the nod?'

'Er, it's a bit like a wink, but a dash zingier, don't you know. Never mind. Don't play games with me, Doctor.'

'Games? I don't play games. Life is too serious for games, Lord Ballashiels.'

'So where are the stelae?'

'I am not at liberty to say. And that is not the reason I invited you to meet me.'

Ratty found his nether regions squirming once again, and tried to regain control of the discussion.

'I think you will find, Doctor, that it was *I* who invited *you* to this powwow.'

'Does it matter?' asked Otto.

Ratty was unprepared for this latest deflection. He was making no headway at all. The return of the mildly intoxicated bar drinker from the gents' gave him some relief. Aware that Otto was observing the man's return, Ratty gave a smile and a hesitant wave towards him. To the aristocrat's horror, the man returned the gesture with a smile and a wink. He then nudged and whispered something to his companion at the bar who turned around and blew a kiss at both Ratty and Otto while stroking his broad moustache.

'I was not aware of your personal inclinations, Lord

Ballashiels, but I want you to know that I do not judge you.'

How did Otto continue to maintain the upper hand? If this meeting had been held in a public bath he would have drowned, Ratty mused, because it was certainly not going swimmingly. He was no more intimidating to his adversary than a daffodil. Otto's last comment simply left him speechless.

Otto calmly continued.

'Lord Ballashiels, one of the reasons I wanted to meet with you again was to offer you, in person, my sincere apology for my behaviour yesterday. Please appreciate that it was an unusual and eventful day, and I experienced stress at levels that compromised gentlemanly conduct.'

'Quite, quite,' mumbled Ratty, failing to prevent his old self from snivelling its way to the forefront. He felt his guard lowering. Otto had a point. Strange things had happened yesterday. No one was quite themselves. Remember the plan, he reminded himself. He had a mission to fulfil.

'I also wanted to inform you, Lord Ballashiels, of the connection our ancestors shared.'

'Bilbo?'

'Indeed. Your great-great uncle conducted archaeological works here in Guatemala at the same time as my great-great grandfather.'

'That's great-great, er, I mean, great.'

'They were rivals, they had their disagreements, and the prize they sought was divided between them, rendering each half of no practical value. What can you do with half of the stele? Nothing. It does not provide the answers. That is why I have made it my mission to complete the work begun by my ancestor Karl Mengele.'

Ratty twitched uncomfortably at the mention of the name.

'There is no reason,' continued Otto, 'for the feuding of our ancestors to continue today. We live in enlightened times. The German Empire has gone the way of the British Empire, shrunk out of existence by conquered nations demanding their independence. Nineteenth-century nationalistic ideals have no place in the hearts of citizens of the modern world.'

'Just one question, Doctor. When you say Mengele, of course it's no relation to the famous concentration camp doctor chappy from the war, is it?' Rather than waiting for an answer, Ratty then laughed down his own question.

Otto looked him firmly in the eye but said nothing. The look was sufficient. He then continued, 'One half of the stele came into my possession following the unexpected death in Brazil of my –' he stopped himself. 'It came into my possession in nineteen seventy-nine. There was little I could do with it at the time, but with the resources of my client at my disposal I have now been able to reunite it with its long lost twin.'

'Do go on, old fellow.'

'Lord Ballashiels, I inherited the stone but no papers, no written accounts. You inherited a stone with a considerable collection of contemporary notes. Those notes made by your great-great uncle may provide the final part of the puzzle, for they are alleged to give context and meaning to the stele.'

'Are you trying to say, Doctor, that although you have both parts of the stele in your grasp, you don't actually know how to use them?'

'Your diary contains, I believe, details of inscriptions, found in a cave, associated with the stele. Carvings that have since been lost to history.'

'If I might say once again, old boy, it seems to me that you have acquired a new toaster but you can't work out how to turn it on without the manual.'

'That, in the shell of a nut, Lord Ballashiels, is correct.'

Ratty felt elated. The race to the treasure wasn't over yet. Neither man could identify the location of the lost Mayan hoard without the missing part of the puzzle. Otto had the stele but needed the diary; Ratty had the diary but needed the stele. His great-great uncle's rivalry was reborn, and Ratty was determined that this time around he would score a decisive victory for his country.

'Hi, my name's Ruby. You must be ...?'

She had waited on the back stairs of the palace for over an hour for this opportunity.

'Oh. Pedro,' replied the young man, predictably mesmerised by the cleavage she had meticulously arranged to elicit just such a reaction.

He is barely more than a boy, thought Ruby. His uniform was too big for him, as though he had borrowed it from his father, and he wore his gun loosely at his side like a cowboy. He held a tray of unappetising food.

'Pleased to meet you, Pedro,' she said, motioning to shake his hand, but realising he was too encumbered with the tray. 'Shall I take that for you?'

He held the tray tight against his waist.

'God, this place, eh!' she said conspiratorially. 'Can't even sort out proper uniforms. Complete chaos! Bet General Lorenzo didn't even tell you I was starting today, did he?'

It took Pedro a couple of moments to tear his eyes from her curves before he blurted out, 'Who?'

'Oh, that's odd. He promised me he'd sort everything out.'

'What?'

'I'm your assistant. Lorenzo said to shadow you for the first day and just pick up the job as I go along.'

'I should ask.' He gestured vaguely upstairs with his shoulder.

'The President will vouch for me.'

She was winning him over, but whether it was due to the mention of the President or her undone buttons was unclear.

He looked at the food on the tray, which was getting cold, then at the stairs behind him, which were steep. What harm could a woman do, anyway? He opened the door to the basement rooms and switched on the lights to illuminate the unpainted interior. Ruby peered into the underground corridor, sniffed the stale air and saw a rusty but unbreakable-looking door set in a thick steel frame.

'So we feed them, right?'

'And check they no escape.'

'Obviously. We wouldn't want that, would we?'

Ruby stood behind him as he picked a large key from the set on his key ring and turned it in the lock of the steel door. When it opened, the impregnability of the cell was only too apparent – the door was several inches thick, armour plated on the outside and inside, with a mortise lock worthy of a bank vault. It swung to ninety degrees to reveal an unfamiliar Guatemalan prisoner standing at the far end of the cell. Seated on a grim-looking bed next to him was Matt.

As Pedro placed the food on the floor, Matt spotted Ruby and stared, his jaw sagging almost to his chest in disbelief. For a brief second their eyes locked and burned with unaskable questions. When Ruby raised her finger to her lips in the classic 'shh' gesture behind Pedro's back, Matt assumed this was the prelude to a carefully honed rescue plan. He sat watching, waiting for her to make some crucial move from her position of advantage behind the soldier. But she did nothing.

The door slammed shut and was locked again. Matt

found himself wondering if he had imagined it all. For her sake, he hoped he had.

The armoured Mercedes re-entered the palace grounds at precisely four in the afternoon. Otto flashed a security pass at the guards, plainly unhappy that to do so necessitated opening the window and letting in heat. He was already sweating profusely despite the efforts of the car's air conditioning system. The constant stop-start nature of the journey had caused him more stress than he cared to experience immediately prior to the administration of injections – it wasn't conducive to a steady hand. But he had arrived. He would be no more than five minutes late by the time he had made his way to Orlando's office.

What he was going to do with the English aristocrat who had accompanied him on the journey, dressed eccentrically in black like a modern day Zorro carrying a school bag, he wasn't sure. The conclusion of their dealings was not possible until he had finished with Orlando, but Otto was determined that the paths of Orlando and Ratty should not cross.

He drove into the underground lot and parked the Mercedes among the government fleet of Mitsubishi Delica minibuses, robotically pocketing the ignition key as he exited. His quivering hands then fumbled for the same key in his jacket pocket, rejecting the first one he pulled out before finding the Mercedes key once more and hanging it noisily on the rack. Normally this would be manned by a civil servant diligently signing official vehicles in and out, but it was currently abandoned owing to the man's recent violent demise, in common with many of his co-workers. Nevertheless, Otto could not help but sign the book and record his mileage before walking up to an inconspicuous service entrance.

Ratty observed Otto's behaviour closely, noting where he had placed each key.

Inside the palace, Otto gave Ratty a firm instruction: 'You are to wait where I tell you to wait, Your Lordship. Please do not move from there until I come for you. It will be no more than an hour. You are a gentleman and I will treat you with the respect your position deserves, so there will be no guards or locked doors. You are my guest here at the palace and it would be inappropriate to confine you to your room by forceful means. You may study your books and your maps. I will then take you to the stele. Please understand how important it is that you do not leave the room.'

The room was a compact bedroom on an upper level. Its grey, porcelain tiled floor blended seamlessly with the off-white painted walls, accented by burgundy red drapes and cushions. There was an en-suite bathroom, a television on the wall and a bottle of water on the dressing table.

'You bash off and do your doings,' chirped Ratty, deliberately standing on Otto's shoelace. 'Don't worry about me.'

The Doctor noticed his lace had become undone and immediately crouched to tie it properly, taking several attempts to get each side of the bow precisely the same length as the other, and failing to register his guest's ingratitude as the key in his jacket pocket was gently removed from him.

Deep down, Otto sensed he was being naïve, but the pressure to keep his appointment with Orlando distorted his thinking. As he reached the bottom of the stairs he was sure he heard the squeak of a door handle turning on the floor above, but in a property with fifty rooms and hundreds of people he wasn't going to give in to paranoia and retrace his steps.

The faux-Versailles hall had evolved into a makeshift bar where palace staff congregated, starting to focus their new lives and enjoying free looted drinks. With no one specifically charged with cleaning the glasses, the only thing to do was to rinse them out with white wine and throw the waste into a bucket. One of these unlovely receptacles had already been accidentally kicked over, and the stench of sticky shoes, sodden beer mats and body odour started to pervade the air. The party was growing. Word of free drinks spread effortlessly around the blood-stained corridors of power. The triumphant administration had much to celebrate.

Well into his second bottle of Château DeFay, Pedro was lowering his defences against the relentless onslaught of female flirtation.

'So,' Ruby breathed sexily, trying not to model herself too obviously on Marilyn – after all, she had no intention of sticking around to sing 'Happy Birthday' to Orlando, 'tell me more. About this job. What happens next?'

Pedro gulped directly from his bottle and began to fall in slow motion. Ruby caught him and, with some difficulty, sat him up straight, trying to ignore the bubbles of wine he was snorting. Then he perked up, waving one hand as if giving a lecture.

'You listen. This is job. Be very, very good. Good job.'

Holding him more or less upright, she nodded keenly and – she tried – admiringly. She just hoped he wouldn't throw up on her.

'During night I pick up the tray and check the prisoners. Hey, maybe you could do me a helping? A favours?'

Ruby smiled. Favours she could understand. Pedro reached into his pocket for the keys, found them and dropped them on the floor.

'You must no lose these. We no have spare.'

Bending over to pick them up like a decrepit old man, he just kept going and passed out before he reached the ground. Ruby watched him fall onto the keys, unconscious. She shoved him aside and picked the keys up. They jangled heavily in her grasp, satisfyingly large and clunky, as befitted the keys to a presidential dungeon. She held them tight. The power of life and death lay in her grasp. She would never let Matt forget that.

Saving him would come at a cost, though. She would need to flee with him. No chance to find out if Orlando had any connection to the Sphinx theft. No opportunity to work on the Tikal project. The shining opportunity to further her career beyond her wildest imaginings would be lost. She would never let Matt forget that, either.

After only five minutes in the broom cupboard Ratty was short of breath. The airless atmosphere in there was slowly cooking him. The cupboard didn't just contain brooms, of course. He could feel a plastic bucket next to his left foot and something heavy next to the other, possibly a vacuum cleaner. A coat peg dug into his back, and cobwebs tickled the edges of his precious new hairdo. As if he were not in quite enough discomfort, he started to feel the twinge of approaching cramp in his leg.

And yet it wasn't safe to emerge. The soldiers whose voices, loud in conversation, had sent him scurrying for cover were still within earshot. They might not have challenged him had he passed them by with an air of confidence, but he had panicked and hidden himself, and if he now emerged, half dead, from the hallway cleaning cupboard, questions would have to be asked and his plan would be in tatters.

The cramp hit full on. He lifted his knee and hopped

on his good leg in an effort to disperse the excruciation. The second hop landed off-centre, nudging the bucket sideways, toppling two brooms and sending Ratty falling onto the vacuum cleaner before the whole jumble of body and cleaning items burst out onto the floor of the hallway. Rough hands dragged him unceremoniously to his feet. Ratty found himself looking down on two diminutive soldiers, one of whom picked up Ratty's satchel and thrust it aggressively onto his shoulder.

'I say, terribly grateful and all that. Got myself in something of a pickle back there.'

The private looked at the corporal with an expression that did not suggest sympathy. This overgrown English schoolboy appeared to have been hiding in a cupboard, listening to their conversation. Those were the facts, and they were sufficient to generate considerable anger. Other circumstances were not deemed relevant, such as the fact that they were talking about soccer rather than grand military secrets, and the fact that Ratty hadn't paid attention to a word they'd said anyway.

'Come with us,' grunted the corporal.

'Awfully kind invitation, but I was actually waiting for Doctor Mengele. We have a meeting in a few minutes after he's finished with the President.'

'Is this true?' asked the private.

'The Doctor asked me to wait in one of those bedchambers along the hallway. Became somewhat adrift, what with all these doppelgänger doors.'

'Why are you here?' asked the corporal. His tone had become more neutral. Ratty's idiotic innocence was starting to shine through.

'I came to assist the Doctor with some Mayan artefacts he is studying.'

'You are an archaeologist? From England?'

'More of an historian, but yes, one is the fruit of the

loins of Blighty, if you like. Or perfidious Albion if you don't, ha ha.'

The two soldiers spoke quickly to each other, as much to ascertain the reason for Ratty's unexpected chuckle as to decide what to do with him. One of them had heard about Mayan stones and other items being kept somewhere in the palace. Ratty's story had a chime of believability about it. He seemed a harmless foreign imbecile. They decided to throw this catch back into the water.

'I say, quick adjuration, chaps,' called Ratty as they began to walk away. 'It might be helpful to the Doctor if I tootle on over and make a start before he gets there. I know he's awfully busy. Any idea where one might find the antiquities room?'

As the setting sun fired its dying rays into the overhead smog in a spectacularly colourful, and rapidly changing, display, the celebrations spread further about the palace. The hallways soon lost their echo, muffled by the presence of soldiers and officials drinking and singing tunelessly and making amorous advances that they would regret in the morning. Many staff now congregated around the staircase that led down to the basement and the cells. There was no way Ruby could risk bringing Matt out in front of them. Returning later in the night was her only option. She briefly experienced a guilty pleasure at this realisation: Matt would suffer for a few hours more. It wouldn't fully compensate her for the damage his predicament had done to her career opportunities, but it would help. Besides, the delay gave her a chance to continue her hunt for Orlando's private collection.

This time she easily located the room to which precious packages were rumoured to have been delivered. It was almost directly opposite the chlorine-filled office that the President had so far displayed little interest in using. She tried the handle; the door was locked. Sounds coming from within the room caused her to step away, not wanting to be caught in the vicinity of what must be a restricted area.

The door opened a fraction revealing a nervous rat-like nose.

The door slammed shut again. Ruby banged it impatiently.

'Ratty? What are you doing there? Open up!'

The nose reappeared.

'Goodness! Thought you were the Doctor chappy. Come in, old sausage.'

Ratty let her in and locked the door with the key he had taken from Otto. The room was a small office, kept deliberately stark and neutral, with boxes of historical and esoteric literature and maps stacked in one corner, and piles of flight cases to one side. Some of the cases were open, displaying pottery items set into padded foam linings. But Ruby just stared at her friend.

'What have they done to you?' she asked him. 'Why have they put you in that ridiculous outfit? And what happened to your hair?'

'No time to explain,' he replied. 'Rather pushed for time. Although perhaps we could quickly discuss the poetry of Philip Larkin?'

'Now? Are you crazy? Listen, Ratty, they've arrested Matt. He's in a cell here in the palace.'

He tried not to smile at this revelation. The Mountebank fellow was not Ratty's cup of tea, and the sooner Ruby found herself a more suitable person with whom to enjoy her romantic liaisons, the better, in his opinion.

'If you're after bail money, I'm afraid –'

'No, Ratty, they're going to execute him tomorrow.'

'Golly. What rotten luck,' said Ratty, silently berating himself for thinking the exact opposite.

'It's under control, though. I stole the key to his cell. I'll let him out when the coast is clear.'

'Can I be of any assistance in that department?' he offered in an attempt to redeem his uncharitable instincts towards the American soldier.

'Just get yourself away from this madhouse. I don't want you getting in trouble as well.' She was about to give him a hug and tell him to be careful when the contents of a half-opened flight case caught her eye. She shoved Ratty unsympathetically aside and picked up a clay tube from its foam padding. It looked ancient, greyed by passing eons. And it looked familiar. She pulled back the foam layer and saw others beneath it. Ten of them.

'Ratty! These are the tubes that were stolen from the Sphinx!'

He picked one up and turned it around.

'Is it meant to be empty?' he asked.

Ruby checked the ends of the tube she was holding. It had been neatly sawn open at the tip. There was nothing inside. The same was true of the others.

'Quick, Ratty, help me look in these other containers. Perhaps the scrolls are here.'

'No, old raspberry, I've already checked. And there are definitely no scrolls in those two flight cases there.'

She looked at the containers in question. He shuffled in front of them, blocking her view and reminding her of the evasive squirming he had displayed when she was last at Stiperstones Manor.

'Tell me honestly, Ratty. Did you sell that stele to Otto?'

'Sell? To that schnitzel-nibbling scoundrel? Absolutely not.'

'Good. So why are you here?'

'Me? Here? Awfully glad you asked me that, actually. Yes. Indeed.'

'Well?'

'Time has transfigured them into wotnot, eh?' he continued. 'Heigh-ho and tinkerty-tonk.'

She sighed. Getting a coherent answer from her friend was often a challenge, and right now she lacked the patience to pursue the matter. Her head was starting to hurt. She hadn't eaten all day and had no desire to waste her remaining energy on an eccentric aristocrat. She was going to need all of her strength to rescue Matt.

'I'm going to get something to eat, Ratty, then I'm going to free Matt. All hell might break loose after that, so make sure you're not around. Promise me that?'

'Off you trot, old condiment, and don't concern yourself with me.'

The palace kitchen, when she found it, was surprisingly small. The two chefs – both with sodden rings of sweat under their armpits – were still working on the supply of evening meals. From the looks of them, they were more used to cooking outdoors on portable equipment, moving from one rainforest clearing to another. Jungle hygiene clearly did not translate particularly well to the interior of a palace and the men seemed out of their depth, lost in their new surroundings. The floors were filthy with a crust of squashed nachos and flour, plus what looked like blood, and the surfaces were stained and cracked. The smell of tonight's chilli did little to mask the all-pervading odour of rot, a stench exaggerated by the humidity. A greasy extractor fan half-dangled from the wall, apparently broken, and no windows were open. Ruby looked for signs of fresh food, or indeed anything still in a packet or free from mould, but everything seemed equally hazardous to health.

One of the chefs smiled at her and put together a small

heap of his creations on a tray. Reluctantly she accepted the chef's offerings, taking herself off into a corner to eat a pile of tortillas, cheese and strips of what was hopefully beef. The bits of green might actually be vegetables, she tried to reassure herself. After everything she'd been through, it looked almost edible, and smelled a lot better than the raw ingredients that were decaying around her. She gulped it all down, forced herself to smile and give the thumbs up to the chef, and went to look for a quiet room where she could rest until it was safe to rescue Matt.

The moment she walked out of the kitchen her stomach lurched ominously.

Ratty placed the two halves of the artefact side by side on a wooden table. Together again after hundreds – possibly thousands – of years apart, the two stone discs were ready to reveal the secret they had so long withheld from the world. The recess in the centre of one half was clearly designed to receive the protrusion from the other. It was a primal concept, as simple and elegant as Nature herself: the mating of male and female. Ratty tried to understand the minds of the people who had carved the stones and started the legends that surrounded them. What kind of phenomenon would be worthy of such travail? Why had it needed to be hidden from view, erased from history until someone worked out how to crack its code?

He had no idea, but he hoped it was something to do with treasure. He desperately needed a hoard of Mayan gold to refill his coffers. Perhaps El Dorado really did exist. Perhaps he would be the first one to pull back the ferns, tilt up his pith helmet and gaze in wonderment at the dazzling sight of thousands of tons of mythical gold. Its value was sure to outshine anything Otto might offer him for Bilbo's diary. And to claim the elusive grand prize on behalf of the good guys would earn him Ruby's respect, instead of her resentment when she realised he'd told her a small porky pie about the stelàe. Was that stronger motivation than the money? He couldn't deny the possibility.

'Time has transfigured them into Untruth' echoed through his head in search of meaning. Its significance and the great discoveries would come later, however. Otto would soon start to look for him. He needed to act quickly. The twin stones were too heavy for him to carry out of the palace alone. Despite his new tough guy image, he was still the same scrawny person inside, a classic example of an inbred aristocratic weakling. But the stelae themselves were not important, he realised. It was their message that mattered. It was the location they pointed to that was of value. He picked up the part of the stele that rightly belonged to him and mated it to the other piece, half expecting to see a genie appear in a puff of smoke or for heavy granite walls to slide open.

Nothing happened.

Don't be an oaf, he told himself. These are merely lumps of stone. Now for the important part. He had to line up the inscriptions to create a meaningful message. The difficulty lay in deciding exactly how the inscriptions should be aligned. There were multiple options, like a stone-age version of a bicycle padlock with spinning numbers. The carvings on the Mengele stone now showed that twelve readings could be obtained, according to its alignment with the Bilbo stone. Otto had needed the extra information to be gleaned from Ratty's uncle's diary in order to select the correct alignment.

He pulled the diary from the inside pocket of his leather jacket and laid it on the table next to the stele. The mauve ink which had read 'Bilbo de St Clair, his Diary. Private. KEEP OUT' had started to dissolve in the unforgivingly humid interior of the jacket. He rifled through the fragile leaves quickly.

The diary told of the union of the fortress glyphs with the red squares or diamond shapes. Each half of the stele contained both glyphs, in reverse order. When the rows were aligned together, some of the other glyphs could then be read across the two stelae, giving the co-ordinates of the sacred location. It wasn't a set of simple numbers, of course, like modern map grid references. The division of the world into segments, measured in degrees, minutes and seconds of longitude and latitude, was an arbitrary system, agreed upon by nations for general convenience in relatively recent times. The ancients saw their world in more poetic, hyperbolic terms. The stelae referred to positions relative not to precise sections of the globe, but to named Mayan settlements. Ratty interpreted the glyphs to the best of his ability. He cross-referenced the places named in the glyphs with historical records of place names no longer in use and with topographical maps of the country.

His personal quest was undeniably rather jolly good fun. He felt a closeness to his ancestor, sensing a connection that had not been there before, as if Bilbo were with him now, gin and tonic in one hand, Union flag in the other, ready to guide him to the ultimate archaeological prize.

His hurried research was complete, and an audacious plan occurred to him. It was a stroke of genius, he decided. He would leave the diary for Otto to find. This idea made him especially proud because, of course, the diary he left next to the stele would not be in entirely the same state as it had been when it was originally bequeathed to him. Subtle modifications would lead Dr Otto to a different result from the one Ratty was now pursuing.

He permitted himself a tired smile as he coolly walked

from the antiquities room to the underground car park and helped himself to a set of keys from the unguarded rack. Not wishing to exacerbate any trouble he might already be in, he signed the register, putting his name and the registration number of his chosen Mitsubishi Delica into the book and leaving a few *quetzales* on the desk as a contribution towards the fuel. Besides, those *quetzales* didn't matter to him. In a few hours he'd be in possession of unimaginable wealth. The all-terrain Delica could seat eight adults plus their luggage and it could handle the toughest off road conditions, so he reckoned on being able to help himself to a substantial haul.

Only the security contingent at the palace gates now stood between him and riches beyond his considerable capacity for dreams. Twenty soldiers, tired, triumphant and inebriated. Ratty knew that success depended on whether he could make this his finest hour.

The odds of being able to persuade the soldiers to let him through did not appear favourable. These guards were not educated people. They had no inkling of culture, of history, of philosophy. They were not cricketers or connoisseurs or collectors. Ratty would have been just as uncomfortable encountering them drinking and chatting in the King's Head in his home village. They were, in short, not his kind of people, and even New Ratty lacked the social skills to win over this rabble.

He slowed the Delica to a halt and opened the window. A soldier asked to see his security pass. Dumbing down his classical Spanish to its most colloquial, he began to burble at them.

'I do like your uniforms. Where do you get them? Do you find them rather hot in this somewhat clement weather? So how long have you all been in the army, then? Do you enjoy it? What's the most interesting part of this work? Have you always wanted to do this?'

It was a complete failure. He knew he didn't have it in him to relate to them. His escape was doomed. His attempts at engaging these lowly soldiers were worthy of a monarch on a royal visit making small talk to connect with the plebs – trite, patronising and superficial. None of his questions received an answer.

'You cannot take this vehicle without a security pass,' repeated the soldier.

'Well, now that's a funny thing, don't you know?' continued Ratty. 'Doctor Otto said I wouldn't need one as I'm not really leaving. He's asked me to test drive the official vehicles and write a report, so I'll be, er, taking them out one at a time, starting with this one. Back in a few minutes.'

'You are testing the government cars? But you are from England. Who are you?'

'I'm a sort of expert in car type things, don't you know,' he blabbered.

'What is your name?'

'Right. My name. Yes. I, er, the name's, er, James. James May,' he bluffed, vaguely recalling a television programme he had once seen on the subject of car testing.

The gasps of admiration were drowned by the squeak of the gates being opened. Ratty gave the men an appreciative wave and drove away from the palace. Reinforcing his ruse with a leisurely pace and a notable lack of skill at the controls, he headed northeast to earn his place in history.

The medical session in the treatment room adjacent to Orlando's grandiose office was taking longer than Otto would have preferred, but he could not allow himself to take any shortcuts. Orlando was in a relaxed and triumphant mood, enjoying the personal attention to every aspect of his physiology.

'The archaeologist seems a troublesome character,' said Otto, withdrawing the final needle from Orlando's forearm.

'Ruby Towers? I have her under control.'

'I took her to my house on the pretence of needing her expert opinion on the other half of the artefact,' continued Otto, dabbing the spot of blood on Orlando's skin with an alcohol pad. 'Now I am not so sure we need her. She is too headstrong.'

'You know how much we need her, Otto. She will be useful. And I have her lover in the cells. When she sees him on the scaffold tomorrow she will offer no further resistance.'

'His body will be an excellent specimen for my research,' said Otto. 'But you know I need at least one other fresh corpse. There are too many gaps in my knowledge of the procedure. I can only perfect it by trial and error.'

'I have that in hand,' assured Orlando. 'You will receive two bodies tomorrow.'

By the time the President excused himself from the medical room almost an hour had passed. The ritual cleaning session that normally gave the Doctor so much pleasure could not be postponed or abandoned – Otto would not conceive of leaving his surgical items behind without preparing for their next use, but the knowledge that he had an English aristocrat waiting for him upstairs added pressure that sucked the joy from the obsessively intricate process.

Eventually the repetitive tasks were complete. He walked up the stairs two at a time and rapped determinedly on the bedroom door where he had left His Lordship. Without waiting for an answer, he threw the door open to precisely ninety degrees.

Lord Ballashiels had vanished. It was an act of

cowardice and disrespect, unbecoming of a gentleman, and it grated against Otto's monochrome values. And there was now something of greater concern: if His Lordship had managed to find the room where the Mayan relics were stored, it was possible that he could have stolen both parts of the artefact. Otto marched, breathless, to the relics room, loathing the lack of flexibility in his personality that had prevented him from accelerating or postponing his treatment session with Orlando and, as a result, had jeopardised his life's work.

The door was closed, however, and there was no sign of forced entry. His guest hadn't broken in. Both parts of the artefact must be safe. Otto fumbled in his jacket pocket for his key. It was gone. There was no point in searching his other pockets, because only one of them was assigned for keys. He tried the handle and the door swung open. His horror at finding the room unprotected almost made him forget to measure the angle at which he had opened the door.

A second later his fears were assuaged by the sight of the two stelae, side by side on the table. And what was that next to them? He picked up the battered Victorian diary. Could it really be Bilbo's? Did he really have in his hand the information that would unlock the secrets of the stele? He flicked through the pages, finding references to his ancestor and sketches of the stele. This was it. This was the diary his agents had failed to find when they ransacked His Lordship's hotel room. But why would the aristocrat leave it here and disappear into the night?

Lord Ballashiels no longer mattered. The drunken handwriting in a foreign style would take him a little while to decipher, but he began immediately the process of examining the diary, looking for the information he was convinced was contained there.

With the goal of finding a vacant bedroom fixed in her mind, Ruby forced her weakening body up the stairs. Walking descended into crawling. Crawling became dragging. It took all of her residual energy to make it to the upper floor. Helpless as a day-old kitten, she tentatively leaned against a half-open door and was tempted to cry with relief when it swung open to reveal a large, almost opulent – if somewhat dusty – apartment. Most importantly, it was empty. With guts sore even to the lightest touch, Ruby finally fell headlong onto a large mattress. Now alone, she allowed herself a groan, and, as the horror and terror of the last couple of days swept over her in this oasis of calm and quiet, she began to sob, each convulsion threatening to rip her fragile abdomen.

Lying back on the comfortable sheets, she felt as if she'd been run over by a ten-ton truck. If only she could give in to the demands of her wrecked body: just sleep for a couple of days. She was dizzy and faint. The slightest movement left her breathless. She lay stretched out on the bed, wincing from the pain of the food poisoning. Although she was too exhausted even to be aware of the fact, she was dangerously close to passing out.

There was something she had to do. Something vital. Her whole body hurt. She closed her eyes hoping to blot out the discomfort. A great task lay ahead of her. Very soon. In the basement.

It was Matt. She had to save his life. It would involve getting up off the bed, walking downstairs, unlocking the door and letting him out. It was that easy, so easy. She imagined herself getting off the bed and starting the journey to Matt's cell, picturing each step in detail. The steps grew softer and softer until she could no longer feel them under her feet. It didn't seem odd to her that the building should be subtly melting around her. Her

112

imaginary rescue operation was running entirely satisfactorily, her worries evaporating as fast as the walls as she finally fell unconscious.

WEDNESDAY 21ST NOVEMBER 2012

A toucan in the palace garden squawked, but its scratchy song could not penetrate Ruby's brain. It took the scream of a dying man to shock her eyes into opening. She felt rough, as if her internal organs had been bruised, but she was immensely satisfied with herself. She had a vivid recollection of unlocking the cells during the night, and of bribing the guards at the front gate to let her and Matt out of the palace. They had walked straight to the American Embassy where the Ambassador had given them coffee and Hershey's chocolate, and had then put on his Mickey Mouse hat and started line dancing. It had all seemed such harmless fun at the time. Even the escape from the palace had seemed like a game.

Piece of cake this rescuing business, she thought.

The intense daylight pouring in from the window flooded her senses. The window was unfamiliar. The bed equally strange. And what was that sound that had woken her? She scanned her memory. The palace. Matt in danger. It had to be the middle of the night. She had fallen asleep and now it was time to rescue Matt. The light from the window must be from an artificial source.

Her watch, however, told her otherwise. Eleven.

Instantly it hit her. *No* ... this can't have happened. It just *can't*. She'd slept not only through the time to rescue Matt, but also his appointment with the gallows. It was because of her that he'd died. She forced herself to confront the stark truth over and over: Matt is dead.

It was all her fault. Still weak, she fell off the bed and found herself stomping around in her agony of spirit. What would Matt have thought of her in his final minutes? She could never live with such tormenting guilt.

No, there had to be some mistake. She walked to the window and looked outside for reassurance. The light was unbearable today. The smog over the city had been increasing in translucency every hour as one by one the building and car fires either were brought under control or had simply burned themselves out. There were hundreds of people in the garden. All of the palace staff appeared to be out there this morning, but the celebratory mood of the night before was replaced with a sombre sense of repression, of enforced respect.

One feature in the garden appeared to be the focus of this mood. It was a man, hanging by the neck from the scaffold.

Ruby threw herself back onto the bed in despair. A sharp object stabbed her hip. She had fallen onto something unforgiving. She grabbed at her side, realising that the large bunch of keys pressing deep into her flesh was to blame. She grabbed them.

There, in the centre of the ring, was the key that Pedro had used to enter what was otherwise an impregnable underground cell. And what was it he had said, slurring drunkenly before he fell off his seat? Something important.

She recalled their conversation in the bar the previous night: 'We no have spare'. These keys were vital. Pedro was highly irresponsible in handing them over to her. He must have drunk so much that he was utterly beyond making any sensible decisions. Yet the door to the cell must have been opened in order to get the prisoners out for hanging. A steel door, inches thick, with a lock mechanism as heavy as a bank vault, could not have been opened with a mere handyman's toolkit.

She returned to the window, heart thudding. It took a few seconds for her eyes to adjust. When her focus landed upon the scaffold she could make out that the figure swaying like a broken doll at the end of the rope was wearing a baggy soldier's uniform. Otto stood behind him, checking for a pulse while soldiers hacked at the rope to allow his pathetic limp body to drop free from the noose. As they carried him away, Otto at his side, she was finally able to make out the face of Pedro, frozen in time in an expression of fear and confusion. She gripped the keys in her hand and ran towards the cells, clinging to the hope that Matt could still be alive.

Soldiers placed Pedro's body respectfully upon a table in Otto's treatment room. They nodded to the Doctor and left, unconcerned that he then deliberately locked himself in. Studying Bilbo's diary throughout the night had left Otto exhausted, but the opportunity to experiment upon Pedro was a gift to his research project which he could not refuse.

What had he ascertained from the diary? He pondered this as he simultaneously examined the condition of the young man's body laid out before him. His opinion of his ancestor's great rival had sunk to a new low. This Bilbo character was mischievous, irresponsible, generally unworthy of respect. Quite how this bumbling alcoholic had managed to keep Karl Mengele from achieving the highest archaeological prize was beyond him. The information in the diary was presented in a chaotic manner that grated painfully with Otto's ingrained sense of order. There was a great deal of useless tittle-tattle wrapped around the important passages. Personal stories of sordid liaisons with tribeswomen were not his idea of edifying prose.

Pedro seemed to cough as the Doctor manoeuvred his torso to remove the hidden harness beneath his shirt to which the noose had been discreetly attached and which had prevented his neck from breaking. The Doctor connected a heart monitor and straightened Pedro's limp arms to make them precisely parallel to his body.

There were two sections of the diary, he recalled, that shone through the haze. One revealed the name of the village that was closest to the place where the stelae had been found – the two halves of the artefact were separated by less than a mile when they were discovered. Bilbo and Karl had been treading on each other's toes the whole time during their searches. The other revelation concerned the way in which the stelae were said to be aligned. Of the twelve positions, only one could lead to the correct interpretation of the glyphs. The other eleven positions cleverly gave coherent, meaningful readings in every respect, except that they were wrong. Follow any one of those clues and you would end up miles from the true location.

It had, of course, occurred to the Doctor that he could send a search party to investigate each of the disparate locations now that they could all be interpreted. Mechanical excavators would make short work of each site, and he would have results within a week. Such an all guns blazing approach did not suit his style, however. There was an elegant problem to be solved, and it needed an elegant solution.

He inserted a tube into each of Pedro's carotid arteries and began diluting the blood with cell preservatives. He left the room to enquire whether another execution was imminent. He had been promised two bodies today, after all.

Pedro's pulse slowly began to drop, eventually flat-lining for lengthy periods between beeps until it ceased altogether.

'What the hell were you playing at?' Matt's veins were dilated and his eyes were dull and hard, boring into her like a bull's before it charges. His head was still spinning from the din of the futile sledgehammer battering on the steel door of his cell. When he spoke he had to cover his tender ears to shield himself from his own noise. Ruby quickly forced the dented door open wider to let him out, conscious that soldiers could return at any moment.

When Matt had squeezed moodily and ungratefully past her, she paused with one hand on the door and the other on the key. Then she looked at the Guatemalan prisoner who stood calmly by the far wall and couldn't help but hold the door open for him too.

'I don't think that's a good idea,' protested the temporarily deaf Matt, talking loudly. 'Somethin's odd with this guy.'

'I can't just leave him there!'

'Huh? You were happy enough to leave *me* there yesterday!'

The Guatemalan ignored them both and slowly walked out of the cell. Matt marched up the stairs, hands on ears, not caring when his elbow banged into Ruby's head.

'Why the hell didn't you bust me out of there when you had the chance? We could have gotten out of the country by now. This nightmare could have been history.'

'Shut up, Matt. Not now! I'm giving up a hell of a lot to save your arse. And I think they killed the guard who gave me the keys. Hurry.'

'My cell mate said he broke into the palace through a tunnel that leads into the President's office. Said he was part of the team who dug it as an escape route for the previous President. You know, if the shit hit the fan. There's a swimming pool or something at the end of it.'

'I know the way,' said Ruby, feeling somewhat heroic and useful. This was almost enjoyable.

At ground level there was still no sign of anyone. The ghoulish attraction of a public execution had proved irresistible. The Guatemalan prisoner ambled along behind them, seemingly unhurried. Matt hoped they could lose him. His silence and slowness were freaking him out.

'How come they didn't lock you up too?' Matt's attempt at a whisper came out at normal voice level.

'Turns out I've been working for them all along,' Ruby replied directly into his ear as they walked briskly down a hallway. 'My job offer was never from UNESCO. The President and his cronies just pretended to be from the United Nations to get me out here. They were going to send me back to Tikal today. They wanted me to work on the big sarcophagus that you contaminated.'

'They tricked you? Goddamnit!' Matt stopped walking and waved his arms in exasperation that Ruby had been deceived like that.

'I also found out it was the Guatemalans who robbed the Sphinx from under our noses.'

'Assholes!' he shouted, waving his arms again with more pointless gestures.

'Keep moving and stay quiet, Matt. Act normal.' She paused and thought more carefully about her choice of words. 'No, not normal. Act quietly. Behave like you never lived in Manhattan.'

He winked at her.

'You really know the way to this tunnel? If we don't find it, I'm screwed.'

'Matt, no one's looking for you yet. And I kind of work here so no one's going to challenge me. You can find that tunnel and walk away from this.'

'What about you?'

'I have to stay.'

'Huh?'

A soldier entered the corridor ahead, walking in the same direction without spotting them.

'Orlando thinks the world is going to end,' Ruby whispered. 'I want to know why.'

But Matt had divided his attention between her and the soldier in front.

'Look, if we get split up and you don't make it out of here, I'm coming back for you, Rubes,' he said.

'I won't even be here! I'll be in Tikal,' she replied. 'Were you even listening?'

'Hey!' shouted the Guatemalan prisoner. The soldier turned round. 'Over here! I'm ready for execution now!'

Ah. That would be the crazy one, thought Ruby as she saw Matt break into a sprint. The soldier opted for the easy target and grabbed the shoulder of the unresisting Guatemalan, quick-marching him to the gallows. Matt turned a corner, out of Ruby's line of sight. As the seconds passed she was starting to believe he could still make it when a forlorn-looking Matt reappeared, dragged along by four soldiers. Perhaps he would now demonstrate the legendary hand-to-hand combat skills about which he had boasted in his book. He was twisting and bucking like a fish on a line, but there was no sign of any martial arts prowess and the soldiers were able to maintain their grip.

Ruby ran her hands through her hair, smartening herself as best she could. It was all down to her, again.

'Hey, guys!' she called to the four soldiers as they puffed their way past. 'It's OK, you can let him go. President Orlando has ordered his release.' She hoped her Spanish accent sounded formal and authoritative, because her demeanour certainly wasn't.

Four pairs of distrustful eyes glared at her, but no one stopped or spoke.

'Just leave him with me,' she continued, now trying to sound forceful. 'I don't want any discussion about this. Let him go. Now.' When they continued dragging Matt towards his demise, she added hopelessly, 'I'll sort out the paperwork. It's all on my shoulders.'

Playing on the universal hatred of paperwork had no effect. They were gone, out of the nearest exit to the grounds and enveloped by the small crowd in front of the scaffold. Ruby followed in time to see Otto arriving hastily, looking tired. He administered an injection to each of the prisoners and attached something beneath their shirts. Matt's resistance weakened visibly.

The scaffold creaked as soldiers placed the first noose around the Guatemalan prisoner's neck. The main supporting beam seemed to bend as they tugged at the rope to tighten the knot. Matt stood at gunpoint behind the prisoner, cursing the insanity of his former cellmate.

A retinue gathered around President Orlando nearby. He was pontificating and shouting occasional orders to make use of the time spent waiting for the executions to be completed. Wishing she had taken a moment upstairs to make use of the shower, Ruby chose this moment to push through the others and make an approach to Orlando.

'Can I speak to you, Mr President?'

'Oh, why so formal all of a sudden?' he asked, without looking at her.

'I beg you not to kill Matt. You're a great and powerful man. You don't need his death. *Please.*' He glanced at her pleading face. 'If you spare him I promise to work faithfully for you. For as long as you want.'

Although a soldier was by now pointing a gun into the small of her back, Ruby grabbed Orlando's arm. Orlando shrugged her hand off and briefly dusted down his jacket.

'Vicuña. Expensive. Please don't touch again.'

The condemned Guatemalan man was offered a mask, but shook his head.

'It is important I die a visible and honourable death,' the prisoner explained with words that were slurred as if he were drunk. Ruby guessed that Otto had injected a sedative to reduce their suffering.

Orlando made a tugging sign with his hands to initiate the execution, but before the trap door could be released the prisoner began to mumble semi-coherently.

'I will make an important speech before I die,' he said. 'I am not afraid of death. My life has been a journey with a purpose, and this glory is my destiny. I have always known that I would lead my people to greatness. They will follow my lead and bring prosperity to this land. When I was a child in the foothills –'

'Oh, God,' moaned the President, gesturing impatiently.

The trap door opened and the rickety wooden structure creaked. There was a snapping sound. Ruby tried to turn away, but the prospect of a swinging man proved irresistible to the primitive part of her brain. Or it would have done if there had been a swinging man to see. The snap had actually been a wooden support on the scaffold; the structural failure had softened the fall and the Guatemalan was still alive, already attempting without coercion to climb back onto the platform for a second attempt, although as the sedative took an increasing grip on him, he needed to be carried part of the way.

A replacement wooden brace was quickly nailed into place, and this time it held.

Ruby tried to turn away, but her eyes were glued to the body. She was aware that finding death and execution fascinating was fundamental to the human design, but her attitude nevertheless appalled her. Without taking her eyes off the macabre spectacle she confronted Orlando.

'This is all so wrong. This is barbaric. Your country will never move into the modern age with practices like this.'

'What is so great about the modern age?' asked Orlando. 'Maybe there is a different age into which I would prefer to lead my country. Tomorrow you will be back working for me at Tikal.' It seemed a curious non sequitur, but then little was making sense.

The novelty of execution as entertainment was beginning to wear off. Many people returned to their duties after this second hanging. A group of soldiers cut down the body and carried it into Otto's medical room in the palace, accompanied by the Doctor himself. Another soldier placed an almost anaesthetised Matt on the scaffold with the rope around his neck, then tied a rope around his hands. He offered Matt a mask. Matt drunkenly refused. His blurred eyes were studying the structure to which he was connected. Every joint, every bodged repair, every beam, every nail. He was at the twilight of consciousness, but he could see how the trap door operated and where its edges were. He desperately estimated that the drop below was just that little bit more than the slack in the rope.

A few inches more rope and he would survive. But that was impossible.

If he could jump onto the ledge at the side of the trapdoor, he could survive, but it was too far, and his bulk would slip back into the hole. His neck would still break.

The list of options wasn't quite as exhaustive as he would have liked.

Surely just seconds left now. Darkness encroached on his peripheral vision; the circle of light in his eyes reduced to a white dot. The sedative kicked in completely. His feet wobbled and he fell asleep. Soldiers braced his body to keep him upright, inwardly cursing the Doctor's insistence on sedating the prisoners before the execution was completed. They were forced to wait in this uncomfortable position for some minutes, as Otto had ordered that they wait for his return before the sentence be carried out.

'Please, Mr President, this has gone far enough. What right do you have to terminate the life of another person?' pleaded Ruby, trying to stop the tenseness in her throat from making her sound like a shrieking dolphin.

There was a brief pause, during which Ruby counted some of the remaining seconds of Matt's life, before Orlando replied enigmatically, 'None at all.'

The concurrence of opinion shocked her. Maybe she had found a way to connect with his humanity. Some of the tension eased from her neck muscles.

'So please stop this madness. Let him go.'

'Ruby, you must have faith in me. Your friend will discover that there is to be a life after his death.'

'Not that again. Life after death is wishful thinking. It's a way to comfort relatives. It's selling a product that never needs to be delivered. It has no place in a science-based world view.'

Orlando chuckled. He was either insane, thought Ruby, or he knew something of fundamental importance that she didn't. Given the broad scope of her education, she guessed insanity was the more likely scenario, and that didn't bode well for her chances of reasoning with him.

'You speak of science, Ruby, but science is not complete. It moves forward. Sometimes it also moves backward. What if we were to rediscover forgotten sciences from the past? What would that say about your world view?'

Otto returned to the scaffold. Matt's executioners

pulled the rope tight amid more straining of the old timbers above him. Their preparations complete, the soldiers left the scaffold except for the one whose task it was to release the trap door. The number of spectators had dwindled to about ten. Ruby could see, to her dismay, that Matt was showing some signs of waking up. The sedative was already wearing off, plainly insufficient to knock out someone of Matt's bulk for long. He was going to suffer his hanging fully conscious. His eyes blinked and his body shook in frustration.

'At least give him some dignity,' begged Ruby. 'Get rid of the audience, please!'

The President gave her this small concession.

'Non essentials can leave!'

Matt watched the minor exodus through eyes that widened with fear as he came to the realisation that he had woken up for the last time. But Ruby seemed to be up to something. Reducing the number of people present could give her a chance to act. He felt a growing sense of confidence in her abilities.

'Please don't be tempted to make a speech,' said the President once the area was clear.

'Ruby! Now!' shouted Matt.

'What?' she yelled. Lacking the superhuman strength that movie characters seemed to find in these situations, she felt powerless.

'Your plan! You must have had a plan! I thought that was why you got everyone to go away!'

Her jaw was on her chest. With great difficulty she found her voice.

'Er … no, not particularly.' Then, almost whispering as the full horror of the situation hit her and her eyes filled with hot tears, 'Oh God, I'm sorry, Matt.'

Grinning coldly, Orlando ended their discussion with a peremptory hand signal. Otto administered a second injection, then stood back.

The trap door opened and Matt fell into it.

The night spent in the Mitsubishi Delica minibus on a dirt track in the middle of nowhere had been relentlessly miserable, made all the more unpleasant by his determination to remain in full New Ratty regalia while lying down, including the stiff leather jacket. And with no sheets, no duvet and not even any Belgian chocolates on the non-existent pillow, Ratty felt that he had stretched his survival skills to their limits.

But none of that mattered now because, according to his calculations, he was standing on the spot. The intersection of the lines was not a straightforward latitude and longitude equivalent, for the lines ran between ancient Mayan settlements that didn't restrict their locations to the niceties of horizontal and vertical map divisions. The two lines Ratty had, in fact, drawn between the ruins of Topoxté and El Zotz, and between the ruins of Paxcamán and Uaxactún, appeared more like an 'x'. So 'x' did, indeed, mark the spot.

Or did it? The spot on which he stood looked exactly the same as every other spot around him: damp ferns that engulfed his ankles; trees randomly spaced but uniformly blocking any view of the sky. The map said he was three hundred metres above sea level, and the land sloped down towards a shallow valley. There was no habitation within sight, not even a hint of a bulge in the ground level that might suggest the presence of a buried Mayan temple – nothing but diffused rays of sunlight and the sweet aroma of nectariferous berries dripping with heavy dew, a fragrance tempered by the increasingly fruity odours emanating from within his new outfit. He made a mental note to buy several copies of each item of clothing when he was able to afford it.

Had he made a mistake with his map reading? His biro lines between the items on the map were a millimetre wide, and on a scale of 1:25000 that could equate to an inaccuracy of about twenty-five metres in any direction. He stomped around the trees covering the area that he felt might include the margin for error, but there was nothing out of the ordinary. It was more likely that the creators of the stelae were in error. They didn't have aerial photographs or GPS to help them map with pinpoint accuracy. They couldn't see any of the locations the stelae described from this position on the ground, even if the tree coverage had been thinner in past times.

Ratty crouched down and put his hand into the soft soil. Decomposing leaves and insects covered his fingers as they easily penetrated a few inches before hitting firmer ground. He realised how difficult it would be to dig here, alone and without any equipment. He didn't even have a spade. Even if he could create a hole using a screwdriver from the Mitsubishi, it would be a random pin-prick compared to the size of the area that needed to be excavated. He wasn't sure what he had expected to find here, but some kind of clearly delineated entrance, obscured by a few easy-to-move bushes, would have been ideal. It wasn't too much to ask. He wished he had brought Ruby along with him. She would know what to do.

Sighing at the anti-climax of his visit, he trudged back to the Mitsubishi. He needed to return to England to learn how to locate buried monuments, to acquire the equipment he would need and to get fit enough to be able to conduct this dig alone, in secrecy. But going home would throw him back into a vortex of financial chaos. The banks would tear him to shreds. And that would be nothing compared to whatever vengeful Teutonic tendrils Otto was able to extend to England when he realised that

Bilbo's diary had been tampered with. Ratty wondered what the chances were that the sinkhole would widen and swallow Otto's villa with the disagreeable Doctor inside it.

'Time has transfigured them into Untruth,' he told himself, once again. Ruby's quote was really starting to get on his nerves. He could see only one way of purging the poetry from his head: as soon as he returned to England, before all hell broke loose at the manor, he would pay a long overdue visit to Chichester.

'It has not been possible to connect your call,' said the distant recorded voice of a well-spoken Englishwoman. 'Please try again later.' Otto put his mobile phone back in his pocket, noting that Ratty was out of range of Guatemala City's phone network already. It was of no consequence. The call would have been a mere courtesy, and Ratty's disappearance should not affect his ability to decode the message of the stelae.

In any case, the third body of the day had just been delivered to his treatment room, and he had more pressing tasks ahead. The tall American would use up all of his stocks of the unique embalming and preservation fluids he had developed. He made a mental note to create some more barrels of the stuff at the earliest opportunity. With Orlando now self-enrolled as President, assassination attempts could not be ruled out, and Otto had to be ready to tackle any eventuality at short notice. Orlando was counting on him.

He looked at Matt lying unconscious on the trolley, lips and chin wet with dribble. At least this one hadn't soiled himself, but it had been tough knocking him out on the scaffold. The sedative was pre-prepared in quantities suited to the body mass of typical local men. In Matt it had barely lasted a couple of minutes. As he removed the support strap from the subject's chest and replaced it with a heart monitor, Otto pondered whether a third dose of sedative would be necessary before the live embalming process took effect and started slowing the heart rate to an eventual standstill. No, he decided. The double dose already inside Matt ought to be enough, and the even number fitted comfortably with the grain of his sensibilities.

There was no movement from the body as he inserted the tubes into the carotid arteries and turned on the flow of cell preservatives. This first stage of the embalming process would take three hours to complete before the body was ready for full mummification. He made a note of the time and left the room, locking it carefully behind him before he made his way to the antiquities room, unaware that as the door clicked shut, the eyes of the body on the trolley flickered open.

Otto was now alone with the stelae and Bilbo's diary. Two of his ancestors had striven to achieve impossible things. Otto knew he would, someday, complete their unfinished works for them. Some projects would take him longer than others; his medical training and subsequent research had consumed the majority of his adult years just to equip him with the vast amount of specialist knowledge needed to be able to continue from where his father had been forced to stop. He was pleased that completing the work of his more ancient forbear, Karl, would show results more quickly.

He mated the stones together, noting dispassionately the accuracy with which they fitted after all this time, and turned them to the alignment suggested by the diary. This was it. He had arrived.

He unpacked the boxes of books and maps that lay on the floor, then stacked the empty boxes neatly against the wall. The glyphs had to be translated, their meanings had to be equated to actual locations, and the lines between those locations had to be drawn. It was a process not to be rushed, not least because he loved diligent, careful research. He pictured Karl Mengele trying to carry out the same meticulous investigative work from a flimsy tent in the jungle with only one of the stelae in his possession. No malaria pills, no electric lights during the long nights, no real chance of success while that moronic Ballashiels man was obstructing respectable science.

Slowly Otto identified the glyphs as referring to the ruins of Chukumuk and Los Cimientos. He drew a line between them on the map. Next came the settlements of Utatlán and Iximché. Another line. A shiver of excitement ran through him. A location had revealed itself at the centre of a tall, thin cross. To the north west of Guatemala City, just outside a small town called Chichicastenango, he sensed fate was waiting for him. He checked his watch. Matt's body was almost ready to be mummified.

Matt felt rotten. He'd expected the afterlife to be fun. It wasn't supposed to suck. His neck hurt like hell where he'd pulled the tubes out, and his head was pounding like he'd been trying to out-drink an entire college fraternity. Falling off the trolley onto an unforgiving tiled floor hadn't helped, and it had seemed like hours before he had the strength to pick himself up. But the bruising convinced him that he was still alive, on planet Earth, although he was so disoriented he had no idea what country he was in.

There was a sink. He ran the water and splashed it onto his face before glugging some down his dry throat. His surroundings came into focus and the fog of confusion started to evaporate. He was in a medical treatment room. There were two bodies on trolleys next to him. He recognised one of them as the crazy Guatemalan who had shared his cell. He was a pale blue colour. Not a healthy look. The other guy was covered in sticky brown tar and stank like a fishmonger's dumpster. Even worse.

It dawned on Matt: he was meant to be dead, like these two, and some depraved doctor was about to start experimenting on his corpse.

He needed to get the hell out of there.

He tried a door. Locked. There was a second door, though. It opened with a waft of chlorine when he tried the handle. Beyond was a room with a swimming pool, a desk and some chairs. Cool office, his muddled mind thought. Reminded him of something. He walked around it, fantasising about having such a room in his own apartment. Great place for writing his next book, he decided, thinking it would be cool to write a thriller about a guy who wakes from a coma to a changed world.

Memories started to return. Arriving in Guatemala. The dying fan of his previous book in the pit near Tikal. Hiding in a golden sarcophagus. Having the crap beaten out of him by the soldiers who found him in there. Making the situation worse by getting angry with them, especially when they pretended not to have heard of him. Seeing Ruby's face as she opened the door to his cell. The scaffold and the hanging.

And there was something else. Something vital he was forgetting.

He still had to find a way out.

This really is a cool office, he told himself again. Worthy of a rock star. Or a king. Or a president.

Finally, everything clicked. Something the Guatemalan prisoner had said. A tunnel. A swimming pool. The tunnel entrance was here in this room. He staggered around the edges of the pool, looking for a trap door in the floor. Solid marble tiling held his weight everywhere. He checked the walls and opened cupboards. He crawled under the desk looking for a hidden switch that might make the wall roll back.

Nothing. The surfaces of this room were fixed. There was no secret passageway. That damn Guatemalan was a bullshitter, and now Matt was screwed.

Footsteps echoed in the corridor outside. Matt could hear a key turning in a lock. It wasn't the door to the President's office, it was the adjoining medical room; the Doctor was returning. It was too late to close the door between the rooms. Matt had nowhere to hide. That left him the option of fighting and, feeling as bad as he did, that was not an option at all. Overwhelmed by panic, he dipped quietly into the deep end of the pool and sank beneath the surface.

Immersion eased his pains and freed his mind. He looked up and saw streaks of red, like an oil slick. The blood that had seeped onto his shoulders when he pulled out the tubes from his neck was now staining the crystal waters. It was like an arrow pointing right at him. He saw a blurred figure moving around the edge of the pool. He had been spotted. A few more seconds and he'd have to surface and face execution all over again. Perhaps he should try to drown himself, denying his enemies the satisfaction of a kill. He wasn't a quitter, though. So long as his heart was beating, there was still hope.

He looked behind him and saw for the first time the overhang and the submerged recess, like a tiled cave. Above him an arm reached into the water, attempting to grab him. Without thinking, he swam into the cave. He breathed out the last of the air in his lungs, still heading into the unlit recess. Soon he'd need to inhale, and that meant returning to the evil doctor, but he took another stroke into the blackness. That was it. He was done. He couldn't even make it back to the open part of the pool. His lungs were almost bursting with the instinct to inhale, and it took all of his strength to resist that force.

So he was going to drown. After all he'd been through, playing the role of the hero one last time, he was going to end it here. He relaxed his arms and floated upwards, briefly wondering whether his publishers would exploit his demise with a new release of his book and feeling disappointed that he would never get to write that thriller about the coma guy. Any moment he expected to hit the roof and become wedged there until the life had been flushed from him.

There was no impact. He floundered, instinctively righting himself, cringing at the thought of the agony he would briefly endure the moment his lungs sucked in water instead of air.

But the agony did not come. In near total darkness he felt his head break the surface of the water. He felt air on his face. He opened his mouth and breathed in. It tasted stale, but it was beautiful. He splashed around in search of the sides. The chamber was small and low, and there appeared to be a ledge in front of him. He clambered out of the water and crawled forward on what felt like dry tiles. He could see nothing at all, but the echo of his exhausted breathing sounded like this was a tight space. Without room to stand up, he continued to crawl, and as the sound of softly sloshing water receded behind him, he knew he'd found the tunnel. Once more he dared to contemplate the possibility that he might yet make it out of this country in one piece.

The water sloshed again, far behind him, echoing endlessly along the tiles. Only this time the sound was of angry water, brutally and hurriedly disturbed. Someone was already on his trail. He broke into the equivalent of a brisk trot on his hands and knees, blindly trusting that the passage would continue straight and that he wouldn't slam into an unseen wall. Behind his own animal-like panting he could hear the breathing of another. The trot became a sprint. Was it one person or two? He strained to hear, but the clatter of his bones against the floor had become a dominant white noise, suppressing the sounds of whoever was pursuing him.

Trusting that his kneecaps wouldn't shatter, he kept up the relentless pace. Without visual clues there was no sense of distance. He could be a hundred yards from the President's office, or he could be a mile away by now. There was no way to tell.

Then shadows – fast-moving, elongated limbs – projected onto the walls and the floor, moving with him, in front of him, around him. The shapes were distended, monstrous, spider-like. They terrified him, but he didn't stop. These, he quickly deduced, were his own shadows. Someone behind him had switched on a torch, and that could only be to his advantage because now he would be able to see when he reached the end of the passage.

There was a new sound now, piercing the envelope of white noise that surrounded him. It was a voice. Matt didn't care what it was saying, and the reverb effect rendered it incomprehensible in any case, like an announcement on a loud speaker in a railroad station. Another voice bounced off the walls. There were two pursuers. He tucked his head down low and maintained his speed.

The texture beneath his hands and knees suddenly changed. The tiles gave way to wooden planks, which in turn reduced the aura of noise surrounding him. More importantly, he realised he was at the end. Everything now depended upon whether or not there was a locked door in front of him.

There was no door. The tunnel merely stopped. Ahead was a wall of brick. To the sides was more brickwork. Behind, the light, the voices and the thud-thud of stressed knees grew stronger. Matt reached up. It was the only remaining option. He felt the texture of bare wood. He pushed. The wood moved. He pushed harder and a trap door opened fully. He jumped up through it, and slammed it closed again, throwing the whole weight of his body down on top of it.

Only then did it occur to him to look around. He was in a kitchen – small, nondescript, old-fashioned. A square table stood in the centre with four wooden chairs. An oven. A fridge.

He leapt up, grabbed the fridge and dragged it over to the trap door, noticing without curiosity that it wasn't plugged into the wall. He took hold of one of the chairs and pulled it towards the fridge, intending to make a stockpile of awkward and heavy items to obstruct the enemies below him, but with the chair came the table and the other three seats – all were screwed together. No matter. He placed them next to the fridge.

The trap door was pulsating. Someone was making a valiant effort to open it from below, but with the weight of a major household appliance above them, Matt was confident it would be some time before they gained entry. He scanned the kitchen for other items that would add to the weight on the door. A kettle. If he filled it with water, that would help. He tried to pick up the kettle, but it was glued in place. He had another idea. If he ran the faucets in the sink and let it overflow, the floor would start to flood, and it would all drain down upon the heads of the guys in the tunnel.

He spun the taps. Nothing came out. What kind of kitchen was this? He looked closely at the loaf of bread on the counter. It was made of plastic. Had he ended up in some kind of museum? Pretty dull museum, he thought, opening the door to the hallway. There were paintings screwed to the walls and a vase containing plastic flowers was glued to the little table upon which it sat. He was in a fake house, he realised, set up as a cover for the emergency escape route of the President. It had been made to look as bland as possible in order to disguise the significance of the tunnel beneath its floor.

He unbolted the front door and pulled it open. Outside was a modest suburban street – a mix of small houses, a few apartment blocks and a bar. In all the fantasies he had dared to dream during his brief captivity, he had never expected freedom to be as simple as stepping out into a street. But it wouldn't be like that at all, he knew. This country was hostile territory. Ruby was still in the hands of the bad guys, fooled into their clutches and now working as a slave, no doubt at gunpoint. He'd seen through her brave façade. He knew she was trying to be calm – almost indifferent – about her kidnap for his sake. This wasn't over. He needed to get her out of there, but he needed help, had to find someone he could trust.

He ran to the bar.

'Hey, buddy, can you help me?' he asked the bar owner. 'Need to get to the US Embassy. You have a computer I can use?'

The man said nothing, but went into a back office for a couple of minutes before returning with a printed Google map for Matt to follow.

It was less than a mile across the city. Matt could walk it in a few minutes. He thanked the man and left the bar, counting down the footsteps to safety.

The bar owner locked his doors as soon as Matt had left and picked up his telephone.

Otto had no desire to wait for news of Matt's recapture. The soldiers who had swum into the submerged tunnel entrance in pursuit of the American were armed with handguns sealed inside zipped plastic bags – whatever was left of the prisoner would be of no use to him. He put away his embalming fluids, tidied the mess created by Matt in the treatment room and completed the mummification of the Guatemalan prisoner's body. He had no particular interest in the preservation of the deceased prisoner per se, but this was no ordinary mummification technique and he needed subjects upon which to practise. If he had followed the procedures correctly, the mummification was, in theory at least, reversible. Cryogenic freezing without ice. An afterlife without death. He had first attempted it at short notice, many years before, and that mummified body, now in its fourth decade of stasis, was the most important to him. He couldn't risk making an error in the reanimation process. That was what prisoners were for.

Right now, it was time to return to his villa. He needed to keep a close eye on the effects of the sinkhole. The trip from the palace to his home took just twenty minutes in the armoured Mercedes, although aligning the wheels perfectly with the kerb filled an additional five. Otto opened the door to his basement as soon as he arrived. The first step felt deeper than usual. Otto descended a little further and then looked back at the crack that had formed in the stonework as a result of the disturbance in the ground. He had made this journey beneath his villa daily since the sinkhole disaster, but this was the first time the height of the step had been noticeably different. He would just have to take his chances and hope that the ground had stabilised. At least the government coup had drawn public attention away from the brickwork that had been revealed many storeys below his villa. People were more concerned with rebuilding their lives and their livelihoods than with investigating a subterranean wall that shouldn't have been there.

The villa's basement was a large space, but there was

no furniture, no comforts of home. Tiny slits of windows near the ceiling allowed opaque street light to filter through to the bare stone floor. Otto walked behind the stone steps and unlocked a plain door. Another flight of stairs led down to a room beneath the basement. This second underground level possessed no windows. The concrete floor, ceiling and walls, and rusty air conditioning ducts, suggested this place had once been a nuclear bunker. Metal shelves were stacked with fresh food and medical supplies, some of which Otto selected and placed neatly in his shoulder bag.

He then unlocked a steel door and descended a third flight of stairs and then a fourth. The passage was tight and oppressive, like some ancient pharaoh's pyramid interior. Otto felt no discomfort here. He had dug these underground tunnels and rooms for his father in the late sixties and early seventies before moving to Frankfurt to study medicine. Since his return, he had made this descent thousands of times.

The cracks, however, were new. Never before had he noticed so many fractures in the walls. Only wide enough for a sheet of paper, they were disconcerting nevertheless, and their irregular patterns caused him immense discomfort.

So much that was of value to Otto was stored down here. It represented not only his life's work but also that of the great dynasty of which he was a part. Here were the only things that mattered to him, physical objects that defined him as a person, everything he had inherited: research papers, blood samples, slides, a unique ancient Greek text, photographs and mementoes.

And part of the living experiment itself: a human subject, his sole patient besides Orlando, kept in subterranean isolation for more than four decades.

At the US Embassy, Matt was having an unfamiliar degree of trouble with the woman behind the bullet-proof screen. She was giving him nothing to work with. The shield thrown up by her lack of personality was tougher than the shield of glass provided by her government to protect her; she displayed no cracks into which Matt could squeeze some charm to make her open up and start being helpful. Trouble was, he wasn't exactly a Prince Charming lookalike right now.

She repeatedly thrust a neat pile of forms and a pen through the gap beneath the glass towards Matt, and without pausing he repeatedly pushed them back at her. This continued for some time. Occasionally she returned to tapping on her computer keyboard, as if dismissing him from her mind. It was curiously insulting.

Now she looked up and murmured in a tight voice into her microphone, 'You have to fill in these forms. The top one is for your lost passport.'

Her voice was appropriately robot-like by the time it emerged, distorted and compressed, through the speaker on Matt's side of the glass. Briefly, he conceded to the necessity of excessive bureaucracy and scribbled his name, then thought better of it and abandoned the form.

'I know. I'm not interested.'

'The next one is for your lost tickets.'

'You've already told me. I don't care.'

'The pink one will enable you to get cash wired from home.'

'I just need to speak with the Ambassador.'

'The blue one at the bottom needs to be filled in before I can consider you for an appointment.' As she said this, her top-to-toe sweep of Matt's dishevelled, damp and grungy appearance made it clear such an appointment was somewhat unlikely.

'I know. And I'm telling you to stick these forms up

your ass and tell the Ambassador I'm here.'

'You can fill them in over there.'

'No. Listen to me. My name is Matt Mountebank. I am an American citizen. You've probably read my book. I have just escaped from the new President of this country. He tried to kill me. And I think they tailed me here. I'm sure I saw a car following me. So I ain't leaving, honey. The President also kidnapped my girlfriend. I need to inform the US Government of what is happening here.'

'Certainly, sir.'

'What? Oh, great.'

'And you can start by filling in these forms.'

'Right. Give me those. I'm tearing them up. I don't want to see them again. Which door do I go through?' Matt scattered bits of form onto the floor.

'This is getting you nowhere, sir. Why don't you sit down? There's a coffee machine right there. In any case the Ambassador is not in the building.'

Matt flung himself into a chair. The woman began sorting through the day's mail, but every few moments she looked warily across in Matt's direction. He made sure he flashed the widest smile whenever she looked his way.

About half an hour later the reinforced entrance swung open to admit a tall middle-aged man in a suave suit, flanked by his bodyguard. The wealthy-looking man was old-school American – clean-cut, cropped hair, obviously ex-military. A dependable, reliable, incorruptible authority figure.

Judging by the dragon's face, this was someone she respected. Before the woman could say a word, Matt was on his feet, hand out assertively and saying, 'Good day, sir. My name's Matt Mountebank. I'm in trouble and seriously need your help.'

The man pumped his hand firmly with what felt

141

suspiciously like a Masonic handshake. He looked Matt squarely in the eye with just the right amount of wariness yet concern, saying, 'Charles McDermott. US Ambassador to Guatemala. How can I be of assistance today?'

'I want to report a kidnapping.'

'I see,' McDermott said calmly, gesturing to Matt to sit down with him. The woman had the grace to look ever so slightly humiliated by this turn of events. 'Of a US citizen?'

'Well, no. It's my girlfriend. Well, kinda girlfriend. It's been rocky, if you know what I mean? Anyhow, she's a Brit.'

'That's really something for the British Embassy. Or the local police.'

'The guy who kidnapped her is the new President.'

'Do you have any identification?'

'They took it off me when they tried to kill me.'

'In that case there are a number of forms to be filled in before we can check who you are and the validity of your claim.'

The Ambassador had barely got the words out of his mouth before Matt was on his feet, losing it rapidly. McDermott flinched and stood up.

'More bullshit, bullshit. I'm Matt Mountebank. Are you guys listening to me? Don't you *recognise* me? Even the goddamn Guatemalans know who I am. Listen, a woman has been kidnapped –'

'Now, Mister Mountebank. You listen. You may be telling the truth. You may be here about a very serious matter. But frankly I'm not in the habit of taking seriously everything some wild-eyed bum says right off the bat. Now if you'll just calm down and co-operate, we can get the show on the road. *If* I decide there is a show to be gotten on the road, that is. First off, though, please fill in the forms Ms Lavelle will get for you.'

Matt tried to block his way, but the Ambassador's bodyguard stepped quickly between them. Matt figured that any minute this man would disappear into his office and forget all about him, and he'd be stuck in a tedious battle of wills with Ms Lavelle for all eternity.

'Look, there's much more at stake here,' Matt blurted, trying a different tack. 'Apart from the kidnapping, the new President is behind that theft from the Sphinx. And he's stolen a huge Mayan thing.'

McDermott looked at him coldly. Matt was not getting through. Within seconds he might get his security thug to throw him out. Matt went on, speaking fast, aware that time was running out.

'It's an amazing archaeological artefact. Some kind of ancient – I dunno what it's called. Made of gold. It was big. Real big.'

'Look, I know those forms suck. There're some fast track papers in my office. They come pre-approved by me. Two minutes and you'll be done. Colin will run upstairs and get some for you.' He signalled to his bodyguard. Colin did not look impressed by the proposal.

'Sir, I must remain with you,' he grunted, more out of hurt pride than out of concern for his boss's safety.

'I'm with a US citizen in a US embassy with a hundred guards around the perimeter. I'll be fine. Go get the papers. Second draw down on the left.'

With exaggerated reluctance, Colin sprinted up the stairs, out of sight. A movement outside of the window caught Matt's eye. The embassy guards appeared to be running towards something, mouthing words that Matt couldn't hear through the thick walls and bullet-proof glazing. There was a flash of light, surreal in its silence and detached beauty. Then another flash, this time brighter.

The spray of glass fragments came from nowhere, as if the air in the embassy had simply crystallised. Instantly the noise from the aftermath of the explosion outside whooshed into the building, accompanied by the zip of bullets spraying from beyond the railings.

'Aarrgh! Shit!' shouted the Ambassador, clutching his arm. Blood gulped out from between his fingers and he fell heavily onto the ground, groaning. Matt threw himself onto the floor.

'Get down, sir!' shouted Ms Lavelle to the Ambassador through her microphone before running out of her reception booth via a rear security door, but he was in shock and sat still, exposed there in the lobby, his baby blue eyes staring glassily at nothing.

Another bullet caught the Ambassador full in the chest. He keeled over. Colin the security guard ran back into the lobby and stared at the Ambassador who was now gurgling horribly, blood pouring from his mouth. He was choking on it.

'Shit, what'd you do?' he asked Matt.

'Zip. I just dove on the floor.'

'Who the hell are you anyways?'

'It doesn't matter. Help me get this man into a back room.'

'You're kidding me, man! You set this up. You're under arrest. You have the right …'

The Ambassador started convulsing.

Conspiracy to murder a high-ranking government official, such as an ambassador, would be a capital offence in some states, thought Matt. And if he were tried in Guatemala he wouldn't stand a chance anyway.

The convulsing stopped. The breathing stopped with it. With the security guard now pinned under the dead weight of a fresh corpse, it seemed an appropriate moment for Matt to bid farewell.

'Getting help,' he lied, darting outside and slipping away amid the black smoke and confusion.

THURSDAY 22ND NOVEMBER 2012

The blackness of the old hangar was instantly dispelled by a clunk. The fulgent light of four steaming super-troupers now held the monstrous gold artefact in their luciferous grip. Patches of umbra and penumbra criss-crossed the plain concrete floor as if it were a chequered Masonic mosaic. Around the walls of the hangar had been assembled steel racks of tools, testing equipment, a coffee machine and a rusty filing cabinet. One corner of the building had been screened off to form a separate bedroom and shower area for its sole nocturnal occupant.

'Impressive,' said Ruby, bitterly. 'Almost up to professional standards.' She no longer cared whether her tongue would get her into trouble. Matt's execution had undermined everything. Nothing seemed important any more. And her contempt for anyone and anything connected with Orlando was obvious.

Lorenzo looked pleased with himself, as if his conscience had been purged of impurities. He obviously hadn't shot anyone for a few days, thought Ruby.

'Some things come from my new office at the capital, so careful please. You will be finish before I return from my next assignment, so I no miss it.'

'We also fixed the plumbing and cleaned the toilets, now that we are to have a woman working here,' added Paulo, perfectly sincere but sounding almost as if he were deliberately winding her up.

'It just goes to show what two tiny minds can achieve,'

she grumbled, turning away from them.

Ignoring her, Paulo produced a typed sheet of paper from his pocket.

'We considered getting in welders and odd-job men for the heavy work, but for security reasons we decided to limit it to expert scientists. Tomorrow you'll get a metallurgist, a pathologist, an atomic scientist and a jet propulsion expert.'

'A what and a what?' Ruby's disinterest in the proceedings was suddenly halted by these unexpected descriptions. She assumed she had either misheard or that Paulo's normally impeccable English had failed him.

When he didn't bother to repeat the list, she let it drop, assuming a basic mistranslation. Meanwhile she needed to take her mind off Matt. Emotions were overwhelming her and no one was giving her space to grieve. She climbed up one of the ladders to look at the artefact. The large indentation at the rear was still plugged with mud. Nothing had been tampered with since Matt had disturbed the bones.

Again, that image of him in a noose. She couldn't shake it.

'The cleaning equipment is in the kitchen area, Ruby,' said Paulo as she came back down the ladder, even though he could see she wasn't paying attention. 'You can draw up a roster if you're not prepared to do it all yourself.'

'Food, anyone?' asked Lorenzo. 'The kitchen is no much to look at, but we can make soup or some nacho dips. Whatever you want.'

The men opened some nachos and a jar of spicy dip. Ruby had no appetite.

Someone else was in the hangar. Behind the glare of the spotlights Ruby could just make out the shape of a man holding a small box in front of him. As her eyes adjusted to the gloomy end of the hangar she recognised

Otto, staring intently at a digital display on the box he was holding. The LCD readout cast a Mephistophelian glow into the deep lines of his face. He nodded to himself and exited the building.

Moments later President Orlando entered the hangar, closely flanked by Otto and his glowing gadget. Paulo and Lorenzo stood up respectfully, while Ruby deliberately ignored the President's arrival.

'Don't get up, Ruby,' said Orlando, sarcastically. 'I'll join you.'

The President indicated that they should be seated, pulling up a chair for himself next to Ruby. Paulo offered the President the bowl of nachos, but Orlando declined with a wave and Otto stepped forward with a sachet of pills which Orlando swallowed without water. Otto then walked slowly around the artefact, holding up his gadget close to the gold surface while the others talked.

'The television address went well,' Orlando said. 'I got the highest ratings in Guatemala since the second moon landing in July nineteen sixty-nine.'

'You mean the first,' grunted Ruby, sounding like an annoyed teenager. 'July sixty-nine was Apollo Eleven. And don't you have a nation to oppress?'

Orlando ignored her, almost as if *she* were the ignorant one. 'The country is stabilising rapidly. I have direct control of the urgent matters that are crucial for the country and for the world. Administration of local affairs would distract from what matters, so I have good men in place to do that work for me. As I have here, of course.'

'I'm a woman,' Ruby growled.

'Indeed you are. It is the service of good men *and women* such as you that leaves me free to come here to the key projects.'

'I'm not free, though, am I?'

'Come now, Ruby, you know you're not going

anywhere. It makes no difference whether I put a guard on you or not, just as it makes no difference whether the United Nations signs your pay cheques or whether I do.'

'So far no one has signed any pay cheques.'

Orlando's joviality tensed into a glare that would have chilled the heart of most people who knew him, but Ruby had tested her boundaries with him before. He had endured from her a degree of verbal ribbing that would have put others in jail. When his face broke into a smile, she began to sense something inside Orlando: a weakness, a need. It was buried beneath his arrogance and his power and his beauty. If she hadn't despised him so strongly, she would have been intrigued.

'I have a timetable for this project,' Orlando announced. 'I need results fast. The dismantling of the artefact will take two days, and the analysis and recording of the component parts will take a further three days. Is that understood?'

Ruby's jaw fell.

'Two days? Three days? What is this? Not that I give a shit any more, but you must know that's impossible. Ridiculous. You can't expect … Look, come on, think about it. Apart from anything else, that kind of schedule would totally undermine scientific integrity.'

'You will not allow that to happen. Your team must work efficiently. I have other work for them when they are finished here.'

'What about me? Will you let me go when I finish this or do you have a gallows waiting for me?'

'You misunderstand. The next week is just the beginning. You cannot imagine what plans I have for you after that. The world is on the verge of finding out what I already know. Much will be different soon. You've joined the winning side. Be excited, Ruby. Be very excited.'

'After you murdered Matt? Why on earth would I be

excited by anything you say?'

Orlando leaned closer and put his arm loosely around her, for once seemingly unconcerned about his expensive tailoring, and for once she was too despondent to shrug off this invasion of her personal space.

'Ruby,' he whispered, 'I have told you before and I will tell you again. Yesterday's execution was not the end for the soul of this man. I said he would find that there is life after the noose. I think he may have found it sooner than we anticipated. You have to trust me.'

Now she squirmed out of his arm. This was worse than the comforting words of a toothy vicar and she wanted none of it.

'I want to go, Orlando. I can't do this any longer.'

'Don't be tempted to leave my employment, Ruby. It will not be possible to watch over you every minute of the day, but you must understand that if you should be tempted to abandon my second favourite archaeological project, you will be found. What then happens to you depends on how much I feel I need you.'

'*Second* favourite?' she asked.

'What?'

'You said this thing was your *second* favourite archaeological project.'

'Indeed.'

'May I enquire as to what is your *favourite*, then?' Her professional curiosity was returning. 'Could there possibly be anything even more amazing than a golden artefact with bodies inside that could date from an antediluvian era?'

'My favourite,' he began, 'was another of your projects. The Sphinx. You did an excellent job in Egypt. I want to assure you that the work you carried out has been of great benefit to my nation and, subsequently, to the world.'

The stolen scrolls. The significance of the theft had faded in her mind amid the trauma of witnessing Matt's execution. Not only did Orlando possess them, he must have translated them.

'Can you tell me what they said?' she asked, bypassing her instinct to release a torrent of verbal abuse in his direction.

Otto cleared his throat loudly. Orlando stood up and followed the Doctor out of the hangar without a word.

When Paulo and Lorenzo had also gone, Ruby walked in endless circles within the hangar, remembering the good times with Matt as well as the bad times. She had to admit that the bad times probably outnumbered the good ones, but all of the memories were now precious to her. Their clumsy first kiss in a tunnel within the Great Pyramid of Giza. Their first argument, moments later, about which was the way to the exit. Could such a strong personality as Matt really cease to exist? It was so much to take in. Pressure began to build around her eyes. Her head started to ache. Finally, she took advantage of her solitude and let the tears flow. She screamed and cursed at Orlando's callous personality. She tried to convince herself that Matt was dead because of bad luck and circumstances beyond her control – she couldn't take the blame. Grieving was hard enough without adding guilt on top.

Between bouts of sobbing, she came to a decision. Given that her options were minimal and that she needed to busy herself with a project to take her mind off Matt, she decided to take on the challenge of the next few days with all of the skills and professionalism at her disposal. Yes, technically it was colluding with the enemy, but like Alec Guinness's crazy colonel in *The Bridge on the River Kwai*, she felt that collusion was best for her morale during this difficult time.

When the tears eventually dried, she cleaned her face and wiped her eyes. There was a long and lonely night ahead. She might as well prepare the artefact for the next day. As she rubbed some of the bodywork clean, she could feel no seams or joins, no panels or rivets, just an endless monocoque shell. A thing of incomparable beauty.

Hours later, with the majority of the object now clean enough to work on – with the exception of the massive mud plug at the rear, which would need shovels and wheelbarrows to clear out – she went back to the kitchen and tipped away the rest of the nachos. With a yawn, she decided her day was done. There was, however, time for one more peek at the bones before she switched off the lights. She climbed the ladder, lifted the hatch and stared inside.

There appeared to be two bodies, roughly side by side. Many of the bones seemed broken, some obviously recently from when Matt lay on them, but mostly the breaks dated from the moment the people had died. Fragments of clear broken glass lay among them, and flaps of fabric still clung to the metal sides of the compartment.

If this was a sarcophagus, thought Ruby, surely there must be more bodies. This compartment took up less than five per cent of the whole artefact. Maybe there were another ten or twenty similar compartments somewhere inside. Other sets of bones would still be undisturbed, minimising the significance of the damage already caused. It had to be a mausoleum.

As Ruby leaned over to close the hatch, something caught her attention. On the same side of the compartment as the access ladder on which she was leaning, shielded from view until she'd stretched across, there was a protrusion of tarnished metal sticking out of a square panel.

Just like a small switch.

Ruby closed the hatch and climbed down, her head buzzing with possibilities that her education had trained her to believe impossible.

FRIDAY 23ʳᴰ NOVEMBER 2012

Michel Lecour walked boldly into the hangar soon after sunrise, catching Ruby by surprise as she clumsily made coffee after a fitful sleep. He introduced himself as a scientist from the European Space Agency. He sprouted expensively styled black hair, and his skin glowed with a healthy Mediterranean hue. His classic jungle suit was made from thin beige cloth and he wore his porous shirt open a couple of buttons. Given that he had been travelling for most of the previous twenty hours, his elegance was impressive. As she prepared to shake his hand, the somewhat diminutive Gallic boffin turned on the charm, making twinkling eye contact as he lifted her hand to his lips.

'*Enchanté.* This is a nice place you have here,' he said. Ruby was disconcerted to find herself smirking, possibly even simpering, but while she wrestled with her image, annoyingly Michel's attention had already wandered. His eye snapped to the reason for his presence: an outrageous hunk of battered gold; an ancient, impossibly heavy artefact skulking menacingly in the centre of the hangar.

He almost skipped over to it, looking up with reverence and exclaiming, '*Mon Dieu!* I cannot believe it! This is the best example I have ever seen.'

Ruby missed this as she was adding more water to the kettle.

'Coffee?'

'Of course,' he replied.

155

She extracted a second cup from the cupboard.

'What's your speciality?' she asked.

'Propulsion systems.'

Ruby looked at him, searching for indications of irony. He smiled pleasantly, but sincerely. So she had found herself on an archaeological project teamed up with a rocket man. Oh well, she figured, he wouldn't be any use scientifically, but at least he was pleasant to look at.

As if to emphasise the pointlessness of his presence there, she responded, 'That's a bit modern for me. My expertise goes in the other direction, to the past.'

'Mine too,' said Michel, pulling up a stool and sitting in a position from where he could take in the whole artefact. Before she could question him further there were voices outside the hangar – Lorenzo and Paulo, talking excitedly in Spanish. Behind them walked three other men, all conversing in French.

'Ruby!' called Paulo when he spotted her. 'Good morning. You had a pleasant night?'

'I'm a prisoner who's just seen her boyfriend killed by an undemocratic régime, the same bunch of crooks who are also to blame for the theft of the scrolls I found in the Sphinx. How do you think I slept?'

Their hosts' smiles barely flickering, Paulo and Lorenzo hastily showed the three Frenchmen inside, where Michel was waiting for them.

'OK,' said Lorenzo, 'we no have much time. Ruby, I see you've met Michel. He is propulsion expert. We also have Professor Lantier from University of Marseille. He is world expert in metallurgy.'

'Call me Jean,' he said, shaking Ruby formally by the hand. 'I'm the one they call on to test for stress fractures when things break catastrophically. And, well, this is a fine wreck you have here.'

Lantier was the oldest of all the scientists present, old enough for this assignment to be his last before retirement. He was almost completely bald, except for a thin wisp of white fluff that wrapped around the back of his head. The top of his cranium must have gained its deep suntan after he had lost his hair, but had more recently become unhealthily blotchy. His features seemed kind and trustworthy.

Paulo continued the introductions.

'Ruby, this is Doctor Berger. He is the pathologist who will work on those bones.'

Dr Berger smiled at Ruby. She found him somehow unnerving. In his late forties, he sported a thick beard which she was glad not to have to kiss. She proffered her hand, which he shook vigorously, holding on just a fraction too long. No first name was forthcoming, and Ruby was happy to leave it at that.

'Finally we have our atomic specialist, Professor Philipe Eyzies.' She swung round to find herself confronted by an unexpectedly young man, almost a youth. Despite his glittering credentials, he was still in his twenties, and would be tutoring people close to his own age at whatever university he came from. Must be one of those nauseating child prodigies, she thought, finding him more than a little irritating. Why was his hair so long? For such an intellectual star he seemed oddly keen on being cool. And why was he here at all? Ruby recalled telling Lorenzo on their first meeting that the artefact emitted radiation, but in truth the radiation detected was minimal and was not much above the kinds of levels that can occur naturally.

'Pleased to meet you, Philipe,' Ruby said with a smile.

Philipe merely gave her a curt nod then turned away.

With the introductions over, she boiled more water to make coffee for everyone, hoping they saw her as a hostess rather than a maid. They sat on stools in a tight circle, sipping the liquid stimulant appreciatively. Ruby felt cautiously optimistic to be in the presence of these civilised and, at least in some cases, friendly faces. It was like all those first meetings of new colleagues on a major expedition or dig – a gathering of people with differing skills and backgrounds, all of whom were vital parts of the overall mission. Half of this particular group had expertise that was irrelevant to this mission, but Ruby was confident she could quickly train them to be useful as low-level assistants. Normally a team would be larger, but under these aberrant circumstances she had to be grateful for what she could get.

'Most of us have worked together before,' explained Lorenzo, 'but Doctor Towers is new to the team. She studied Archaeology at Cambridge, and has worked all over the world at high profile archaeological sites. She now work for the Guatemalan Government, appointed by our great President himself!'

There was a smattering of embarrassed applause from Michel, Jean and Dr Berger. Philipe just stared at her impassively. Ruby wondered whether she should explain to the assembled company that she was a political prisoner, but Lorenzo's next words appeared to make blatant her status.

'You are all aware that research into this artefact must be quick. You have five days, and that time can no be extended. Ruby is Project Director, and she will catalogue all findings on the computer, but she is no allowed to use Internet. Paulo will video and photograph each stage of the work, and he can provide Wi-Fi dongle for those who need it – apart from Ruby. The usual secrecy measures apply. Ruby is to remain on site, there will be two guards at the entrance to this airstrip at all times, and the rest of you will all be staying at the Hotel Villa Maya at Flores.

Now, if you will excuse me, I have another project to oversee.'

Lorenzo left the building.

'My dear,' said Paulo, 'the men would appreciate some more coffee before we get started.'

'Make it yourself.'

A chorus of 'ooh-la-la' erupted from the Frenchmen, but her point had been made. Paulo sorted the refreshments and then activated two video cameras that would record, from different angles, everything that occurred. From his personal bag he picked out a small digital camera and began taking close-up shots.

Dr Berger silently set to work inside the artefact's top compartment where the bodies had been found. He took stills, followed by a few seconds of digital video, before lowering himself inside completely to examine the context and arrangement of the bones.

Paulo moved quickly around the exterior because he knew the others would soon need to burn into the golden bodywork with fine-tipped oxyacetylene torches to gain access to the interior.

Jean Lantier, the metallurgist, was making a detailed examination of the sections that appeared to be deformed, some of which damage, he realised immediately, was due to the rough and ready excavation. He took measurements from one side, then compared them to the other side. Like Paulo and Dr Berger, he used his own photographic equipment to record a detailed study.

This pleased Ruby. The vast quantity of photographic evidence, much of which was duplicated, would be a valuable future resource. She sat down at the computer. The first thing to do, she figured, was to familiarise herself with the software on the machine and create new files to log every action of each member of the team, noting the *modus operandi*, any problems and, of course, the all-important results. She was pleased to find a copy of Word on the hard drive, and opened a new file in which she would summarise the proceedings so far in the examination of this ancient, curvaceous sarcophagus containing a switch-shaped feature. If she could find evidence of a rudimentary understanding of electricity in the culture that built this thing, the implications could be enormous. This was going to evolve into a classic archive, she told herself – a thorough analysis, from various scientific perspectives, of the greatest archaeological discovery ever made. It would be read by the entire academic community. She felt proud, despite the extreme circumstances, that she had been chosen to oversee this extraordinary find. If only Matt had been around to see it.

While the others worked at clearing out the mud from the indented rear of the artefact, Ruby clicked on the e-mail icon. No freshly-despatched digital missives would arrive without the dongle, but she was keen to know if any correspondence was stored on the laptop itself. Rather naïve of Lorenzo to leave his computer in her hands with all his personal stuff, she thought. Perhaps he assumed she would be completely computer illiterate, being a woman, and so wouldn't know how to find his private files.

A list of archived messages appeared before her. One thing struck her as interesting: many of the messages were from French names and .fr e-mail addresses. She clicked the program's 'close' button and returned to her Word file.

Ruby initially paid little attention to the men's manual work going on behind her. She tapped away furiously at the keyboard, speedily deluging the computer with information. Faster the better. That way she could spend quality time training each of the members of her team who lacked archaeological experience, ensuring they followed correct procedures. She was also keen to be around at critical times, whenever historic breakthroughs occurred, but she was busy typing when the first one happened.

'Ruby, come and see this!' called Professor Lantier.

The men had already cleaned out a large quantity of compacted dirt from a bell-shaped cavity at the rear, which had revealed a new type of surface material that was certainly not gold. They had then created a great deal of noise while removing a small section of gold panelling from the base of the artefact. This small inspection hole had been Ruby's suggestion – it would indicate whether the thing was really a multi-layered sarcophagus, as she strongly suspected.

Ducking under the timber supports, she bobbed up beside Professor Lantier.

'You see this?' he asked, shining a lamp inside the hole. Ruby peered in, expecting to see a cavity similar to the one at the top containing the bones. But this was no cavity. The hole they had cut was only one square foot, enough to test the settings on their cutting apparatus to ensure there would be no damage to whatever was behind the wafer-thin gold outer layer. Behind the hole were parallel lines of narrow gauge pipes, wrapped in a dull, faded substance. She climbed out from beneath the artefact and stood up.

'It's just as I expected,' said Professor Lantier, 'but in far better condition. The minimal amount of corrosion is extraordinary given the timescale.'

'What do you mean, "as you expected"?' asked Ruby. 'We've just opened up the belly of a sarcophagus and we've found what looks like pipes. This is insane. Nothing like it has ever been found. It's like some kind of giant coffin with underfloor heating.'

'Mmm, I think heating would not be appropriate, Ruby.'

'Appropriate for what? Why do I get the feeling that everyone here knows a lot more about this than I do? Has one of these turned up in France, too?'

Ignoring her questions, Professor Lantier murmured, 'What you have seen is a cooling system. Gold doesn't corrode, being generally a non-reactive element, which is why the thin outer shell is so impressive even after all this time. The really clever bit is inside. The superstructure isn't made of gold. That would make it too heavy. There's a small part exposed just to the side of the hole we made, and as I expected it's an advanced alloy.'

'There you go again,' protested Ruby, 'you keep saying this is as you expected. What do you mean, "expected"? How on earth can you have expected this?'

Professor Lantier glanced at Philipe, who shook his head.

Paulo took Ruby to one side for a quiet chat.

'Ruby, my dear, come and sit with me.'

'I am not *your dear*.'

'There have been other finds.'

'Where? What other finds? Nothing has been published in journals.'

'There isn't time,' said Paulo. 'The world can't wait.'

After an hour of searching Chichester's mediaeval cathedral, Ratty paused and stood still. It was good to be back in England, but this kind of thing didn't suit his new image. He felt like one of those tourists on a *Da Vinci Code* trail, desperately looking for clues that weren't really there. What made his task so fiddly was that the stonework on the floor was worn smooth by centuries of pious shuffling feet, rendering most of the inscriptions illegible. Those on the walls were fine, but many were too high for him to read and he found his opera glasses of only limited benefit in the half-light.

'Time has transfigured them into Untruth.' Ruby's words had been so enigmatic they were nonsensical to Otto, but Ratty had recognised the reference to a poem by Philip Larkin. It was also a reference to a disastrous undergraduate date Ratty had shared with Ruby. For this romantic occasion they had journeyed for three hours in Ratty's Bristol Blenheim from Cambridge to England's south coast. He had parked next to the toilets in a nondescript car park on Selsey beach, facing the choppy grey waters of the English Channel. They sat, saying nothing, just like the elderly couple in the adjacent car who were drinking coffee from a flask and wordlessly watching the waves.

Eventually Ratty had turned to Ruby and told her that they were looking at the spot where an ancient cathedral once existed. The sea had gradually encroached on the land until it was lost for ever under the English Channel, another slice of history vanished beneath the waves. Not wearing her archaeologist's hat, which would have caused her to question the validity of that legend, but instead wearing her bored, pissed-off would-be lover's hat, Ruby had toyed in her mind with the words 'deal' and 'big' before Ratty had suddenly said, 'Chip-chop. Let's take a look at the new one they replaced it with.'

Thirty minutes later they were standing inside Chichester Cathedral next to a dingy hole in the floor which was covered with a protective layer of glass. Ratty had put a coin into a box on the wall and lights began to flicker in the hole, revealing a section of Roman mosaic tiling four feet below the ground.

'This cathedral is almost a thousand years old,' he had told Ruby, as if she hadn't known already, 'but the mason chaps who threw up this Norman monstrosity built it upon the ruins of an earlier civilisation. Completely covered up all traces of the fellows that had lived and worshipped here a thousand years before them. And yet, when one thinks about it, in many ways the civilisation that was here first was far more advanced than the later one. They had hypocaustic heating, sanitation, slaves ...'

With a solenoidal clunk, the lights had gone out in the Roman hole, and Ratty had guided his date over to the other side of the building, pausing at a mediaeval tomb. The top of the tomb was decorated with two life-sized stone effigies – one was a knight with a large round chest wearing full *Monty Python and the Holy Grail*-style battle costume, and the other was a woman dressed in long flowing robes. Her feet rested on a pet dog, his rested recklessly on a disproportionately small lion, crouched in a sphinx-like position. Rather sweetly, they were holding hands.

'An ancestor,' Ratty had proclaimed. This had not been what Ruby had expected from a promise to meet some of his family in Sussex. He had then intertwined his arm with hers. Physically, they weren't an obvious couple. Her face exuded an unconventional beauty, bronzed by regular field work. Suitors who gazed into her eyes would joyously drown in wide pools of molten chocolate. The only person who had ever gazed into Ratty's eyes was his private ophthalmologist. An unkind observer might have commented that on Ratty's pallid arm, Ruby appeared not so much his lover as his carer.

The pair of effigies was the subject of a famous poem by Philip Larkin, *An Arundel Tomb*. Ratty wasn't sure if it was the way he had read the Larkin poem in its entirety out loud, or the fact that he had then suggested how nice it would be for the two of them to spend eternity together like the people in the effigy, but for some reason Ruby had then disappeared and wasn't seen by him again until he returned to Cambridge. One day he would unravel the mysteries of womanhood, he had told himself. One day.

Right now he was preoccupied with a more important mystery. The line of Larkin's poem had been quoted to him in Guatemala, entirely out of context. He really had no idea what she was on about, but the power of her words was enough for him not only to risk his life, but to change it. He now looked back on that meeting with Otto and Ruby as a significant juncture in his existence. At that moment he had transfigured. How could a small chunk of poetry do that to him? What subconscious connection had those words made within the dark, labyrinthine culverts of his mind?

A party of schoolchildren filed past, forcing Ratty to step aside. Time has transfigured them into Untruth, he told himself once more, returning to his thorough perlustration of the stone effigies. The years had not been kind to this tomb. Ratty began to pick out the lines where repair work had been carried out. The knight's feet were clearly glued on. The top of his head showed faint repair seams. His nose was black, awkwardly glued on to grey stone, giving him an oddly comical Bacchanalian appearance. Ratty wondered if his ancestor's bones still lay beneath the effigies, or whether they had become separated during the tomb's less than restful history.

'Time has transfigured them into Untruth,' he said, out loud this time. Heads briefly turned his way, then once again he was left to his ponderings. Did the line from the poem mean that the repairs carried out to the stonework rendered it no longer genuine in some way? Was the original purpose and meaning of the tomb utterly unlike that which was currently assumed to be its *raison d'être*?

With Ruby apparently in a permanently incommunicado state there was no one to answer his questions. He waited beside the effigies for a flash of inspiration. Nothing happened. He looked up, hoping for a divine beam of enlightenment to blaze through the stained glass windows above him in a manner that he recalled seeing in a scene from *The Blues Brothers*. Nothing penetrated the blanket of cloud above the cathedral, however.

Reluctantly he returned to the poem itself, handwritten in red and black calligraphy and stuck to a stone pillar next to the tomb. He read it slowly, carefully. The words Ruby had quoted formed the beginning of the final stanza. And the line that followed them suddenly jumped out at him. A connection had been made, not with her quotation but with the subsequent line. Ratty felt a shiver of excitement pass through him.

He mouthed the words quietly: 'The stone fidelity They hardly meant'.

Could it be that elementary?

Nachos provided little gastronomic satisfaction for the French contingent in the Tikal hangar, feeding only their desire to discuss, during lunch, the failings of Guatemalan cuisine. Even the reticent Dr Berger voiced an opinion or two about corn. Michel produced a bottle of Côtes du Rhône from his bag and shared it among them. Ruby was not a keen lunchtime drinker, especially in humid climates, but one bottle between six was hardly decadent. She held out her paper cup and asked a question that had been burning inside her.

'If those pipes were for cooling,' she began, 'does anyone think it might be a form of cryogenics, a mummification technique to preserve bodies in low temperatures?'

Everyone stared at her as if she was nuts.

'What?' she blurted in confusion, taking a grateful slug of wine into her throat.

'It is a cooling system, but not for people,' explained Michel, without really explaining anything at all.

Ruby was fed up with being the ignorant one in the group. She gestured for him to elaborate.

'The cooling is for the propulsion system,' explained Michel.

'What are you talking about?'

'The propulsion system. The engine.'

'Don't be ridiculous! This thing is thousands of years old!'

'Have you really not been told?' Michel looked around to see if he had overstepped the mark. It didn't seem to him to be a breach of secrecy if Ruby was told more about this project than she appeared to know so far. She was going to find out soon enough, in any case. 'Ruby, this artefact is a machine. A very ancient mechanical device.'

'A machine to do what?'

'Do you not see from its shape?'

She looked up at its partially crushed and mangled form, but could not discern any kind of mechanical shape.

'It is a flying machine, Ruby.'

She looked away from the artefact into the eyes of her companions, slowly reading each pair. She saw, in turn, compassion, impatience, surprise and disdain in those eyes, but there was no indication of joviality, falsehood or dishonour. Finally, she spoke.

'You're kidding, right?'

Michel shook his head. If it hadn't been for the earnest expressions of the company in which Ruby found herself, she would not have been able to take this seriously at all.

'Ruby,' Michel said, 'look at it. Just look. Forget your prejudices. Forget your education. This thing once flew.'

'Well, of course it has a vaguely streamlined shape, I suppose, and those stubby bits could have been wings before they were crushed, but it's nothing like any aircraft I've ever seen. I just assumed any weak resemblance was coincidental. It seems to have all the aerodynamic properties of a pebble.' She looked long and hard at the artefact, but still couldn't picture it in the air.

'Its systems are vastly different to those of our modern age,' Michel continued. 'The aircraft did not use aviation fuel as we know it today. They had a source of power which we understand in theory, but have not yet been able to put into practice. Philipe has been studying it, and hopefully – if this example is as intact as it appears to be – this could move our research forward considerably. You are aware, are you not, of the principle of cold fusion?'

'Yes,' she said, 'I'm familiar with cold fusion. The theory, that is. No one's been able to crack it so far.'

'And you are aware, no doubt, of the low levels of radiation emitted from this craft. They are nothing to worry about, but there are clear signs of a weak source of radiation at the heart of the structure. This aircraft had as its power source – as I expect to be able to prove very shortly – a cold fusion engine. A lightweight form of nuclear power.' He trailed off briefly to let his words sink in, but Ruby simply continued looking at him, mouth slightly open in a less than dignified way. Inside her head, a desperation to believe was battling with the hard-headed scepticism of the professional archaeologist. Her face showed the maelstrom within.

'Such an engine is capable of producing almost limitless power without the risk of overheating and without the subsequent problem of disposing of radioactive water used in the cooling process,' continued Michel. 'It was safe and incredibly efficient. I have been privileged to examine fragments of such power sources before, but I have never had the opportunity to dismantle and catalogue an entire self-contained system. I think that is what I will find when we dig further into this vehicle.'

'How come we never managed to crack the problem at

Cambridge – er – or any of the world's top universities?' asked Ruby.

'I'm not sure,' said Michel. 'My guess would be that our thinking has evolved along different lines to that of the ancient people. They simply tackled the problem from a perspective that we haven't thought of. It is that perspective I hope to discover. Who knows what other problems it may solve for us?'

Ruby's science head returned.

'When I checked the aircraft over with the Geiger counter, I got two different types of readings. There was one specific source, but also a much weaker reading everywhere else, and a different sort of radioactivity.'

This was Philipe's speciality, and he was visibly chagrined at the revelation that Ruby had carried out her own investigations.

'You are correct in your observations. I need to do more tests before I can hypothesise in an informed way,' he told her coldly.

'What do you expect to find in other parts of the, er, aircraft?' she asked the team in general, scarcely believing she had actually said it.

'There are many systems involved in a machine like this one,' replied Michel. 'We don't know for sure yet, but I expect to find engine management systems, radio systems, possibly some kind of radar since there's no evidence of a human pilot. There should be a life support system for the passengers, some kind of landing gear if it landed in the normal way, which we have yet to ascertain. The dissimilarities are a matter of evolution. The ancients evolved a technology that could do the same as ours, but in different ways. Their science didn't evolve through Copernicus, Newton, Galileo, Einstein, like ours did. They would have had their own scientific forefathers, their own constrictive religions, their own day to day problems that needed solving and their own military requirements.'

'The discovery of all this ancient technology did not surprise me,' said Professor Lantier. 'I was in Baghdad, before the first Gulf War, on an invitation to examine some clay pots that dated back about two thousand years. Each one was about six inches high and contained a copper cylinder. The cylinders had been soldered with a lead-tin alloy, and their bottoms were capped with copper discs and sealed with bitumen. A further bitumen layer was used to seal the top of the pot and to hold in place iron rods suspended in the centre of the copper cylinders. The rods showed evidence of having been corroded by acid. What I held in my hand, in effect, was an electric cell, capable of discharging a current of one or two volts, and it was contemporaneous with the time of Christ.'

If he expected his words to be received in stunned silence, he was disappointed. The Baghdad batteries were well known curiosities, and everyone present had read or heard something about them.

'They found jewellery that had been electroplated, didn't they?' asked Ruby.

'I suspect that was the main use,' Lantier replied. 'One cell was found at a house that had belonged to a magician, so again, we have a clue there. Perhaps he created whizz-bang effects to impress an audience. What is also likely is that they were used to provide electric lighting.'

'Yes,' agreed Michel, jumping in enthusiastically. 'There is much evidence in history and in the Bible that the ancients possessed electric lighting. The book of Genesis, for instance, translates the word *tsohar* as window in reference to the source of light within Noah's Ark, and yet in other parts of the Old Testament it is translated as brilliance or a brightness. What the mediaeval translators cannot have realised is that it most probably refers to electric lighting.'

'What always impressed me,' said Ruby, eager to show off at least a little first-hand knowledge, 'is that in many Egyptian monuments and ruins there are no signs on the walls of any burn marks or soot from lanterns or torches. I hadn't given it much thought before, but if they could electroplate jewellery, they could certainly produce smokeless light from their electric power.'

'Indeed,' said Michel. 'I understand that there are examples of Egyptian hieroglyphs that suggest the use of a sort of electric light bulb, with a cord running from it. Again, this is something that I believe is not an Egyptian discovery, but rather the faded memory of a past knowledge, kept alive by a small number of people for a short period.'

Ever since her misguided involvement in the Antarctic project, Ruby had sought to rebuild her reputation by avoiding the world of esoteric pseudo-science like the plague. Now she had to come to terms with the horrible, embarrassing realisation that they were on to something after all. Years of trying to disassociate herself with the likes of those who dared to question the tenets of a monolithic archaeological establishment had come to an abrupt halt. On the plus side, assuming there was no fakery involved and everyone eventually accepted humanity's new historical timeline, she would reach a superstar status in her career. It gave her a splitting headache.

She walked to a cupboard to look for painkillers. As she opened the door, a stranger clipped her peripheral vision. She swung round to see a mountainous young man in gaudy bright clothes, T-shirt riding up over rolls of pasty flesh. He looked around the hangar in an unfazed, almost leisurely fashion, seeming to find the ancient aircraft insufficiently fascinating to merit more than a glance.

He then waddled into full view, saying, 'Hey! You guys wanna doughnut?'

Ruby shook her head as if to dislodge yet another surreal situation from her mind. How could there be an American doughnut delivery boy in the middle of the rainforest? Even more curiously, despite their overly grand gastronomic philosophising, all four Frenchmen couldn't wait to tuck into the young man's stale doughnuts.

'The door was open,' the visitor said with what he hoped was an innocent smile. 'Hey, you guys archaeologists?'

Paulo took him by the arm and led him to one side.

'You should not be here. This is government property.'

'Jeez, man. I only wanted to offer everyone a doughnut.'

'How did you get past the soldier at the gate?'

The American shrugged indifferently.

'Is Rula Towers here?'

Visibly startled, Paulo pulled himself together.

'Nobody of that name here. I suggest you find some tourist to sell your doughnuts to.'

'Look, there she is!' he cried, looking over Paulo's shoulder into the hangar. 'I'm a big fan. Would she like a doughnut?'

'You can't possibly have known she was here.' Paulo seemed to hesitate, and instantly the fan powered into the hangar, hand outstretched.

'Wow! I can't believe I'm actually meeting you! This is amazing. Can I, like, shake your hand?'

He held out his sweaty, sugar-encrusted palm. Delicately, Ruby shook it, then subtly wiped her hand on the seat of her shorts. Gross though he was, she was

quaintly flattered to have a fan. Archaeologists tended not
to have too many groupies.

'I saw your Egypt series. Bummer about the scrolls.
I'm Charlie.'

Paulo now enlisted help from Michel to deal with the
Charlie problem. Each man grabbed one of Charlie's
arms.

'Wait,' said Ruby. 'What are you doing at Tikal,
Charlie?'

'Oh, we're working on a dig.' He waved one pudgy
hand as if to take in the whole of the surrounding jungle.

Charlie was staring unblinkingly at her and had even
started to dribble. Not the best sort of fan to start off with,
she mused.

'Well, Charlie, it's been great meeting you.'

Paulo and Michel escorted an unresisting Charlie to
the exit.

The stone seat was concave, worn down by backsides that
for five centuries had sought rest in this public place in
the centre of Chichester. It was also draughty, but the
octagonal Market Cross of which it was part made Ratty
feel at home. 'Draughty' was, after all, the most common
word used by visitors to his house when later asked about
their experience by inquisitive friends. The architectural
style of the Cross was also familiar to him: vaulted stone
arches that framed a perfect view. In this case, the view
was of West Street, with a hint of cathedral to the side and
a large dollop of bell tower dead ahead, and framed by
rows of Georgian townhouses converted for modern use
by solicitors, dentists and publishers. At Ratty's home, the
mediaeval wing was connected to the Georgian section by
a vaulted hallway that was partially open to the elements
and frequently provided a view, to anyone of sufficiently
sturdy disposition to want to enjoy such a thing, of storm

clouds rolling menacingly across the hills. So this truly was a perfect environment for Ratty to ponder what 'The stone fidelity They hardly meant' could mean. He could have done this from the comfort of his hotel room at the top of North Street, but here he felt connected to his home and to a long, complex sense of history.

History, thought Ratty. The telling or writing of a series of events. The human story. It was not complete. Not reliable. History was the story presented by the winning side – a distorted tale, skewed and spun to give a desired context to carefully selected facts. Past reality was made unreliable by the agendas of those who chose to recount them. An historian could make a reader think Winston Churchill was either a hero or a war criminal depending on how words were chosen and arguments structured.

Things done in the past were done for a reason, and that reason was not always correctly interpreted by people living centuries later. Was that what Ruby was trying to tell him? Was the Larkin poem saying that the effigies in the cathedral were originally intended to mean something other than how they were interpreted today? Was the knight not designed to lie hand-in-hand with the damsel? Was this arrangement merely a schmaltzy flourish on the part of a Victorian stonemason charged with repairing two damaged, armless, separate effigies of unknown origin? Had history been rewritten by those actions, obscuring the truth behind incorrect interpretations? He was close to understanding the poetic weapon that Ruby had used upon him. Very close.

The phone in his pocket started to vibrate. He withdrew it and glanced at the screen – a debt collector trying to contact him for the fifth time today. Each time he saw that number he turned into a nervous wreck, shaking almost as much as the phone. He rejected the call and stood up, remembering the plan he had devised to help him cope with the challenges that lay ahead. He needed to toughen up. Building physical and mental strength required daily exposure to situations that would test him and push his boundaries outwards, little by little. For that reason, he had blown yet more of other people's money in the hurried purchase of gym equipment and had made enquiries regarding martial arts tuition in his home. Bruises and aches would fade into muscle. Nervous exhaustion would fade into confidence. Lacklustre underachievement would fade into success. Old Ratty would permanently fade into New Ratty. And it was New Ratty who was destined to fulfil the work begun by his alcoholic ancestor.

To this end, he had already made call after call in an effort to hire the finest tutors in Shropshire – well, the finest of those who were prepared to accept post-dated cheques – to provide private tuition in practical archaeology, Mayan history, Mayan language, Spanish language, self-confidence and flirting skills. The idea of taking self-confidence lessons filled him with fear, but he guessed that was the whole point. And the flirting tuition was just as important to Ratty as any of the other subjects. Without flirtation there would be no wife, and with no wife there would be no successors to admire his forthcoming greatness. Each cog was a vital part of the machine.

Tomorrow he would receive delivery of the best ground-penetrating radar system illicitly borrowed money could buy. He needed to learn how to use it efficiently, quickly, quietly – like it was an extension of himself. The tool would help him find the greatest treasure on Earth, not to mention a key that had been missing in the grounds for generations and which meant there was a room in his home that he had never entered.

Back with his companions, hiding in the deep shadow of the outer wall of the hangar, Charlie related his experiences, with a little embellishment.

'I took out these goons single-handed – ker-pow! Rudi was in this cell, naked and in chains. I had to bite through them …'

'Shut up, Charlie,' whispered Matt. 'And it's Ruby, not Rudi. What really happened?'

Relinquishing his fantasy with unconcealed reluctance, Charlie reverted to a normal voice.

'She's in the hangar. You can go on in, but there are guards, up the track. We can't let them see us.'

Matt was unnerved. This had all been too easy. Charlie showed no sign of concern on his chubby face, but his square-jawed Kennedy-hairstyled companion, Brad, was clearly ill-at-ease. The two students were already jeopardising the completion of their PhD research, and the help that Matt had so far received from them had gone way beyond the initial generosity of a ride to Tikal in their kombi van. He couldn't expect any more of them. This next part of Ruby's rescue mission would have to be carried out by him alone.

He crept closer and cautiously observed the movements of the guards. When he was certain their attention was elsewhere he signalled to Charlie and Brad to wait just outside the main door while he edged silently into the hangar.

It was impossible for Charlie to follow any kind of order, however. He tried to imagine himself in a James Bond tux, gun in hand, ready to go back into the danger zone. Fantasy took over and he sidled his corpulence into the hangar behind Matt. Brad sighed and followed his friend into the incongruous concrete edifice in the heart of pyramid country. The two students stood just inside the hangar entrance, almost invisible to those working under the dazzling spotlights in the centre of the building, and watched as Matt walked on, so far unseen, towards the light.

Charlie's nose twitched. He threw his hand towards it, but it was too late. He sneezed. The whole place seemed to shake. Matt froze in angry terror.

Paulo glanced up from his work, shocked at this second interruption.

'This is making me very nervous,' he told Ruby. 'It makes no difference to me if your fan club follows you everywhere, and these French guys don't give a damn so long as they can do their job, but I wouldn't like to be in your shoes if the President found out.'

Ruby didn't bother to look up from her computer. Her work was her only release from thinking about Matt's death, and she needed to concentrate.

'Hey, Ruby!' called Matt in an ear-splitting whisper.

This was starting to annoy her. It was the voice of another fan, she decided, still not looking up from the screen. Also American. Probably a New Yorker, since the accent reminded her of Matt.

Matt took a frustrated breath and marched right up behind her, placing his hand on her shoulder.

'Ruby, it's me,' he said, but this time he didn't need to. There was something about his body odour that had connected with her. She breathed in the miasma that enveloped her, turned around and saw.

He had risen. Orlando had been right about life after the gallows. She scrambled to her feet and staggered away from this reanimated corpse, this zombie, this abomination of nature. Her mouth opened but no words came. Instead, her confused mind spun with questions.

What had Orlando done? Was this a pastiche of Matt,

an animatronic talking waxwork? And if he was the real Matt, how could his neck not be broken? And how could he have come back here?

She put her hands over her eyes in denial. Matt approached her again.

'It is you,' she whispered, once more overcome by his sweaty odour. She lowered her hands and finally allowed her heart to fill with joy and relief. 'I'd recognise that stench a mile away.' They smiled and embraced. 'So, what's it like?'

'Huh?'

'Being dead.'

'The hangings were faked,' replied Matt, refusing to indulge her sick humour. 'The Doc clipped the noose to a strap round my chest to take the strain, but he knocked me out so I couldn't tell you.'

She now realised there was a second reason to be cheerful. If Orlando wasn't the cold-blooded despot she thought he was, then perhaps there was no danger to her. Orlando barked, but he didn't bite. And now she could continue working on this incredible artefact with a clear conscience. This was turning out to be a rather better day than she had expected. Without the combined weight of fear, guilt and sorrow on her shoulders, the coming days could turn out to be the best of her life.

Ruby hugged him again but less intensely this time, already remembering that she didn't want to go so far as to reignite their relationship.

'Never mind that,' he grunted, pushing her off. 'Come with me. Quick.'

'What do you mean? I've got work to do.'

'We've come to rescue you,' he murmured, keeping an eye on the door where the two students were watching him.

'From what?'

Michel came over and cheerily handed Ruby a paper cup of water.

'From the psychos holding you prisoner,' said Matt, trying to ignore Michel's friendly expression.

'Hi. I'm Michel. And you are?'

He stuck his hand out to Matt.

'Matt. Matt Mountebank.'

'Hey,' he said to Matt like an overgrown schoolboy, 'I read your book! Pleased to meet you. You sure took some *merde* from those Iraqis!'

As he clapped his hero on the back, Matt's head reeled, confused by an unexpectedly amenable enemy and a heroine with a surprising aversion to rescue.

A shadow then fell across the golden light in the hangar. A soldier had entered via the rear service door. Ruby shot off to guide the soldier round to the other side of the artefact, away from the unauthorised visitors.

'Beer?' she offered the soldier, holding his attention. He glanced around suspiciously. Ruby signalled to Matt as obviously as she could by tilting her head and swivelling her eyes in the direction of her quarters. He nodded, but the doorway was within the soldier's field of vision. She took a bottle of beer from the fridge and offered it to him.

The soldier was still studying the edges of the hangar, looking for something. When he turned away, Ruby dropped the bottle onto the concrete floor where it smashed at his feet, soaking his trousers.

'What am I like? Butterfingers! I'm so, so sorry. Here, let me ...' she gabbled, while the soldier indignantly mopped himself. Matt ran into Ruby's quarters, quietly pulling the door to behind him but leaving a gap so he could hear what was going on. Charlie and Brad took the opportunity to creep quietly out of the hangar, but the soldier saw them the moment he stood up again.

'Freeze!' he roared. The students halted, hands in the air, faces drained of blood.

'Oh, Lorenzo said they could help us,' Ruby said casually, although her heart was thudding fit to burst through her chest.

'How they get here?'

'Lost.'

'Why I no told?'

'Because you're a stupid ignorant bastard with nacho brains,' said Ruby very quickly and with a sweet grin.

Charlie sniggered nasally. He was more in love with his idol than ever.

'Slowly please,' complained the soldier.

'Because there was no time to arrange it,' corrected Ruby.

The soldier sneered and took another beer from the fridge. He waved his handgun around. Everyone ducked.

'My gun is always loaded,' he advised them as he left.

Ruby found Matt waiting for her on the camp bed.

'Let's go before they find me,' he said in a low voice.

'Why?' Ruby asked, sitting next to him and hoping the fragile bed frame could take their combined weight.

'Don't waste time.'

'Look, Matt, we need to talk.'

Christ, he thought. Typical woman. You escape death and tempt fate by walking into God knows what in the middle of the jungle and what does she do? Want to *talk*.

'Let's get outta here,' he hissed.

'Don't talk in American clichés, Matt,' she reprimanded. 'You know you can be so much more eloquent when you make an effort.'

'Make an effort? Isn't finding my way across an entire country – a country in which I'm a wanted man – to … to rescue you –'

'Listen,' she interrupted, 'I haven't been able to talk to

180

you about this before, but –'

'Never mind that. Come *on!*'

But she just sat there.

'We're safe here,' she murmured, trying to sound decisive. 'Well, *I'm* safe. Not so sure about you.'

He grinned, his face feeling taut and painful as the assorted bruises and contusions he had accumulated on his travels began to complain at the unusual muscle activity.

'I planned to come here to end it with you,' he told her sombrely.

Some men drop from helicopters, swim shark-infested oceans and fight alligators just to leave boxes of chocolates for their ladies, thought Ruby, but this one does it all for the opposite reason.

'Are you insane? End what, exactly?'

'Well, you know … us. After you nearly got me killed. Kinda put me off you a bit, but when I think of Egypt I can't bring myself to end it.'

'There's nothing to end. We had a holiday romance.'

Squatting there beside her, Matt stared into her mesmeric eyes, whispering quickly and urgently, 'You know what kept me going when I was sentenced to death? I realised what you meant to me. Well, when I wasn't busy being mad at you for leaving me there, and when I wasn't pissed that you got me into this mess in the first place, those were the moments I thought nice things about you. I mean, you're a pain in the butt and all that, true, but there's something about you that works for a guy like me. I think we could go places. Spent a lot of time thinking about starting a family with you, actually.'

'*What*?' Ruby's horror could not be contained. The repulsion she had felt years before at Chichester Cathedral with Ratty returned to her in an instant, only this time running to the train station was not an option. She merely leaned away from him.

'You know. You. Me. A few kids running around. Maybe a dog.' Ignoring Ruby's lack of zeal, he wrapped his arms tightly around her and kissed her. She twisted violently and pushed her palms into his face. Still hanging on, he persisted, despite his flattened nose. His words came out sounding like Donald Duck through her pressing hands: 'You'd make a great mother.'

With a heave she managed to throw him off her. He overbalanced and fell backwards. Half of the bed frame collapsed, dropping him to the ground with a thump. She was struggling to cope with the sheer irrelevance of what he was saying. None of that stuff mattered right now; he simply had to get out of there and she had a job to do. And what were those students doing while she and Matt were fighting? What kind of chaos was going on while they wrestled on what was left of her bed?

'Matt, it's wonderful that you're alive – you can't imagine how happy I am that the nightmare is over for you – but you should leave. Now. Don't push your luck by staying in the country.'

'No. You're coming with me. It's all arranged. Charlie has a van with smuggling compartments to get us over the border.'

Twenty-four hours ago she would have jumped at this opportunity. Now things were different. She didn't think of Orlando as a saint, but his threats no longer chilled her. She was with her peers. They were all in it together, all on top of their game. All facing the most exciting assignment that could even be imagined.

Looking Matt straight in the eye, she said levelly, 'I don't want to go with you.'

'What? You're a prisoner. I … Goddamnit, I came here to rescue you.'

'Don't make it sound like such a big deal, Matt. You were the world's greatest soldier. This stuff is like riding

182

a bike for you.'

'It *is* a big damn deal. Everyone thinks they know me. Everyone assumes I'm the hero. Well they don't know me. You don't know me. Even I don't know me, but I've come this far and I'm not leaving without you.'

'This is the most important work I've ever done.'

'Huh?'

'This discovery is more important than me, more important than, you know, the you-and-me scenario. We'll fade into history, but the object out there is actually an ancient aircraft. I know, I know, I didn't believe it either, at first. Don't you see, Matt? This object *is* history. It changes everything we thought we knew. It puts us in touch with an ancestry that we didn't know we had. It forces us to reassess what we take to be the major scientific discoveries of the last century and to realise that they are only re-discoveries of knowledge that was previously lost. It's the big picture, Matt.'

For a couple of beats, they faced each other – she, proud and defiant; he, trying hard to swallow his pride and not look ridiculously, even childishly, disappointed.

'Yeah,' he muttered. 'I'm the guy in the little picture and right now that picture sucks.'

'Matt, just go to the American Embassy. You'll be safe there until they can get you on a flight home.'

'Embassy. Right. Actually, that's kinda not an option any more. Already tried that. The President's hitmen followed me there and attacked the place. The Ambassador was shot. The security guy seemed to think I'd done it. I, er, might need to clear my name.'

Oh God, thought Ruby, unconsciously rolling her eyes.

'Did they recognise you?'

'Everyone recognises me, you know that.'

'So now you have the governments of two countries after your blood. Brilliant. That's quite an achievement.'

183

'You know me, huh? Always like to go the full Monty, as you Brits say.'

'You can't stay here. The soldiers will turn you in. You've got to get away from Tikal, get out of Guatemala.'

He sighed. 'I know. I know. But, Rubes, what about Orlando? He stole the scrolls from the Sphinx. He nearly had me killed. What will that asshole do to you?'

She flashed him a *Mona Lisa* smile. Foul thoughts of Stockholm Syndrome flooded his mind. Had she fallen for her captor? Did she have feelings for the maniac?

'I can handle him,' she said, unhelpfully.

Silently, not exchanging so much as a glance, Ruby and Matt exited her room and re-joined Charlie and Brad in the main part of the hangar.

'Guys, Ruby wants to stay. She thinks this shit is worth the risk.'

'There's no risk,' she declared, consciously suppressing the doubts that were already beginning to taunt her, aware of the possibility that her refusal to let Matt extricate her from this uncertain situation might have more to do with her determination to ram home to him the message that it was over between them than with her conviction that she faced no true peril.

'I agree,' said Brad. 'Paulo says I can stay and help him provided he can get clearance for me. They sure could use an extra pair of hands.'

'So I'll just rescue myself, then, shall I?' sighed Matt.

Charlie's face dropped. His dream of a romantic escape with Ruby in the back of his van had evaporated. He flopped ponderously onto a stool that squeaked under his weight and looked down at the floor as he announced, 'If Rita stays behind, I can't go through with it. The whole rescue deal's off. You're on your own, Matt.'

SATURDAY 24TH NOVEMBER 2012

A northerly meltemi whipped across the Aegean Sea, slicing sheets of white surf from the tops of the waves and filling the yacht's mainsail in an instant. Monika gripped the wheel and dug her heels in. The fifteen-metre boat was almost torn from her grasp, but, determined to stay at the helm and maintain control, she quickly turned it into the wind to take the power out of the sail. She looked up briefly at the cloudless azure sky. It was deceptively calm, almost innocent. The instructor had briefed them about the peculiarities of the local weather systems in this part of Greece, but learning about it was not the same as experiencing its raw, invisible energy through her fingertips. The boat now slowed. She started the engine and called out her instructions.

'Rocco, take in the mainsail. I'm going to motor back. It's too rough to sail.'

He gave her a salute accompanied by a sarcastic grin. But the meltemi was neither one of his practical jokes nor a crazy conspiracy theory: this was a very real danger for inexperienced sailors. She wanted to shelter in the nearest harbour. As acting skipper for the day, she had to consider the feelings of the six other crew members, some of whom now wore distinctly uneasy expressions as they held on tightly.

None of them really wanted to be here. All of their resentment for this team-building weekend found its way back to her, in one way or another. If she hadn't complained to senior management about the attitudes of her fellow workers, they wouldn't have been forced to endure this trip together.

With the mainsail furled neatly inside the mast and the yacht now making a bumpy seven knots under diesel power, Rocco came to sit next to her at the helm.

'You know the real reason they sent us here?' he asked her.

Monika sighed. After the brief drama of the transition of the wind from force three to force six, she wanted to relax a little. Rocco's presence was rarely conducive to such a state.

'Go on, enlighten me,' she groaned.

'The Chinese. It's obvious. They found out that I was tracking their returning probe from Mars. We got a tight lock on it. They must have arranged for us to be sent away until it reached Earth, before we had a chance to get an image of it in close-up.'

'And why would they bother to do that?'

'The same reason that anything gets hidden. Because they had something to hide.'

'Last week you were telling me you didn't think the probe was coming back at all. Then you managed to find it, in between bouts of sabotage against my workspace, and now you think we were all pulled from our desks because they didn't want us to see it, like it's towing a bunch of Martians or something.'

'I'm telling you, they wanted it hidden.' As he spoke, his eyes moved furtively, as if, even on the open sea, someone might be spying on him.

186

'Well it's landed now, anyhow. End of story.'

'End of story? Monika, this is just the beginning. Have you heard about the receiving facility?'

'Of course, but that's obviously anti-communist propaganda. It's the weakest of all your conspiracy theories.'

Rocco shook his head, unfazed by her cynicism. He leaned closer to her, but he still had to shout over the sound of the wind, the diesel and the waves.

'Everyone who has been in contact with it is in quarantine,' he said, as if that proved anything.

Monika felt like pointing out that the first few Apollo crews to return from the moon also spent time in quarantine. It was a public relations thing. Any serious scientist knew that the conditions on the lunar surface would sterilise all forms of life and disease into oblivion, but the public needed reassurance nevertheless.

'They don't know what they have, but it's serious,' he continued. 'You wait. This is going to be big. No wonder they needed us out of the way.' Rocco grabbed Monika's shoulder and looked over the port side, genuine fear showing in his eyes.

'Get your hand off me,' she yelped, uncomfortable with the unsolicited physical contact.

'They're after us. It's a trap. That could be a Chinese sub,' he panted.

She shielded the sun from her eyes and tried to focus on the object he was looking at. As her eyes adjusted to the sparkle of the water his paranoia became clear. If every floating piece of driftwood was going to ignite this kind of response from him, it was going to be a tedious voyage.

'Forget about China,' she ordered, still trying to maintain authority over her crew. 'Think about something else. How's your Nazi-hunting going?'

'The Vatican helped Hitler escape, you know,' he stated.

Monika tried not to react. She was having a tough enough time dealing with the forces of nature that tried to push the yacht off course, and in so doing offended her sense of perfectionism. She couldn't wait to reach the harbour and get the untidy ropes into neat curls and loops.

'Others too,' he added. 'Bormann. Mengele. All made it to South America with enough gold to buy their safety. I've been following their trails – public records, private papers, photographs, witness statements.'

Suddenly the yacht whipped to starboard, causing its occupants to yell at Monika for failing to anticipate a swell that caught them side-on. She straightened the wheel and looked at the surrounding sea, but she was no longer seeing it. An idea had taken over. It pained her to consider asking Rocco, of all people, but she had to admit that he had the skills she needed.

'Rocco, I need a favour when we get back. Can you do some research for me?'

'Er, sure. What is it?'

'Can you help me find my father?'

From the coffin-like compartment inside Charlie's old camper van, Matt replayed the kiss in his mind, unsure whether it really counted. When his lips had touched her forehead she had responded instinctively, blindly kissing him back on the lips. She tasted good – raw, salty, sexy – but she hadn't woken up. The whole episode could have

188

been a dream for her. For all Matt knew, Ruby might have thought she was snogging George Clooney. Given the possibility that he might never see her again, it was not the romantic farewell he would have wished for.

There was a small, crudely-cut hole in the plywood, in line with his mouth. He slid back to put his eye against it. The interior was a kaleidoscope of dancing orange and brown shadows and shapes as the van ploughed its way through the Guatemalan dawn. He stretched his spine, trying to find a position that would minimise the jolts that continuously shook him. No such position existed within Charlie's smuggling compartment.

The van stopped. Matt saw the lid open above his face, and Charlie's chunky features beamed down upon him.

'Hey, Charlie, you greedy bastard,' grumbled Matt, making no effort to mask his anger at Charlie's attempt to strike a new deal over his escape.

'Twenty grand? Greedy?' protested Charlie. 'I could spend that on doughnuts in a month.'

Matt climbed out of his hiding place and felt enormous relief when he sat on a regular seat. He hoped he wouldn't have to go back in the stinking box until they reached border territory, but while Charlie returned to the front seat and concentrated on driving, Matt's mood darkened. What if they were compromised here and he didn't have time to get back in the smuggling compartment? How could he get away? Which direction would provide the best cover? He found himself thinking like the soldier in his book, the hero everyone thought he was, but they passed village after village with no difficulty. For the next half an hour until the border with Belize there would be nothing but jungle, a deep green façade either side of them behind which everything was inky black.

A bright flash of glinting metal among the foliage suddenly caught Matt's eye. He dismissed it until a series of objects became visible, just behind the line of trees. There was the occasional blinking glass of a vehicle windscreen, and – unmistakably – long tank barrels. The camouflage netting slung over them did little to hide them from the road. Half a mile further he spotted army trucks, jeeps and armoured personnel carriers. Hundreds of them were lined up, parked out of the sun under trees.

As Charlie drove on, Matt noticed that, far from thinning out, the military presence strengthened. The Volkswagen was now only just outside the tiny border town, but all around them were soldiers, tanks and supply vehicles.

Then they were in the town and suddenly all evidence of the Guatemalan army vanished. Matt lowered himself into the hidden compartment and shut the lid, onto which Charlie scattered handfuls of odoriferous clothes.

The border post was familiarly oppressive to Charlie. He had passed through the US-Mexican border and the Mexican-Guatemalan border on the way to the dig, and the intimidating atmosphere of excessive and inexplicable Third World bureaucracy backed up with guns had pervaded all of them. Tensing inside, but putting on a brave face, he parked the van and lumbered into the run-down passport inspection office.

Inside was a large map of Guatemala on which, Charlie was interested to note, Belize appeared as a Guatemalan region, marked in the same small-size lettering as other local areas.

The Guatemalans had never given up their territorial claim.

Charlie handed his passport across a desk to a middle-aged soldier with a large moustache. The soldier glanced at Charlie, then stared inside the passport for a full minute, enjoying his moment of glory while the obese American boy shifted uneasily from foot to foot. Slowly he picked up his rubber stamp, still staring at Charlie, and flicked through the passport to find an empty page to mark the exit visa.

Next, the vehicle insecticide spray and customs inspection. On the Guatemalan side an officer slid open the door and glanced inside before waving Charlie through the gates to Belize. Easy, thought Charlie.

The next inspection, however, was thorough. Charlie watched helplessly from the Belizean passport office as uniformed men conducted a plenary search of the messy interior of his van, and felt his legs turn to jelly when the sound of excited voices announcing a discovery was accompanied by the clicking of gun safety catches being released.

Authorisation to add a man to his crew in Tikal reached Paulo via an oddly-worded e-mail from the palace. Permission appeared to be conditional upon the additional man being made available for another governmental research project immediately after the completion of the dismantling of the artefact. The nature of the subsequent work was not made clear, and something about the tone of the message made Paulo disinclined to ask questions, so he shrugged and decided not to mention it, but his mood had changed and Ruby sensed that he had become unsettled, almost fearful. This triggered a resurgence of her own disquiet, and she began seriously to question whether she had made yet another bad call in refusing to go with Matt.

Brad began helping to dismantle and rebuild sections of scaffolding as the team worked its way around the artefact's outer skin, removing panels of gold-plated bodywork. Each panel they removed was photographed and catalogued, and placed on a wooden pallet at the edge of the hangar. A bizarre grey superstructure was emerging, tightly and efficiently packed with complex systems. Involvement in an archaeological find such as this was so far removed from sifting through soil looking for fragments of pottery that Brad couldn't believe what he was doing now could be classed as the same subject. He dutifully did everything Paulo asked of him, but he did it with his mouth open wide in constant astonishment.

'Please permit me to check my e-mails, Ruby.'

She looked up. Dr Berger stood at her side.

'Again? That's the fifth time today. My work is starting to pile up thanks to all these interruptions,' she protested as she saved her file and vacated her seat. She stood around, tutting, while he inserted the Wi-Fi dongle and checked for the specific e-mail that had so far failed to materialise. On this fifth attempt, however, something arrived that elicited an expression on his face which was not entirely unlike a smile.

'Carbon dating is extremely accurate with human tissue,' he explained to Ruby, as if she didn't know. 'I have just received results which suggest that we can be very confident these people died twelve thousand, four hundred and ninety-seven years ago.'

He stood up and offered the warm seat back to Ruby. She sat down to resume work on her lengthy report document, trying not to get distracted by the carbon dating results. The precise date was roughly in line with her visual analysis and educated guess, but to have it confirmed like that was an event of fundamental importance. She stared at the words in her document, but they didn't sink in. The certainty of the antiquity of this flying machine, coupled with the uncertainty of her future, made concentration impossible.

She sat back and noticed that Dr Berger had forgotten something. The dongle was still in the laptop. She was still connected to the Internet. She glanced at the others –

all were engrossed in their activities and paid her no attention. Here was a chance to tell the world of her incarceration, she realised, immediately opening a browser window and logging into her Hotmail account. She opened a new message and selected a few key contacts as recipients, and began typing a passionate cry for help.

She stopped writing and looked blankly at the wall.

The reckless side of her nature led her finger to the delete key. She had to take some chances in life, the devil in her head was whispering. She had to go with the flow of this situation, stay in control of her wits and come out of it a winner.

She deleted what she had written and shut down the program, then whipped out the dongle, went over to Dr Berger and handed it innocently back to him.

Ruby returned to her computer. The Word document now exceeded twenty thousand words, but there was at least as much again waiting to be entered. She still couldn't focus on the broader task, so she decided to glance at some of Lorenzo's saved e-mails. There was an ongoing correspondence with a government official in Paris, containing discussions of the ways in which the French could work with General Orlando if he were to become the Guatemalan President and how they were supporting his cause. Another French contact had written that two men died in an explosion during the testing of a reactor. It was followed by a note confirming the names of the team members who would be working on Project B, and their date of arrival. It was the same day that Ruby's team had begun work, but the names were different.

'Michel, can I borrow you for a minute?' she called.

He came and stood by her, his hand resting casually on her shoulder.

'Are there other projects at Tikal besides us?'

'Of course. There are only a few weeks available for the world to prepare, so obviously we have multiple teams working on this stuff.'

'What are you talking about?'

'Oh, I probably shouldn't say. But I can tell you we're Project D. The scientists from Project B are staying at our hotel.'

'So what is Project B?'

'They're not allowed to talk about it, and we're not allowed to discuss our work with them. All I know is that they are based somewhere here at Tikal too.'

'Do you know if there's a Project A or a Project C?'

'Oh yes. There are dozens of others.'

'Where's it all going, Michel?'

Michel seemed about to speak when Philipe, who had been edging closer, glared at him. Michel acknowledged the silent reprimand. He shrugged at Ruby.

194

SUNDAY 25TH NOVEMBER 2012

'You have a lot of paperwork building up, my dear.'

A mound of scraps sat on the desk in front of her, secured from being blown away by any breezes in the hangar by the weight of a grubby coffee mug. The workload was obvious. Ruby didn't need Paulo to tell her she was slipping behind.

'It's under control,' she hissed, thinking it would be even more so if he left her alone to get on with it. 'These French guys are scribbling notes and reports throughout the day. They're generating a vast amount of technical information, their handwriting is appalling, and I'm doing my bloody best, all right?'

'We are working to a tight deadline,' added Paulo. 'There is much at stake here. Maybe you could keep working while we take our coffee break?'

'Maybe you could go take a running jump,' she replied, standing up and joining the others at the little canteen table.

'I brought a local newspaper in from our hotel, Ruby,' offered Michel. 'I thought you might like to read it, since you have been so isolated these past few days.'

He handed it to her. It was mostly about the new President, with articles – seemingly written at gunpoint, thought Ruby – about how his policies would increase the prosperity of all Guatemalans. Suddenly she laughed out loud.

'The paper says Guatemala is on course to become a

world power!' she exclaimed. 'Who on earth believes this kind of rubbish?'

With the exception of Brad, the assembled faces showed surprise and a detectable degree of offence at her remark. Michel held out his hand for the return of the newspaper, whispering, 'You really do not know, do you, Ruby?'

'What?'

Once again, Michel was silenced by a look from Philipe. This was really starting to get on Ruby's nerves.

'What is it with you, Philipe? You're always stopping people from telling me anything. Arsehole.'

Philipe replied in the kind of French that she hadn't been taught at school and returned to his work. 'You will know what you need to know, Ruby,' he called from across the hangar, 'but only when you need to know it.'

'Is there anything we can all talk about?' she asked the remaining coffee drinkers at the table.

'The past,' suggested Michel.

This was her kind of territory. She relaxed.

'The past. OK. So from what we know,' she said, 'there's a gap of about eight thousand years between the people who made this aircraft and the Sumerians with their emerging pre-Egyptian civilisation, during which we've found nothing to indicate any sign of sophistication at all.'

'That is true, Ruby,' Michel replied.

'In that case, this technology the ancients developed, it didn't go anywhere. It just died away.'

'It is not the fact of the disappearing technology that interests us as scientists. The fact is obvious and indisputable. It is the speed at which it declined and the reasons for that decline. If we can solve those mysteries, our society will be much enriched.'

'Do you have any theories, Michel?'

'I have many. We have documentary evidence of more recent societies rising and falling. They seem to slide back into mediocrity. Their civilisation becomes primitive, and they lose their collective memory of their former greatness. Often this happens due to war, natural disaster, unscientific belief systems, accident or a gradual neglect, but whatever happens, they leave an imprint on our planet, even if it is hard to see.'

'Such as the buried foundations of their buildings?'

'More than that,' said Michel. 'I mean the positions of their buildings. The alignment of their structures. Anyone can place bricks next to each other. It takes mathematical and astronomical knowledge to align those bricks with magnetic north and to portray an accurate scale model of a star constellation on Earth.'

'That's not proven,' she replied with an unfamiliar lack of conviction.

'Remember that the Mayans believed they came from the constellation of Pleiades, Ruby. Why would they not attempt to represent those stars in the alignment of their temples? Tikal has been shown to mirror the stars of Pleiades.'

'Not objectively or scientifically,' Ruby said. 'Someone just took a map of all the temple mounds around here and joined the dots to suit the theory. There are so many dots you could do anything with them.'

'Are you equally sceptical about the pyramids at Giza? There are only three dots to align there to get a match for Orion's belt. Plus, the Sphinx, of course, and its relationship to the constellation of Leo.'

'Surely that depends on whether you think the Sphinx was contemporaneous with the pyramids, or whether it was built much earlier,' Ruby announced, realising that she was digging herself into a hole from which she could only escape by adopting an unproven theory about the age of the monument. If only she could find out what message the stolen scrolls contained, all such speculation could be ended permanently.

'Why?' asked Michel.

'If the Sphinx really is as old as its weathering patterns suggest, then it could be the same age as this aircraft, and the same age as the dying civilisation. This aircraft proves that there was a society far older than Pharaonic Egypt. The Sphinx might have been built as a marker of that ancient time, and maybe records of that time were stored inside it in the clay tubes I found.'

'Ah yes. The quest for the Hall of Records, I believe the New Agers call it. The Holy Grail of archaeology. Edgar Cayce and his drug-induced ramblings.'

'There's no need to be cynical. Not now that we know all this. We know they're probably right.'

'Don't be so sure, Ruby. It's just a hunk of rock. We don't know when it was carved, and without those scrolls we never will. Experts will argue about its age, but we have to accept it might have nothing to do with our work.'

'We'll see,' she said. 'We'll see.'

MONDAY 26TH NOVEMBER 2012

After twenty-four hours in solitary, Matt was intrigued when two Belizean police officers took him to an interview room where an attorney was waiting.

'The name's Roland Baxter. Sorry I couldn't come sooner.'

They shook hands. Baxter's grip was limp and sweaty. He wore thick-rimmed glasses, Buddy Holly style – only without the style. Despite this, the cultured English voice sounded confident, which was reassuring to Matt. He needed a strong ally to fight his corner for him.

'I've been given a brief outline of your case, and I must say it's fascinating. Quite a drama.'

'Can we get rid of these apes?'

Baxter spoke to the policemen, and they agreed to leave the two men alone for fifteen minutes.

'Fire away,' said Baxter.

'Can I trust you?' asked Matt.

'Of course. I'm a lawyer.'

Matt gave him a cynical stare. His question had not really been resolved to his satisfaction.

'Whatever you tell me is just between the two of us, unless we both decide otherwise,' Baxter continued.

'You know I'm Matt Mountebank, right?' Matt paused for effect, folding his arms and tilting his chin. 'Go on,' he continued, 'tell me you've read my book. *Eye of the Desert Storm*.'

Baxter looked at Matt blankly.

'Sorry, your name doesn't ring a bell. I tend to read legal journals mostly.'

Matt recounted the series of events that had occurred since his arrival in Guatemala. Baxter nodded a couple of times when Matt had finished, and then calmly read through his notes to remind himself of the salient points. The fact that the whole of human history would be changed by Matt's revelations obviously hadn't registered with him.

Baxter cleared his throat, sounding as if he had a small bird trapped in his windpipe. Then he looked steadily at Matt as if about to ask what he fancied for his condemned man's breakfast.

'It's hard to know where to start. It looks like you're in a bit of bother.'

'You have to get Ruby out of Tikal.'

'And how would you suggest I do that, Mister Mountebank?'

'Ruby will be able to give evidence in my defence. Figure something out. We just need proof of the ancient airplane she found and everything that was triggered by that discovery.'

'Ancient aircraft, yes. Yes, you mentioned that.' Baxter sighed slightly and fiddled with his pen.

'You don't believe me, do you? What's the goddamn point of me telling you all this if you don't believe me?'

'No, Mister Mountebank, you misunderstand. It is totally irrelevant what I believe. I will work for you and put your case to those to whom you wish me to put it. I don't need to believe you; I only need to act on your instructions. Now, there is the matter of my fees. The State of Belize will pay for me to defend you on the illegal immigration charges, and I can offer a certain amount of legal advice with regard to the ambassadorial murder charge if the Americans decide to attempt to extradite you, and of course I can assist you if the Guatemalans request you to be returned to them, but you will have to pay me to work for you with regard to any additional projects. How am I to be paid for this? I assume you have no money and no prospect of obtaining any.'

'I am a bestselling author, remember? I made a fortune after the first Gulf War. It's all in my account in New York. I can give you the codes to access the account yourself and take your payments that way. I know they'll be able to trace me here, but I want the authorities to know about all this. It's the only way to get me off the hook.'

Baxter slid a notepad and a pen over to Matt and asked him to write down his bank details. He then slid the pad into his briefcase and said, 'You're in an awful lot of trouble, Mister Mountebank. An awful lot. I'm not sure there's a lawyer in the world who could disentangle you from this mess.'

Professor Lantier was lecturing the team as they tidied the hangar, their initial studies of the ancient aircraft now complete. Lantier's final discovery had been an atomic pulse-powered system which he considered to be part of the autopilot technology.

'To fly itself,' he droned, 'this aircraft must either track a series of geostationary satellites and compare its three-dimensional grid location with a stored memory of the geography and topography over which it flies, or it must be able to see for itself. There is no sign of a suite of radars that could do the job of the human eye, so we have to assume satellite navigation was their preferred method, and therefore we can assume that they were capable of leaving the planet.'

'If they put satellites up, how come NASA hasn't spotted them?' asked Ruby, trying to regain some degree of healthy cynicism, if only for her sanity. Ancient aircraft, now satellites …

'Because orbits decay,' answered Professor Lantier. 'I doubt that many of their satellites even lasted a hundred years, let alone twelve thousand. They would have burned up on re-entry. Even remote geostationary orbits decay eventually. They may have created structures on others planets, though.'

'Like on the moon?' asked Ruby.

'I was thinking about the Cydonia region on Mars, but it's really a long shot.'

Ruby had once read a crackpot book about some sphinx- and pyramid-like monuments that were said to be visible from a set of 1976 Viking spacecraft photographs of the surface of Mars. One of the photos seemed to show a human face, and dotted close to it were square-shaped objects that may or may not have been pyramids. At the time she had sneered – as only an academic can – at such ridiculous ideas, fabricated by what real archaeologists termed 'pyramidiots'.

'The Cydonia Sphinx is a ridiculous idea,' said Ruby. 'We don't understand how the pyramids in Egypt could have been built, even allowing for an unlimited workforce. Imagine creating similarly impossible monuments on another planet with hardly any men, all wearing spacesuits, with limited oxygen. It doesn't add up. If you go to Mars and build anything at all, you'll build shelters and oxygen distilling factories and sealed biospheres. The top priority when you get there is not going to be public art.'

'Not with our modern rationale, that's true,' said Lantier, 'but who knows what inspired those people? The Americans went to the moon primarily to prove to the world that capitalism works better than communism, after all. Anyway, we may soon find out the answer. I believe the Chinese landed robots at Cydonia with the intention of returning samples to Earth.'

President Orlando abruptly appeared in their midst. Emerging from behind a stack of pallets, he admired the achievements of the team.

'This is good. You have made excellent progress this week. Ruby, how are you? It is always a pleasure.'

'I'm sure it is, Orlando, otherwise you wouldn't do it.'

Some of the others gasped audibly, while Brad went on working, not having a clue about the identity of this immaculately dressed man.

'You will no doubt be aware that Project D constitutes the most complete example of its kind that has ever been found,' announced Orlando, 'and the preserved condition of everything is first class. We will have a thorough understanding of this technology and an ability to replicate it very shortly. Soldiers will arrive here later to pack the materials for air freight to France. Most of you will leave for France by private jet.'

'Why is everything going to France?' asked Ruby.

The French scientists stared incredulously at her, but she continued to look at Orlando.

'It has been expensive to run a rebel army large enough to take over the State. The French were most co-operative in supporting my plans, and in return I am sharing some knowledge with them. They have research facilities and experts that I do not have in my country. But right now I need a volunteer.'

In one smooth movement he turned and pointed at Brad. Suddenly the cosy little scene became a frenzy of activity. As if from nowhere, two soldiers hared out of the shadows and Brad was dragged brusquely out of the hangar. His protests – in which being a citizen of the United States figured largely – were ignored.

Paulo ran to Brad's side. 'Do not worry,' he said

unconvincingly. 'You are merely being sequestered to the next research project under the terms of the permit I negotiated for you.'

'But they hurt me!' complained Brad.

'It is simply, er, the Guatemalan way.'

'Well this is the American way!' Brad lashed out at Paulo, causing him to duck. The Wi-Fi dongle fell from his pocket onto the ground.

Orlando led the scientists out towards waiting cars without giving them the opportunity to say goodbye to Ruby. When Brad had gone, Paulo left too. It was a sudden and unceremonious end to some incredible archaeology.

The plaintive cries of Brad still echoed in her mind as she sat once again at the computer, her senses numbed by the swiftness of his transition from contented assistant to terrified prisoner. After long evenings spent catching up with the backlog, she had virtually finished the scientific journal. Ruby had managed to type more than fifty thousand words into the computer, describing scientific disciplines and ancient technologies that she barely comprehended. It was a great sense of achievement, but next to Brad's uncertain fate and her fears for her own future this revolutionary document meant nothing. She was like a plover bird plucking meat from the jaws of a crocodile. This deadly symbiotic relationship with the President had given her at once the best and the worst days of her life. The endorphin rush of skirting so closely to danger had previously balanced out her cold understanding of the risks. She had been split down the middle – confused and focused, uneasy yet confident. No longer was this the case, however. It was now clear to her where she should attempt to be, and it wasn't here.

She spotted the dongle, still lying on the ground. She snapped it into the laptop and logged into her e-mail account. The mass of unread messages was getting ungainly, and it slowed down her search for the people who actually mattered to her. She just wanted a sign that Matt was still alive. That would at least calm one small part of the vortex within her.

It was almost drowning among the spam, but eventually she found it: the most recent missive from Matt, a semi-incoherent message pre-dating his flight from New York.

'IM ON MY WAY. LOVE U HUN'.

Despite their appallingly loose relationship to the English language, his words warmed her. She wouldn't have expected any better from a military man, even one who professed to be a writer. Ruby typed her reply.

'They took Brad, and it didn't look good. Matt – I'm scared.' She dithered about telling him she was scared, but opted to be open about her feelings for once. She then wavered about adding an 'X', typing it, then deleting it, then typing it again. Signing off with a kiss risked being over-interpreted, but she felt it would be impertinent to omit such a small sign of affection given how she had treated him. There was no guarantee he was ever going to receive the e-mail – it felt as reliable as throwing a message in a bottle out to sea, but it was all she could do.

She pressed 'send' and waited for confirmation that it had been processed. Nothing happened. The connection was sometimes intermittent. Patience would fix it.

Her time alone in the hangar would shortly be up. She wandered aimlessly around it, glancing repeatedly back at the computer to check for a sign that it had completed her instruction. As she walked close to the main entrance, two dust-encrusted Mercedes pulled up outside. Orlando emerged from one of them.

'Ruby?' he called, marching straight into the hangar.

Shit. The computer was still showing her e-mail

account page. She quickly grunted hello to him and inched towards the computer, intent on switching it off before he could ask any questions. He stuck an arm out and stopped her.

'Your work here is done.'

'I just need to power down the computer,' she protested.

'And I need to get you to the hotel where you will prepare for your next project.'

'Another artefact like this one?' she asked, trying unsuccessfully to wriggle past him.

'There are many artefacts, but none like this one. No, your next role is entirely different. Things are moving fast. I am moving thousands of men into Tikal. Work has already begun. As for you, I need you at the hotel. I need your voice. Your face. Your body.'

The comment chilled her.

'You must be joking,' she grumbled in disgust.

'Just have faith in me, Ruby. How many times do I need to tell you?'

He nodded to his car. Two soldiers jumped out and forcefully ushered Ruby into the other vehicle. They shut the doors and drove her away. To Ruby it felt like a repeat of Brad's frightening abduction – no explanation, no time to prepare, no idea how she would be treated.

Orlando walked further into the hangar and sat down at the computer.

TUESDAY 27TH NOVEMBER 2012

Otto woke up at the sound of breaking glass. Humid air washed over him and he could hear the singing of the crickets. He jumped out of bed and cut his foot on one of the shards that had sprayed across the bedroom floor. Had someone deliberately broken his window? He would check later, because right now he needed to hop to the bathroom to take care of the bleeding.

Noises started. Creaking timbers and cracking bricks. Windows frames were twisting. More panes shattered. Walls were straining. Sickening vibrations shuddered across the floor, threatening to topple him as he cleaned his wound. Now fully awake and alert, he knew he didn't have much time. The sinkhole was widening. The foundations of his villa were moving. His underground research centre could be crumbling. His life's work was under immediate threat.

He strapped his foot and threw some clothes on. He needed to begin the evacuation.

The hotel was, in many ways, typical of the resorts to be found in the Petén region: cream ceramic tiles on the floor, bedside lamps mounted on novelty twirling tree branches, ceiling fans unhurriedly chopping the quiet air, balconies with views over a crocodile-infested lagoon.

'Evian?'

Orlando opened the door of the fridge and selected a small bottle of mineral water. His guest was surprised to see that the fridge stocked only mineral water and what looked like vials of medicine.

'Glass?'

'Bottle's fine.'

He handed it to her and invited her to sit in the armchair. She sank deep into its embrace, almost permitting herself to relax.

'So, Ruby, tell me about your anxieties. Your misgivings. Your fears. Your failure to trust me.'

'Why am I still here?'

'Why do you think I still want you here?' he parried, sitting on the edge of his bed.

'I'm not really sure that you do. I think you might be toying with me, and then you'll throw me away.'

'Why would I do that?'

'Because you're the President of a putrid tin-pot dictatorship and you can do whatever you bloody well want.' Although she could feel the angry heat rising in her voice, she spoke with a hedging smile. 'Why don't you just let me go home?'

He glanced briefly at her, but merely murmured, 'I do so love it when you flatter me in your own special way, Ruby. You know I can't let you go home. I have great plans for you.'

'But I've done what you asked me. I'm scared I'll be summarily despatched to a cockroach-infested prison like poor Brad.'

'The volunteer from the hangar? He's not in prison.'

'Thank God for that. What have you done with him?'

'He is merely assisting Doctor Otto in another research programme.'

'What about the stolen Sphinx scrolls? Is that one of your research programmes?'

'Doctor Otto has a particular interest in those too. He has made a thorough study of their message.'

Ruby's expression lit up. 'Really? He's translated them? What did they say? What were they written on? What condition were they in? Have they been carbon dated? Where are they now?'

Orlando chuckled at her over-excited rapid-fire questions. 'They are now in the heart of Tikal, where they belong. And they confirmed what we already knew,' he told her, 'with a few extra details, perhaps, but the message is the same.'

'And are you going to tell me?'

'It's about something the ancients triggered.'

'What does that mean, Orlando?'

'I can't tell you everything now, but you will soon find out. The world will soon know. Twelve millennia ago, there was an advanced civilisation like our own.'

'I know that!' she fumed impatiently. 'What do you think I've been doing for the past week?'

'If that is to be your attitude, then I will ask you to leave.'

'You mean I can go home?'

'No, I mean to go back to your room. If I allow you to go home, you will soon find you have no home to go to. Too much is at stake, Ruby.'

'All right,' she sighed. 'I'm asking you calmly and politely, what has the ancient civilisation done that I don't already know?'

'Ruby, they have done something terrible.'

'All civilisations do terrible things. They always end up fighting, causing their own downfall. My whole life has been spent studying traces of the mess they left behind.'

'This is different,' said Orlando. 'They caused their own downfall, true, but they also set something in motion that could destroy the modern world. Ruby – this ancient civilisation might eradicate their descendants.'

'Us?'

'Everyone, Ruby. The entire planet. The day is almost upon us. Those Christians were so nearly right with their idea of the Second Coming. The Mayans knew it a thousand years ago. They devoted their lives to a meticulous counting of the days and the years. They worked out elaborate celestial clocks and calendars to count down the time to when it would happen.'

'I know about all that, Orlando. They believed the world was reborn every twelve thousand years or so. The last time they experienced a great upheaval was the flood at the end of the Ice Age. According to their calendar, the world was due to be reborn on the twenty-first of December this year. But that doesn't mean the end of the world. No sane historian thinks that.'

'And it won't be the end of the world, if you stay by my side.'

'What for?'

'I need a face. Someone to symbolise my country and its new discoveries. Someone who is respected. A monkey could have written the report in Tikal, but it had to be you so that you would have first-hand knowledge of all aspects of the project. Your background as a respected scientist, not to mention your good looks, makes you the perfect person for the job as front woman for my plans. You will do television interviews, present documentaries, give speeches and meet with presidents and kings.' Then, more seductively, he added, 'And you will be with me, helping to guide the planet into its new phase. It's probably the best job in the world.'

As he spoke, Ruby was taking a long slurp of her water, but the last comments made her spit it back into the bottle. Snorting slightly, she regained her composure before replying.

'Why should I help you when you treat me like a slave?'

'Slave? You were at the heart of the research. I even put you in charge of part of it.'

'In charge? They treated me like a bloody typist.'

Orlando laughed, but beneath his veneer of geniality he was sombre. 'You will never get a chance like this again, Ruby. The truth is, I need you. Things are going to change quickly. History is already changing under me. The technology of the ancients is being reinvented. Tikal is being transformed in preparation. Stick around, Ruby. When we're done with rewriting history, we're going to *make* history.'

WEDNESDAY 28TH NOVEMBER 2012

The ex-police van, hurriedly purchased the previous day, now contained almost everything needed to salvage Otto's life's work from the yawning sinkhole, and the boxes were stacked with all the requisite precision and neatness that were essential to his sanity. The only item remaining was a living person – someone who needed to be moved from the underground home he had inhabited since birth to the safety of the armoured van. This kind of transition could not be undertaken lightly. There were huge psychological implications in exposing his patient to so many new experiences at once – new rooms and corridors, daylight, sky, other humans, vehicles. Explaining him away as a mental patient was one option, but his physical appearance would force further nosey inquisition. Ideally it would be done at night, but Otto was concerned that the sinkhole would not wait for him.

It didn't. Amid screams from the members of the public closest to the hole to the effect that more of the sides were falling in, and while what remained of the villa was seen to shake before settling at an angle that was achingly displeasing to the eye, one very loud voice yelled out that someone was down there.

The figure crawling over the rubble and detritus at the bottom of the sinkhole was difficult to discern from street level. After the initial shock and excitement there were calls for hush. There was no bright searchlight immediately available for the police officers at the scene, but someone had the brainwave of reflecting sunlight to the shadowy recesses of the hole using a domestic mirror. A suitable looking-glass was located and the sun's intense rays were directed to the bottom of the pit.

Everyone could now see that the figure was male. He was entirely naked, and his skin was so pale it looked almost translucent. Close to him was the strange brick wall that had been spotted when the sinkhole first appeared, many levels lower than a human structure would normally be found. The wall had partially collapsed, creating a hole through which the man had apparently crawled.

Attempts to engage in a dialogue with the individual were not successful, however, and the priority became to find a way to lower a rescue worker into the pit. As a police officer radioed a request for mountaineering equipment, Otto let himself into the ruined villa. The condemned building now sloped in the direction of the sinkhole, creating a feeling of drunkenness in Otto as he entered the dining room. Here, the former grandeur of the house was still evident, but its strange angles and partial destruction made it resemble the interior of the *Titanic* as she started to slip beneath the waves.

Otto desperately wanted to straighten every uneven floor and lintel, but somehow the impossibility of that desire freed him from the lunacy of attempting to pursue it. He ripped a curtain down and took it with him into the cellar. As he made the journey downstairs one final time he saw fresh cracks in the concrete, some of which seemed to be growing before his eyes.

When he reached the lowest level of his laboratory, the air was different. Gone was the stale mechanically processed air to which he had grown accustomed. Now the air tasted sweet and cool. And it moved. He followed the breeze until he came to a chamber that had split open at one end, creating a magnificent view of the bottom of the sinkhole. And there was his patient ... lost. Bewildered. Hurting.

Otto sat quietly by the gaping brickwork and waited for the rescue attempt to begin.

There was a trickle of soil part way up the vertical wall. The gentle movement triggered an avalanche of collapsing earth all the way to the top, growing louder and widening the mouth of the hole. Otto shielded his face from the choking dust with the curtain, occasionally checking through the haze to see if the rescue was underway. Finally, a rope flopped to the ground and he saw the silhouette of a brave soul starting to climb down.

Otto climbed through the brickwork, carefully keeping the curtain over him so that his presence would not be obvious to those at street level. He moved unsteadily over the loose earth to get to his patient and wrapped the curtain around the naked man, guiding him back through to the laboratory. With the thick dust in the air and with the focus on the abseiling rescue worker, no one saw that the mysterious, pale man had vanished. In fact, they soon could see nothing at all, as a further landslide sucked down a portion of the road and forced everyone to move back from the edge. Otto's villa moved again. The police decided to abandon the rescue and pull their man back up. They tugged at the rope and it came up easily – too easily. Frayed strands of rope soon emerged from the dust with no one attached to the other end.

Concentric cracks began to open up around the hole, each forming a ring that stepped lower towards the centre. A circle of buildings shifted, their roofs splitting loudly in half, their windows shattering. The crowd around the sinkhole began to disperse in panic. The mouth of the hole appeared to yawn, engulfing those who were too slow or too fascinated to move. The roof of Otto's villa curled and the higher levels of its cellar system were fully exposed, hanging in space, seemingly unsupported. Another concentric ring appeared, carving its way instantly and violently through the centre of the house and beyond. The cellar walls could take no more. They disintegrated and fell into the void, followed by the entire property above, as if vacuumed down into the ground, but no one remained close enough to witness it. No one other than two men, wrapped in a dusty fabric, who staggered out of the villa seconds before its demise.

Thursday 29th November 2012

'Go in there, get changed, then meet me in the lobby.'

Before Ruby could question him or protest, Orlando was gone. Having nothing better to do, she walked into the room and opened the wardrobe. Designer outfits – Emporio Armani, Prada and Gucci – hung neatly from the rail. Exquisite bags sat in a line on the end of the bed. There were high-heeled shoes, a little gaudy for her taste, but obviously expensive. She turned to the make-up, all set out neatly in a professional make-up artist's toolbox. An impressive collection. She quickly picked a Gucci dress and matching shoes and bag, applied a light dusting of the latest mineral-based foundation, some neutral lip-gloss and some mascara. It was blissful. Just as she was about to leave the room, she thought, what the hell, and swept a line of black liner across the top of her lashes. Now she looked subtly, but suitably, awesome. If the world was going to end, as the paranoid President seemed to believe, she was going out in style.

Arriving at the hotel lobby, Ruby looked like she had just stepped off a catwalk. Dozens of male heads turned her way, medals swinging, leather holsters creaking. The hotel had been taken over by the military hierarchy, and any sense that this was once a vacation resort had been subsumed by campaign maps, crates of ammunition and the stench of overdressed and under-washed men.

Orlando came striding along the corridor.

'They were having trouble setting up the autocue,

Ruby, but I think we have it sorted now. You look great. Follow me.'

'What? What autocue? Hey, I'm talking to you. Have you dressed me up to film something?'

He took her by the hand and half-dragged her to a bedroom. Thoughts of a grubby régime financed by presidential pornography rushed through her head. She clamped her hands around the door frame as Orlando inelegantly pushed her into the room, and she only relented when she noticed amid their tussling that the improvised studio set contained no bed. Instead there was a bright green cloth covering one of the walls, two television cameras, some other technical gear on a table and a sprinkling of bright lights. A crew of five was busily adjusting equipment settings.

'Why wasn't I told about this?' demanded Ruby, rising to the challenge of her new diva's look.

'What you have to do now is perfectly simple. You need to stand on the small cross marked with tape, just in front of the green screen. This is the autocue, and all you do is read out the words that appear in front of you.'

'I've never done autocue before. How fast does it go?'

The director, who today doubled up as the autocue operator, stepped into the conversation.

'I will go as fast as you speak. It's Ruby, isn't it?'

She shook the hand of the portly man who was dressed in black from head to toe, with a small goatee beard. Very beatnik, thought Ruby.

'My name's Jean-Pierre. I'm the director of this film.'

'This film!' echoed Ruby. 'What film? I don't know anything about this. Who are we making this film for?'

'Initially, Ruby,' said Jean-Pierre, 'we are making this to be broadcast at the IAC.'

'The International Archaeology Conference?'

'Your film will be shown to the assembled experts,'

Orlando explained, 'and to a selection of the world's media. After that, of course, it will be shown on every news channel around the globe. Your presentation of the show will give it the credibility we need in order to be taken seriously. This is no easy matter for the world's scientists to digest, and many of them will claim we are attempting a hoax. Our discoveries will hurt their pride. The tone of this broadcast will help to persuade them that we are not fooling with anyone.'

'I'm not sure about this,' she said.

'You cannot deny the appeal of fronting such a broadcast, Ruby?' asked Orlando.

'It's repugnant. I'm being forced to become the face of a dictatorship.'

'And yet?' he nudged, widening the obvious gap in her divided feelings.

'And yet, you give me no choice.' She almost sounded pleased.

A woman abruptly appeared in front of Ruby and wordlessly dabbed some powder onto her nose and forehead, then led her over to the small cross on the floor. Ruby looked into the autocue camera and saw the words: 'Hello. I'm Ruby Towers. I'm here to talk about a recent discovery in …' That was all she could see on the screen, but it didn't look too difficult. She cleared her throat and prepared to give it a go.

Jean-Pierre told everyone present to shut up and cued Ruby for a practice run. She ground to a halt almost immediately, shading her eyes against the glare and trying to see beyond the autocue.

'Hello. I'm, er, sorry. Can we start again? The words started moving and kind of took me by surprise.'

'No problem,' called Jean-Pierre from the laptop that controlled the script. 'From the top, Ruby. At your own pace.'

'Hello. I'm Ruby Towers. I'm here to talk about a recent discovery in Central America that adds a new and exciting chapter to our previously unknown ancient history. It's not a discovery that many of you will immediately accept. It's shocking, it's unexpected, and it will force an unprecedented reinterpretation of our sense of identity and history. Before I show you what we have found, I just want to remind you of some obvious facts.

'*Homo sapiens* reached its current evolutionary state at some point between thirty and sixty thousand years ago. Perhaps earlier. We don't know exactly when, but you can safely assume that a person born twenty-five thousand years ago had exactly the same brain capability as you or I. That's the first fact. The second is that ... oh God, sorry, it's going too fast. I can't keep up.'

'No, it's you, Ruby,' said Jean-Pierre. 'If you want to slow down, just do it. I will always follow your pace. Try to relax and it will be fine. Pick up from where you were.'

'The second is that in our known history it took us only a few thousand years to develop from cavemen to spacemen. The final part of that process, from simple society to today's computer age, took no more than two hundred and fifty years. Because we have no record of any previous advancement before our own, we naturally assume the recent generations were the first to soar to these great heights, but there is no reason why it could not have happened before, at any time in the past thirty thousand years. Now, remember that period included the end of an Ice Age, a phenomenon catastrophic enough to globally raise sea levels – excuse me, sorry to stop again, but I can't say that.'

'Which bit?' asked Jean-Pierre.

'Enough to globally raise sea levels. It's not correct.'

'You don't believe in the science?'

'No, I don't believe in using split infinitives. It's not

an elegant way to speak. "To globally raise" sounds like I'm uneducated. Can you put "globally" either before or after the verb, not hammered into the middle, please?'

Jean-Pierre took a deep, frustrated breath as he re-keyed the text. Seconds later he cued Ruby again.

'Now, remember that period included the end of an Ice Age, a phenomenon catastrophic enough globally to raise sea levels, reshaping coastlines everywhere. If there were advanced societies at that time, this factor could, if combined with other disasters or war, have reduced them to the primitives we always thought they were. Untamed nature over a period of thousands of years is a powerful force that obliterates signs of human achievement. So, if there had been a great civilisation on this planet before the ice melted, there is every possibility that we would find no trace of it today. Except, we have found trace of it. Astounding traces in various secret locations. Ruby points to ... oh, sorry, I wasn't meant to read that bit, was I?'

'You're doing a good job, Ruby,' said Orlando. 'You make me proud of my choice of front person.'

'Yes,' added Jean-Pierre, 'you're doing fine. At this point in the script I would like you to point at the green screen to your right. Our editor will superimpose the image of the aircraft artefact there, but please don't take your eye off the autocue, otherwise you will get lost and we will have to start again.'

Ruby practised pointing at the screen without actually looking at it, then returned to the script.

'This artefact is twelve thousand years old. It was built shortly before the end of the Ice Age, and it contains technologies significantly in advance of our own. I know you will all be saying "that's impossible" and looking for some indication that it is a fake, but I do assure you it's genuine. I was privileged to witness its discovery and to manage the team responsible for dismantling and cataloguing every part of it. We have full documentary evidence of our work, in video, photographic and written form. Two human bodies inside the craft were carbon dated to twelve thousand years ago. In itself, the discovery is the most important addition to our historical understanding since Darwin's theory of evolution. You may find what I am saying as hard to accept as the religious establishment in Darwin's time found his theories abhorrent and blasphemous, but Darwin's ideas nevertheless became the bedrock of accepted knowledge.'

'Just a small point, Ruby,' interrupted Jean-Pierre, 'you're drifting away from the cross. I need you to remain absolutely still so that we have enough room to put the aircraft in the shot throughout this. We're going to add in some graphics and some close-ups of you with the second camera, but essentially the style is very straightforward, like you are giving a lecture. I want those feet anchored to the cross on the floor.'

'Sorry, I forgot. There's so much to think about, and all these people. It's quite stressful out here.'

'You have made television programmes before, have you not?' asked Jean-Pierre.

'Yes, many times, but only on archaeological digs, where I just have to talk about what I'm doing off the top of my head. It's much more laid back, more like chatting to a friend behind the camera.'

On the last series she'd filmed, that friend had been Matt, standing just behind the cameraman, throwing cue questions at her, then making faces while she answered. Matt's constant unprofessionalism had annoyed her at the time, but in retrospect it had been kind of fun.

When everything had been performed to Jean-Pierre's satisfaction, Ruby sat in the corner of the studio and started to take in the significance of the scripted words she had just read out. All the disparate pieces of information began to fit together. She remembered now the moment she'd first seen the aircraft in the pit, and the stratum in the soil above it that looked like molten glass, and how it had reminded her of a similar layer she had once seen in India. Could it have been the result of a nearby explosion of nuclear intensity that had fused the topsoil into this hard crystalline layer? If the ancients could power their craft with a cold fusion system, they certainly had the potential for atomic weapons. And every society in history had the potential for war.

There could have been a devastating war in antiquity, she realised. It could either have coincided with the end of the Ice Age, or it might even have been a contributory factor. No advanced civilisation could survive two catastrophes like that. If all of this had taken place over twelve millennia ago, then it was no wonder that the evidence was so hard to find. The world and human society had taken a long time to heal. Five hundred generations. The renaissance was too slow. The memory of the pain and folly was lost. The world had been rebuilt and was now capable of repeating its mistake.

Was this circle of history the great threat that the ancients posed to the modern world? Or was an ancient war somehow directly responsible for a looming cataclysm? She felt sure the scrolls stolen from the Sphinx would explain all, but there was no way she could track them down while she remained under constant guard.

FRIDAY 30TH NOVEMBER 2012

The chain attached to the van's front fender strained slightly, jolting Otto from his light slumber with a sharp clink. He needed to give it some slack by driving forward a couple of feet. When the tension was released he saw the chain slither and straighten through the grass, like a long silver snake plunging its head into a hole. A shovel arced into the air, throwing up another clump of soil which landed haphazardly on an adjacent heap. Otto exited the cab and approached the edge of the hole. His feet were level with the eyes of the labourer – the man whom he had rescued from the sinkhole. Five hours of strenuous digging had created a pit five feet deep and three feet wide. Soil strata were visible down the sides. Tree roots that once passed through this space had been severed.

The stelae, according to the interpretation given by the diary that Lord Ballashiels had given him, pointed to this spot precisely. The quest begun by his Victorian ancestor could be almost at an end.

The Patient was coping well with the new form of exercise. His muscles were already well toned, as close to perfection as Otto had been able to obtain with the subterranean programme of diet and exercise that had been practised, with Teutonic regularity, for so many years. The only medical complication today appeared to be caused by the chain around his neck, which was chafing the skin despite its lining of cotton. Using his precious possession for this kind of activity disquieted Otto. What else could he do, though? The strong body at his disposal was the only resource upon which he could call.

Inwardly he cursed that the structures of law and ethics in every country on the planet should conspire against his research, forcing him to lead a life of self-reliance. He trusted no one. The Patient did not officially exist, and therefore counted as no one. The Patient did not even have a name. He was simply a living embodiment of an experiment that was slowly maturing.

The degrading shackles were of no consequence to the Patient. He had an expression on his face which Otto hadn't seen him wear since he was a child – he seemed contented. The mouth wasn't giving too much away, but there was something of a glimmer in his eyes. Spending time in the open air, in natural light, in contact with nature, seemed to make him blossom.

It was time for a break, time for his patient to take on some hydration and for Otto to examine the hole. The Patient needed help climbing out, but Otto was not forthcoming in that respect. He stood by, looking down while the man in the hole slipped in his attempt to scramble out. Otto grew impatient, but he would provide no physical assistance. Finally, the Patient crawled out, leaving Otto a clear view.

The depth of the excavation should easily have reached through sufficient millennia to have exposed whatever it was down there that marked the spot. The alluvial layers were plain to see and Otto was in no doubt that he should have found something significant by now. There was, however, nothing at the bottom but a reddish mud. There was no way of knowing precisely what he was going to find, but he was certain that the stelae did not exist simply to point the way to damp soil. A subterranean cavity must be down there somewhere, possibly capped with stone for security and durability – that was the most likely scenario.

With the evening sun starting to dissolve into the rainforest that capped the hills behind him, the Patient's silhouette was starkly outlined to Otto. He had never viewed the Patient from such a perspective before, and was struck by the pure humanity of the shape. To control the entire existence and health of so excellent a creature made him proud of both his own work and that of the man from whom he had inherited it.

Otto handed the Patient the shovel and instructed him to jump down and push it deep into the mud to see if it met with any resistance in the next few inches. But the Patient did not move.

'He who is unable to live in society, or who has no need of it because he is complete in himself, must be either a beast or a god.' It was only a whisper, but Otto recoiled as if he had been shouted at.

'I know that,' Otto replied, 'but how did *you* know that?'

'Which am I?' asked the Patient. 'The beast or the god?'

'It is not that simple. I ask again: how did you know those words?'

'All men by nature desire knowledge,' whispered the Patient, quoting from the same source.

'You desire it, but where did you find it? I did not teach you this philosophy.'

'You gave me fish. I taught myself to make a rod. Then I caught my own fish.'

The sun must have emboldened him, thought Otto. Back in the underground laboratory he had never dared to speak without permission. Where was his sense of respect? What had happened to his meek manner, his pet-like, unquestioning deference? This was not the creature on whom Otto, for so many years, had freely experimented; this was something more. The Patient had grown in spirit. He was no longer the passive half of a single soul dwelling in two bodies. It was as if he were greater than the sum of his component parts, more than just a living set of legs, arms, head, body and organs. It was as if he were a *man*.

At some deep level, Otto knew this was a man – fully functioning, emotional, abused and deprived. He knew it in the same way that a diner tucking into a juicy steak knows – but tries to forget – that the meat was once part of a conscious animal that could experience pleasure and pain.

Otto returned to the truck. From his black leather bag, he pulled out Bilbo's notebook and his own notes. Had he missed something? He started from scratch, re-checking the photographs of the stelae, the interpretation of their inscriptions, and the legends and records of the local Mayans in antiquity. The price of failure was high, and with every passing hour he feared his rival, Lord Ballashiels, might use the knowledge that he surely possessed to attempt to be the first to locate the prize.

The last of the tutors departed, post-dated cheque in hand. Ratty had completed all of his intensive tuition courses. He felt fitter, stronger, wiser and, most peculiarly, sexier. His student date with Ruby at Chichester Cathedral, he now knew from his flirtation studies, would have developed into something interesting if he had grunted disdainfully rather than enthusiastically reading a poem and attempting spooning techniques that had gone out of fashion with togas. More importantly, he was nearly ready to return to Guatemala, where he would solve the mystery of the stelae and claim the treasure that awaited him.

He waved the tutor off and walked back inside,

ignoring the mound of unopened and unfriendly-looking mail that was becoming something of a feature within his portico. The remainder of this afternoon, he decided, would be allocated to the enigmatic poetry that had been bouncing around his head for so long. He made straight for his library and had just reached the top of the mahogany ladder when he heard the doorbell ring. He cursed under his breath in classical Greek. He was a long way from the unforgiving parquet floor, high amid the dusty upper shelves. He gripped the rungs and waited for the uninvited visitor to leave, but the bell rang repeatedly – and it literally was a bell, worthy of any parish church – suggesting that whoever was pulling the rope wished to see him on a matter of some urgency.

Shaking his head in frustration, he climbed down and went to the window. The view afforded him a peek at the entrance portico, where stood a man in a grey suit. Definitely not a welcome sight. Ratty had encountered the type before, and they invariably wanted to extract money from him towards outstanding loans, interest and collection fees. If these people needed their money back so desperately, why did the fools lend it to him in the first place? He closed all of the shutters, lit the chandelier and climbed back up the ladder.

His head almost brushing against the flaking paint of the ceiling, he browsed past a collection of bound student theses from Cambridge, Harvard and one or two lesser universities, feeling a shimmer of contentment that he had read all of them, and continued on to the poetry section. Finally, he found it. A 1964 edition of *The Whitsun Weddings*, containing thirty-two of Philip Larkin's finest poems including *An Arundel Tomb*, from which Ruby had quoted.

It would have been so much easier for Ruby to have explained what she meant, he told himself as he climbed down, but she had refused to discuss the matter when they had met at the President's palace in Guatemala City. It could be weeks before he heard from her again, and as the commotion at his door confirmed, he simply didn't have that much time to complete his quest.

He sat at his leather-topped *bureau à gradin* and opened the book. 'Time has transfigured them into Untruth. The stone fidelity They hardly meant,' he recited without looking at the pages. Then he re-read the entire poem, noting that the line referring to 'little dogs under their feet' was factually incorrect. Larkin implied in his poem that both effigies on the tomb displayed stone dogs beneath their feet, whereas only the woman had a dog in that position. The knight's feet rested on a small lion, lying in a sphinx-like position. Was Ruby referring to this poetic inaccuracy? If so, why? It didn't make sense to him.

'Lord Ballashiels!'

The voice sounded close. Ratty got up and crept towards a tight gap in the shutters. The man was pacing impatiently outside his window.

'I know you're in there, Lord Ballashiels. I've come to collect outstanding monies you owe. This is your last warning. I have a warrant to enter the property by force and seize your possessions if you don't open the door.'

Phew, thought Ratty. That was a relief. For a moment he'd thought the man had come about one of the mortgages secured against his house. This was just one of the smaller unsecured loans.

Returning to the poem, he considered the theme of the passing of time distorting the original intention of the sculptor of the effigies. If the maker of that tomb in Chichester did not intend to display the sentimentality that it now showed, perhaps the glyphs on the Mayan stelae could no longer be interpreted as they were intended by their creators. The passage of time hadn't changed the glyphs, but it had changed thought processes. So the way those glyphs were understood could be fundamentally wrong.

That was all very well, decided Ratty, but it didn't explain why Ruby's words had affected him at such a deep subconscious level. He had risked his neck to get away from Otto without losing the stelae, and a comment about the detail of the connotation of the carvings wouldn't have meant enough to him to warrant such action.

A sharp rapping noise came from the window. Ratty jumped. He could see an ugly nose pressing against the glass through the slit between the shutters.

'I can see you in there, Lord Ballashiels.'

There was no avoiding him now. Ratty opened the shutter and lifted the stiff sash window a couple of inches, revealing a bulbous, stubbly face with small eyes and cauliflower ears.

'How much do I owe you?' Ratty asked, determined to get straight to the point. He had better things to be doing than dealing with the vulgarities of usury.

'Just under twenty-five grand,' replied the man with a solemn tone that suggested such a sum was a great deal of money to him. In the context of Ratty's overall negative wealth, this was a paltry amount. Small change. He would settle this with just a few nuggets of gold from the treasure he was confident of finding as soon as he returned to Guatemala. The problem lay in convincing these finance-obsessed people that such a plan would work. So far all of his attempts to persuade the lenders to wait for his Mayan hoard had been met with derision.

He slid the window shut and trudged to the front door.

'Do come in, old fruit. Follow me.' Ratty led the meaty debt collector along the impressive hallways and staircases up to the turret room. 'Make yourself comfortable in there while I look for my cheque book.' Ratty ushered him inside and waited while the man tried to sit on a rickety Hepplewhite chair. Then he left and silently locked the door.

Frustratingly, the bell rang again. He made the long journey back to the entrance, smoothed back his dyed hair and pulled the heavy iron handle. A woman was standing there.

'Is Lord Ballashiels at home?'

Ratty looked at the young woman. She had cropped auburn hair, freshly tanned skin and wore a repulsively unfeminine grey suit with flat black shoes. In her right hand was a plastic leather-effect briefcase and in her left hand she proffered a business card.

'And you might be?' grunted Ratty, using the casual, disinterested tone he had not quite perfected.

'Cindy Evans,' she replied. She pushed the business card into his palm. Ratty studied her curves – despite her grim clothing, he was not displeased by her appearance. 'Is your master at home?'

He looked at the card. She was a banker. A 'personal relationship manager' from the unfortunate institution to which he owed the bulk of his debts. This was the big one. He had been expecting this.

'My master?' he enquired, leaning moodily against the door frame. 'I have no master. There is no one to whom I am answerable. I am Lord Ballashiels, but you can call me Justin.' He enjoyed the startled look which this revelation triggered.

'Lord Ballashiels, the bank has written to you many times demanding a meeting to discuss your situation and you've ignored every request. Not only have you missed a number of payments with us, you also appear to have taken out a substantial mortgage with another company, which you somehow managed to get secured against this property even though the deeds are held as security by my bank. What you have done has crossed the line into fraud.'

'Ah, yes, those loans. Glad you mentioned them, actually. Hoping to pay them off soon, as it happens. Got a little project in the pipeline. Bit of archaeology. Guatemala. Kind of a treasure hunt, in fact. Should be enough to –'

'As you have ignored all communications,' Cindy interrupted, 'my bank has already applied to the County Court to repossess. The order has been granted. Bailiffs and the police are on their way. I'm sorry, Lord Ballashiels, but you could also be looking at a custodial sentence for obtaining money by deception.'

Ratty sighed. All this interfering from financial institutions was a most unwelcome intrusion in his life. New Ratty would shortly become Homeless Ratty and possibly Jailbird Ratty.

A black car drew up behind Cindy and another unsympathetic-looking bank manager type stepped out.

'Lord Ballashiels?' called the man. Another grey suit, thought Ratty, wondering if his profligate expenditure of these bankers' money had rendered them unable to afford any colour in their lives.

'Yes, yes, you've come about the money,' replied Ratty, without even bothering to ask the man's name.

'I have to warn you, Lord Ballashiels,' said the man, 'that my bank has supplied the Crown Prosecution Service with the evidence they need to issue a warrant for your arrest on suspicion of fraud. Unless you can repay all outstanding sums immediately then you will shortly be taken away for questioning.'

'Do come in, both of you. I'm sure we can discuss this over a cup of tea.'

Cindy and the banker followed him into the hallway, marvelling at the faded and broken grandeur of the manor.

'Walk this way,' Ratty said. 'Not far now. Just up these stairs.' He led them up the stone steps to the turret room and unlocked the door. The first debt collector had not found any item of furniture that could take his weight safely and was leaning patiently against a wall. 'Do go on in.'

Cindy and the other banker stepped inside the cluttered and musty turret room, their eyes too busy scanning the jumbled array of antiques to notice immediately that Ratty had closed the door and was locking it from without.

'Wait there, old bean counters!' shouted Ratty from the staircase. 'I'll just bash off and find some pennies for you!'

Now he had truly crossed the line. He shivered with excitement. It felt great. He was high on the thrill of criminality. The house was already lost. His liberty was already threatened. There was nothing left to lose.

He ran to his bedroom and threw some clothes into a battered leather portmanteau. Through the uneven panes of a leaded window he spied Constable Stuart, the village police officer, cycling along the driveway towards the manor. He sprinted down to the library and picked up his passport. The bell tolled, echoing along the gloomy corridors. He grabbed the cases of archaeological scanning equipment and flew out of the back door to the disused stable block where his elderly Land Rover sat waiting, untaxed and un-roadworthy, but – crucially – out of sight of Constable Stuart at the front door, who had yet to get over the novel delights of campanology.

The engine started, reliable as always. Nothing else on the vehicle functioned, but that was of no concern as Ratty bumped across the fields to the rear of the manor. As the constable vainly applied brute force to a mediaeval door that had proven strong enough to foil Cromwell's cronies, Ratty tossed the turret key out of the window, joined a remote country lane and headed for Heathrow Airport.

SATURDAY 1ST DECEMBER 2012

The mound of earth outside was damp with morning dew, which gave it the appearance of freshly-dug soil, as if someone had continued burrowing all through the night. But the hole had not been touched since the previous day.

The Patient yawned and rubbed skin that was sore from the cold steel of Otto's needles.

'I feel,' said the Patient, 'that you perform these tests on my person out of nature, compulsion and habit. I sense that reason, passion and desire no longer play a part.'

Once again, Otto recognised more than a hint of Aristotle in the Patient's comments. Yesterday the Patient had refused to elaborate on the remarks he'd made regarding his self-teaching of philosophy. There had been no books available to him in the underground laboratory; decades ago, Otto's father had taught the Patient the basics of reading, but had given him nothing to read. He intended to maintain in the Patient a mind that was a blank canvas, a raw material. Otto had no cause to change this. For the Patient suddenly to have acquired sufficient knowledge to quote from philosophical works was astonishing.

'The type and state of my motivation are not your business,' Otto said. 'And I ask again, by what means have you acquired knowledge that did not come from me?'

'All my knowledge came from you. I learned that you placed a small piece of metal in the door and twisted it to enter my home. I saw that object many times. Its contours remain in my memory. I reasoned that a similar object would gain me entry to *your* home. It was my first project. I built a key. I released myself.'

'When did you do this?'

'It serves me no purpose to measure time. One night I climbed some steps and then retreated. Another night I climbed to a new level, and then retreated again. You displayed no sign that you knew of this, so I climbed more levels. After many nights I found your library. It became my nocturnal domain. I learned to read the books. It was hard at first, but it became magical. The roots of education are bitter, but the fruit is sweet. The books told me of a world I had not seen. They told me stories, they taught me languages and medicine and history. I learned of war, love, hatred, prejudice.'

'And philosophy?'

'I have read every book in your collection. Several times.'

'Why did you not leave?' asked Otto.

'You told me I was special, that I needed to be protected from a cruel and dangerous world. I simply wanted to learn about this world. I knew you would take me to see it, some day. And you did.'

The colour slowly drained from Otto's face. He was deflating. He felt foolish, outwitted by a creature he had assumed to be a meek ignoramus. A desire to apologise for the years of abuse began to swell within him, occupying the space left behind by his retreating self-confidence. He fought the feeling. The Patient owed him everything, he told himself. He had taken good care of The Patient; he had been responsible for his food, his health, even his life.

A strained silence ensued until the Patient said, 'You will not find what you are looking for here.'

This was taking things too far. Otto regained some redness in his cheeks as he angrily retorted, 'You will speak when spoken to. I have heard enough from you.'

'No, you have not,' replied the Patient in a calm monotone. 'I say again: you will not find that which you seek under this soil.'

'How can you know what I seek? And how can you know that it's not here?'

'You seek the truth demanded by your destiny. And it is not to be found in the hole that I have dug for you.'

'You do not know what you're talking about.'

The Patient coolly breathed in and waited a few seconds before replying, 'I know more than you can possibly comprehend. And I will lead you to the site that you seek.'

'How?'

'Graphology.'

'What?'

'It is the study of handwriting.'

'I know that,' grunted Otto. 'I have a book on the subject.'

'*Had* a book. And by the condition of its binding I deduced that you had not read that book.'

The Patient picked up Bilbo's diary.

'Have you read that diary?' Otto asked.

'I read everything I see. The diary's handwriting is a classic example of the nineteenth century English script of a male in late middle age, conducive with the distorting effects of excessive alcohol in his body.'

'Bilbo was an irresponsible amateur. He was not suited to serious archaeological investigation. His interference has caused a delay of over a century to what will, no doubt, be a great discovery.'

'And you have read this diary yourself?' asked the Patient.

Otto sighed, always uncomfortable when being quizzed. 'How else could I have found the correct alignment of the stelae to which it refers?'

'It is possible to fail in many ways. To succeed is possible in only one way.'

'I aligned the stelae according to what I read in the diary.'

'You have read it, but you have not *looked* at it.'

'Of course I looked at it.'

'The ink type was common in its day. Both the pigmentation and the cursive style are consistent throughout the diary with the exception of one page.'

He flicked through to the page in question and showed it to Otto.

'It looks the same as all the other pages,' Otto grumbled.

'Now hold the page horizontal to your eye so that light bounces off it.'

Otto did as he was instructed. The majority of the ink on the page was flat and dull – light sank into its dry matt surface – but some words were shiny, and from this angle, dents in the paper beneath them were clearly visible. Although the colour and the shape of all the words were consistent, the writing implements that had made them were not. In a convenient space at the bottom of the page, someone had made an addition to Bilbo's text using a modern steel-nibbed fountain pen rather than a quill.

Otto swiftly re-read the affected page. It was the most important part of the diary: an account of the inscriptions Bilbo had found in a cave that indicated how to align the stelae in order to find the location to which they pointed. Bilbo's roguish intimacy with the natives had gained him a crucial advantage over the aloof Karl: they had opened up to him one evening after sharing a bottle of his finest gin. They had told him of the cave. He had drawn its inscriptions carefully in his diary and then chipped away on the cave wall until no trace of them remained for Karl to stumble across. Bilbo's diary still displayed the hand-drawn copy perfectly clearly along with his contemporary notes about their meaning, but the final note on the page was not contemporaneous. It was simple. It was stupid. It just said that the legend was encoded.

'The alignment of which the cave inscriptions speak is apparently a deliberate falsehood. The true alignment is to be found by turning the male stele clockwise by one more glyph marking than told of in the cave.'

Only an idiot would have made such a moronic alteration, thought Otto. Only an imbecile could expect to get away with it. He resolved never again to trust Lord Ballashiels.

The seat near the toilets at the back of the plane was nowhere near as bad as Ratty had expected. If it hadn't been for the excessive length of his legs, it could almost have been regarded as comfortable. As soon as he was in the air he reached down for his satchel and pulled out his notes and maps, squeezing them onto the fold-down table. He wanted to go through his calculations and measurements of the places he had linked on the map, taking the original clues from the two parts of the stele which pointed to four locations in Guatemala and finding the point at which they intersected. And that point was precisely the location he had visited before, albeit he had only scratched the surface. Yet something made him uneasy about the steps that had led him to that conclusion; he had found the location too easily, and when he had been there previously it had seemed strangely featureless for such an important site.

The stewardess arrived with the drinks trolley and he treated himself to a gin and tonic, then sat back and watched the route to Miami unfold on the small television screen in front of him. When he grew bored of the slow progress on the animated map screen, he flicked channels to find something dull enough to help him sleep. A pre-recorded news report ought to do it. He plugged in his earphones. Trouble in Guatemala dominated. Something to do with the closure of its airports and a military build-up at its borders. He was going to have to be careful driving into the country from Belize. When politicians started commenting on the prickly political situation in Central America his eyes grew heavy.

Sleep came quickly. His head slumped limply to one side as the white noise of the airliner's interior sent him deep into dreamland. Ruby was in his reverie, talking to him, her voice loud and confident, clear and purposeful. It was so real, as though her face was pressed against his ear. A jolt of turbulence forced his eyes wide open again, but Ruby's voice continued in his ears. And there she was on the television. Looking good. Looking great, in fact. He wondered if he might be in love with her.

SUNDAY 2ND DECEMBER 2012

A haze of dust fell to the floor of the van as the stone surfaces ground against each other. The Patient held one half while Otto turned the other. This time the reading of the alignment would not be distorted by the despicable trap Lord Ballashiels had set up in his uniquely shambolic way. The towers and the rubies were aligned, and the glyphs revealed their message: a fresh set of glyphs to be deciphered; the ancient forgotten place names to be cross-referenced with places on a modern map.

The first glyphs were the Mayan symbols for 'Two Springs' and 'Devil'.

'El Diablo at El Zotz,' said the Patient without looking at any documentation. 'It is in the Petén region, close to Tikal National Park.'

'That's incredible,' conceded Otto.

'You will find El Zotz on the map. The ruins were given that name in nineteen seventy-seven due to the presence of thousands of bats.'

Otto sighed. 'You really are a walking Wikipedia, aren't you?'

The Patient raised his eyebrows, uncomfortable at the first reference to a world he had yet to experience. With the exception of a collection of modern works on the subject of organ transplant, most of the books in Otto's library had predated the Internet. Many even predated electricity.

'I believe the next glyph refers to Islapag, which you

will find on post nineteen o-four maps as Topoxté.'

Otto located El Zotz and Topoxté and drew a line on the map, noting that it cleanly bisected the Tikal National Park. The next glyph in the alignment symbolised birth in heaven. The Patient was on to it immediately.

'Siaan K'aan,' he said. 'A Mayan site to the north of Tikal, known since nineteen sixteen as Uaxactún.'

A bony white finger traced it on the map. Otto was astonished by this man's learning. But there was more to come.

'The final glyph we need to identify,' said the Patient, 'is a reference to the settlement of Paxcamán, close to the southern shore of Lake Petén Itzá.'

'Paxcamán?' checked Otto, scanning the map.

'Yes, known for the distinctive red ceramics of the Post-classic era.'

Otto was no longer listening. He was drawing the final line on the map, creating the cross and excitedly noting the grid references of the point of intersection. It was just inside the Tikal National Park, about ten kilometres to the south west of Tikal's city. He held the map up to show the Patient.

'That is the location,' said Otto, standing up and folding away the map along its original creases. 'We have to hurry.'

'You wish to go there?'

'Of course. Come on.'

'I will come,' said the Patient, 'although I tell you now that you will not find that which you seek at that spot.'

'Not this again,' groaned Otto. 'Just come with me and be silent.'

While the global media buzzed with reports of the film she had fronted for Orlando, Ruby remained isolated, witnessing nothing of the profound impact her revelations had made upon academia, Facebook postings, tweets, and even within the real world. She simply stared at the crocodiles from her hotel balcony, wondering if anyone out there was paying the Guatemalan discoveries any serious attention, and willing the afternoon temperature to cool. The shores of Laguna Petenchel would once have been home to ancient Mayans, she knew. Beneath the teeming foliage lay the untouched remnants of this lost world. Layer upon layer of clues, memories, skills, beliefs and practicalities. For a moment she was all archaeologist, all intellectual enquiry. She became briefly the Ruby she was meant to be – the Ruby she wanted to be, not the Ruby she was forced to be.

A breeze picked up and the air became comfortable to breathe. She yawned, fell onto the bed, cleared her mind and drifted in and out of sleep. Dreams erupted from nowhere, whole life cycles played out in milliseconds of real time, all the while dragging her deeper into the kaleidoscopic world of her subconscious. Somehow among the Brownian chaos of zapping synapses, however, she retained a critical awareness, as if she were an objective observer on a journey into uncharted lands. Were the lives she witnessed inherited memories, embedded in her DNA, stretching back hundreds of generations? After all, what is an instinct other than a hard-wired memory, passed down to protect progeny from the dangers experienced by the ancestors? She witnessed stone workers carving monuments that glistened in a subtropical sun. She saw herself tower over the people, venerated by them, adored and respected by them. She was colossal and she was abundant. She was healthy, yet the people were sick. Many faded before her caring eyes. Nothing made sense to her. She relaxed and went with the flow.

Then the breeze dropped and the temperature climbed,

and she was pulled into the sweaty reality of a locked room and an isolation that had remained unbroken for more than twenty-four hours. She thumped her pillow, cursing Orlando for once again having lulled her into a false sense that she was important to him before treating her with complete disdain and disrespect. And how long would it be before his contempt for her welfare descended into indifference for her life? She started to wonder whether the toothy reptiles in the lagoon would be a safer choice of companions than the heavily-armed soldiers that filled the rest of the hotel.

Back on the balcony, Ruby leaned on the railing and gazed forlornly at the enchanting and deadly view. A crocodile glided into the water and began to swim. She followed its route, noticing that it landed on a well-worn patch of bank. She began to study the movements and behaviour of the ancient creatures, watching closely as they gathered in certain sectors of the bank, swam in parts of the lake according to their territorial instincts, rested for predictable periods of time after feeding. This was a form of history more alive than any she had studied. The habits of these beasts would have remained unchanged since the time of the dinosaurs. Observing them scientifically wasn't simply zoology, it was paleozoology. She wished she had a greater understanding of reptilian behavioural characteristics, but her own deductions would have to suffice if she was going to take her chances out on the lake during one of the long nights ahead of her.

Monday 3rd December 2012

Matt was led by the Belizean officers once more to the interview room, where Baxter was waiting.

'What's the news?' he asked his lawyer.

'Not good. Except that it appears to vindicate part of your story. That ancient aeroplane is on all the front pages together with your friend Doctor Towers. It's not going to be enough of a defence to justify your alleged crimes, but it might be a starting point. I'm going to have to think about in which direction we take your case. Things are starting to happen out here. Mexico is reported to be pleading for military aid from the United States to protect its southern borders. Commercial flights in and out of Guatemala stopped after an airliner was shot at. The country is now isolated, and there are reports of internal train movements, even though the country's railways have been closed for years.'

'Orlando sure is stirring up some shit,' said Matt.

'Your bail hearing is set for Wednesday. As you're an illegal immigrant there's no chance of bail being granted, of course. Then we'll be looking at a trial date next year. Plenty of time to work on your defence before then.'

'This is insane. Forget the defence bull crap. You gotta bust me outta here! There's a war brewing. I gotta get Ruby.'

'Bust you out? I have to confess that's not a service that's ever been requested of me before. I rather doubt that it's something I am able to offer.'

'You don't realise how dangerous this Guatemalan president can be. He's still got Ruby. He's preparing for some serious sword swinging. I've seen the army he's building. Soon he'll have the world by its balls. I was there. I saw it. I have information that other governments need to be able to prepare themselves. This is serious, Baxter. None of the charges against me matter a goddamn hoot if World War III is about to break out.'

'Perhaps your former regiment might want to assist you in the "busting out" department. I could put you in touch with them if you wish.'

Matt looked at the floor. 'Yeah. Maybe. Probably not. I kinda worked solo. And that was all a long time ago. No one would remember me. There has to be another way.'

'I fear that a war would have to commence in order for your value to increase sufficiently for a government to overlook your misdemeanours.'

The first glimpse of the border sent a shiver of fear running down Ratty's back. He had left the main road and was bouncing along the dirt tracks that connected remote Belizean farms and hamlets north of San Ignacio. The track meandered left and right, but was mainly parallel to Guatemala's flat, intimidating face, which lay just behind a narrow band of rainforest. The full strength of its menace revealed itself whenever Ratty's track reached higher ground and he was able to see across the valley. Tanks. Missile launchers. Armoured personnel carriers. More tanks. Helicopters. And thousands of soldiers relaxing, smoking, drinking.

It was a force that Old Ratty would not have contemplated attempting to outwit. Old Ratty would have turned around, tail between his legs, but New Ratty kept going. The Guatemalans couldn't possibly occupy the entire length of the border between the countries. There had to be a hole through which he could slip.

Where the border fence was visible from his track there were always soldiers present on the other side. Where the border was obscured he would have to park and hack his way on foot to get close enough to check it out. He tried this three times within the space of ten miles, bravely tackling unsavoury-looking furry spiders, deftly stepping away from snakes at his feet and not so deftly avoiding faecal deposits that were large enough for him to conclude that they were of dinosaur origin. And at the end of each mini-adventure he found Guatemalan forces lurking on the other side.

Finally, the track started to head eastwards, away from the border. He had come as far as he could on this route. He turned around, backing the rented Toyota Hilux pick-up onto a steep, grassy bank, then pointing it south back to San Ignacio. After negotiating the bustling small town once more, he followed a twisty route through the Mountain Pine Ridge Forest Reserve, a track consisting of Mars-red dirt lined with tall, noble Caribbean pines that passed through spectacular granite mountains with waterfalls a thousand feet high. He was miles from the border, with hours of strenuous driving ahead before the tracks started to get anywhere close to Guatemala, but, when they did, he knew that he would be at least forty miles due south of where he had last witnessed a soldier.

Douglas Da Silva Forest Station was the first hint of civilisation to appear inside the forest. It was a collection of small dwellings on a hilltop, linked to the outside world by either a dusty road or a dusty airstrip. Ratty pulled over adjacent to a sign instructing all vehicles for Caracol to book in here. He checked his maps. The Mayan ruins of Caracol lay just twenty-two miles ahead. They would be his last stop before the next attempt at a border crossing.

He looked up again to find a soldier tapping abruptly on his window.

'Caracol?'

Ratty pressed a button to open the window. The soldier wore Belizean fatigues, with a rifle slung over his back.

'I think it's straight ahead,' answered Ratty, showing him the map. 'Just stick to this road – you can't miss it.'

'I meant are you going to Caracol?'

'Would you care for a lift, old boy?'

'You must wait here for the next convoy. There will be an army escort leaving soon. We come with you to protect against bandits on the next stretch of road.'

'Gosh. Jolly decent of you.'

Half an hour later, a brown sign on a rusty steel frame welcomed everyone to Caracol Archaeological Park. Ratty purchased a visitor's permit and parked in the shade, away from the other vehicles. He unfolded a map across the steering wheel and located his position. Caracol covered thirty square miles of rainforest, extending all the way to the border. It could be the best place to attempt a crossing.

When the other members of the convoy started to explore on foot, Ratty self-consciously started his engine and drove slowly down a track heading deep into the site. No one appeared to take any notice, and once he was away from the main entrance it was possible to travel for miles without seeing anyone. A few students, a handful of full-time archaeologists and a gaggle of tourists were insufficient in number to populate this vast, abandoned Mayan city. He would hang out until sunset, he decided, and attempt the border crossing at night.

To his right was a large mound, fifty feet high, in otherwise flat land. Trees and shrubs protruded from it, but it was clearly not a natural feature: its sides and proportions were too perfect to have been formed by chance. Ratty knew he had encountered his first Mayan pyramid, and by the looks of it, this one was completely unexcavated, abandoned to nature and digested by the forest. He stopped the car, curious to see what his ground-penetrating radar equipment could reveal about what lay beneath the soil.

Balancing on the steep side of the pyramid with the scanner was fiddly, especially with the headset display restricting his vision so he couldn't see where he was putting his feet. He fought his way through the denser vegetation around the base to a slightly clearer patch half way up. The display showed stone blocks just inches below the soil. Their outer layer was tumbled, each brick having long ago been dislodged by roots before becoming entombed in ever-deepening layers of decomposing organic materials. He adjusted the settings to see more deeply into the stonework. The patterns were regular now, showing much less disruption from invading creepers and trees. Deeper still, the clean-cut stones faded into rubble, a loose in-fill material not intended ever to be seen.

It was only when he adjusted the settings to the maximum penetration range of which his scanner was capable that he saw something shocking in the heart of the pyramid.

Under the pale starlight and a handful of garden illuminations from the hotel, the lake was a sheet of graphite, almost invisible. Ruby found its stillness neither inviting nor threatening, just beautiful. As she eased her body into its coolness, she felt the serenity of a midnight dip, the electricity of complete immersion in the natural world. But this was no ordinary swim. She had made the decision to escape from Orlando's control, preferring the known risk of the crocodiles to the uncertain fate that awaited her if she did nothing. If she could gain her freedom she might also be able to save her professional reputation from the foul stench of association with a dictatorship.

From her balcony she had studied the reptiles' behaviour for hours. They were creatures of habit, with two particular patches of muddy lakeside beach on which they liked to spend their time. Crepuscular rather than nocturnal, they were most active at dawn and dusk. Now, six hours after sunset, seemed to be an appropriate time to enter their world, and it had been simple enough for her to clamber down the balcony support post to the grassy bank.

Only her head protruded above the water, but from here she could count nine shapes on one of the banks, and three on another. It correlated with her daylight observations. They were all asleep. Nevertheless, she gripped the little plastic bag of meats she had saved from her lunch, hoping the need to use it as a decoy would not arise.

She had a clear plan for her escape: she would find a road, hitch a ride to the capital and bang on the gates of the British Embassy, hoping to avoid a repeat of Matt's experience at the American one. From what she had observed at the hotel, the country was becoming heavily militarised and citizens might have difficulty moving around without paperwork, but she would deal with one thing at a time. Besides, it all depended on her making it away from the hotel to the other side of the lake; getting safely past the lake's toothy inhabitants was now her sole focus. Freedom was a hundred feet away. She pulled herself smoothly along, minimising the ripples with a slow breast stroke, pausing regularly to count the black shapes on the shore. Nine and three. She was still alone. She pushed on further for a few strokes and repeated the count. Nine and three. And again.

Nine and two.

She scanned the waters around her, gripping the bag of meat even tighter. Would she be able to see if the errant crocodile honed in on her? Would its nose and ripples be visible from her low vantage point? Or would the first she knew about it be the pincer grip around her thighs, dragging her down to a pitiless fate? She was strangely calm and analytical. She was ready. She took the meat from the bag and held it out of the water, ready to throw it at the first sign of approaching danger.

There it was. Hard to see, just a small blob moving in her direction, the tip of the creature's nose the only clue. She threw the meat and started swimming desperately towards the far shore. Seconds later she glanced back for another quick body count.

Zero and zero.

She was out of decoy meats and twelve crocodiles were heading her way.

She swam harder, looking back repeatedly at the rapidly advancing row of noses. Still about twenty feet to go. Even if she could outswim them it wouldn't be over. The bank might be slippery. She might stumble or become entangled in weeds. Crocodiles could sprint short distances over land, and she would be tired after the swim.

She wasn't going to make it. She screamed, more in frustration than in fear.

A gunshot pierced the air. Had she been spotted? She looked back at the hotel. A volley of shots now rained down behind her. Orlando's goons were trying to kill her. The water convulsed. Tails whipped and spun. In the mass of white water, she couldn't make out the crocodiles and just kept swimming until with deep relief her fingers touched the mud and she was able to scramble ashore on her knees.

The shooting stopped. The crocodiles were no longer

moving. There was a brief silence before the most astonishing and unexpected sound hit her ears: a round of applause and cheering. She stood up and looked back at the hotel. Dozens of soldiers were watching her, clapping. She felt a tap on her shoulder. Orlando stood there, accompanied by a guard.

'Thank you, Ruby,' said the President.

'Huh?' she replied, reduced to the kind of incoherence she normally associated with her American former boyfriend.

'Thank you for demonstrating to my men the meaning of courage. They have all enjoyed your escape, and they were protecting you every step of the way. No one expected you to make it as far as you did. I am sure that when the big day arrives, they will be inspired by you to fight with all the bravery I require of them.'

Orlando's guard placed handcuffs on her wrists.

'Huh?' she gasped again, silently reprimanding herself for her monosyllabic gibberish.

'I have given you too much freedom. I have trusted you, Ruby. I have treated you well. I have given you the chance to remain by my side where I will shortly need you, but you have abused that freedom. You have insulted my faith in you.' He leaned closer and whispered in her ear. 'Ruby, too much is at stake. I cannot afford to lose you.'

TUESDAY 4TH DECEMBER 2012

A line of student archaeologists woke Ratty with their whistling and clanking of tools. He half expected Snow White to be following up the rear. He peeked at them from his foetal position in the back seat of his car and remembered he was still in Belize. His temporary parking spot adjacent to the unexcavated pyramid had turned into a long stay on account of the jetlag that had overwhelmed him after nightfall. Even his excitement at making a significant discovery inside the pyramid could not cancel out his exhausted body's demands for rest.

When the students were out of sight, he climbed out of the car and stretched his stiff frame. The rear of the pyramid served as his bathroom and the lower slopes at the front became his kitchen as he prepared himself for the challenging day ahead, all the while thinking about the profound implication of what he had seen with the ground-penetrating radar.

He pinched himself. Such a thing was impossible. It had to be the result of his brain subconsciously adding something to the digital image in front of his eyes. He had been weary, after all. The mind could play tricks under those conditions. He opened up his maps and tried to concentrate on the problem of entering Guatemala. A rough track within Caracol would take him all the way to the border. There it stopped, but on the archaeological map it showed a Mayan path continuing westwards. He rather hoped to find a wire fence marking the border because it would be fun to drive through it with irresponsible velocity.

The ground-penetrating radar unit had the capability of recording the images it displayed. Ratty re-scanned the same part of the pyramid he had examined the previous night, this time with the equipment set to record its discoveries. Then, with everything safely stowed away again, he immediately set off for the border. He now knew what he had seen, and it had not been a misinterpretation or a delusion. It was, nevertheless, impossible.

He reached the fence. It was eight feet high and consisted of rusty interlaced wire with a strip of barbed wire at the top. The base of the fence had been curled up to permit reasonably comfortable pedestrian passage beneath it. He guessed the archaeologists regularly passed through here. The footpath marked on the Guatemalan side of the Mayan map looked to be a traversable continuation of the track on which he currently sat. He backed the car up a few yards. He checked his mirrors. All was clear. He began to accelerate towards the fence. Upon impact, as the wires stretched, snapped and whipped around him, he had no thoughts of possible Guatemalan military presence. The only thing on his mind was the centre of the pyramid.

For what he had seen was not rubble. Not soil. Not anything that deserved to be encased for all time beneath a thousand tons of brick. What he had seen was beauty. Poetry. A symphony in stone. It was a face. A pure and lovely woman's face staring at him through time and technology.

It was a face that he recognised.

The Jurassic Park-style entrance to Tikal was now a heavily guarded military checkpoint. Orlando's cavalcade of armoured cars was waved through and continued along the deep jungle track until it reached the visitors' car park.

There were no tourist vehicles any more, just tanks, APCs, green trucks and portable buildings that had been hastily set up in the last few days. In front of the former visitors' centre was a welcoming party – a line of soldiers and officials saluting the arrival of their President.

'Wait here,' Orlando told Ruby, next to him in the car. She was still handcuffed, desperate for some moisturiser to soothe her chapped wrists. 'This won't take a minute.'

He stepped out and slowly walked along the line of men, occasionally shaking hands and uttering banal comments.

He loves every minute of this pointless charade of loyalty, thought Ruby. Those people were probably just as obsequious to every other president – until they strung them up on the lamp-posts.

When Orlando reached the end of the line, a man in a white suit accompanied him back to the car and both men got in.

'Ruby, what a pleasant surprise!' said Paulo, making himself comfortable beside her. 'No teeth marks, I see. I heard all about your little adventure. Thought you could be like Tarzan, did you?'

Ruby found that, for the first time, she was actually pleased to see him, not even wriggling when he kissed her on the cheek. There was no shame in her failed escape attempt. Her moonlit swim across the lagoon had earned her the respect of everyone who had heard the story.

'You're looking well, Paulo. It's nice to see they don't enforce the wearing of wrist jewellery on everyone. It wouldn't suit you.'

'Indeed. So, Mister President, I would now like to take you on a tour of our installation. Thanks to the enormous resources you have provided, we have been able to achieve a miraculous rate of development here. If our driver would like to turn left after this building, I will explain what we have accomplished.'

They turned a corner and drove down a road that was gleaming in the sun with its new covering of tarmac. Here, what had been a simple unexcavated temple mound surrounded by trees a few weeks before was now a building site, devoid of both trees and life.

'We will see many examples like this,' said Paulo. 'As you know, Mister President, but Ruby probably doesn't, it was recently discovered that the centres of the temples at Tikal contain more than stone. They have each been built around something that the Mayans of a thousand years ago discovered and treasured. Previous archaeological works at this site were purely superficial. They cleared the soil from the stones, cleaned them up and investigated any doorways that were found, but no one actually dismantled a major pyramid.'

'I'm not surprised!' snapped Ruby. 'That would be sacrilege. We haven't even had time to record them with the three-dimensional scanners. We owe it to future generations to look after them.'

'Anyway, no one had looked inside until our scientists pointed Geiger counters at them. They went around the whole of Tikal pointing their Geiger counters at every temple mound. A few of them gave weak readings. One of them nearly went off the scale.'

Orlando was enjoying watching Ruby's reactions.

'And no one knew about this?' she asked. 'How come no one ever got radiation sickness?'

'Simple,' said Paulo. 'It was an unexcavated mound. No one ever spent more than an hour or two there. It wasn't one of the pyramids that people come here to see. This is just the peripheral stuff, not as tall or impressive as the ones in the Great Plaza. Most tourists would look and move on. The mound was fenced off and a team was sent in to check it out. They dismantled the pyramid, brick by brick, until they got to its centre. The source of the radiation had simply been sealed in Mayan stone a thousand years ago.'

'Just a thousand? So it has no connection with the aircraft we excavated?'

'On the contrary. The Mayans of a thousand years ago uncovered something strange in their jungle, something that was to them alien and god-like. They built a temple over it and kept it preserved. What we found when we looked inside was the melted, distorted remains of some kind of reactor ...'

Paulo paused for effect, but Ruby seemed too awestruck to chip in and the President knew all of this anyway. 'It looked as if it had exploded, or as if there had been an explosion nearby that had damaged it. We found a kind of concrete, some metal fragments, plutonium fuel cells. Our scientists tried to work out its function, and it seemed very different to the design of modern reactors. It's too early to tell whether this ancient design would have been any more efficient, or safer, but we have a team working on a reconstruction.'

'And is that where we are now?' asked Ruby.

'No. The other temples weren't completely destroyed, as you can see with this one. Once we were sure of the kind of thing we were looking for, it was only necessary to remove half of one side of each pyramid. Concrete was used to stabilise the structure while the core was dug out. As you can see in this instance, a concrete roof and extended walls have also been added.'

Ruby was jolted into speech. 'It's horrible. Like you've built a small warehouse on the side of an ancient monument.'

'That is exactly what we have done. The new building on the side of it protects the items we find in the centre of the temple, and allows us the space to examine the find *in situ*. Some of the things we find are too fragile to be moved easily. Sure it looks bad, but isn't it better to know more about our history than to leave intact a few mounds of earth that people occasionally come and stare at for five minutes?'

'No. A more sympathetic approach would be a careful removal of the bricks, extraction of the find and rebuilding of the temple to its original state.'

'But there isn't time,' objected Paulo. 'The clock is ticking. You can't expect us to sit idly and wait for –'

Orlando held up his hand. Paulo realised he was entering a subject area to which Ruby had not yet been fully initiated.

'Ruby,' said Orlando, 'you do not see the truth. Not yet. But you will know when the time is right. Paulo, please explain what was found at this temple.'

'Actually this one was particularly unusual. Inside was a pile of human bones, about fifty sets in total. They were carbon dated to roughly twelve thousand years old, and were in a poor state of preservation, but this temple was one of the ones registering a weak reading on the Geiger counter. All of the bodies were mildly radioactive.'

'Were they linked to the reactor?' asked Ruby.

'That's what we thought at first, but the type of radioactivity was wrong. The radioisotopes used in the reactor leave a different kind of radiation imprint in humans to the sort we found in the bones. These people weren't killed by exposure to the reactor, or even by an explosion.'

They drove on along the road. The forest was untouched until they arrived at the site of the next temple mound, where again the trees had been cleared, the side of the pyramid cut open, and hideous concrete walls and a roof had been quickly and shoddily put up. At this site, there were also portable office buildings and cars. Large doors into the new concrete extension of the pyramid were open, revealing unrecognisable objects on benches and people poring over them.

Ruby cast an eye over the artefacts, but soon gave up trying to make sense of them, exclaiming in her frustration, 'I can't make out anything! I thought I would recognise stuff having dismantled that aircraft, but it all looks like junk. How do they know what they've got?'

'Everything we have found is badly damaged,' sighed Paulo. 'Not just through corrosion and the effects of the enormous period of time, but it has all suffered from explosive forces. Some of the remains are therefore difficult to identify, particularly as we are talking about objects that we might not recognise even if they were in perfect condition.'

'Do you know if all of these things originated from the same site, or were they brought to Tikal by the Mayans?' asked Ruby.

'An intelligent question for a pretty little lady,' replied Paulo, instantly cooling the warmth Ruby had briefly felt for her old acquaintance. 'We have people examining the tiny soil fragments embedded in some of the artefacts. From the samples already analysed, the soils do not always match those found in Tikal, and they do not, on the whole, match each other. However, they all originated within a relatively small distance from here. Nothing was carried more than a few kilometres. So Tikal must have been a significant place more than twelve thousand years ago. Possibly a city or a military base.'

'The Mayans must have kept on finding this stuff all over the place,' said Ruby. 'Whenever they found something, they brought it here and stuck a temple on top of it. They must have thought these things were relics of the gods or something. Hey, but what about other temple sites? What about the ones in Mexico and Honduras?'

'Don't forget Belize,' added Orlando smugly, trying to look mysterious.

Ruby stared at him for a few moments before bursting out, 'Oh no, that's it, isn't it, Orlando? That's what it's all about? You don't really give a shit about Guatemala's old territorial claim over Belize. You want to go in there and rape its heritage. And then do the same to all of your neighbours. Please tell me I'm wrong. I really don't want to be right about this.'

'Ruby, how often have you been right about my intentions? We will soon have amassed knowledge of the ancient world that will enable us to replicate any of the technologies they enjoyed in their day.'

'*Enjoyed* in their day? Did you say *enjoyed*? Yes, I suppose the people of Hiroshima enjoyed the technological advances of the Americans. We've just seen the evidence. Everything in these people's day was blown up. It ended with a nuclear war. We don't want to risk bringing it all back again and repeating their mistakes.'

'How could we do that, Ruby? We are a different civilisation. We are their descendants. Of course we will not make the mistakes of the older generation. They have shown us how they went wrong.'

'What do you mean? Have you found any written records from the era? Some ancient film footage perhaps?'

'Oh no,' said Paulo. 'Film could not possibly last that length of time, but the scrolls were well preserved.'

Orlando looked at Paulo, and the latter ceased talking.

'Scrolls? You mean the scrolls you stole from the Sphinx?' Neither man gave any response. She carried on her questioning regardless. 'Are you telling me those scrolls were contemporaneous with this ancient civilisation? Are you saying the Sphinx is twelve thousand years old and was built by people from this place?'

Silence. Ruby got the hint. She changed tack.

'Do you think the Mayans knew about the war that killed their ancestors?'

'They would have seen plenty of evidence of that destruction,' explained Paulo, relieved to be able to talk again. 'The temples may have been built as a reminder, for future generations, of the follies of the past. There would have been verbal accounts of the war, songs and poems, that kind of thing. Myths. We now believe that their tradition of smashing their pottery was less to do with releasing the spirits contained in it and more to do with commemorating the devastation of the nuclear explosions that took place many generations before. An event like that is hard to shake off in folklore.'

Paulo went on to explain the contents of some of the other pyramids. There were various types of weapons, the workings of which remained a mystery. There were pieces of metal and associated corroded electronics that some speculated might have been connected with receiving satellite signals. The poor state of the remains made it impossible to be sure at this stage, but the navigation system found in the aircraft Ruby had studied made it obvious that the ancients were space farers, so the theory was potentially valid. The Mayans seemed to have built a temple around every trace that then remained of their ancient predecessors. Whether their motivation was to erase their ancestors from history, to protect against their influence or simply to worship objects of mysterious origin was unclear.

They drove on until they reached a plateau overlooking the Great Plaza. Ruby couldn't bear to look at what might have been done to two of the finest and grandest pyramids of Central America. When she had last seen them facing each other on the grassy plaza, their peaks higher than the surrounding jungle, they'd been fully restored and cleaned. It had been an awe-inspiring sight.

Paulo and Orlando were already out of the car before Ruby dared to open her eyes.

The plaza was unchanged. Her relieved lungs emptied themselves loudly.

At least, it appeared unchanged at first glance. The pyramids and the surrounding temples, palaces and stelae were all there, but the detail was wrong. There were ventilation shafts sticking out of the sides of the pyramids. She could see the steps at the base of one had been removed to accommodate a doorway, large enough to admit a truck. Around the lower levels of each pyramid were windows. Tourists no longer strolled on the plaza, just troops armed with machine guns.

'The improvements are subtle, Ruby. I hope you approve of them,' said Paulo.

She didn't know how to respond. She was delighted that the main structures were mostly intact, but she abhorred the way in which their insides must have been hollowed out to create whatever kind of military installation this was.

'Why couldn't you just bring in some portable buildings and work from there?' she asked.

'Oh, we did that too,' said Paulo, pointing at the courtyard behind one of the palaces in which stood an assortment of pre-fabricated structures.

'And what is the purpose of these modifications?'

'It's a kind of centre of operations,' Orlando explained, his eyes shining with his inner vision. 'From the nearest pyramid we have the new command centre for the whole Guatemalan army. From the other one we assemble the knowledge and lessons learned from all of the different areas of research going on around us, and we decide how to implement that knowledge. Sometimes we are able to combine one or more of the ancient technologies to create what should turn out to be remarkable new developments.'

'And by that I suppose you mean you've invented new ways of killing people.'

'Killing people? You know that's not my style. The real skill comes in preserving people, using people, and taking the enormous power they collectively possess and putting it to positive use. I think I have found a way of tapping that resource more effectively than anyone else has ever done.'

'What are you going to do, lobotomise us all?'

Paulo cut in to prevent Ruby from digging any deeper holes for herself.

'There is just one more facility we have not yet seen,' he said. 'Apart from the sleeping quarters, medical block and canteen facilities, of course. In the trees behind the Great Plaza we have constructed a series of large units in which the samples from other sites will be housed and studied. There's no point in visiting them because they're still empty.'

'How very euphemistic,' said Ruby. 'I really thought more highly of you than this, Paulo. What you're saying is that the finds you plunder from other countries, having fought your way into them and killed a lot of people, will be put in there. Can't you see the reality is that people will die? How can you begin to justify that?'

'I don't justify it,' Paulo replied meekly. 'Don't give me a hard time. I'm just doing my job. I'm not a soldier. I'm just putting up some buildings because I've been asked to. If I take a moral stance and refuse to do it, someone will fill my shoes instantly. Believe me, I have tried to minimise the impact of my work on the monuments at this site, but that has to be balanced against the time limits within which we have to work. It all boils down to a compromise in the end, but it doesn't matter. I know what we are working towards and why. It all makes sense.'

'This stupid new era? You believe all that, do you?'

'I don't need to *believe* it. I *know* it. One day you will know too.'

'When are you expecting your first delivery of stolen artefacts, Orlando?'

'Belize is proving a little tougher than we thought, but we'll get through. It isn't far to the most important sites. Just have to get past those damn British soldiers. What we don't yet know is whether any of the thousands of smaller temples contain these relics. There won't be time to investigate more than a few of them. Mexico is looking promising. We should be moving in any time now. Likewise, Honduras.'

Listening to this, Ruby felt one moment as if her face and neck were on fire, the next as if she'd been dunked in an ice bath. The sheer scope of this was breath-taking. She tried to reassure herself that this was just madness – but then, the gold aircraft was real, the residual radioactivity was real, the scrolls were real. Feeling as if her voice came from a long way away, she heard herself saying, 'What about the United Nations? You'll never get away with this. If you start acting like a Bin Laden or a Saddam Hussein there'll be sanctions and reprisals in no time. You'll have a massive coalition army coming after you.'

Orlando was permitting himself a sneer, insofar as it was allowed to wrinkle his almost totally smooth brow. 'Your grasp of archaeology is good, Ruby. Stick to your specialist subject. You know nothing about international politics. That is my subject and that is why I am doing this. Honduras is poor; there's no oil there. No one's going to help them. We roll into Mexico and everyone will turn a blind eye. That leaves Belize. Again, no natural resources. The only fly in the ointment is the British, who want to defend that patch of jungle, even though they know perfectly well it was stolen from Guatemala. But they're on their own in this, and my boys know what they're doing.'

He was probably right, Ruby told herself. There would be no coalition. The countries he planned to invade were not significant on the world stage. The developed world would make sanctimonious noises and continue their nice little lives and nobody would know what hit them.

'Let me tell you one more thing, Ruby. Even if the major powers did decide to put up a coalition army against me, do you know how long it would take before a single soldier appeared on the scene? They would be stalled for weeks by attempting diplomacy first. They'll try anything to keep out of trouble. By the time they've packed their soldiers and their body bags onto the boats, we will have entered the new era and they will be irrelevant. They might as well go home. Which is where you must soon go, Ruby. Your new home. There you will stay until I have need of you.'

'For what, Orlando? I still don't get it. Why do you allocate so much of your time and effort to keeping me like a pet?'

'I told you, Ruby. I need you.'

She looked at him for a beat. Was she a toy for the man who had everything? If he enjoyed her company, he wouldn't keep locking her away.

'So you need me. I get it. Tell me this, though. Do you know *why* you need me?'

It was Orlando's turn to pause and think before answering.

'Because it is written that I need you,' he whispered, as if ashamed to admit it.

'And what the hell does that mean?'

'There is an ancient script.'

She looked at Paulo's face to find signs of a snigger, but his expression was as earnest as Orlando's was embarrassed.

'I've read a few old documents in my time, Orlando. So tell me about this one.'

'A Greek text. Thousands of years old. It reads that knowledge will one day come to he who possesses a stone in a castle. A particular stone in a special part of the castle. A ruby stone. In a tower. It matches your name. A coincidence? Perhaps. But fate delivered you here, to me.'

'Fate didn't deliver me. A fraudulent offer of employment brought me here.'

Then something clicked. The stele Ratty had hidden from her in his turret. The diamond-shaped inscription Bilbo had copied in his diary – he'd said it had originally been coloured red. Ruby red? And it was adjacent to a carving of a battlement. A castle tower …

A freaky fluke, she decided. At odds with her mother's account of the origin of Ruby's name, which had everything to do with the type of port she'd been drinking on the night of her daughter's conception and nothing to do with ancient history. The connection was undeniably weird, but hardly sufficient to justify kidnapping.

'Come on, Ruby. Let's get something to eat, then I'll take you up there,' said Paulo.

'Up where?' Ruby felt deflated. 'Are you going to let me out of these 'cuffs?'

'I'm sorry,' said Orlando. 'You know the answer to that. I want nothing more than to have you by my side willingly, unshackled. It pains me that I have to do this, but your presence remaining within my reach is more important than your comfort. There is much riding upon you, Ruby. Far more than you could possibly know.'

The absence of soldiers did not make Ratty's progress into Guatemala any easier. The four-wheel drive capabilities of his vehicle helped him through the wildest parts of the track, though some of the deepest ruts and soggiest mud pools were only traversed after several attempts. The sudden appearance of an adjacent ravine left him with knuckles that were even whiter than usual and crossing the Chiquibul River – during which the water became deep enough for his car briefly to float – left him with some hairs on his head turned newly grey beneath the black dye.

Some strenuous miles later, the ancient, meandering Mayan pathway merged with a dirt road. His satellite navigation unit disputed the existence of the road, but that didn't prevent him making steady progress along it, and soon, to the apparent delight of his electronic guide, he was on a recognisable route, heading north towards El Naranjo. There was a disturbing quantity of military hardware heading in the opposite direction to him, but, with his progress impeded by neither bushes nor border bureaucracy, he found himself with time to reflect upon what he had seen in his scan of the Caracol pyramid.

The face. Rendered in vulgar, almost neon, shades of orange, yellow, blue and green by the scanning equipment in order to highlight its texture and topography. There was a hint of an enigmatic smile and a knowing glint in the eyes. The face seemed to be several feet across, and was mostly intact except for a crack that gave one cheek an age-weary appearance. Without digging the thing up, Ratty had no way of discerning the real colours that lay behind the digitised gaudiness, but its smooth surface reminded him of fine Romanesque sculptures crafted from pure white marble.

He found himself thinking of the wide, full lips on that

ancient stone face – cold, inhuman, inert. And yet his thoughts strayed beyond their lifeless context. He was imagining the lips to be curiously desirable, enticing, kissable. It was madness, of course. He was having romantic fantasies about a chunk of chiselled stone that had been buried for thousands of years beneath a pyramid. It made no sense at all. And yet it made perfect sense because he was attracted to that face at a deep animalistic level. It was a face that was always in his head, guiding him, castigating him, confusing him, yet never loving him even though he loved her.

The majesty of the twin pyramids dominated the area – two timeless creations that would far outlive the generation of scientists and soldiers now scurrying around at their base. Paulo and Ruby entered the Great Plaza.

'Did they find anything inside these main pyramids?' asked Ruby, partly from professional curiosity and partly just to keep a conversation going.

'We excavated them very carefully. We cut through thick stone walls and found a chamber at the base of each of them. Both chambers were about the size of a small house, and had been perfectly sealed from moisture and air for all of these years.'

'Why do you think they created those chambers?'

'I have an idea that they were waiting for something, or someone, to put in there,' said Paulo. 'Or maybe it symbolised to them that they didn't want to see the destruction of the previous era in their own era, that there would be no need in the future to build temples on old war artefacts. I don't know really. Anyhow, we have enlarged and ventilated these rooms and added ante-rooms with windows. This is the nerve centre of the whole operation. It's the most exciting thing I've ever been involved in, Ruby.'

'But it's wrong! Can't you see? Don't you have a conscience? Don't you bastards sodding well *care*?'

The expression of indignation on Paulo's face seemed false to Ruby. Even so, she found it comforting to recognise a spark of humanity still inside him.

'I'm not allowed to tell you the whole story, and that hurts me because I know you would feel differently if you had that knowledge. Trust me on this one, Ruby. Soon we're going to be living in a very different world.'

They reached the base of Temple II. He offered her a slug of mineral water from the bottle he carried in a leather contraption around his chest.

'And where am I going to be living in the meantime?' she asked between glugs.

'Orlando asked me to prepare a special place for you, my dear. Ready?'

Paulo started to climb the pyramid, striding up the enormous blocks that constituted the stairway. Although an entrance had been cut into the steps at ground level, there was still enough width remaining for someone to pass comfortably on either side.

Ruby looked up, straining her neck in an attempt to see the top of the pyramid. From this angle it was so high and so steep that she couldn't quite see its summit. She followed Paulo steadily upwards, panting as the heavy humidity quickly drenched her with sweat. Sometimes he stopped to help her, but mostly he let her struggle, tier by tier, some almost as tall as her.

'Don't look down,' called Paulo from above, without looking down himself. 'It's a much steeper angle than a modern staircase. We lost a man last week.'

The higher they went, the narrower the staircase became. Ruby looked up and finally saw that Paulo had reached some kind of platform area and was standing there, catching his breath. A few more steep steps and she was up there with him, on a ledge high above the jungle canopy. Despite her determination to appear tough, she had to lie on the floor to regain some strength in her jelly-like legs for a few moments before forcing herself to stand. Shakily, and once again accepting some water, she realised she could see for miles. The patches cleared by Paulo in recent weeks were not detectable amid the overall ocean of green. Aside from the clear Great Plaza beneath her, and a couple of other peaks belonging to the taller pyramids, there was no sign from here of any of the industry that was taking place at Tikal. The treetops stretched as far as the horizon in every direction.

'Impressive, isn't it?'

Paulo had spoken from inside the small structure that sat at the top of this pyramid, about six feet in from the edge of the stone platform. It was a single room, about ten feet wide, with an ancient-looking wooden lintel above its door. This, Ruby realised, was to be her new home. Still a little unsteady, she walked inside. There was a camp bed, a couple of boxes containing food and soft drinks, a covered bucket and a drum of water on a metal stand. Attached to it was a length of hosepipe.

'The plumbing is a bit basic up here, for obvious reasons.'

'Paulo, couldn't you get anything else for me? I could be up here for weeks.' Ruby swung round and round, taking in her situation.

'Weeks? I don't think so. The world only has days left.'

'And what about these handcuffs? Come on, Paulo, give me a break.'

'I really hate to do this to you, Ruby,' he said, unlocking her handcuffs. 'I have to follow my orders, no matter how much I disagree.'

'Oh no, you're not serious, are you?'

He began to lock them around Ruby's ankles. Where her wrists had been loose in the cuffs, her ankles were a tight fit.

'Are these your orders? Ouch! That hurts. Spineless arsehole!' She tried to slap him hard on the side of his face, but he merely caught her weakened hand in one of his bear-like ones.

'I really am so sorry about all this, Ruby. I did offer to put you in the standard sleeping quarters, but the President insisted I put you up here in this manner. After your previous escape he felt this was essential. I'm sorry, Ruby, but you really make things hard for yourself.'

'Bullshit. You're a coward, Paulo. Why the ankles?'

'There is no door. There are no locks. You are free to move around the top of the pyramid, but with your ankles tied there is no way you could safely negotiate the steps. They are too steep and you would never make it. Please do not even try. There are soldiers below who have been ordered to look out for any escape attempt. When you are needed by the President, someone will bring you down.'

'Can I at least have something to read, Paulo?'

'Look, I know it's not going to be easy for you up here. Just try to sleep a lot. Get plenty of rest, and enjoy the view. You're seeing Guatemala as the Mayans saw it from up here.'

He started making his way down the treacherous steps.

'Paulo,' she called after him, 'the only Mayans who saw the view from up here were the sacrificial victims just before they died.'

WEDNESDAY 5TH DECEMBER 2012

The flickering fluorescent light caused demonic shadows to flash across the grid of faces staring at her, and the mediaeval weaponry hanging on the panelled walls behind them did nothing to lessen the sinister tone. Monika straightened her hair and tapped her microphone and checked her watch. She tidied the white tablecloth that draped across her knees and cascaded down to the stone floor. She placed her two pens on the table and made sure they were perfectly parallel. Anything to avoid eye contact. She sensed passions in the room. The journalists wanted blood. She was determined not to let them pick up the scent.

Two of the other panellists had joined her and were settling in to their chairs and sipping water, but there was one seat that remained conspicuously empty. Rocco must be planning some kind of stunt – a dramatic, headline-grabbing late arrival. She knew it had been a mistake to invite him to take part in the mini-conference. He'd been acting with a degree of eccentricity that surpassed his usual weirdness these past few days, refusing to comment on his search for her father, but disappearing for hours at a time, holding private Skype conversations from the meeting room, printing downloaded medical research papers about sexual studies on their office inkjet and shielding them from her view. She didn't need this kind of distraction. Facing the press in the function room of this castle was stressful enough for Monika without worrying about Rocco.

One of her colleagues started proceedings by introducing them, explaining their roles at ESA and apologising for Rocco's unexplained absence. Then the first question hit them.

'How much notice will you give us if an asteroid is going to kill us all?'

Monika sighed. She knew this kind of questioning was unavoidable. Her team was viewed by cranks as being at the front line of the defence of the planet from the celestial attack that would inevitably occur at the end of the Mayan calendar. She had hoped to inject a little science and common sense into the media reports, but as the questioning continued, her hopes faded. Then, half way into her negative response to an idiotic question about whether the space shuttle could be brought out of retirement to launch terminally ill mining engineers on a one-way mission to land on a comet and blow it up, just like in a movie, she felt something grab her leg beneath the table. Her kick resulted in a muffled yelp, followed by a hand tapping at her thigh. She finished her belittling answer and referred the next question to a fellow panellist.

A face appeared below the tablecloth. It was worried. It was mouthing something. It was Rocco. She pretended to drop one of her pens and bent down to pick it up.

'I found him,' whispered Rocco. 'Your father. I didn't want to believe it, but I've been double-checking my research and I'm sure.'

She put her hand across his face and shoved him

back beneath the table. He seemed to settle for a minute, but then a hand emerged and placed a piece of paper on her lap. She flicked the hand away and picked up the note.

A name was written on the paper. It meant nothing to her. *Gerhard.* She knew no one of that name.

When the press started filing out of the room, Rocco crawled out from beneath the table and ushered Monika to a quiet corner where no one would overhear them. He looked drawn, weighed down by sleepless bags beneath his eyes. He was also anxious. Monika wondered what fresh paranoia had incapacitated him today.

'His name's Gerhard,' he panted, as if revealing something of devastating profundity. Monika looked at him expressionlessly.

'I know,' she said. 'You wrote it down for me.'

'But that wasn't his real name,' continued Rocco. 'He was hiding something. He studied medicine in the seventies. With your mother. There was a research project. Physiological responses during sexual activity. Your mother took part in it nine months before you were born. She is recorded as being partnered for the experiment with Gerhard. Therefore, he is your father. I have a copy of the research paper.'

'I was the result of an experiment? No wonder you were reluctant to tell me.'

'No, that's not it. Experiment, one-night stand, what's the difference? It doesn't matter. I had to find out who this Gerhard really was. I followed his trail. I'm so sorry, Monika. It is not a happy result.'

A thin scattering of altocumulus boiled into fireballs of amber and canary yellow high above the Tikal National Park. Ratty checked the time: it was almost six. The sun was rising quickly, creating a spectacular dance of colour and energy that threw sepia light over the sacred site. He hadn't waited for daylight, however. He was a one-man custodian of Greenwich Mean Time and had been up for hours, configuring his archaeological scanning equipment and taking care to ensure that the quality of his morning shave was not compromised by his enthusiasm to begin his work.

He could see now that the site had not been disturbed since his last visit, and felt pride at the success of the ingenious deception that had sent that frightful Otto chap scurrying to the wrong end of the country with his Teutonic tongue slobbering over a mouth-watering red herring. Ratty picked up a ball of twine and stretched it between all of the trees in the vicinity, creating a tangram in which each segment could be scanned individually. Nothing would be missed, and the scans would not overlap unnecessarily. He tied the final knot, then stepped over the string to get back to the car and load himself up with the ground-penetrating radar. With the kit strapped to his body *Ghostbusters*-style, he felt dynamic, invincible, unstoppable.

He switched on the viewing goggles and placed them over his eyes. Instantly the soil beneath his feet vanished, replaced by a *gratin dauphinoise* of geological strata in a rainbow of colours. It was disorienting, like stepping out onto a glass floor. He slowly scanned left, then right, then stepped backwards.

The twine flicked around his legs as the pressure of his body stretched and snapped its tiny fibres, but not before the destabilising encounter had sent him tumbling backwards onto unfeasibly expensive equipment. He whipped off the goggles and shifted his body weight to relieve the pressure on the scanner. Fortunately, the high price of the radar was justified by its robust construction, and no damage had been done. He put everything down and rummaged in the car for a knife with which to slash the network of string. Segmentation of a site was good archaeological practice, he reasoned, but not when working alone.

He set up the equipment again, and looked around himself before committing to a wholly digitised view of the world. He swept the radar unit smoothly over the ground, keeping to slow and gentle movements in order to give the machine a chance to process and display the data in real time. The whole area appeared to be natural sediments interspersed with stones, beneath which was a layer of bedrock. He moved forward, sweeping the scanner left and then right.

And then he stopped. The first archaeological discovery of the day glared at him in an intense pink glow in his virtual reality goggles: the bones of a foot, unmistakable because they all seemed to be intact. Five sets of phalanges ran directly to the metatarsals and on to the cuneiform bones. Ratty passed the scanner back over them and adjusted the focus. They were perfect, immaculate. To be showing clearly at this setting they had to be close to the surface. That meant they could have been buried recently. A shallow grave. He shivered.

Then he blinked.

No, he told himself. That was impossible. It had to be a trick of the video display unit. What he was seeing could not happen.

The phalanges were moving.

Considering her enforced elevation and the quantity of construction and destruction taking place around her, there was frustratingly little for Ruby to look at. The girdle of ceiba and mahogany trees that encased the Great Plaza reached almost as high as her platform atop the pyramid, and the people walking fifteen storeys below her looked like toy soldiers. The sounds that penetrated the forest barrier were a cause of unceasing despair to Ruby. There was once a time when even the Guatemalan dictators had acknowledged the significance of Tikal and its surrounding biosphere, and it had been preserved responsibly – even through civil wars and bloody revolutions – but not now.

She had long given up hope that Matt would show up and whisk her to safety. The more she thought about his timidity in Egypt and the ease with which Guatemalans had been able to overpower him on more than one occasion, the more she began to question his legend. Soldiers rarely made good writers, and good writers were rarely any use in a fight. Matt wasn't a great writer, but he was competent – good, even – and she had yet to see him initiate any kind of combat or self-defence. Had he lied to her? Was he a fraud? Had he made a fool of her and of his readers? She found the idea intensely irritating.

Annoyance turned to boredom. Boredom finally turned to sleep. Dreams filled her mind, scenes that were epic in their scale and terrifying to witness. Hot deserts swarmed with legions of sick and dying people, remnants of an ancient race coming together, with their failing strength, to build something. They toiled in long lines, united and dedicated, squeezing every drop of power from muscles weakened by a poisoned and polluted air. Some dropped to the ground as they laboured, and others unquestioningly took their place. The project was larger than any individual, more important than the final days of their abbreviated lives. They were creating something eternal, finding a way to connect to a future they would never see. She viewed these awesome sights as if detached, floating above the passionate slaving, the insect-like single-minded devotion of the masses, and then sank in among these strange people, absorbed in their long forgotten nightmare.

The bones were curling, rippling up and down like a wave. Ratty switched the radar unit to recording mode and tried to stand completely still in case he was accidentally scanning his own foot. The phalanges continued to move with eerie regularity. It was time to fetch the shovel.

He removed his video goggles and blinked in the bright morning light.

'Good morning, Lord Ballashiels.'

Ratty blinked some more. Standing immediately in front of him was his least favourite German. The expression of displeasure that Ratty saw etched into the man's face looked deep enough to have been carved with a knife.

'Gosh,' stumbled Ratty, unravelling himself from his equipment and placing it on the ground. 'Almost stuck a spade through your tootsies. Awfully –'

'Lord Ballashiels,' interrupted the German through teeth that refused to separate, 'your presence here was to be expected, though I have to confess that it gives me no satisfaction.'

Ratty looked over Otto's shoulder at a man standing quietly behind him, dressed in clean blue overalls of the type that world leaders tended to don in times of national crisis in order to look like they were getting their hands dirty.

'I don't think we've been introduced, old fellow.'

The Patient keenly took a step forward, but Otto held an arm out to prevent him from assuming a place at his side.

'It is merely a patient of mine,' said Otto.

'Jolly nice to meet you,' burbled Ratty. 'Sorry, didn't quite catch your name, old chap.'

'It is of no importance,' declared Otto before the Patient had time to consider a response.

Ratty looked at the Patient's face. The shape of the mouth suggested that he considered the opposite of Otto's statement to be true. Even with the edges of his mouth turned down, it had no effect on the rest of his face, which seemed blessed with infinite suppleness. The Patient's skin had an alien-like translucency that glistened with a combination of protective sun cream and a child-like radiance. Ratty thought his features seemed vaguely familiar, but was unable to place them.

'One can't exactly call you "the Patient",' he said, chuckling nervously. 'Would you care for a nickname? One has plenty to spare.'

'What's in a name? That which we call a rose by any other name would smell as sweet,' said the Patient in a soft virgin voice with an accent that seemed to belong to everywhere and nowhere. Otto nodded as if agreeing with the words, but the Patient's eyes hinted at an undertone of irony.

'Yes, quite. Romes and Jules, two-two. Jolly good. Well, it's been a pleasure to meet you, er, mister Chap. Good Lord, is that the time?'

'That which you both seek is not to be found here,' stated the Patient flatly.

'Quiet,' barked Otto. 'Lord Ballashiels was just leaving, weren't you?'

'Yes. Got to, er, see a fellow about a coatimundi.'

'Goodbye, Lord Ballashiels,' said Otto. He said it as an order.

Ratty turned towards his car, then paused and turned around again.

'Sorry, Mister Patient, did you say something about this place?'

'No! It did not. Now go, Your Lordship.'

The Patient stepped forward, now level with an irate Otto.

'There is nothing to be found here,' said the Patient.

'Lord Ballashiels and myself have both studied the stelae, the glyphs, the legends and the maps and we have come to the same conclusion that this is the location protected by the ancients. You know nothing of our research. We have been logical and meticulous.'

The Patient smiled. The desperate rivalry between his two companions was no concern of his. The fact that their quest had been instigated by their ancestors and to some extent symbolised an historic enmity between two nations was irrelevant. The Patient possessed a profoundly inquisitive mind, however, and was growing impatient to visit the true location described by the stelae.

The frustrating shortcomings of both Otto's and Ratty's methodologies caused him to blurt out, 'To find that which you seek you must follow the correct path.'

Otto and Ratty glanced at each other in shared confusion. Otto silently counted to ten on lips trembling with fury as he sought to cope with a level of impertinence to which he was unaccustomed. It seemed that the closer he came to fulfilling his life's work, the more obstacles life threw at him. Years of diligent progress in controlled conditions had given way to the storm of challenges within which he now floundered. In recent weeks he had frequently found himself behaving in a less than chivalrous manner, and it appalled him. The blow that he now sent in the direction of the Patient's cheek flew cleanly through his principles, smashed apart the history of care and devotion he had lavished upon this being, and left him with a heart full of sadness. There was no impact – Ratty's recent exposure to the martial arts ensured that his training could override any limitations caused by his innate cowardice. An aristocratic hand clamped around Otto's wrist in an instant, pulling back the punch before it had a chance to connect with the Patient's face.

Otto's eyes filled with tears as Ratty released his grip. Submission to base animal instincts and a tendency towards primitive violence reminded Otto of his mortality and underlined his imperfections as a human. He stepped away from the Patient as if to prevent a repeat attack from a fist that he could not control.

The Patient stood passively on the spot, serenely taking in the proceedings. Ratty took a step backwards, away from the two men, and picked up his scanning gear.

'I think I'll bash off now. Starting to get awfully hot in these woods. Doctor Mengele, I will bid you farewell. Mister Patient, I heartily suggest you seek a second opinion.'

'I do not understand,' said the Patient.

'Find yourself a new doctor chappy,' said Ratty, scurrying back to the car with his ground-penetrating radar kit in his arms.

The lengthy – possibly indefinite – prison sentence that would soon be Matt's fate, according to the opinion of his lawyer, was still preferable to taking his chances in the winged warehouse in which he now stood. The space was vast. It was much too large to take to the air. Amid the exposed metal alloy ribs of the fuselage Matt felt like Jonah in the whale, isolated from the world in a cavernous hell.

To make matters worse, the C-130 Hercules didn't even have jet engines. Somehow it was going to attempt to get off the ground with propellers. The military policemen who had driven him here to Belize City Airport stood outside the aircraft at the foot of its loading ramp. Baxter handed him a document. It had to be at least fifty pages long, and the typeface was tiny. Matt held it in his cuffed hands and bounced it in the air, as if weighing it would negate the need to read it. He saw his name on the first page; the rest he was happy for his lawyer to précis for him.

'So is this the extradition treaty?' Matt asked.

'Goodness me, no. That's between governments. They wouldn't let you see it. These are merely the charges that are being brought against you in the United States.'

'Jaywalking? Parking next to a fire hydrant?'

'They merely apply to the incident in Guatemala City. Any criminal activity in Belize has been looked upon as being in relation to your attempt to evade justice and so will be dealt with as associated charges related to the main charge.'

Matt rubbed his arm. It was still sore from the blood test he had undergone as part of a medical examination that morning.

'Is it normal to have a medical before extradition?' The shake of Baxter's head suggested not. 'I got the works, you know. Fitness, eyesight, body fat, probes into every orifice they could find. And you think that's not normal?'

'A medical examination would normally be done to a condemned prisoner shortly before execution.'

'Reassuring.' Matt's fingers fidgeted away the tension. Baxter laughed. 'Is any of this good, Roland?'

'There's a subtext. Be patient. This is highly unusual and it may not be as black and white as it appears.'

'And is *that* good?'

'In your circumstances, anything other than a lengthy spell in prison is good.'

Voices outside the aircraft distracted them. The military policemen stood to attention and saluted. An army officer walked up the ramp, followed by a dozen soldiers in full combat clothes carrying heavy kit bags. Either the US was giving Matt a lift on a flight that was taking some soldiers back home anyway, or they considered him sufficiently dangerous to need half a platoon to keep him under control. The latter idea tickled his vanity. The actions of the officer, however, surprised him.

'Captain Mountebank?' asked the officer. His jet black eyebrows seemed to move up and down independently from the rest of his face, a twitch he had long since given up trying to control. He was otherwise a tall, healthy-looking fighting man with a thinning crew-cut and sunburnt ears.

'Er, kinda. Yeah,' mumbled Matt.

The officer knelt down and released Matt's handcuffs.

'I guess you've seen the inside of a few of these babies before,' he said.

Matt had never been in such an aircraft in his life.

'I got a lot of guys dying to meet you,' the officer continued with a smile, pointing at the soldiers gathered around, ducking their heads and shuffling their feet in a quiet orgy of embarrassed hero worship. One of the soldiers was holding a copy of Matt's book. 'But first we have to make a deal.'

'Huh?'

'I'm Lieutenant Nichols, Special Forces. The United States Government has been hunting you for days, but now that we have you, things have changed a little. We are prepared to drop all charges against you, but we need a signed conditional undertaking from you, which I can witness, that you have not, at any point in time, committed or attempted to commit homicide in any degree against any employee of the United States Government, or any United States citizen, in the United States or any other country of the world, whether or not officially recognised by the United States, and furthermore –'

'OK, enough. Just give me your goddamned pen and I'll sign.'

'Let me finish. There are strict conditions in this document.'

It was only now an olive branch was held out to him that Matt truly understood that within him had been growing an intuitive fear, a deep-rooted terror. The rest of his life had almost been thrown away. The wealth, the apartment in New York, the adoration of his readers, the restaurants, the filming, the travelling – not to mention Ruby. Everything that he cared about could have been switched by an uncaring system for a grey prison cell. There was only one chance to live a full life, he realised. Get it wrong and there was no 'undo' button, no 'control Z' to make the mistake go away. He had to take the freedom deal, no matter what provisions were attached to it.

'But I'm outta the frying pan, huh?' he asked.

'With regard to any potential prison sentence, yes, but as I explained, the deal is strictly conditional.'

He didn't care, but he asked anyway. 'What's the condition?'

'That, in return for taking you out of the frying pan, we drop you into the fire.'

Shaking fingers fumbled to open the emergency kit bag. First aid items, water ration, medicines, tow rope, suncream – all were tossed aside until, finally, he found the tin he was looking for. He held it in his trembling right hand and opened it with a click. He doubted it would have a particularly beneficial effect at this temperature, but he poured it down his throat in any case.

This was a new low for Ratty. Not only was this gin and tonic ready-mixed in the can, it was tepid. No, worse than that, he thought, it was positively warm. Right now he would have killed for some ice cubes. Even ice made from tap water would have brought a smile to his face.

He had sped away in the Toyota after his earlier encounter, not stopping until he had put a couple of miles between himself and Otto with his odd-looking patient. Now he had a chance to settle his nerves and reflect on the surprising success of his martial arts and fitness training. Otto really seemed to have been put in his place by Ratty's blocking move. A thank you note to his instructor, Mr Thompson, would be a nice touch, he decided.

From the safety of the remote track on which he was now parked he could review his options and consider the words of the patient fellow who seemed adamant that he was looking in the wrong place. What was it he had said? Something about following the correct path. Given the complete absence of any signposts pointing to lost treasure he doubted that finding the correct path was possible, other than by the means with which he had already endeavoured to do so.

The map of the region, on which he had drawn straight lines between the locations described by the stelae, didn't show any paths in the area. There was nothing close by other than Tikal itself. The direct line methodology had to be correct, for there was no other way he could link the four places. If only he hadn't taken such a circuitous route to get here. If it hadn't been for the military presence at the border he could have arrived almost a day earlier. The whole site could have been scanned before Otto's unwelcome arrival if he had been able to drive straight there. Maybe it could have been done even earlier if the flight across the Atlantic had been more direct, instead of hugging the coastline of North America along an invisible lane in the sky.

An idea was starting to assemble itself in his mind. He swilled down the rest of the gin and tonic and stared at the map, trying to distract his taste buds from the horror they had just experienced. The stelae had been carved more than a thousand years ago. They didn't have accurate maps then. He crushed the can in his hand and threw it onto the floor behind his seat. Could it be, he found himself wondering, that the chaps who made the stelae intended not to point to the intersection of direct lines between the four places, but to a crossroads? To a point dictated not by two-dimensional maps but by real geography? He looked again at the map. There was a marked absence of any ancient pathways. He tried to imagine how the ancients would have navigated between the four settlements. Was there an obvious route with an unmistakable intersection? The landscape had its ups and downs, and the marshlands to the south would have caused a necessary detour, but there were no clear routes that jumped out at him.

The car shook. In the mirrors Ratty could see someone leaping out of the open rear of the pick-up truck and landing on the ground next to his window. He cast the maps aside and fumbled for the ignition key.

A hand tapped at his door window. Ratty slowly turned to face the tapping sound. He recognised the translucent skin of his stowaway immediately. He opened the window.

'I seek,' said the Patient, 'a second opinion.'

Ratty opened the passenger door, and the Patient climbed in.

'Perhaps you'd care to give me your name now that the German fellow isn't around?' The Patient simply looked at Ratty from his seat. 'Right-o. Perhaps another subject?'

'We must drive north from here,' said the Patient.

The unique accent tickled Ratty. He tried not to snigger at 'noo-rth'.

'Ah, yes, the quest. Are you sure you should be coming along? If you're Doctor Mengele's patient, perhaps I should take you to a hospital.'

'No.'

'Or should one get you back to Doctor Mengele himself?'

'I consider that relationship to be terminated.'

'Don't blame you. He does seem a trifle odd. I've heard that even the National Health Service has better doctors than he.'

'Whenever a doctor cannot do good, he must be kept from doing harm.'

'Quite, quite. He's something of a Hippocratic oaf, then.'

A sense of humour did not appear to be on the Patient's radar. He looked blankly ahead and repeated, 'We must drive north from here.'

'Look, I don't want to be rude, but we've only just been introduced, I still don't know your name, and I'm on a rather important archaeological mission that I wasn't planning to share.'

'It is all right. I trust you,' said the Patient.

'Erm, quite, but the question was really about whether I can trust you.'

'I have nothing to gain and nothing to lose.'

'Erm, right. So, the trust thing?'

'You have already proven to me that I can trust you,' said the Patient. 'You protected me from attack.'

Ratty beamed proudly. 'It was rather splendid.'

'Actions have consequences. Virtue deserves virtue.'

'Well, indeed.'

'It was my intention to lead Doctor Mengele to the item he sought. It is now my intention to lead you there instead.'

'So you want to go fifty-fifty?'

'I do not understand,' replied the Patient.

'On the treasure. Half each. After my expenses, of course. Just have one or two small debts to clear first.'

'I seek nothing but truth and knowledge.'

Ratty wasn't much of a businessman, but this sounded like a fair deal. He reversed back onto the dirt track, looking uneasily in his rear view mirror lest anyone else should pop out of the boot. He pointed the Toyota in the right direction and headed through the trees to where the Patient wanted to go.

'This patient thing. I hope it's not contagious, old boy.'

'I am neither old, nor a boy,' replied the Patient with an arid logic that seemed to have an obvious Teutonic lineage. 'And I enjoy perfect health.'

Despite the low frequency throbbing and droning of the four Rolls Royce turboprop engines, it was the silence that was deafening. No visible reaction had so far appeared upon the face of the man at the centre of everyone's attention. Nichols and the dozen Special Forces soldiers stared from their seats at Matt, waiting for him to accept the deal upon which they depended. This guy, they decided, was ice cool. A super warrior. Emotionless. Ruthless. They wanted him badly.

The reason for the expressionless exterior was that inside Matt felt numb. He looked cool on the outside because Nichols's words had chilled him to the core. He ought to have been considering the proposal carefully, but his mind had simply stopped processing information.

Some of the soldiers lost interest and started chatting among themselves. Nichols realised he wasn't going to get an instant response and relaxed his posture.

'Think about it,' said Nichols. 'Take a few minutes, but not too long. We still have the briefings ahead. You know what these missions are like.'

That was precisely the problem: Matt had no idea what these missions were like. A part of him had always known the deception would one day catch up with him. He'd expected it to come from an investigative journalist, to be played out publicly and with much mocking derision in the press and online. He was prepared for that day. He knew what he would say. He knew how to twist it to make it seem like an academic exercise, a literary experiment, a practical joke. At least the royalties couldn't be undone. A legion of angry, misled readers couldn't actually do him any harm. Future sales of the book would fall off a cliff, but that was fine with him. The ride had been fun while it lasted. However the revelation played out, he'd never anticipated that it would necessarily put him in the path of danger. A literary ruse was hardly a crime. A work of fiction purporting to be non-fiction was a work of genius, an artistic accomplishment. Other arts had their cheats too – Matt didn't think his writing was as misleading as pop stars who have to mime during live gigs.

For his book to put him in this situation, though, was beyond anything his creative mind could have envisaged. It had taken him two years to write, and had been based on an amalgam of experiences that real Special Forces fighting men had written about, topped off with a heavy dollop of his own imagination and dramatic talent. It was showmanship on paper, a terrifying tale of bravery and gallantry. It was David against Goliath, the story of how Matt was dropped behind Iraqi lines alone, with a heavy bag of survival and combat kit, on a mission so secret that even the regular Special Forces didn't know about it. Or, crucially, about him. He had written about an unknown elite within the United States Army – a group of individuals that never trained together, never met each other and were never integrated into the military infrastructure and hierarchy. He had invented this Stealth Operations Lone Officer class, or SOLO, and he had described it as so Beyond Top Secret that any government or army official would deny its existence. It gave him a mystique that became legendary. Conspiracy theorists wondered if there were thousands of such fighting men living among them. Foreign armies studied the concept, and, he was proud to discover, some of them had even introduced it to their forces. Crucially, the invention of the SOLO class made his claims very tricky to disprove. He had spent the Gulf War travelling the world alone – indeed, solo – so no one could point to his continued presence at home as proof of his deception.

The book had started out as an exercise in writing: how would it work if he wrote a first person account of a secret wartime mission? He had found a literary voice that suited the subject. He had researched all technical and military details meticulously. He had created a book so gripping that the third publisher his agent sent it to signed it up immediately. The first hardback print run was a modest two thousand copies. Publicity relating to its launch was quickly subsumed by other events that dominated the news, and sales failed to rise beyond half of the printed stock. Matt's little joke looked set to dissolve away, undeserving of a paperback edition, soon to be forgotten.

Then the Bill Clinton incident occurred. The President, relaxing during a vacation, was snapped holding a copy of Matt's book. Whether he was reading it – and whether he actually liked it – nobody knew, but the photo saved the book. It was propelled into the bestseller charts across the world. A chance photo had changed Matt's life.

And now an intricate work of fiction had evolved into an alternative history that threatened his future.

It didn't feel right to be sharing his vehicle with this stranger. His elastic face constantly switched between wide-eyed wonder and a stoic, knowing look that subtly undermined Ratty's new-found confidence. The Patient was visibly astounded by the simplest things. Birds and monkeys forced contortions of the neck as he tried to stare at nature's passing creations. Roadkill fascinated him, and he insisted on stopping to examine a recently-deceased Baird's tapir. He prodded it and jumped back, as if confused by the notion that it was no longer alive. He spoke little, but when he did he would randomly come out with the queerest phrases, sometimes in his amusing slant on the English language, other times in classical Greek or Latin. All were perfectly comprehensible to Ratty.

'Quite the philosopher, aren't you?' said Ratty.

'I know one thing,' replied the Patient, 'that I know nothing.'

Hmm. Socrates, thought Ratty. Hardly a denial of philosophical tendencies.

The journey continued slowly over rough forest tracks in the direction dictated by a man with no name who combined the *joie de vivre* of a puppy with the combined wisdom of all of history's greatest thinkers. Today was going to be memorable, Ratty decided.

The track merged with a small road, and a signpost indicated that they were heading to the ruins of Tikal. Ratty twigged. Tikal was the crossroads. The junction. The X on the map. The Patient really knew where to look. They were going to find the treasure.

The military road block at the entrance to Tikal

suggested otherwise. The Patient showed no emotion or interest in the group of armed men who stood menacingly in front of them. Ratty felt his body erupt in a spray of sweat. He slowed the car to a halt and prepared to explain that he was a lost tourist. A soldier approached the car, but stopped abruptly. He shouted to his colleagues and they quickly formed themselves into a neat line along the roadside. He ran to join them and waved Ratty's car through. All of the soldiers saluted as the Toyota and its surprised occupants drove past.

If I had tried that at the border I could have avoided a considerable detour, thought Ratty. Having a face that shouted in-bred English aristocracy had its advantages. These chaps knew their place. They recognised a toff and doffed their caps accordingly; that kind of response rather took him back to his childhood. Still, those salutes were unexpected. Nice, but not really necessary.

The remainder of the journey to the centre of the ancient city was uneventful. The visitors' car park was bursting with trucks and metal shipping containers. There were pallets of building materials, piles of timber, bags of cement, cranes and excavators. Soldiers and civilians moved like armies of ants, working in dedicated unison, their paths traced by small twists of dust. Ratty parked inconspicuously beneath a tree and looked at the map of the site that the Patient was studying. They faced an obvious complication to their quest: there were thousands of ancient structures spaced over several square miles. The city was clearly on the route between the other four sites, but where within the city would the treasure be hidden? And with hundreds of workers around, how could they investigate and excavate without attracting unwanted attention? Even the mysterious Patient was unable to provide an answer.

'It is not once nor twice but times without number that

the same ideas make their appearance in the world,' he said.

'Well quite,' replied Ratty. 'So is that a suggestion as to where we dig?'

'Make the journey then, make it now: you will follow the same path.'

'Provided there's room to get the Toyota through the trees.'

'You do not understand,' said the Patient. 'Think.'

'Not quite got the old grey matter in top gear. The cogs are somewhat seized up.'

'You travel from El Zotz to Topoxté and you arrive here. Or you travel from Paxcamán to Uaxactún, and again you pass by here. What do you see?'

'Crikey. A quiz.'

'Pyramids. Temples. Towers of stone.'

'The Great Plaza,' suggested Ratty. 'That seems to be where the tourists used to go. Must be the city centre. The village green. The Trafalgar Square. Is that it?'

The Patient looked at him with an annoyingly enigmatic expression. Ratty sighed.

'Come on, old bean. Let's take a gander at this place.'

Inside the military transport plane the mottled olive bundles hanging from aluminium racks swung to and fro. Matt counted them twice. Fourteen. Enough for everyone on board, including himself. Even as he was putting on his camouflage uniform he still couldn't believe he had really chosen this option. Part of him hoped it was all a sick wind-up, and that he would simply go to prison after all. He didn't rate his chances of emerging from the mission in one piece. He tried to think of himself as a journalist embedded with a fighting unit behind enemy lines, surrounded by and protected by soldiers who would do anything to take care of him and get him home safely. But there was a profound difference. None of these soldiers was assigned to look after him. Worse still, some of them even seemed to look up to him. They thought they were going into a conflict with a battle-hardened warrior at their side. He pulled on the black boots they had given him – hoping he was tying them like an old soldier – and sighed. The lie was growing at an exponential rate.

The briefings were a blur. He knew his life could depend on paying close attention, and that made it even harder to concentrate. There were technical terms he didn't understand: acronyms and slang that no one thought it necessary to translate. Something about new explosives that weighed less and punched harder than the old stuff. Maps were handed round and co-ordinates shouted out. For a man who had difficulty enough in coping with the simple fact that he was in a flying machine, any words sent in his direction were wasted. His only refuge from the sharp tension within him was humour. When it was time to ask if there were any questions, he put up his hand.

'Yes?' asked Nichols.

'Do I get air miles on this flight?'

The ripple of laughter helped to soothe his nerves, and only served to reinforce further his reputation as a cool and fearless soldier among the other men as they passed around the bundles. Nichols handed one to Matt.

'You need any help with this?' asked the Lieutenant.

Matt was holding the parachute pack upside down as he shook his head. Nichols turned it around for him and helped him climb into it, checking all of the buckles and fastenings as he did so.

'The rip cord?' asked Matt.

'Very funny!' laughed Nichols.

'No, I mean it. It's changed since my day,' bluffed Matt.

'You probably trained on the old T-10 design. We're now on the ATPS – Advanced Tactical Parachute System. It's a slower landing, forty per cent less impact force, which means we can jump with more kit and fewer injuries.'

'I, er, knew that. And the, er, rip cord?'

'Hasn't changed. Don't worry.'

'Fine. But how would you explain it if I had my film crew here?'

'You haven't, though. So I won't. Just do nothing. You'll be hooked up. The chute opens automatically. Just bend your knees and keep your tongue in.'

'So what do I do with this?' Matt indicated the cord with a metal ring attached.

'Reserve chute. Usual procedure. If you don't see the main chute open after three seconds, this ring releases the reserve. But you don't wanna do that.'

'Because?'

'It's a faster drop with the reserve. With the kit you'll be carrying you'll break your legs.'

Matt wondered if there was any way to break his legs now and avoid the jump altogether. He went through the motions of preparing for the drop, copying the tightening of straps and connection of clips from the other guys, but in his mind he was sheltering in another place, safe in the warm harbour of Ruby's arms as she affectionately caressed his neck instead of it being rubbed raw by a parachute buckle.

Beneath the low-level glass conference table, a small fountain gurgled, spewing spotlit water into a channel cut through the floor. Chesterfield sofas surrounded the table, their red leather shining with a glow never possessed when the hides were alive. Three walls bore large portraits of President Orlando in various military and civilian costumes, proudly displaying the medals he had awarded himself. The fourth wall consisted of a giant screen, currently showing a map of Guatemala and its surrounding countries overlaid with patterns of troop movements and the Mayan temples they were targeting. Beneath the screen was a table on which a selection of weaponry was laid out. The floor was carpeted in a plush purple that wouldn't have looked out of place in a seventies porn movie, and the atmosphere was silently and refreshingly air conditioned.

Frankly, Otto had expected more tasteful interior design from his President, but this was the interior of a Mayan pyramid and, as such, there was little precedent to follow. The only redeeming feature of the room was a glass cabinet in which ten ancient scrolls were displayed. These scrolls were the *raison d'être* of all that was happening in Tikal, and Otto's diligent hand-written translation had become the guiding principle behind all of Orlando's lavish projects and preparations. The subsequent loss of that translation in the sinkhole had not arrested their progress; Otto and Orlando knew the message and carried it in their hearts.

Otto proceeded to carry out the tests and treatments upon Orlando. The repetitive and intricate tasks brought him another step closer to healing the pain of the Patient's defection, although he was confident that they would soon meet here, at Tikal. The Patient had seemed curiously intent on visiting the site described by the stelae, and Otto had finally come to the conclusion that the intersection of the paths was within this ruined city, not outside it. But when and if the Patient showed his face, Otto was determined that it would be for the last time.

'I trust the self-medication went smoothly in my absence,' stated Otto, drawing a small sample of blood into a syringe.

'You provided me with everything I required,' replied Orlando, failing to answer entirely to Otto's satisfaction.

'Yes, but did you manage to take all of the medications at the appropriate times? You know how important it is for maintaining your indestructibility.'

Otto removed the syringe and swabbed the skin.

'I know, Otto. You have no cause for concern. But do you not think it is a pity that your tests cannot analyse my mind?'

'Your mind is healthy because your body is in as close to a state of perfection as I have been able to maintain.'

'I am concerned,' Orlando whispered. 'I worry.'

'You have a great responsibility. To worry is part of your role as our leader.'

'For you, Mengele. I worry for you.'

'That is not necessary.'

'The sinkhole took your home. I have fond memories of that villa. You were fortunate to survive. I know you have continued your work – from a truck, I believe – and I'm concerned that the quality of your research may have been compromised by the upheaval. That is why my people have been preparing a new medical facility here at Tikal. It is basic, but it will serve the needs of the soldiers and scientists. And there are private rooms reserved for you.'

'I am grateful,' said Otto. He wondered if the rooms would be sound proof, or whether he would have to resort to medicinal options for silencing the Patient when recaptured. The truck possessed the advantage of being something he could park away from suspicious ears, but to be able to work in a static, stable environment once more would be priceless.

He looked at the weapons on the table. 'And so,' he continued, 'if I am to have a new laboratory, there is nothing that need concern you from the point of view of medicine.'

'What about dreams?'

Otto regarded him blankly. The world of dreams was of no interest to him from a medical perspective. They were not quantifiable, so they were not important.

'Dreams as in ambitions, desires, fantasies, or unconscious brain activity?'

'I just want your reassurance that you can still fix me, no matter what.'

The Doctor showed no reaction to that question. He was still staring at the guns on the table as he handed some pills to Orlando.

'I have the same capacity to care for you that I have always had. Nothing has changed.'

'I have had ... I have experienced ... I, er, have recurring dreams,' said Orlando with uncharacteristic hesitancy. 'A conflict. A brightness. A blur.' He put the vitamins and supplements into his mouth and mumbled, 'It always ends the same way. Blackness.' He glugged a glass of water to wash the pills down. The liquid also soothed his throat, dry and rough from the strain of vocalising intimate revelations of personal weakness.

'There is no scientific evidence that dreams are premonitions. Belief in dreams is primitive cultural mumbo jumbo. And you, of all people, have no reason to fear anything.' Otto edged backwards towards the weaponry table, failing to recognise that morbid dreams might be symptomatic of a gap in Orlando's medication, that his patient might be slipping from his tight control just at the moment when he needed him most.

'You really think I'm immortal, Mengele?'

'I've never used that term,' replied Otto, checking that Orlando was facing away from him as he silently swiped a pistol from the table and put it into his pocket. 'You are still susceptible to the natural limitations of a healthy human lifespan, but you are, to an extent, indestructible within that timeframe. I still have the ability to repair you. And if I can't repair you then I can halt any progression of a malady until such time as medical science is ready to reverse it.'

Orlando turned his head to face Otto. The President appeared reassured. He had always known of his situation. It gave him two lives, two chances at everything. His personal doctor was running a research programme that stretched back to the 1940s, a quarter of a century before Orlando had even been born. Somehow it was all for his benefit. He had been selected for greatness, to live his life with a unique insurance policy that gave him the confidence to take risks, to fear no one, to take control, to take power. No person could permanently disable him. No disease could strike him down. No accident of nature could harm him. Otto could fix everything. Orlando was like a computer with mirrored hard drives: there was no risk of any data loss.

And yet at no time in his life had he ever stopped to wonder how his doctor would be able to perform the medical miracles which had been promised to him, should he ever require them. It was a fact of his life that he had grown up with. Issues of legality, morality or practicality did not concern him. He was special, and that was that. Orlando knew he was The Chosen One.

The attempt at moving unseen through the Tikal monuments was spectacularly unsuccessful. It took less than five minutes for Ratty and the Patient to be spotted creeping suspiciously from tree to tree alongside the Maler Causeway. The young Guatemalan soldier who found them froze on the spot, terrified, and then ran to a nearby temple complex where construction and conversion work was taking place. Before Ratty could

drag the Patient to a suitable hiding place, a line of
soldiers and builders rushed out of the temple towards
them. Ratty tried to remain cool, harnessing the wisdom
of eastern philosophers and hand-to-hand combat
specialists that he had learned in his martial arts training.
Sun Tzu was his favourite, and he remembered that a
battle could be won before it had begun if one side took
the psychological upper hand.

'The supreme art of war is to subdue the enemy
without fighting,' he reminded himself. Whether that
applied to two unarmed men facing a battalion of proper
soldiers he wasn't sure. He glanced at the Patient who
showed no fear. In fact, he showed little interest in what
was happening. The texture of a ceiba tree had caught the
Patient's attention, and he was running his fingers across
its immense, pale bark, oblivious to anything else.

Ratty stood firm, straightening his leather jacket,
slicking back his hair, looking like an underfed bodyguard
next to the Patient. An officer emerged from the group of
people and marched briskly towards Ratty and the Patient.
He stamped his feet on the crushed gravel track and
stopped, then threw his arm up into an angular salute. The
Patient looked at his new visitor, head slightly cocked in
the manner of an inquisitive dog. The officer spun round
to face the soldiers and builders behind him. He shouted
at them and they stood to attention in an instant, all
throwing perfect salutes at Ratty and the Patient.

Quite a hospitable bunch, thought Ratty. These
Guatemalan chaps were charming hosts – attentive and
respectful to their guests, if a little over the top in their
apparent sincerity. He just hoped that they didn't ask to
see his entry ticket. The discovery that he hadn't paid to
get in might sour the atmosphere of *bonhomie*.

He looked across the row of salutes in front of him.
Dozens of pairs of eyes were locked in his general

direction as he gave them a pathetic wave of his hand. And yet, they were not looking at him. He followed the line of their gaze. Their attention was wholly upon the Patient. An awkward impasse followed, as if they were waiting for a response from the Patient. There is something deeply queer about the whole situation, thought Ratty. Had he inadvertently got himself involved with a Guatemalan army general? Was the Patient a well-known soldier who had gone as potty as a potato and escaped from an institution?

In the midst of the stifling embarrassment felt by all present, the Patient suddenly began to walk away. Ratty's neck rotated left and right between the Patient and the line of soldiers and workers, the sweat from his chin dribbling onto the upturned leather lapels on his jacket. He took a deep breath and scrambled after his new friend.

'I say,' he wheezed, 'Patient chappy. Any idea what that was all about?'

'Everyone I encounter shows me great kindness and respect,' replied the Patient. 'With, it seems, the sole exception of Doctor Mengele. Perhaps that is a natural function of long acquaintance, but it is not an observation recorded by philosophers.'

'Quite, quite. It will be dark soon, so perhaps we could return to our hunt for the ancient crossroads – do you have any thoughts?'

'Nothing exists except atoms and empty space; everything else is opinion.'

'Most helpful.'

The Patient continued to stride purposefully along the causeway. He walked as if he had been here a thousand times before; as if he owned the place. Given the reaction of the soldiers they had so far encountered, Ratty began to wonder if the Patient had the title deeds to Tikal stuffed inside his overalls.

A small wooden sign indicated they were at the North Acropolis. Ratty followed the Patient into the complex of ruins, unnoticed by nearby workers beginning to tunnel into the side of a small temple. From the blackened edge of the North Acropolis a series of ledges and steps led down to the Great Plaza below them, dominated by the enormity of Temples I and II. The two men paused to take in the view. Did these two pyramids mark the spot? If so, the area was too vast for them to excavate, and too conspicuous for them to get away with it.

Something was pressing into Ratty's lower back.

'Thank you for returning my Patient to me,' said a Germanic voice. 'I trust he has not been bothersome.'

Ratty turned to see Otto holding something in his right hand that looked suspiciously like a handgun, while in his left was a collection of items including a steel chain.

'No, no trouble at all. Don't mention it. Remarkable chap, your Patient. And fit as a fiddle.'

The Patient made no attempt to resist the imposition of a metal collar and chain and the placing of a canvas bag over his head. Ratty felt like he was intruding on a private role-playing session or a meeting of the Grand Lodge. Disquieted and embarrassed, he fidgeted and looked away.

'Goodness, *tempus fugit* and all that. Best be off.'

The gun swung back in Ratty's direction.

'Please accompany me, Lord Ballashiels.'

The cargo ramp opened slowly. Vortexes of cool air picked up everything that wasn't strapped down. Matt instinctively shielded his eyes from the anticipated bright light, but the doors opened only to blackness. After a couple of hours chasing the sun westwards, they had lost the daylight race. He strapped on the night vision goggles and looked outside again. The blackness was now green, but still devoid of shape and detail. He had been advised that nothing would appear in view until he was a few seconds from the ground. Whether that would give him enough time to avoid landing on a cactus field he wasn't sure, and didn't really want to know.

In his helmet and goggles and full jump suit he felt detached from the world, alone with his fears, trussed up like a Thanksgiving turkey with the heavy paraphernalia necessary for a successful jump and completion of the mission. He groped at the line that linked his parachute to a metal rail inside the aircraft and wondered what it would feel like to entrust his life to the sack of fabric on his back. Could he activate the reserve chute if the main one failed? Would he remember to keep his legs together and bend his knees upon reaching the ground? Would he remember not to scream like a baby?

At this last minute, with everyone lined up for the jump, he came up with a plan: he would close his eyes until it was over. The line moved towards the void. Heavily laden feet shuffled sideways, forcing him along in the same direction. His heart rate jumped. His stomach was lurching wildly. His tongue was as dry as desert sand. The shuffling was continuous now. He was in the middle of the line, about the sixth or seventh to jump, he reckoned. Ruby's image popped into his head. Would he ever see her again? A few more seconds and –

His feet were no longer shuffling. He was freefalling, slowly tumbling, sucked towards the Earth in an invisible hurricane. With a jolt he suddenly hung upright, apparently motionless. He opened his eyes. There was nothing to see. The silence was broken only by the soft creaking of the parachute lines. Suspended in the middle of nowhere, lacking any sensation of movement up or down, left or right, he was more alone than he had ever been before. And yet he felt a connection, a human presence. The land beneath him was hostile territory, but not entirely. Somewhere down there beat a friendly heart.

The green blur in his goggles quickly took the form of trees. He looked for a gap, as he had been instructed to do, and tried to use the very limited steering ability of the parachute to aim for clear land. Whichever ropes he yanked, it didn't seem to make any difference. He would hit the ground wherever fate decided. Bend the legs, he reminded himself, pinching his knees together. A rapid rustle of leaves and snapping branches passed his ears. He tensed for the impact, pointing his toes downwards to maximise the cushioning effect of his joints.

There was no impact. A second jolt left him swinging once again, but this time there was no air moving across his face. The wretched stillness of the jungle's dense atmosphere bathed him in an instant sweat. He looked down. The tree had caught him just a few feet from the ground. He pulled a knife from his pocket and prepared to cut the cords above him, but when he looked down at the drop again it seemed a little too far to fall safely.

Something hit his foot from the side. A soldier was standing beneath him, attracting his attention by hitting him with the business end of an M16 machine gun.

'Pull your reserve,' whispered Nichols.

Matt did as he was told. A useless parachute fell to the ground, attached to him by its cords.

'Now snag those cords around a branch, release the main and climb down the reserve.'

Seconds later Matt was standing on solid ground. Or, at least, he attempted to do so, but the bones in his legs appeared to have been replaced with jelly and refused to give him the necessary support. He pretended to sit down deliberately, making a play of checking his equipment while Nichols gathered the rest of the team around him. Amid the clicks of weapons being prepared, amid the glow of GPS screens, amid the hubbub of whispered tactics, a feeling inside Matt was growing stronger, convincing him that Ruby was almost within reach.

'Awfully nice, er, place you have here,' stumbled Ratty. 'The architecture has a hint of Art Deco about it – elegant and yet potent. The angles create an overtone of dominance reminiscent of Albert Speer's finest works, er, I'm thinking Reich Chancellery of course, with its lethal magnificence which is, er, magnificent.'

He dusted a patch of stone with his bare hands and carefully lowered himself down, stretching his tired legs and getting used to the shackles that now rudely bound them at the ankles. The forest canopy was an invisible presence all around, pricked here and there by invasive shards of light from halogen lamps rigged to keep the construction processes moving throughout the night.

'Reminds me of my turret at Stiperstones,' he continued. 'Solitude, sense of history, and a jolly nice view. Always a mess, though. Did I ever tell you about the break-in grandfather discovered during the war? Burglar chap didn't find what he was looking for. Too much muddle. Apparently he left a couple of rooms tidier than he found them and even arranged some of the books in the library alphabetically by author. Probably didn't have time to go for the full Dewey Decimal. Scuttled off before dawn, empty-handed. Grandfather was profoundly embarrassed. Kick-started a spring clean that lasted until VE Day.'

He had so far made no impression on his companion. She sat still, arms crossed, with an expression – as far as he could make out in the faint light of the stars – of matronly disapproval.

When finally she deemed it appropriate to speak, Ratty scanned her words and her tone of voice, seeking affection. He found none.

'What the bloody hell are you doing here?'

'A chap called Paulo Souza brought me up here.'

'I know, I was here. Paulo's an arsehole. A double crossing, backstabbing, money-grabbing vandal.'

'Seemed like a *bon oeuf*, actually. Said he would take care of my rental car for me. It's due back in a few days and one hates to incur the wrath of the little people.'

'Never mind the bloody car, Ratty. Why are you here at all? Don't tell me you've gone and done something I'm going to make you regret.'

Ratty felt himself cowering at her words, pulling back his body from the tongue that whipped sharply near him. She could be so unforgiving, so judgemental. Her world view seemed black and white, right and wrong, nothing in between. She was a force of nature, as irrepressible as the jungle below him. He had missed her so much.

'If you're referring to the stele that was the subject of our last encounter, you need not fear. All is under control.'

'So you didn't sell it to that creep?'

'Absolutely not, old radish.'

Even in the darkness, Ratty could tell that Ruby's body language relaxed at this point. He heard the tinkling of the metal cuffs as she slid close to him and felt a salty kiss on the corner of his mouth.

'I'm sorry I doubted you, Ratty,' she whispered. 'I knew you'd do the honourable thing.'

He had considered telling her that the stele had ended up in Dr Mengele's hands after all, but her unexpected and utterly welcome outpouring of affection convinced him to do the dishonourable thing. It would be easier if she didn't know. Instead he would play the part of the hero. He would be her Perseus, her Odysseus, her Tom Cruise.

'Listen, old fruitcake, I found the other part of the stele. I have the complete set of glyphs. They point to the intersection between four Mayan towns: El Zotz, Topoxté, Uaxactún and Paxcamán. And that intersection has to be somewhere here in Tikal.'

Ratty felt Ruby's bare unwashed arms around him, squeezing him in a delightful, malodourous embrace. He tried to kiss her, but without sufficient visual clues as to the position of her face he only managed to plant his eager lips in her hair, triggering an unromantic sneeze.

'What else do you know?'

'Er, nothing. I don't know what I'm looking for or exactly where it is, but I did remember to bring a shovel and an awfully good ground scanner thingummy.'

Ruby sighed and lay back on the warm stone, staring at the heavens.

'It doesn't matter now. President Orlando is steadily ripping this place to pieces. If there's anything here, he'll find it. It's over for us.'

'Twaddle and twiddle with knobs on,' replied Ratty. 'We can still solve this mystery. Atop this pyramid sits the finest historical brain of our times. And you can be of some help too.'

She giggled. He laughed. Her laughter turned to tears that blurred the constellations above her. She had only just identified the main components of Pleiades, and now they merged into a pale white stain in the sky.

'Ratty, do you know Pleiades?'

'Intimately. Keeps the old joints from seizing up.'

'Not Pilates. The constellation Pleiades. Up there. Can you see it?'

'Ah, the Seven Sisters. The legendary birthplace of the Maya.'

'Do you think it looks like the layout of Tikal, Ratty?'

He looked at the pricks of light in the sky, then at the

light leaking from each temple visible from their vantage point. A vague correlation might have been possible, but it wasn't easy to tell.

'Even if the stars are mirrored on the ground,' said Ratty, 'it doesn't tell us where to stick the old shovel. Pleiades was used in the configuration of other Mayan towns, not to mention the Cydonia monuments on Mars.'

'Don't bring that nonsense into it.'

'But you are acquainted with the theory, are you not? Viking mission. Summer of the drought, flared trousers and James Hunt. NASA photographed a face on Mars. Like a Sphinx looking up at the sky. A nearby cluster of hills looks queerly like a village of pyramids.'

'I know all about that rubbish. I read a book about it.'

'Quite, quite. Nevertheless, if those features were created by the hand of man, it's not unreasonable to point out that the constellation of Pleiades might have influenced the layout of the Martian pyramids. Its Sphinx was out on a limb, just like one of the stars in the formation – I think the fellow's name is Atlas.'

It took her a considerable effort to repress her academic instincts. She knew the visual data for Martian constructions was utterly inconclusive, and that any theories about structures on the red planet were the result of misguided optimism. Any serious discussion about the Cydonia anomalies could not take place without further information, and for now that depended on how much the Chinese were willing to talk about the results of their robotic sample return mission. Until such time, the subject was limited to the lunatic fringe. And yet the world was different now. History wasn't what it used to be. Humanity was not at the zenith of its evolutionary arc; it was rediscovering its prior greatness, relearning what it once knew, bouncing back from millennia of recovery after the traumatic end of its finest hour. In this crazy new world order, Ruby had to be more open-minded than before. Academic rigour could come later.

'I still maintain that the Mars ideas are the moronic, sensationalist peddlings of naïve and opportunistic long-haired pea-brained fools. Martian pyramidiots, in fact. On the other hand, if I were to give them the benefit of the doubt, which I don't because it would be ridiculous to do so, I would make the following deduction: if the Cydonia region is laid out to the same plan as Tikal, which it isn't, then there's a problem. Which there isn't, because it isn't. Are you following this?'

'I'm sorry,' said Ratty, who was still staring at the stars, his mind steadily emptying of all other thoughts. 'Were you talking to me?'

'I'm saying that if Tikal and Cydonia are both representations on the ground of the constellation of Pleiades, then there's a problem – other than the sheer stupidity of the idea. The star called Atlas is represented in Cydonia by the face, or the Sphinx as you call it. Which it isn't, of course, but let's assume it is. But at Tikal that point isn't represented by a Sphinx, because there isn't one here. Its relative position means it could only be represented by Temple IV.'

'Tikal's largest pyramid?'

Ratty and Ruby exchanged unseen glances.

'Down,' whispered Nichols, simultaneously signalling with his arm for the benefit of those wearing night vision goggles. The men dropped to the ground like well-trained dogs and shuffled into the undergrowth on their stomachs. Matt grumbled. Getting down was hard. Standing up again was almost impossible without help when hauling a quantity of weaponry and explosives that almost doubled his body weight. He was terrified of scraping something and generating a spark. It was the same for the others, of course, but they knew what they were doing and they had youth on their side. Matt fleetingly considered a discreet disposal of his load, knowing that it would have no detrimental effect on his fighting ability, which was zero in any case.

Nichols peeped through the ferns. A Guatemalan patrol was heading their way – four men, all in green camouflage, strolling with rifles over their shoulders. One of them paused, as if he had heard something, and the others mocked him. Ignoring their taunts, he looked around, but he was looking at head height. One more step and he would have tripped over a heavily-armed American. The man retraced his steps, lit a Lucky Strike, and continued patrolling. Soon the red glow disappeared.

Once they'd strained to their feet again, Nichols led his team closer to Tikal. Through their goggles they spotted a guard post. Its single lamp shone eerily white, illuminating a lonely Guatemalan soldier. They boxed around him, cut their way through the rusty wire fence intended to keep non-paying tourists out, and were inside the perimeter of the old Mayan city. Moments later they paused at the periphery of a pool of light. A Mayan temple stood before them, the brutal vandalism at its heart dramatically illuminated by floodlights that helped workers who were in the process of shoring up its precarious surviving walls with concrete. There was no need for Nichols to issue orders. Two of his men stayed behind, while the others moved on.

The same happened at the next three temples they encountered. Matt felt his heart rate increasing steadily as they penetrated deeper into the complex. With every step he took, and with every pair of Americans that peeled away to fulfil their part of the mission, he felt his chances of getting out of there in one piece diminish. He couldn't shake the sense of enemy soldiers encircling him, any one of whom might return him to his outstanding sentence of death.

He had an M16 machine gun in his hand and a small pistol in the grab bag – two tools of dispassionate steel, which he barely knew which way to point, to defend himself against thousands of armed Guatemalans. It was beyond hopeless. And yet, as he considered the futility of his situation, lying on his stomach below moist fern leaves waiting for another patrol to pass, he saw something glowing in the remote recesses of his imagination. It was a distant possibility, utterly unconnected to the official aims of this mission. It was a chance for personal glory.

At Nichols's instruction, Matt scrambled to his feet again only for Nichols and the others to dive for cover in response to a sound that might have been a branch snapping. They spun around in a fluid motion with weapons aimed, then started firing at invisible assailants. On instinct, Matt ran behind the nearest tree and slipped out of his rucksack, standing immobile, terrified. The professionals were following some kind of well-rehearsed procedure for this eventuality. So was he – he was getting the hell out of there, taking only the grab bag with him. It contained a cut-down selection of items designed to get him out of trouble: spare ammo clips for the machine gun, M9 pistol loaded with fifteen rounds, utility knife, bolt cutters, torch, some survival items and a hand-held enemy radar and infra-red detector. As he sprinted into the night he thought he heard Nichols shout something in a voice strained with physical pain, but the rustle of leaves as he crashed through them blurred any such noises into a background hum.

At the edge of the Great Plaza he paused to catch his breath and take stock of his situation. The men were split up. Nichols was possibly hurt, and the other guys had already peeled silently away in pairs, leaving Matt alone.

Leaving him without their protection. An untrained novice no longer embedded with the Special Forces upon whom he had depended.

It was exactly what he wanted.

The medical laboratory behind the Great Plaza was as austere and functional as the conditions under which the father of its new occupant had once worked. Constructed from steel shipping containers clamped together, the blue corrugated walls and ceilings and unpainted plywood floor created a space more suited to the transportation of boxes than to medical research. Two iron beds sat starkly in one section, lit from above by bright construction lamps tethered to the ceiling, powered from an extension lead that snaked across the floor. A fan running at full speed in one corner kept the temperature close to bearable. There was a sink of sorts – a small unit powered by an electric pump, fed by a plastic barrel of water beneath it. Empty modular plastic shelves, of the type normally found in domestic garages, provided storage. Two long picnic tables sufficed, Otto presumed, as desk and workbench. A month ago it would have been depressing; today it delighted him.

The Patient co-operated passively as Otto made him lie down on one of the beds, chaining each limb to the ironwork in links that were aligned in perfect symmetry with the metal framework. There had been not the slightest hint of protest since his hours of freedom had been curtailed. A weak flame of suspicion flickered within Otto, but he paid it no attention as he straightened the untidy extension lead on the floor. The Patient was going nowhere and his face was covered; there was no cause for concern.

Despite the lateness of the hour, doctors from the adjacent clinic – another structure flung quickly together from shipping containers – had offered to assist in unloading the equipment from Otto's truck, but he had refused their generosity. He turned instead to the help of low-ranking soldiers who would not question his possession of certain items of medical equipment – a collection of specialist machines and surgical tools that would have raised curious eyebrows among more knowledgeable men.

Otto placed a cloth over the Patient and injected a sedative as soldiers unloaded the first items into his laboratory. There would be no awkward questions to answer and no rumours started, so long as the Patient went unnoticed. When the final item was delivered and the last soldier had left, Otto closed the heavy metal door and slid the bolt to secure it, ensuring that the handle was tucked down flush at precisely ninety degrees. He was now alone with his most important things, and for the first time since the loss of his villa he had power, water and enough space to work. More importantly, he would be able to establish a routine. The improvised normality would return a sense of peace to his soul and shield him from the turbulence outside the metal walls.

He had barely begun to straighten the boxes stacked haphazardly by his military assistants when that turbulence encroached upon his world. His bubble of steel was insufficient to isolate him from the crackle of machine gun fire. He winced. This laboratory was close to the Great Plaza, at the hub of Orlando's activities. Guatemala's blend of military and archaeological power was starting to exasperate the rest of the world. When the walls strained loudly against explosive forces, Otto felt no surprise.

The pulse of compressed air knocked the breath out of Matt. The vacuum that followed it made him gasp until oxygen filled the void and replenished his lungs. Behind him, an orange glow climbed high above the trees, illuminating the surrounding forest in a fiery wash. Then came dull thuds from a lethal drizzle of bricks blown out from the temple they had once formed. Some turned to dust on impact with other stone structures; most landed harmlessly, indented into soft soil. The sinister pounding seemed interminable to Matt as he sheltered in the night shadows, close to Temple I. The operation, he realised, was still on. The first target had been taken out and the mission clock was ticking.

A cavalcade of lights bounced through the trees, headlights blended with torchlights, all coming to a halt within the Great Plaza. Vehicle doors opened and slammed in anxious haste. Feet skidded and padded in different directions. Matt squinted through his night vision goggles as the processor tried to compensate for the excessive brightness that bleached the image. At the side of the smeary picture a figure caught his attention. The man moved slowly amid manic soldiers, walking with unique dignity. Matt wasn't certain, but something about the man seemed familiar. Others ducked and cowered, cautious of an unseen enemy among them. This man, though, appeared to be devoid of fear. He walked upright, confidently approaching Temple I. Two officers saluted him as he stepped effortlessly up the steep steps to the new entrance carved in the pyramid's face.

Matt took his chance. The plaza was chaotic. One more headless chicken was not going to attract any attention. He ripped off his goggles and walked purposefully in the direction of the pyramid, head down. He didn't even want to think how far he was from his comfort zone. Two Guatemalans stood between him and the entrance to the temple. Matt gripped his weapon hard, knowing that even if he had the nerve to use it against them, it would be suicide to do so – the noise would bring others running.

As he drew closer, an explosion from behind the trees solved his problem. The two men charged towards the blast, shouting orders. Matt silently ran up the steps and was inside the pyramid in seconds.

A man rose from a leather sofa.

'Ah, a familiar face. To what do I owe the honour? Or should I say, dishonour?' asked President Orlando. Matt spun round, checking for the presence of anyone else. 'It's perfectly safe. There's no one else here. Of course, I have ten thousand men in Tikal who will descend upon you in a short space of time and tear you limb from limb, but for the moment we appear to be alone. Juice?'

Matt levelled his machine gun at Orlando.

'Where's Ruby?'

Orlando ignored him and poured himself a glass of fresh green vegetable juice. Attempting to take aim with trembling arms drained of strength, Matt gripped the gun tightly and squeezed a single shot at the glass in Orlando's hand. The recoil pushed him back a step and the bullet missed the President's beverage by a couple of inches, smashing into the glass display cabinet and shredding some of the priceless Sphinx scrolls. It however was close enough to force an instinctive retraction from Orlando that flicked green juice humiliatingly all over his cream double-breasted jacket and over what remained of the scrolls.

'You have five seconds to tell me where Ruby is before I shoot your goddamn legs off, asshole.'

If it were possible to be possessed by another spirit, Matt thought, it would probably feel like this. Those words could not possibly have come from him. Threatening the President of a nation in the midst of his own army was madness. He was having an out-of-body experience, fighting to regain control of himself. The shakes started to spread.

The President wiped slimy juice off his clothes, unable to hide his horror as chlorophyll molecules clung immovably to the fine strands of fabric. The close brush of a speeding bullet was of no consequence in comparison to the permanent staining of what was to him no less than a work of art in silver mink and ultrafine Merino. Neither did the destruction of a set of documents from twelve thousand years ago affect him – it ensured that no one besides himself and Otto would ever know what they said.

'It is no surprise to me that a man of your breeding has no respect for exquisite tailoring,' Orlando stated with flat disdain, exuding superiority and control despite standing at the wrong end of a gun. 'And it appears that you have destroyed the scrolls that you failed to prevent my people taking from the Sphinx. We made no copies, you know. Nice work.'

The unpredictable forces inside Matt instigated an action that allowed his nerves to settle: he put his gun on the floor and raised his hands in a conciliatory gesture. Why the hell had he done that? His instincts were still running amok. He stepped back from the gun and breathed deeply, slowly. Orlando displayed no interest in his actions; with or without a weapon pointing his way, the President was ice cool. Matt wiped the sweat from his face, relieved to note that the palpitations of his muscles had ceased.

'Please,' he whispered. 'It's real important to me. I won't hurt you. Just let me have my girl.'

'You blew up one of my pyramids,' said Orlando.

'No, not me. That was, like, other guys. I'm not really, you know, with them.'

'Tell me what else they are planning and I will consider discussing Ruby's situation.'

'You gotta tell me where she is. Those guys, they're here to slow you guys up until the US can work out what your game is.'

'I see. An inconvenience, but they will not succeed. Neither will you, because Doctor Towers is secured on top of one of the pyramids.'

A complex series of muscle contractions pulsed through Matt. A passenger in his own body, he felt his hands scoop the gun off the floor while his legs propelled him towards Orlando's throat. The barrel of the weapon now pressed horizontally against the President's larynx. Matt could not sense the floor beneath his feet. Rivulets of sweat dripped from his nose onto his lips, but he tasted nothing. A primal force was carrying him to new heights of lunacy.

'If your friends intend to destroy other temples,' choked Orlando, his warm throat wrapping itself around cool metal as the words tried to form, 'you will have Ruby's death on your own hands.'

The destruction of the other temples was precisely Nichols's intention. The explosive charges would be set in place wherever a pyramid was found to be housing a research facility. Timers would be started, documents and technological samples grabbed. They would be shooting their way out of that jungle city before the main firework display.

Matt felt a panic pulsing through him. Twenty minutes. Ruby's life. Ruby's existence. Everything he cared for. Soon to be erased. One piece of information could, however, delay her entry to the great history book in the sky.

'Which pyramid?' he growled. The President started to wriggle away from the gun. Matt recoiled at the sudden movement and whipped the weapon up to his shoulder. 'Which pyramid, asshole?'

Orlando looked at the door, still open to the night, facing the pyramid across the plaza. Matt followed his gaze, expecting to see soldiers, but there was no one. Before he could turn his head back, he felt strong hands seizing his gun. He didn't pull the trigger; it was pulled from him. Orlando dropped in an instant, the green stains on his suit now drowning in deep shades of red.

'I hate to mention a topic unsuitable for mixed company, and I apologise for my Boeotian leanings, but I fear I can suppress no longer the need to spend a *quetzal*,' frothed Ratty.

'Get it over with. I don't like what's happening down there. We should be ready.'

Ratty shuffled to the furthest point from Ruby at the top of the temple and relieved himself over the edge, surveying with fascination the remote animations of distressed soldiers. He craned his neck to follow a bundle of partially illuminated figures carrying a limp body from a chamber within the closest pyramid. They were shouting and screaming and heading for a cluster of metal rooms nearby. As they went almost out of sight he stretched his body a little further, trying to correct his balance by adjusting his feet, but he had forgotten the shackles. His right ankle moved, but only an inch. The momentum lifted the left foot from the ground, and his centre of gravity moved beyond the spot where his limbs could control it.

'Goodness me!' he yelped, tumbling into the void.

'I think Tikal's under attack, Ratty. It could be our chance to get down from here without being seen. What do you think? Maybe we should chance it. Perhaps we can wear away the cuffs on the corner of the stone if we rub them really hard for a few hours. Maybe we can take the steeper route at the sides one step at a time with a safety line between us. The drop looks dangerous, but at least they're not guarding the sides. Ratty? Hello? Am I talking to myself?'

Ruby stood up and looked around, unable to see much with pupils contracted from watching the fires and flashes below. 'If you're looking for the washbasin and the scented hand-towel you might be disappointed. Ratty?' Hands outstretched, she hopped towards where she thought he would be. Other than a strong odour of warm urine – which she could have sworn reminded her of gin toddy – there was nothing to indicate his presence. The platform just ended. Ratty was gone.

She dropped to her knees, walking her fingers to the edge of the slab, wincing as her skin informed her of the presence of something damp.

'Ratty? You OK?' With the commotion at ground level, she was unsure whether she had heard a reply. 'Ratty? Where are you?'

She thought she could hear something – a faint wisp of breath, a gossamer rasp floating above the jagged resonance of ground-level conflict. It didn't sound healthy. The drop down to the next ledge was more than her body height. She recalled it being something like eight feet. Half way around the platform there were intermediate steps leading down, but getting about in her chains was slow and there was no time to lose if Ratty needed help. Besides, those intermediate steps were in full view of the soldiers down on the Plaza. Eight feet was hardly Beachy Head. She could shimmy down, even though in the night shadows it looked bottomless. Gripping the moist stone, she swivelled her legs over the edge and let herself hang against the ancient wall by her fingertips. Climbing back up was not an option. The only move available to her was to let herself fall. An act of faith, trusting her life to her memory of the pyramid's structure. Her instincts warned her of an impending descent into infinity. Too late now. The fingers started to lose their grip.

She bent her legs and stretched out her toes to cushion the impact, but when it came the landing was unexpectedly soft. The subtle sounds she had picked up from the higher level now grew into a discernible moan, and then morphed into curious words.

'I am Bellerophontes, cast down from heaven, toppled from my fine Pegasus. I am Theseus, flung from the peaks of ignoble Skyros by Lycomedes. I am –'

'Stop wibbling,' said Ruby. 'You fell over while taking a piss. And, er, thanks for breaking my fall. Can you get up?'

'Bit of a bang on the bonce, I fear, but nothing a stiff G and T couldn't fix.'

'We've found a way to get down without being seen, anyhow. You've proved we can survive these drops, even with the ankle cuffs.'

'I did?' Ratty sat up, rubbing a sore cranium.

'Come on,' Ruby whispered. 'There's something I want to look for.'

'Of course. The stelae point to Temple IV. We're going to find the greatest of all the Mayan treasures.'

'No, not that. The stolen Sphinx scrolls. They're here somewhere. I'm going to find them.'

'Can we discuss the poetry of Larkin, first?'

'Not now, Ratty. Get up. Help me down to the next ledge.'

The dream was more intense this time. Orlando had been slain by an invisible foe, skewered on an unseen scimitar, just as in earlier nightmares. But when he fell from lush green lands into a foggy, colourless chasm, he carried with him an endless interlinked chain of despairing, wailing souls. He felt as if he had experienced the moment of death of every one of his ancestors, the combined hurt of every person and creature that had ever carried his DNA. He had dreamed with a pain that was real – a focused, intense agony that he felt to his core.

The cacophony of screams ended suddenly, the pain receded and silence engulfed him. He was alone, speeding through a tunnel like a speck of dust in a vacuum hose, his attention fixed upon a distant, warm, welcoming glow.

The light intensified. He relaxed. The worst was over. He was at peace.

But something arrested his motion towards the light, cancelling his momentum. Every muscle in his body resisted the backwards pull, tearing him between two mighty gravitational fields, a rope in a cosmic tug-of-war. He felt the strain of the transition as he moved from one world to the other, wrenched from a deep coma to an unwelcome reality.

Shapes turned slowly before him, forms without form; analogue noise unhurriedly tuned from the chaotic blizzard of oblivion to a clear frequency. The President's face flexed, meaningless expressions flickering on and off, reacting involuntarily to the coalescing visual stimuli.

The transition was over – he was in a metal room, jaundiced eyes wide open – but the sense of pain he had experienced while unconscious was still there. A shadow passed over his face, blocking the glare from one of the construction lamps. His eyes adjusted some more. There were cables and tubes sticking into his body, connected to a rack of machines. Then came an intense beam of white light, shining directly into one yellow eyeball and then the other, leaving him unable to see clearly.

'Welcome back,' said Otto, still busying himself as he spoke. 'You lost a great deal of blood. It took a saline drip and two litres of your reserve plasma stock to get you back.' He tweaked the settings on a monitor and took notes of the blood pressure and pulse readings.

Orlando's face distorted again, trying to form words, but lacking the breath to project recognisable sounds.

'Don't speak. There is nothing to fear. I have everything I need for the operation,' said his doctor in a tone that was at once reassuring and chilling.

'My immortality,' wheezed Orlando.

'No, we don't call it that. I have explained before. You are merely difficult to kill.'

'I died already. You brought me back.'

'There was a drop in blood pressure which led to the heart ceasing to function for a certain time, but it took me just a few minutes to restart it.'

'How did I die?'

'Gunshot wound to the liver, causing blood loss and some internal bleeding. Not enough of your liver remains for regeneration. I will transplant a new liver, otherwise you will die again.'

On the adjacent bed a figure connected to a drip and no longer hooded twitched, reanimating quickly now that the sedative had worn off and in spite of having had a considerable quantity of blood removed. Orlando caught the movement in his peripheral vision and turned his stiff neck. The Patient did likewise.

Identical twins stared at each other for the first time, confused, fascinated, scared. Brothers, helpless and vulnerable, just as they had been during the brief hours they had spent in each other's company forty-five years previously. On the day they had entered this world they had been equal, indistinguishable, and yet their fates could not have been more divergent.

Otto was too busy preparing his surgical equipment to notice the Patient's movement. When he heard him speak, he dropped an arterial clamp in surprise.

'I am happy,' whispered the Patient, 'that our separation is over. It seems that you have some of my blood inside of you. We are, in so many ways, part of each other.'

'What is this freak show, Otto? Get him out of my medical centre. I have no need for a body double.'

'Body double?' replied the Patient before Otto could think of a response. 'That is right. I am a double of your body. And you are a double of mine.'

Otto finished preparing the surgical tools, replacing the clamp that had fallen on the floor with a clean one. He selected a syringe and the bottle of sedative.

'You were not supposed to communicate with it,' grumbled the Doctor. 'We must not allow fraternal emotions to interfere with the great medical triumph that is about to take place. I will sedate it for a second time.' Otto approached the Patient, then stopped and put the syringe back on a shelf. 'No, in fact there is no need. I will proceed immediately with the general anaesthetic. Don't worry – it will not be able to disturb you again.'

The blue and white anaesthetic machine rolled over towards him like an obedient robot as he tugged at its power lead. Otto straightened it relative to the walls of the room then flicked a switch and held the mouthpiece to his ear, listening for the flow of gases: nitrous oxide, oxygen and sevoflurane. The sound was reassuring, and the sweet smell of the sevoflurane convinced him all was well.

'Stop.'

Otto turned his head to the Patient, preparing to overcome the inevitable resistance to an operation from which he would not wake up. But it wasn't the Patient who had spoken. The President repeated his instruction.

'Stop. Switch that off, Otto. This is going too fast.'

With barely concealed frustration, Otto turned off the machine.

'Without the transplant you will not survive the night. I must proceed quickly.'

The President ignored him, turning his head once more towards the Patient.

'I am Orlando. What is your name?'

'My name? I have yet to acquire one. I am merely your twin.'

Orlando looked back at the Doctor.

'Otto, what is going on? I die, and when I come back to life I have a brother with no name. What is he?'

'It is you, Orlando.'

'I don't understand.'

'After you were conceived, your zygote split –'

'I know the biological causes of twinning, Otto. He is not me; he is my brother.'

'That is merely a sociological label which has no bearing on nature or reality. It is a clone, created by nature at the earliest stage of your development. In no genetic sense is it a separate individual. Societal norm may be to regard both bodies as brothers, but scientifically it is a clone of you. It is a hundred per cent you. It is your backup, the physical reserve that makes you virtually indestructible. It is what you misguidedly refer to as your immortality. You have been blessed with two sets of genes, one set entirely redundant.'

'Where has he been for the past forty-five …' Orlando stopped himself and turned to his brother. 'Where have you been all your life?'

'I had a prolonged gestation,' replied the Patient. 'I have only just been born. Doctor Mengele built a womb beneath the ground in which he nurtured my body.'

'Nurtured?' asked Orlando.

'I have kept your spare biological materials in excellent physical condition,' cut in Otto. 'I have taken care of them for you until such time as you need them.

And that time is now. We must proceed with the surgery.'

'Otto, you always implied that you had access to a collection of organs in vinegar or in the freezer or something. Pioneering research, you said. Tissue storage technology that could replace any part of me. Never this. Never a living being. This is a whole person. This is my brother.'

'I repeat, it is not your brother. It is not another person. It is you. It is an entire duplication. It has served no function in life other than to provide for your medical needs.'

'If you take his liver he will die.'

'If I don't, you will die. It is nobody. It does not exist in any legal sense. It has no name, no official status in the world. No one will miss it. You, on the other hand, are the President. You are not only vital to this country, but the resources you provide are essential to the resolution of the great historical mystery of mankind's first technological age. That is the sole purpose for which you were created.'

'Created?' asked Orlando and the Patient, almost in unison.

Otto paced back and forth, searching desperately for soothing guidance from his inner Aristotle. But it was too late. He had said too much.

Large hands cupped under her armpits. Stale breath wafted over her neck. Ruby tensed. Arms stronger than her own lifted her down from where she hung on the lowest ledge of the pyramid. She was finally on the ground, but whoever had spotted her didn't seem to be intent on releasing his grip. And that grip was inching towards more intimate areas on her front – areas that she generally regarded as out of bounds for Central American soldiers.

From her peripheral vision she could tell this man was

acting alone. Even with their legs in shackles, she felt that she and Ratty might still have a chance to escape if she could temporarily disable her captor. She wriggled forwards to create a small gap between them and rammed her fist behind her, thumping into his balls with unforgiving force.

'What the hell was that for?' he yelped, releasing her and falling to the ground.

'Matt?' she spun round, lost her balance and fell next to him.

Ratty dropped himself down from the final ledge. He looked at the pair of them on the ground. Matt was curled up, his grimace obvious despite the lack of light.

'I came back for you,' panted Matt. 'I've rescued you.'

'I say, look, Mountebank, this really isn't on,' whispered Ratty.

'Isn't on what?'

'This rescuing business. Jolly nice of you to pop by, but I have everything under control. I've already rescued Ruby myself. You can run along, old chap.'

The smirk on Matt's face helped to wipe away the pain.

'Come on, Ruby, leave him,' whispered Matt. 'I'll cut those chains and we can still make it to the chopper rendezvous.' He rummaged in his bag and produced the bolt cutters, his bulky forearms strong enough to snip easily through her metal cuffs.

'No, Matt. There's something I need to do.'

'Yes,' chipped in Ratty. 'She's coming with me. Frankly, I think she's fallen in love with me, so why don't you tootle off?'

'I'm not in love with you, Ratty,' said Ruby with a flat sigh.

Ratty hopped away from her in shock, falling on to his backside. When he spoke, it sounded as if he were struggling to hold back tears.

'But I didn't sell the little stone chap. I made my own way to Tikal, and then I rescued you.'

'You found a way off the temple, and that was helpful. Yes, I suppose you rescued me, but it doesn't mean I'm going to swoon and fall for you, Ratty. It's not that simple.'

'Tell me about it,' grumbled Matt, handing the bolt cutters to Ratty and expecting him to make a fool of himself by being too weak to cut through his own chains. When the tool did its job quickly and cleanly, with no apparent struggle on the part of its operator, Matt was disappointed. How could this effete clown consider himself a rival for Ruby's affections? He just didn't get the English. 'I even read about goddamn Mayan archaeology for you, Ruby. I know about their calendar. It has chunks of twenty days, called a urinal.'

'*Uinal*,' corrected Ruby. 'And is that blood?' She pointed at Matt's stomach and started to study him in the pale light of a distant lamp. 'Yuck. Are you hurt? And why are you dressed like a soldier? And is that a real gun? Put it away before you hurt someone.'

He looked down at the inky stain on his front, a patch of the President's blood, the mark of an apparent crime for which no mercy would be shown. He felt suddenly cold. The adrenaline rush that had seen him through the struggle and had powered his nimble escape had subsided. His mind went blank. The preceding events became a blur. He felt his strength sapping. The hero's plinth that he had briefly usurped was no longer his. The plain New York writer, creator of stories, spinner of fantasies, dropped to his knees.

'Ratty, he's hurt. Help me get his jacket off.'

The last thing Ratty felt like doing was assisting in the undressing of his love rival. He let Ruby do the deed while he stood by, mumbling a succession of abusive epithets in ancient Greek. Ruby soon found that the blood had not originated from within Matt. She covered him up and stared pityingly at the non-functioning lump of a man plonked at her feet. He was in shock, reduced to total incapacity, a completely useless man.

Nothing new there, then, she told herself.

Ratty picked up Matt's gun and bag with one hand, and helped Ruby pull him to his feet with the other. Between them they began to drag the American from the scene.

There was something Matt had to tell them. Something important. He fought to recall the information swimming hard against the receding tide of his memories, floundering. He had found Ruby, but that wasn't enough. There was some kind of danger, but what was it? He needed to explain to them about – no, it was gone.

It was a story Otto had never wanted to tell, and it gave Orlando no pleasure to hear it told, but he insisted on the full details. Brazil had been a long time ago, Otto explained, and the world had been a different place back then. The shadow of World War II dulled the brightness of that country, its population steadily polluted by an influx of former Nazis seeking a new life, anonymity and – most elusive of all – sympathy. But for one notorious SS officer the motive had been different. The experiments he had carried out on thousands of sets of twins in Auschwitz had been regarded as sadistic and vicious. Otto tried to explain the mass murders in the context of the larger historical picture. He tried to justify them, which was something he felt uniquely placed to do. No one else had ever been privy to the reasoning behind that loathsome episode. The prevailing historical opinion was that Josef Mengele was insane, a psychopath given unprecedented opportunity for evil. Otto knew differently.

'The knowledge acquired by Josef Mengele could have been achieved in other ways, but it would have taken decades,' Otto continued. 'In just two short years he was able to develop his science ready to move to the next stage. After the war he was forced to emigrate to South America, taking with him nothing but his medical research notes, the only surviving copy of an ancient Greek philosophical text and the Mayan stele he had inherited. It was in the small, remote Brazilian town of Linha São Pedro that he was able to merge into an ex-pat German community and further his research.

'Some years after his arrival, I was born to German parents who had also escaped the European post-war mania for retribution and come to South America to seek a new beginning. But they were hunted like wolves, forced to keep moving, never settling. My mother couldn't take the isolation, but my father had no choice but to continue seeking ever more remote abodes. In the early fifties they separated, and left me at the door of Doctor Mengele. He adopted me. He began training me to continue his medical research even while I was still a child.

'During the next fifteen years he perfected in vitro fertilisation techniques, building on the knowledge he had gained during the war. He was at least ten years ahead of the rest of the world in this respect. Many women of Linha São Pedro gave birth to twins whilst under his care. Finally, in 1967, a young, fertile virgin girl came to Josef for medical attention. Without her full understanding, he hyper-stimulated her ovaries with human chorionic gonadotropin. Her eggs were removed and fertilised in a petri dish with sperm from a healthy young male. When this virgin girl found herself pregnant with twins she was eager to give up her babies and avoid a life of shame.

Josef and I promised to take care of them and not to reveal her secret. That is how you were created.'

'How,' said Orlando, trying to remain composed, 'but not why.'

'Both of you were taken immediately to Guatemala. That is where your destiny was to be fulfilled. That destiny is playing out right now, and I must proceed with the operation.'

'Tell me more about the young male who donated the sperm,' whispered the Patient.

'There is no more to tell,' deflected Otto, looking once again at the anaesthetic machine. 'Be silent.'

Orlando and the Patient turned to face each other. The look in their eyes confirmed that each was thinking the same thing. Their first moment of fraternal bonding had taken place. It was instinctive, as if they could read each other's thoughts. Together they had made a profound discovery. One of the major unanswered questions of their lives had been resolved.

'You still have not told us why we were created,' stated Orlando. He paused in order for the Patient to continue on their behalf.

'I have done my research over the years,' said the Patient. 'I learned a great deal from books, studying alone in secrecy every night, so I have my theories, but I would appreciate an explanation. I think we both deserve to hear it from our own father.'

Wisdom is knowledge, the Doctor reminded himself. His patients demanded knowledge of the primary cause of their birth, the explanation for their very existence, and in Aristotelian terms that was something to applaud. The reason why something happened, he generally believed, should always be reducible to a formula, a basic principle. But contrary to his philosophical leanings, the reason for the creation of these twins was not a small idea or concept, just as it was not a random event in the manner that most births are. The Mengele destiny ran deeper, stretched further, than anyone imagined. The Nazi association was a mere episode, a transient opportunity taken to extreme. The propagation of the Aryan race was of no interest to any Mengele. There was no profound loyalty to Hitler or his vile ideologies. Otto certainly had no interest in that subject. He had dropped the Gerhard pseudonym and resumed the use of the Mengele name of his adoptive father when, in 1979, he had learned that Josef had suffered a stroke while swimming off Bertioga in Brazil during a brief visit to some old friends. Once Josef's body had been mummified and sealed in his casket there was nothing to hide any more. Otto was indifferent to a war that had ended before he was even born. Mossad had nothing against him. There was no reason for him not to bear the true name of his adoptive father.

Impatiently he recounted the story of the stelae, of the noble adventures of Karl Mengele, skipping over the details which he was confident the two men already knew, which was most of them. He was trying to expound the why. The why was in his soul. He had grown up with it. Indoctrinated. Brainwashed. It was his life. It was the motive for every action he ever took. And yet, when he tried to elucidate it, he faltered. It was too obvious to explain. Too fundamental to be put into words.

'The stele was just the beginning,' Otto continued. 'The location that it leads to is very close to this place, and we will soon find it. And when we do, we will control all the knowledge that matters. But how we deal with the information we learned from the stelae and the scrolls, that is the why. How we direct our planet to cope with the future, that is the why. And how we prepare ourselves for the threat that will come from the past, that is also the why. Mengele created a human system, designed to span several generations, designed to prepare humanity for the significance of the end of the Mayan calendar. I am part of that system. You, Orlando, are part of that system, as is your collection of back-up cells and tissues.'

There was little in that speech that was news to Orlando, and even the Patient had surmised much of it from his extensive learning and his observations of Otto.

'This project is not something that can be resolved by an individual,' continued the Doctor. 'The resources of an entire nation are needed. That is why you were put in power, Orlando.'

'I was not put in power, Otto. I led my people. We fought hard, we fought well, and I took power.'

'And where do you suppose the funding came from? Who paid for the wages of your fighting men for all those years? Who bought the weaponry you needed?'

'You directed the funding requirements from the beginning, Otto. You told me it was from our supporters in the French government.'

'Wrong. A Swiss bank account, stuffed with the bounty of war. Jewish gold. Stolen money. A fortune set aside in the nineteen forties by a man intent on funding a revolution that he knew he would never live to see. When our reserves ran low there was a requirement for some additional support from the French in return for a promise of shared technological research, but essentially it was Mengele who paid for everything. It was the stolen wealth of the German and Polish Jews that was used to fund your work. They could never know it, but their sacrifice was not in vain. They each played a small part in our scheme, and in doing so they will one day be credited, by historians looking back on this period of history, as contributing to the saving of the planet. But, Orlando, that will all be thrown away if you don't receive a new liver. I will not permit the operation to be delayed any longer.'

Temple IV was just a few hundred yards along the Tozzer Causeway from the Great Plaza. Most of the commotion was happening in the other direction, particularly around the North Acropolis and Temple I. Gunshots and shouts still penetrated the night, and as Ruby and Ratty half-dragged Matt through the black shadows past Mundo Perdido, the Lost World Plaza, they were aware of a scuffle taking place to their left. An American voice stood out among the disorder. He sounded frightened as he pleaded for mercy.

The voice connected with Matt. The thousand-yard stare in his eyes dissipated. His blood pressure increased, efficiently flooding his limbs with strength. The memories came back. His limp hands abruptly turned to rock and gripped his companions hard.

'We have to get outta here,' he growled. 'I came in with a Special Forces team.'

Ruby jolted out of his grip, her annoyance easily sensed by the two men.

'Matt, this is no time for more of your bullshit stories. Listen, Orlando told me the scrolls are here. We have to find them.'

'They're going to blow this place to bits,' Matt protested. 'We have to get to the RV point before it's too late.'

'Stop it, Matt. You've been living this fantasy for years. I've humoured you because I respect you as a writer, and because, I suppose, I felt something for you, but I've come to realise that your book had to be a work of fiction. I know you too well. You were never a soldier, and certainly never part of any elite Special Forces. When you say stuff like that, you just come across as a delusional loser, a sad fantasist. It's time to grow up. You are who you are. You're a writer, a nice guy, and you came back for me. That's enough. You don't need to invent stories to impress me. Come on. Help me look for the scrolls.'

'Those scrolls? The ones you found in the Sphinx? I think you should forget them. The pyramids are gonna blow.'

'No one's going to blow up these pyramids. Not even the Americans would do that.'

'But it's true – I'm part of a Special Forces op.'

'These lies are going to get you in trouble one of these days, Matt. Dressing up as a soldier is not the same as –'

'Will you just shut up for a second?' he whispered indignantly, wishing he could scream at her. 'I've just shot the goddamn President. I couldn't be in more trouble if I tried.'

The voice of Nichols rose high in the night air. It had a tone of desperation, every decibel produced with great effort, laced with pain. Matt stood up straight.

'Give me that,' he instructed Ratty, taking the machine gun from his hands. 'It's not a goddamn water pistol.'

'What are you doing?' gasped Ruby.

'Wait here,' he replied, sprinting towards the Lost World Plaza.

Ratty and Ruby stood in silent bewilderment, unsure what had just happened and what they should do about it. A comforting arm found its way around Ruby's neck and was indignantly shaken off.

'Why don't you love me?' she heard whispered in her ear.

'Ratty, this is not the time or the place to talk about this stuff. Matt could be in danger. Come on.'

She grabbed his hand, flooding his brain with endorphins from that simple contact, and dragged him to the stone wall that surrounded the Lost World compound. They crept behind the fortification looking for a place where they could climb up and gain a vantage point.

Immense stucco masks of the Mayan sun god gazed down serenely upon the dimly-lit plaza, their chiselled features worn by passing aeons into smooth ripples of stone. The pyramid at the centre of the Mundo Perdido complex, on which the masks were set, formed a tower of breath-taking grandeur. Millions of tonnes of stone squatted arrogantly in the landscape, part of an ancient astronomical observatory in slow decay.

'The Lost World Pyramid and Plaza takes its nomenclature from Sir Arthur Conan Doyle's novel of the same title,' wibbled Ratty as they climbed a mound of overgrown rubble that provided unobstructed access to the top of the ancient wall. 'The first archaeologists to study this area considered the green mossy pyramid and hanging vines to be a perfect evocation of the –'

'Shush, Ratty. Look.'

She pointed at the scene immediately beneath them. Ratty stared down in horror. At the base of a series of weathered steps that had been out of bounds to the public even before the military takeover due to their treacherous incline, Matt was shouting. He was doing his best to intimidate, showing himself to be the leader of the pack. He threw himself into the role, acting the part. It was a tricky part to play, especially when the pack consisted of five Guatemalan privates lined up as an execution squad, intent on shooting their prisoner.

Nichols went quiet. Mountebank was in control now. Nichols's fate rested with the famous, if enigmatic, officer who had shocked the firing squad into halting with an insane display of primeval belligerence. The performance had convinced the Guatemalans to lower their rifles. Nichols put his good arm over Matt's shoulder, and the two of them began to edge backwards out of the plaza with Matt's gun still aimed at the enemy.

The whole incident elevated Matt's military experience on to a new stratum. Real soldiers practised scenarios like this, quickening their responses, toughening their nerves, but despite his false credentials, Matt felt comfortable with the shouting and screaming, with the hysterical and intimidating jumping up and down like a monkey on a trampoline. He felt completely prepared. This was a scene he had lived in his mind in intricate detail. He had studied the psychology behind tribal supremacy, leadership among simian groups, and he had written an almost identical scene in his book. And, unlike the medical scene where he saved an injured soldier's life with a tourniquet, this chapter had not been the last-minute embellishment of an over-zealous editor. This was something he had worked out for himself, and the theory was translating into practice beautifully. He had carried out a high stakes rescue perfectly. This was medal-winning stuff.

He shouted an instruction at the Guatemalans to stay put as he and Nichols continued their slow reverse manoeuvre against the wall, four heavy feet dragging furrows through the dirt. Nichols was weakening, placing a greater strain upon Matt's shoulder. The parallel with fiction was about to end. In his book, Matt had stolen a pick-up at this point and they had sped away to safety. There was no such opportunity for a rapid escape here, but, restricted by the tunnel vision response to the immediate threat, he hadn't been able to plan that far ahead.

Something jabbed the small of Matt's back. Nichols saw it through his fading peripheral vision.

'Shit,' he whispered. 'Company.'

Matt lowered his aim, and the five soldiers sprinted over to help the new arrival to take care of his captives. The pack had overthrown their leader. Matt was nothing now. All the manic chest-beating and hollering was quickly forgotten. Nichols was slipping in and out of consciousness. Amid the Spanish shouts, Matt heard him whisper one more thing.

'Five minutes. They blow in five minutes.'

Despite his increasing jaundice, Orlando felt a degree of potency returning to his muscles as the drip steadily delivered more essential fluids to his veins and the local anaesthetic, grudgingly applied to his stomach, removed the gnawing agony of his injury. With a great effort, he pushed himself up onto his elbows in order to face Otto more squarely and to give himself a clearer view of his newly-discovered brother. He also had a chance to see the interior of this field clinic with its blue paint, bare shelves and unopened boxes of research materials. On top of one such box was a ring of keys.

'I died this evening, my brother,' Orlando said, looking at the padlocks that secured his sibling to the steel bed frame. 'Otto brought me back. I always knew that I would survive death in most of its forms. That is what I had always believed, though I never realised at what price. But if he had not succeeded in bringing me back to this world, I now realise everything would have been all right. A copy of me would have survived. You are my immortality, my brother. I died already. I'm not immortal, and yet I will not truly die. I know there's nothing to fear. I worked hard and took many risks. It has not been easy. Forty-five years up here, strutting in the sun, fulfilling that Mengele dream. You, meanwhile, never saw the sun, never experienced the world going on above your head. We could have shared the dream, shared our journey through those decades.'

The Patient stared calmly at his brother during this speech, showing no emotion. However poetic the words, the fact remained that he would shortly be put to sleep for ever and he had learned not to react visibly in response to any threat from Otto. He watched as his brother summoned more energy to his arms and pushed himself to a fully seated position.

'You must lie back down,' stated Otto. 'Movement may cause further blood loss.'

Orlando breathed deeply, consciously trying to replenish the tiny reserves of strength that he had already depleted. With a cry of pain, he swung his legs off the edge of the bed. Otto tutted, frustrated by his patient's pointless gesture.

'What gives me the right to take the liver of my living sibling?' panted Orlando, still short of strength. 'Josef worked all his life for a result he would never see. Father, brother, I believe I have done the same. There is no shame in that. Many people contribute to great things that flower after they are gone. I have had my time. I have come close. It is my wish to hand over the baton to my brother, that he may blossom in the sun. I refuse to let you operate on me, Father. Brother, I hand you my name and my life. I have no further use for it.'

The Doctor had heard enough. He needed to regain control of his rebellious patient. He hit the button of the anaesthesia machine once again and yanked the tube of flowing gases towards Orlando's mouth.

Summoning every molecule of energy in his muscles, Orlando ducked through the sweet outflow of the approaching mask, lunged for the set of keys and threw himself to the floor beside his brother's bed, knocking it slightly askew, setting the anaesthesia machine spinning on its wheels and shaking up a tray of neatly arranged surgical instruments. He expected Otto to stop him immediately as he released the first padlock, but the Doctor was unable to prevent himself straightening the machine and then aligning the bed once more to be parallel with the wall. The Patient grabbed the keys with his free hand and set about unlocking himself while Orlando slumped, a dead weight, to the floor. By the time Otto had set all of the surgical tools back in their perfect positions the Patient had risen from his bed. He stepped over his brother and stood facing Otto.

'Get back on the bed!' ordered Otto.

The Patient easily pushed Otto backwards, letting him fall on the plywood floor with a thump that rattled the tray of surgical instruments again.

'Orlando,' said the Patient, 'we truly are a single soul dwelling in two bodies.'

There was no response. Orlando had begun bleeding once more, his strength completely gone. The Patient picked him up with strong arms and placed him gently back on his bed. He looked down at Otto; the Doctor's face was contorted with anger. A sturdy foot applied to his chest was sufficient to prevent him getting up.

'Listen to me,' grumbled Otto. 'You do not understand what you are doing. There is a global perspective to this. I must be allowed to continue. Listen to me.'

'Otto,' replied the Patient calmly, 'I have been listening to you all of my life. I have been extremely patient. I have had no opportunity to do anything but listen to you. I feel I am ready to make my own destiny now.' He picked up the hissing gas hose and rammed the mouthpiece onto Otto's face, pushing it tight as he counted the seconds. By the time he reached number four, any sign of resistance had ceased entirely.

It looked like a piece of the night sky was falling. A black Ratty-shaped figure fell quickly above them, accelerating from the top of the wall and landing heavily upon two of the Guatemalans inside the Lost World Plaza. As faces turned towards the distraction, Matt grabbed the M9 pistol from his bag and fired at the two nearest soldiers, letting his arm spring back from the recoil after each shot. He was tuned back into his fictional alter ego, the fearless hero who could blast his way out of any scrape. The men dropped instantly, like characters written out of his book, annihilated by the hand of the omnipotent writer. The two who remained on their feet, sensing the return of Matt the raging animal, sprinted away from the epicentre of his wrath. Those knocked to the ground by the falling shape scrambled out from beneath it and stumbled away.

Matt inhaled deeply, then panted like a pop legend about to run onto a stage before fifty thousand fans. He was hyping up his strength, feeding his body with the power of success. One of the retreating soldiers appeared to be summoning assistance on his radio. Matt had seconds to get himself and Nichols out of Mundo Perdido to a place of relative safety before the Guatemalans regrouped and returned. He pulled Nichols's limp arm across his back and tried moving. It was virtually impossible to carry him. Two hundred pounds of unconscious man plus heavy kit did not drag easily. Nichols had already lost his main rucksack, but the equipment still strapped to him weighed a considerable amount. Matt unhooked the grab bag and webbing and threw it on the ground.

'Oof,' complained a voice at his feet.

Matt looked down, concerned that one of the soldiers he had felled might be sufficiently alive still to be a threat.

'Awfully sorry to drop in like that,' continued the voice. 'Lost one's footing on the mossy stone. Bothersomely damp, don't you know.'

'Take his other arm,' sighed Matt, yanked against his will from fictional hero mode back to the reality of being stuck in a jungle city with an incompetent aristocrat. 'Help me get him outta here.'

In the shadows close to the Tozzer Causeway, Ruby was waiting for them out of sight. She leaned nervously against the flat surface of a crumbling stele, its ancient message long since lost to the ravages of nature. Without a word she picked up Nichols's legs. With three now carrying him they were able to jog towards Complex N, a site of small temple mounds and ruins close to Temple IV, a place that had so far evaded the attention of the Guatemalan military.

Word of the fracas at Mundo Perdido was spreading. Soldiers not caught up in other skirmishes were directed to the complex. Paulo Souza received an order to cease his work at the Temple V research base and to take charge of the situation in the Lost World. He took the long route, preferring to avoid the central areas where there appeared to be more fighting. His path brought him face to face with Ruby and her companions. Despite the soft starlight, he recognised her immediately. She glared at Paulo with a harshness that released butterflies in his stomach. Her look reflected all of the wrongs he had committed against her: the deception he had crafted to persuade her to work for him in Guatemala; the remorseless manner in which he had carved the heart out of many of the Tikal monuments; and the placing of shackles around her ankles upon the temple. His guilt was not in question, and he accepted it, but there was no time to discuss his failings. He ran on past Ruby and the others at Complex N, heading towards a group of Guatemalan soldiers. He shouted to attract their attention and pointed with his arm.

He was pointing in the wrong direction.

'What do we do, what do we do?' sputtered Matt, laying Nichols down and exposing the shoulder wound.

'Help me find where Orlando's keeping the scrolls,' Ruby replied.

'I told you, forget the scrolls, Rubes. We got a man down.'

'The field dressing,' barked Ruby. 'Treat the wound first. Stop any more bleeding.'

'Right. Field dressing. Knew that,' mumbled Matt as he dug into his grab bag and pulled out a medical pack.

'Ratty, hold his neck while we put the dressing on. Ratty?' She looked to where Ratty had been kneeling next to them and found him lying on his back among the low ferns, out cold at the first sight of the ugly flesh wound. 'Oh God, come on, Ratty, wake up.' Her attention turned back to Matt and his unconscious buddy. The field dressing was in place, but Matt was no longer cradling the patient. He had crawled a few feet away from them and was retching his guts out.

'Not good with gore,' apologised Matt, not accepting that he was simply a victim of the natural reaction to the aftermath of a life-threatening situation. He'd been through enough of those, after all, he figured.

'Help me get him in the recovery position,' sighed Ruby.

The two men turned Nichols onto his side and moved his arms and legs to a position that would maximise his comfort and circulation. His eyes opened weakly.

'Where are we?' he whispered.

'Close to Temple IV,' Ruby answered. 'Who are you?'

'How long was I out?' he asked, ignoring her question.

'A couple of minutes, I think,' she replied. 'It wasn't easy to see everything from where I was standing.'

'Mountebank,' he said, confidence returning to his voice, 'Temple IV is on the target list. We have to find shelter.'

Matt looked at the scene around him. Temple IV was invisible from their perspective, its two hundred and thirty feet of stone cloaked by trees. There was no indication that the tallest surviving pre-Columbian structure on the continent was only yards away. But Matt didn't wait; he dragged Nichols by his good shoulder to the base of a low stone wall and laid him parallel to it. Ratty and Ruby wandered over, unhurriedly, motivated more by a concern to remain sociable than to seek shelter.

'Get down,' ordered Matt.

'As in "and boogie", or as in "assume a prostrate position"?' asked Ratty.

'Temple IV is on the target list,' explained Matt. 'If the rest of the team has done its job, it's going to blow any second.'

Ruby stood up, furious. 'What target list? What's going on?'

'I tried to tell you, Rubes. I'm part of a mission. Special Forces. We've been targeting the research stations Orlando cut into the temples.'

'What does "targeting" mean?' she asked accusingly.

'Ma'am, we are not authorised to discuss mission objectives with civilians,' stated Nichols.

Ruby poked her finger into the dressing on his wounded shoulder until tears filled his eyes.

'Targeting means we get into each location,' he cried, years of interrogation training crumbling under the force of a woman's finger, 'retrieve any research data possible, plant a timed explosive device, get the hell out of there.'

'What? Haven't those temples suffered enough damage? If you put bombs in them, you'll destroy thousands of years of historical evidence.'

A distant blast pulsed through the air, a rumble of artificial thunder that sent a circle of shrieking birds high into the sky.

'Get down, Ruby!' shouted Matt. 'Temple IV could be next!'

'Don't be ridiculous,' she replied, still standing, still

fuming. 'There hasn't been any research here. Orlando hasn't touched it.'

'Every major temple is on the target list, regardless of whether Orlando's actually excavating it,' explained Matt. 'We don't know if the guys made it through, but if they did ...'

'We should run away,' said Ruby.

'We can't!' snapped Matt. 'Man down, remember? And soldiers everywhere. Gotta find shelter.'

'Smithson,' said Ratty, suddenly alert. 'Harvard, 1967. This is Complex N, is it not?'

'Group N, Complex N, whatever you call it, yes,' said Ruby, 'but what are you blathering about now?'

'Smithson excavated a tomb. Wrote a thesis for the Harvard Department of Anthropology. Got himself a distinction, as I recall.'

'So what, Lord Dumbass?' asked Matt.

'The entrance should be right here,' Ratty replied, pointing at a semi-overgrown doorway cut into a temple mound.

Another explosion rocked the night, closer this time. No one needed further persuasion to get below ground. Nichols was dragged on his back, this time down rough-hewn steps into an excavated tomb. As Ruby looked back up through the entrance it was as if the scattering of stars peeping through the hazy night air suddenly exploded, lighting the interior of the tomb in a flash, leaving everyone with a retinal impression of the skeletons and spiders at their feet. Outside the tomb, Temple IV shattered into the sky above them. Splintered stone bricks rained down upon the whole of Complex N, burying the tomb entrance beneath a dusty layer of priceless rubble.

THURSDAY 6TH DECEMBER 2012

The morning sun ticked inexorably higher, pushing the Caribbean night westwards and waking Central America with an intense display of radiance. Sunlight dappled the tips of the rainforest, an emerald carpet spreading across the treetops of the Maya Biosphere. The forest canopy here was unbroken, primeval, a world renewed. There was no sign of the familiar stone chambers that, yesterday, had peeked above the trees atop ancient jungle pyramids. No sign of the temples that had sat like tiny stone islands amid a sea of green. From above there was simply no sign of Tikal.

A solitary figure climbed out through a small gap in the debris that had fallen outside his door. He stood on top of the loose stones and looked behind him at the shipping containers that hours previously had protected him from a rocky avalanche. One of the containers was unrecognisable, as if a giant hand had grabbed it at one end and crushed it. Any sign of royal blue paintwork on the corrugated steel walls was gone. The surrounding scenery was equally unfamiliar, an undulating moonscape blanketed in grey dust. He brushed his clothing and stood up straight. He was tired. The night had been long, the conditions brutal. Somehow he had kept going, hour after endless hour, willing the electricity not to fail.

He walked across the remains of the plaza. Some ceremonial stelae had survived, still pointing roughly skywards like neglected gravestones. The green lawn was more of a muddy battlefield, potholed and littered with bodies and bricks. He viewed the desolation with curious, analytical eyes. It was neither a bad thing nor a good thing. The destruction had merely occurred. It was a fact, and he was looking at it. The sight of mutilated bodies did not connect with him at any emotional level, and he greeted the mutilated temples with equal indifference. He threaded his way around the remains of Temple II. A particularly large rubble mound necessitated an awkward detour up the hill to the North Acropolis, which had survived almost intact, and then he scrambled back down to the West Plaza and on to the Tozzer Causeway.

His destination now lay immediately ahead. It was the precise location described by the twin stelae found by Karl Mengele and Bilbo Ballashiels in the nineteenth century. The point where the ancient pathway from Paxcamán to Uaxactún intersected the route from El Zotz to Topoxté. According to Mayan legend, the site contained a long-lost repository of knowledge that would empower whoever discovered it with the means to survive the upheaval predicted to accompany the end of the thirteenth *baktun* – the current Long Count period of the Mayan calendar, now just a few days away.

He had yet to encounter a living soul on his journey. Those who had not fallen to the attacking Americans during the night had retreated to quarters at the periphery of the reserve. Rapidly migrating rumours of a dead President had sent many of them out of the area altogether, seeking the comfort of home to wait out yet another unpredictable political vacuum. The relentless destructive machine of research and discovery had halted. Tikal had already regained its natural soundscape: toucans, woodpeckers, grasshoppers, rustling forest animals and softly whistling branches punctuated by the occasional shriek of a howler monkey. The long centuries of the current *baktun* were almost over. The process of renewal had begun.

At the end of his short walk he found the road impassable. When mounds of dust attempted to swallow him feet-first, he turned back and headed to one side. Boulders the size of cars blocked his way. In the other direction, a once-proud ceiba tree had snapped in two, leaving a stump and its undulating thick grey roots with nothing to support. He was able to climb over its scarred horizontal trunk and drop down to an area of low-lying rubble at the base of what had once been Temple IV. He knew that the dust, the boulders and the bricks had been part of the pyramid. It had lost half of its height and all of the stone facing on its eastern side, including the external staircase. It no longer dwarfed the forest; it would now sprawl in humble obscurity.

He steadied himself on the loose stones and turned his neck upwards. The pair of stelae that had led him to this scene had provided him with some clues as to what he might find there. He had expected some kind of durable marker to indicate the spot where the wisdom of the ancients had been concealed. He was prepared for a sign, another stele, a monument. The pyramid temple itself could not have been the marker. It was only one and a half millennia old, not nearly ancient enough to be what he was looking for. But it was in the right place. It had been constructed, along with all the other temples at Tikal and in other Mayan cities, on top of something created by earlier generations. Now that its top and side had been blown off, he could see clearly what lay beneath. It was beautiful. It warmed him. It connected with him deep down. The stresses of the previous night became distant memories. The future started here and now. He smiled.

'Hey, Lord Dumbass,' grumbled Matt as he opened

unseeing eyes, not caring who he woke. 'Get your arm off me.'

'Mountebank? Terribly sorry, old chap. Thought you were someone else.'

The batteries in Matt's army-issue torch had lasted long enough the night before to convince them that the rocky chamber contained no other exit. The choking dust that had accompanied the arrival of the debris reduced the torchlight visibility to just a few inches. And though the night vision goggles enabled them to find and crush a dozen furry spiders and a scorpion, and to reassure them that no bats were in residence, the image eventually faded with the power. It was hopeless to attempt a strenuous dig back to the surface under those conditions. Everyone had covered their faces as best they could and lain still, waiting for the dust to settle. Coughing subsided; edgy sleep came and went.

The burial chamber in which they had spent an uncomfortable night was a squeeze for four dead people, let alone four living ones. The tight, sloping access tunnel had halved in length. The detritus blocking the entrance would have to be cleared by hand, working blindly. Ruby knew that if one of the obstructing rocks turned out to be too heavy for the strongest among them to manage, their chances of survival would be bleak.

'We have to find a way out,' she said, already trying to pick up an invisible stone. 'Those scrolls are in Tikal somewhere. I'm sure of it. Between us we can find them.'

'Rubes, forget the scrolls,' said Matt.

'Why do you keep telling me to forget the scrolls?'

'Because there are no scrolls.'

'They're here. Orlando told me. Don't you realise? The Sphinx is a time machine. The scrolls are a message from the past, sent into the future for the benefit of the world. We have to get them into safe hands and find out what that message is.'

'Mmm,' said Matt. 'Tricky.'

'I know, but we have to try.'

'There was an accident, Rubes.'

'What?'

'They got ruined.'

'Don't be stupid, Matt. They're the most valuable artefacts on the planet. They would have been well protected. Orlando wouldn't damage them.'

'He didn't. It was me.'

'What was you?'

'I kinda destroyed the scrolls.'

'Stop it, Matt. You're scaring me.'

'I didn't mean to do it.'

Matt trembled during the ensuing silence as Ruby attempted to process the enormity of his claim. At length, she spoke with a force that reminded Matt of an erupting volcano.

'You destroyed the scrolls? The sole surviving written records of humanity's lost past? The archaeological treasure I spent a whole chunk of my career searching for? Tell me it's a sick joke, Matt.'

'I'm sorry, Rubes.'

'OK,' she said, her voice already hoarse, her breath coming in rapid gasps, 'let's be scientific. Tell me precisely the extent of the damage. I need to know how much survived and in what condition. We may still be able to salvage some of the text.'

'I don't know. Nothing. They kind of exploded into dust and then the dust became a sort of goo.'

'How?'

'There was a bullet, then a spray of glass fragments, and then green juice. And probably some of Orlando's blood. It was collateral damage when I shot him.'

'No!' she screamed, and it sounded as if she were

lashing out blindly at him. 'If I could see you I'd throw this bloody rock at you,' she added, her voice wobbling on the precipice that marked the transition from civilised speech to primeval wailing. 'How could you be such an imbecile? Such a vandal?'

'Would now be convenient to have a little chat about Larkin?'

'No, Ratty,' she barked, finding his idiocy almost a relief from the horror of Matt's confession. She wiped her eyes and took deep breaths. She needed to focus. The scrolls were gone, but she had to go on living. She had to find a way out. 'We need to form a chain,' she said. 'I'll pass the stones back. Someone stack them at the far end of the tomb. Is anyone ready to take the first stone from me?'

Slender hands softly cupped themselves around hers. The rock was transferred. The escape was underway. The blind tunnelling progressed for several minutes, Ruby passing to Ratty, Ratty to Matt. A pile of stones started to form at the back of the chamber next to Nichols, but there was still no ingress of light from anywhere. Ratty was clumsy, finding it harder than the others to judge direction and distance, quickly losing the rhythm of movement as soon as it got started. Matt became impatient with him, grumbling and swearing under his breath. Ruby announced that it was already time for a short break.

'I say, would anyone care for a cigar?' offered Ratty.

'Since when did you start smoking?' Ruby challenged, sounding like an unamused wife.

'Smoke? Never could get the hang of all that malarkey. Charming local fellow, Paulo, gave me a rather splendid Nicaraguan.'

'Do you have any matches or a lighter?' sighed Ruby.

'Good grief, no. Forgot to ask for one.'

'So why offer it? If any of us had matches we'd be using them to see, dummy,' said Matt.

'Mountebank,' wheezed Nichols. 'Grab bag. Feel inside it. Should be a flint and striker.'

'What the hell's a flint and striker?' Matt replied, feeling the unfamiliar objects within the bag.

'Creates a spark. How could you not know that? Get the cigar lit. We'll be able to see for a few minutes.'

Matt pulled a random device from the bag. It wasn't the flint and striker, but it had a button. That meant it had power, and maybe he could get some light from its display. He pressed it and recoiled when it beeped loudly and simultaneously dazzled him with the seedy glow of a faint green diode, indicating the presence of a radar signal.

'What the hell?' whispered Nichols. 'Everyone quiet.' The sound of moving rocks agitated him. 'I said shut it. Quiet, woman. They're on top of us.'

'Don't you "woman" me,' she hissed back at him. 'And for your information I didn't touch any stupid rocks.'

The sound continued, louder this time. Ruby stepped back. The full force of the morning light flooded through a small hole. She grabbed a rock and made the opening larger. A hand outside did likewise. Now there was a face. She squinted through dilated pupils to see the features of her rescuer. With the sun at his back he was just an indistinct shape, a living shadow. The spicy aroma was unmistakeable, however. Oscuro Presidente. Rolled in Nicaragua. Smoked by Paulo. After Orlando, he was the person she least wanted to meet again.

The Patient had observed. He had noted. He had been fascinated. He had learned. The sight of the raw, exposed heart of Temple IV had taught him much, but he would need technological assistance to take his work further.

He turned his attention to the man who had arrived at

the nearby remains of Complex N. The Patient recognised the ground scanning device he was using. It appeared to be the machine belonging to the English aristocrat who had brought him to Tikal, a man who had been the first to show him what he believed was known as kindness and sympathy. A man who came closest to his understanding of the concept of a 'friend'. But this was not the kindly Englishman using the device. He knew of this man. It was Paulo Souza.

The Patient stood on a boulder overlooking Complex N as Paulo appeared to pluck a person from a hole in the rubble at the base of a small temple. Three more people emerged from the same hole. They were grey from head to toe, blinking in the daylight, dusting themselves and each other down. One of the grey people had the same body shape and peculiar mannerisms as he recalled his friend having. The man was tall, slim and had a tendency to stoop. The Patient felt a pleasurable sensation accompanying this realisation. He wondered if this was a normal reaction to the unexpected recognition of a friend.

There was a female. She appeared agitated, angry, fierce. She was pointing at things and slapping Paulo. Then she hit some of the other men. None retaliated. She was an interesting human, he mused. There was a man who moved in a way that suggested strength and another who was weakened by an ailment. From this distance it was difficult to diagnose his condition, even for a man who had spent a lifetime secretly studying the collection of medical textbooks in Otto's library.

The Patient decided to pick his way through the debris field and join them.

'Mr President?' gulped Paulo, suddenly aghast that his apparent defection had been discovered by a man who had been seriously wounded just hours ago and now seemed miraculously healed. He had always dismissed rumours of the President's immortality as the ignorant superstitions of the peasant class. Now it felt to him as if the laws of physics and nature, as he understood them, had been rewritten.

'Shit, it's that asshole President,' mumbled Matt, hoping to be unrecognisable under the chalky layer of dust that was caked on his face and edging behind Ratty just in case.

Having expressed her vitriol at Paulo and at Nichols, one for beginning the destruction of Tikal and the other for completing it, Ruby lacked anything coherent to say to Orlando. It seemed all over for him anyhow. The soldiers had scarpered, the research project had been destroyed. Whatever he had been preparing himself and his people for, well, he'd have to take it on the chin with the rest of them.

'I say, it's Mister Patient chappy,' chirped Ratty with a smile and an effete wave.

'Patient?' asked Ruby. 'This megalomaniac is one of the most impatient people –'

She stopped speaking when the man inexplicably approached Ratty with a broad grin on his elastic face and embraced him like an old friend.

'Paulo,' said the Patient, 'attend to the injured man. He has an impact wound to the shoulder and a broken clavicle. He needs hydration and a sling to take the strain.'

A flash of realisation hit Ruby. Her mouth opened wide in pure unmitigated annoyance. She walked to Matt and slapped him hard in the face for the second time this morning. Then she went up to Ratty and did the same to him, albeit for the first time, realising as she did so that he would probably enjoy the physical contact no matter how bruising.

'What the hell?'

'I say!'

'That was for lying about your soldier boy stuff,' she yelled at Matt. 'I've had enough of your fantasies. To think I let myself believe you when you said you'd shot Orlando!'

'Who the hell do you think this blood belongs to, then?' whispered Matt, pointing at the bloodstains on his clothing. They were now inconveniently invisible beneath the dust.

She just glared at him.

'And as for you, Ratty, I should have known you were in cahoots with Orlando all along. I can't believe you let me suffer all that I've been through when you were bosom buddies with my kidnapper from the start.'

'I hate to contradict, Rubes old *caldo de pata*, but this is the Patient chappy. He was recently in the care – and I use that word entirely perversely – of Doctor Mengele. The Patient's a jolly nice bloke. Never mentioned anything about having a totalitarian régime to run.'

Ruby rubbed more dust from around her eyes. If this was Orlando, there was something anomalous about the texture of his skin. The President looked great for his age, she had to admit, but right now he seemed to glow with a luminescence that was positively childlike. And he hadn't recognised her.

'My friends,' announced the Patient, gesturing to all present, 'and I hope that you are – or will become – my friends, for, after all, without friends, no one would choose to live, though he had all other goods. I certainly have all other goods now – I have been granted executive powers by the President to rule this nation for a short period. But those powers and the wealth that must inevitably accompany them are of no concern to me. I merely hope that I can do justice to my brother whilst I wear his shoes. Aristotle wrote that he who is to be a good ruler must have first been ruled. My life until yesterday has been one of total subjugation. I have been dominated, humiliated, experimented upon and treated with a degree of disrespect that not even the lowest animal should have to endure. If the wise philosopher is correct, I shall excel in my role.'

'Well, jolly good luck to you, then,' applauded Ratty.

'The best friend is the man who, in wishing me well, wishes it for my sake. I thank you for that, Lord Ballashiels.'

'Forget all that Ballashiels twaddle. Call me Ratters.'

'Brother?' asked Ruby after a delay of sufficient seconds to absorb meaning from the Patient's casual mention of his sibling. 'You're Orlando's brother? So what happened to him?'

'All in good time, my friends. I would like to show you something first.' He looked over towards the stump of Temple IV, still impressively high above them even after half of it had gone.

When he started walking, no one questioned whether to follow. Despite fatigue, thirst, hunger and discomfort, no one stayed behind. Four strong-willed, independent-minded individuals – plus Ratty – all tagged along without a word. The serene personality of the Patient had an almost hypnotic effect on their exhausted minds. The tattered rabble followed him unthinkingly across the debris field, climbing as high as the stones would take them.

The mound levelled off a little short of the highest intact part of the pyramid's face. The Patient leaned against the surviving course of blockwork and peered inside. One by one, the others did the same. No one spoke. The natural orchestra of the rainforest spoke for them. What else could they say? There was nothing to add to the symphony nature already provided: a timeless, endless chorus that had been playing – unchanged – when the pyramid was originally sealed, and ten millennia before that when the exquisite item within it was created. This thing had outlasted every human since the Ice Age. It was as close to an eternal marker as mankind had ever been capable of constructing. It was a symbol of its age, a weighty anchor in the ever-flowing oceans of time.

The nose and mouth had partially shattered, but it was evidently a human face. It gazed skywards with the melancholy eyes of disappointment, of waiting in vain. They were fixed upon a point in the heavens, on a place that was no longer there. Leo. The constellation was half way through its precessional cycle, now about as far from this point as it would ever be. But twelve thousand years ago, those eyes would have locked precisely on to that star system. The leonine body would have made sense, been the marker of its age, for this was a time machine, built to convey a message from a forgotten past to the present day. It was beautiful. It was as elegant as the twin stelae that had guided them there.

Ruby blinked several times in disbelief. There was something familiar about those eyes and the shape of the broken face, but the shroud of dust and debris denied her the opportunity to make a connection. The outline of the object in its entirety, though, was plain. She was looking at a Sphinx.

THURSDAY 20ᵀᴴ DECEMBER 2012

The first winter snows rolled in low across the marches. The old house was no match for the icy air that mercilessly squeezed through keyholes, cracked glass and ill-fitting doors. The invading frost quickly overwhelmed the Edwardian oil-fired radiator system. Ice began to form on the insides of the leaded window panes. Tapestries on the walls became brittle. Suits of armour creaked disconcertingly as the metal cooled and shrank. In the mahogany-lined library, however, a fire was glowing cherry red, its coals projecting a small arc of comfort that was not quite sufficient to remove the chill when Ruby's bare neck made contact with the leather wingback armchair. She wore a dressing gown that was somewhat on the large side and covered most of her legs, and Ratty had found her a pair of thick woollen socks to warm her feet. She opted not to complain about the moth hole through which one of her toes was peeping.

Ratty walked across the room, wrapped tightly in an old picnic blanket, and peered out through the window at the white oblivion.

'It's a tad early,' he chirped.

'What is?'

'The end of the world. Should have been tomorrow.'

'Not funny, Ratty. I'm scared. What if the Mayans were right to count the days? What if the scrolls are true?'

Ratty shrugged, overwhelmed by the size of the global threat. The Mayans had been obsessive in their measurements, mathematically accurate across vast millennia, compulsive in their desire to protect their descendants and to keep the warnings alive. They had ingrained their counting system into a religion, into a social structure that was as solid and dependable as the temples they had constructed to house it. They had done everything they could to perpetuate their message.

Then, five centuries ago, came the first expeditions of an unknown nation from across the sea, a different religion, a population dedicated to the blunt, violent exportation of their God, indifferent to the Mayan people and positively antagonistic to their culture and beliefs. The genocide began, the counting ceased, the abandoned temples were subsumed by the rainforest. The ancient warning from the ancestors to the descendants was forgotten.

Also very nearly forgotten was a backup plan: the message spelled out in the written word, sealed, entombed, secure; the wisdom of the ancients sent slowly forward through time to aid a generation they would never know; a repository of knowledge, a chamber of secrets, a hall of records. The concept had become legendary, its existence theorised, disputed and dismissed.

SPHINX SCROLL # 01

I have a memory of hair on my head, but when I touch my skull I feel nothing. I remember breathing clean air, but now my lungs rattle inside my chest. Scar tissue that once sealed old wounds is losing its grip. Movement is excruciating, and even the process of writing is more than I can bear.

Though I cannot use my hands to write, I can still produce recognisable sounds from the flaking bark within my throat. I have a brave and talented female in my presence who is prepared to scribe my every word. These words will survive far longer than my fading presence for, like a fallen ceiba tree in the rainforest, forces of decay are working interminably upon me. These scrolls are my immortality, and I hope they will serve a worthy purpose.

As the heavens drag our planet into the great Age of Leo, we enter a future far darker than I could have ever imagined. There may be other groups like us in the world, but I have no way of knowing where they are or – more importantly – if any future generations will flow from them. The accounts I intend to write may therefore never be read. I have come to terms with the idea that I could be living at the sunset of humanity. We have had our day on this sphere, and perhaps it is time to hand it to another species. But should one strain of our flawed DNA succeed in swimming upstream to an uncertain future, and if there is to be no other record of the achievements and blunders of our kind, I hope the warnings I intend to recount will provide the tools to save our descendants from the miserable existence we have endured.

I suppose I should begin with our place in time. Two thousand years have passed since the arrival of Quetzalcoatl. His legacy of enlightenment was a powerful force that we all believed would forever moderate and control mankind's natural tendency towards extremism. How naïve that mindset now seems when I look back at the violent death of his last descendant, Hocol, and the astonishing speed with which that incident triggered an end to all progress in peaceful science and society.

A million open-mouthed spectators watched the demise of Hocol with a mixture of morbid fascination, distress and shame. There were a few moving moments of silence. They were all thankful that they were not personally affected by an event that was to alter cataclysmically the path of human history.

Never before had so many people been so wrong.

'Any sign of them?' Ruby asked, putting down the translation that she couldn't stop herself reading repeatedly, desperate for an answer.

'Not a sausage.'

She wondered if they'd become stuck in a snowdrift. Ratty's old Land Rover could cope with the British winter, but whether Matt could really handle a manual gearbox while sitting on the wrong side of the car and driving on the wrong side of the road was more open to question.

A clock chimed. Ratty turned a Bakelite switch on the front of something that looked like a small antique cupboard. Nothing happened. Then the faint voice of BBC Radio 4 crackled to life, gaining in strength by the minute as the valves reached their operating temperature. The news bulletin was half way through before he could hear it clearly. Media hype about the supposed end of time, or end of the world, or end of the universe – depending on an individual's degree of pessimism – was getting crazy. The New Agers were counting down the hours until doomsday. They were hiding in caves, or dancing on hills, or even making love on the streets with no fear of repercussions. Scientists argued that the planet would continue its eternal balletic dance around the sun, a reliable rock with no intention of ending it all, oblivious to the fears and dreams of its passengers. The world would keep turning with or without them.

Ratty waited for the everyday political stories. There was news of an announcement from Guatemala that it would begin a reconstruction programme aimed at repairing the damage caused to a number of Mayan sites in Central America, with the goal of re-opening them to tourists within two years. The funding for the project would come from the dividends it was receiving from the licensing of the ancient technologies found there. The United States had also pledged to aid the reconstruction of Tikal, the most severely damaged of all the Mayan sites. President Orlando Barillas, not yet fully recovered from his recent liver transplant, but already back in power, welcomed the news. Then came a minor story about the unmanned Chinese mission to the Cydonia region of Mars that had succeeded in returning a sample of the red planet to Earth. The exact quantity and nature of the sample were currently state secrets; only its location at a receiving centre in Hainan was public knowledge.

Ratty tutted disparagingly at the news. His part in the discovery of the ancient scrolls in Tikal had already faded from the tweets and blogs of the chatterati. His fifteen minutes of fame and glory had already slotted into history and the world had moved on. The ephemeral nature of his hero status was of no concern to him, however. He had set out to achieve his personal goals, and to a limited degree he had succeeded. Should any descendants one day spring from his loins, they would have a true-life adventure to read. He had earned his place in the family's wall of greats. It had come at a cost, though. The house had been repossessed in his absence and sold at auction to an anonymous purchaser who allowed Ratty to lease it back again, but mysteriously did not require any rent to be paid. The enigmatic landlord had even paid his outstanding debts, which Ratty considered to be awfully civilised of him. And by the skin of his wonky teeth, and some timely support from the old school tie network, Ratty had avoided jail, much to the disgust of the three debt collectors who had only been rescued from his turret – and its deplorable lack of mobile phone signal – when

Constable Stuart had finally located the hastily abandoned key two days after Ratty's departure for Guatemala.

A car horn tooted. Ratty began the long walk to the front door, returning minutes later with his other house guests. Matt handed a small shopping bag to Ruby. She looked inside.

'What do you call this?'

'This,' he replied, 'is what's left when everyone thinks the world is about to end. As if panic buying a few tins is gonna make a difference. All they had was these eggs. Not even organic or free range options. Six tiny eggs from factory hens.'

'A hen is only an egg's way of making another egg,' said the Patient, already nosing through yet another of the classic texts in Ratty's library.

'Well that's helpful,' said Ruby, 'but it doesn't change the fact that we'll still be hungry after we've shared this omelette.'

She took the eggs and her copy of the translated scrolls to the kitchen and the others followed, settling at the long rustic table. The cold flagstone floor sapped the heat from their feet, and Ruby tried to keep her exposed toe from making contact with it.

They were a sorry bunch – tired, isolated, emotionally spent. Their discovery of the Tikal Sphinx seemed an age away. Which was almost what it was – soon to be confined to the preceding *baktun*, the last recorded Mayan calendrical period. The planet was entering uncharted territory, a *baktun* that the Mayans had not thought it necessary to record.

'So that's it, is it?' asked Matt.

'So what's what?' Ratty enquired.

'It's over. We did our bit. We found the scrolls. You guys translated them. We told the world. Gave it fair warning. If nothing happens tomorrow, we'll look a right load of asses.'

'Would you prefer it if the doomsayers are correct?' asked Ruby, breaking the first egg into a dish.

There was no answer. Ratty looked at the radar scanner leaning in the corner of the room, a piece of technology entirely at odds with a kitchen that had changed little since Georgian times and didn't even possess an electric kettle. The scanner's paint still bore the scars and dust picked up at Tikal, but it had provided valiant, reliable service not only in saving their lives in Paulo's hands, but also in identifying the presence of a cavity within the Sphinx. The pale grey tubes of clay that they'd found inside the cramped chamber were a huge disappointment to Ratty. He knew then that there would be no gold hoard waiting for him, but New Ratty was not someone who would accept permanent defeat. His day would come again. He made a mental note to complain to his anonymous landlord about the lack of a kettle.

The Patient had recognised instantly the value of the clay tubes. As acting Guatemalan President, and with the assistance of Ruby, Matt and Ratty, he had facilitated their extraction from the Sphinx. The scrolls contained within the tubes needed to be opened in a controlled environment and examined with the appropriate equipment. Ruby had assured him that in her country she had access to the finest facilities in the world, and so the tubes and the four of them had travelled on an urgent diplomatic mission to the United Kingdom. The writer of the scrolls appeared to have anticipated the death of his language, and had assisted future translators by providing a pictorial key as well as versions of some passages written in other contemporary languages.

At no point did the Patient show any signs of stress, regret or concern about the events of the night Tikal was destroyed. He gave his father no further thought. The choice he'd had to make had not been difficult. Three men. Two livers. One of them had to lose. Putting into practice medical procedures that he had only studied in books was a task of Herculean proportions, and some of his cuts and stitches lacked the level of finesse that he would have preferred, but his brother had survived and that was what mattered to him. It wasn't as if he had actually ended the life of his father in any case. He saw it as more like a temporary break in Otto's personal timeline. The Patient had followed Otto's written instructions for the mummification procedure to the letter. Not the primitive, barbaric version practised by the ancient Egyptians and other cultures of their epoch – Egyptian mummies were watered-down, pale imitations of the real thing. Their population had carried a vague memory in their collective consciousness of the way it used to be done, but they had no understanding of the science. Without that essential knowledge, all of their rituals and beliefs were a waste of time, mere empty symbolism. Otto would join his adoptive father, entombed, mummified, gliding blindly through centuries that didn't want them, waiting for a new culture to rise and restore them, perhaps even to appreciate them.

In spite of his indifference to Otto's demise, the Patient carried within him something of the desire to fulfil the Mengele destiny, to give the world the intellectual tools for survival. Otto had come close to that fulfilment, but the Patient had been able to take things further. And for what? The early history of mankind recorded in the scrolls was fascinating, and the warning was chilling, but it wouldn't stop the end of the world if there was nothing to stop.

With a cooking pan in one hand and the translation of the scrolls in the other, Ruby instinctively continued reading as she prepared breakfast.

The death of Hocol has triggered so much that I cannot forget a single detail. I saw the golden craft on which Hocol had travelled as it flew over the city. It banked to the left, creeping around the edge of the hills, reflecting a swathe of light from the setting sun that blinded me for a split second.

Hocol would have lain motionless next to his interpreter, Parem, in the luxury of their padded compartment. I saw a thin wisp of smoke rising rapidly as the small missile rose inexorably towards its target. No sound reached me until after the impact, a muffled grinding of metal upon metal followed by a drop so sudden and so violent that Hocol's face must have impacted with the roof of the cabin.

The machine was not destroyed, but it was fatally damaged. From the ground it appeared to dive, arcing low enough to touch the treetops. The power unit sparked and coughed, then briefly fired again with an exhalation of black clouds as the craft regained some height. A thin smoke trail smiled weakly across the sky.

For some seconds the craft maintained a fragile altitude. As the wings twisted in an effort to maintain lateral stability, a gap quickly opened up between the craft and the stained part of the sky it had left behind. It was riding on nothing more than silent momentum. The laws of physics that had propelled the elegant machine from the Earth no longer applied.

The automatic pilot chose a gap between the trees in which to crash land, unaware of the boggy consistency of the ground. The area is marshy at this time of year and could swallow an aircraft whole without leaving any visible trace. It is possible that Hocol survived the crash itself, only to drown or suffocate in the aircraft under the mud.

As a direct descendant of the great Quetzalcoatl, the legendary leader who brought knowledge, culture and technology to the primitives of South America, Hocol had a hard lineage to live up to. His life had become a continual dance of stamping out little sparking fires in the bracken to prevent the forest from burning. That he would not live to see the final inferno was a well-disguised blessing.

He had viewed Tikal as the latest hotspot, a busy and troubled metropolis, over-populated and politically overheated. For some years, the city had resorted to the practice of casting out its poorer classes, forcing them into a primitive existence in the forest. It was a policy I hated to have to instigate, but, harsh though it was, it ensured that the most efficient workers and the brightest and the best were able to flourish at the expense only of the expendable. There were one or two little safety nets through which one had to fall before qualifying as an outcast, but in recent times the number of people slipping through these nets had reached frightening proportions. And yet there was no way in which the underclass could be supported by the state. It would have meant complete economic collapse.

Watching from the wings with jealous and resentful eyes, the ever-growing numbers of disenfranchised citizens posed a threat to the stability of a state that could no longer afford to carry passengers. The sounds of civilisation could not penetrate the forest, nor could the songs and cries of the forest reach into the city. We were each aware of the existence of the others, but I ignored it as an unpleasant thought in the far reaches of my mind.

'Why go to all that trouble, writing the scrolls, sealing them in vacuum tubes and building the Sphinx to hide them if it's just a made-up story?' asked Ruby, putting down the papers.

'If it is untrue, which I doubt, then it must be an allegory,' said the Patient.

'Why beat about the mulberry if you're trying to warn someone?' asked Ratty.

'To warn the right people, without the wrong people understanding,' said the Patient.

'So who the hell is right and who is wrong?' asked Matt.

'That eternal question has no answer,' the Patient suggested. 'It all depends upon where one is sitting.'

'Of course,' said Ratty. 'Indeedy. That is what you did when you quoted Larkin at me, Rubes. "Time has transfigured them into Untruth". Old Otto wouldn't have been able to interpret it in the same way. He didn't share the history we shared, the connection with that poem that is unique to us. You know what, Rubes? That poem changed my life. And yet I was never frightfully sure what you honestly meant by it.'

Ruby curled her upper lip, about to answer him, when the Patient stood up.

'Philip Larkin died in nineteen eighty-five,' he announced. 'On his deathbed he ordered the destruction of his private diaries. The evidence supports a hypothesis that the diaries contained writings related to his father's visits to Nazi Germany.'

'Those facts about his father are public knowledge,' said Ruby. 'They can't be the sole reason for burning his diaries.'

'Correct, but the twenty diaries that Larkin's *father* wrote during the war are held in the University of Hull and are closed to researchers,' said the Patient. 'They are

371

closed for the same reason that his son's diaries were burned.'

'And how would you know what is written in diaries that are held in a city that you've never visited and which everyone is forbidden to read?' asked Ruby.

'Because I have read the papers written by my own grandfather,' explained the Patient. 'I know of the involvement of Sydney Larkin in the Mengele story. I know that during one of Larkin's visits to Germany in the thirties, Josef tried to recruit him to search for the other half of the stele here in Shropshire. I know that Sydney Larkin broke into this very manor house during the war, but was unable to locate the stele amid the clutter. He then became distracted by the manor's library and wasted much time in attempting to impose a sense of order among the shelves. I know that the poem *An Arundel Tomb* is allegorical. The two effigies upon the tomb symbolise the two Mayan stele. The poem highlights the fact that the interpretation of the stelae's inscriptions has become distorted with time, and even hints at the Sphinx to which they lead. The poem talks of "little dogs under their feet", but when you see the stone effigies it is clear that they are not both dogs. One is a lion. A Sphinx. The poem contains a deliberate mistake, leading to the answer of the mystery of the stelae.'

'Gosh. Goodness. Is that true, Rubes?'

'Er, if you insist. It's a better answer than the one I was going to give.'

'May I trouble you for that answer in any case? It would settle a disquiet that has been threatening to disrupt my renal regularity.'

'I was pissed off at you, Ratty. You didn't read my message about the importance of the stele. You were about to hand it to someone whose intentions seemed dubious to say the least. I didn't have time to think about it. I just needed to say something to get a reaction from you without Otto reading anything into it. It didn't matter what I meant. I just had to get you to think about what you were doing. When you read me that poem years ago it made me run away. Doubtless my disappearance made you think. I just wanted to remind you of that night. It was an instinct, a quick, easy way to connect to a side of you that appeared frustratingly dormant while you were sitting in Otto's study.'

'This whole damn thing makes no sense,' grumped Matt, steering the discussion away from Ruby and Ratty's gossamer thin romantic history. 'If the scrolls are not literal, how could those Mayan jungle Jims see into the future?'

'We all see the future,' replied the Patient.

'Bull.'

'You know something of the future. So do Ruby, Ratty, myself and the whole world.'

'Come on, man. Get real. If I could see the future, I'd be winning the lottery every week and if you could see into the future you'd have seen this coming.' Matt flicked the Patient's ear with his fingers.

The Patient remained stoical, refusing to give Matt the satisfaction of a response, waiting for the American's ego to deflate. It didn't take long.

'To continue the point I was making before that unhelpful interjection,' said the Patient, 'I maintain that certain aspects of the future can be foreseen. For example, I know that Ruby will shortly serve us some small, but doubtless delicious, portions of omelette. I know that the sun will set tonight and will rise tomorrow. Looking further ahead, I know that these snows will thaw and spring will follow this winter. I also know that the stone from which this house was constructed will continue to decay, as will the cells of all of us present. And, more importantly, I can see further. I know that the wobble in the Earth's axis will cause the constellations to appear to rotate around the night sky over a period of twenty-six thousand years. I know that Comet McNaught will return in ninety-two thousand years. These are things beyond the span of any human life, and yet I know they will occur. The details we cannot predict, but the broad brush of our future is there for all to see.'

A sigh emanated from Matt with a resonance that his companions could feel through their chests. He was tired of listening to statements that he considered obvious. In fact, he was bored, period. The frustration of being refused entry to Ruby's bedroom in the East Wing had been gnawing at him. He knew that Ratty's suite was on a different floor in another wing, but that wasn't sufficient comfort to dispel the gut-wrenching feeling that perhaps, despite the skin-crawling repulsiveness of the idea, something was going on between them during the long winter nights. Occasionally, he thought he could see in their eyes the same sparkle he had once shared with her, but sometimes the Patient displayed a similarly inexplicable fondness for His Lordship. The President's twin didn't appear to be in any hurry to return to Guatemala; he seemed content to remain at Ratty's house for ever. Matt walked to the window, staring at nothing, sensing everything. He had gotten the message. His services here were now superfluous. His publisher had asked him to write a second book, this time an honest thriller. He was ready to write his story of a man waking from a long coma to a changed world. It was time to go home, provided the world was prepared to do him the favour of not ending too soon.

'The message in the scrolls is a clear caveat from the ancient past,' said Ratty, pausing to eat a mouthful of his tiny breakfast. 'Whether or not the peril is literal, one must consider what it might mean for the planet. For instance, you might look at the twentieth century and summarise its first half as a period plagued by devastating war and wotnot, but it didn't happen in a jiffy. Events took a few years to turn queer. If the scrolls tell of great unpleasantness happening now, it could be that it begins somewhere, very small, and it might be years before we know what it is.'

Matt was reminded of the incubation and growth of his own little lie, which after some years had exploded in a shower of truth upon everyone who had believed in him. He didn't care. He had found his own truth, and it was stronger than his fiction.

'Let's assume our ancestor fellows have been dreadfully naughty and done something irreversible that could hurt us today,' Ratty continued. 'If the scrolls are not literal, what might they mean? Presumably it isn't some kind of cyclical natural disaster that they predicted. Could it be that they planted seeds of ideas in their fellow chaps that would fruit after many generations?'

'You mean like the way religions grow?' asked Matt.

'You might be able to predict the growth of ideas, but not the timescale,' said the Patient. 'It is the same with our DNA. That is what survives of us into the future. It was Dawkins who said that we are mere survival machines for our genes. Disposable shells, to be used and abused. It is not we who can look ahead to eternal life, but the DNA that we carry imprinted within our cells.'

'Hey, the Dawkins guy. Never could get why he sells more books than me.'

'A not entirely relevant contribution to the discussion, I fear,' stated the Patient. 'Take the genes that created Hitler, for instance. That particular strand of DNA was blindly carried through the millennia from his ancestors, a quietly ticking time bomb waiting to destroy the mid-twentieth century. But the timing could never have been foreseen.'

'Perhaps it's you,' joked Ruby to an unamused Patient. 'You and Orlando share the genes that almost triggered another world war. Perhaps the ancients saw it coming somehow.'

'Or the aircraft you dug up,' suggested Matt. 'That was in the ground for twelve thousand years. Maybe there's something else they buried, something bad.'

'I don't think we're really getting anywhere,' said Ruby. 'All we know is that an awful lot of people think the world will end tomorrow, and if the scrolls come true in any recognisable interpretation then we're in a whole lot of trouble. The message is what it is. I don't think there's any ambiguity in our translation. Maybe the timing is approximate. Maybe pre-Egyptian mummification was based on advanced science. Maybe we'll all be in for a shock in one or two *uinals*. Or maybe there's something that we missed in our understanding of it. I've been studying the first couple of scrolls again this morning. I'm going to carry on and read the rest of them to you. Pay attention. Take it all in afresh, and make your own conclusions.'

A chorus of groans provided the background tone as she picked up the pile of papers.

'Why don't you at least skip the next bit about Hocol's life story and how the Peruvians invented powered flight?' asked Matt. 'We've all read that stuff too.'

Now it was Ruby who groaned, selecting the next few pages and casting them aside before finding a starting point from which to read.

SPHINX SCROLL # 03

Our nation pushed forward the boundaries of human

knowledge. Libraries filled with texts on every tangible subject, scientists became superstars. They proved that this simple biological creature, the human being, related to and not much different from any other vertebrate life on the planet, could understand and control the physical world around it.

The problem was, however, that the scientists were right. The human animal, designed only to fulfil its basic biological functions, was now in charge of complex social systems, with control of nature, presiding over weapons of mass destruction. The evolution of morality was slower than the evolution of technology. Superstition, distrust and blinkered selfishness progressed further than ethics.

The lack of advancement in philosophical thinking and the failure as a race to learn humility and respect created the greatest dilemma: weaponry moved into the nuclear age, but attitudes and beliefs did not. Humankind was left behind by creations that it had not learnt to control.

'This guy could have been writing about the twentieth century,' chipped in Matt.

'The wheel has come full circle,' added the Patient.

'Will you please be quiet and pay attention to the scrolls?' Ruby didn't look up from her pages as she spoke. 'We have a lot to get through.'

'But you're not seriously going to read everything?' asked Matt. 'Come on, just give us the highlights.'

'Shush,' said Ruby, pressing on regardless.

SPHINX SCROLL # 03 [CONTINUED]

The aircraft in which Hocol died was the zenith of advanced nuclear engineering. He had lived long enough to experience this wonder of science, but it was to kill him.

The simple savages of northwest Europe and of northern America remained blissfully ignorant of his death, of course, as they did of most things, but the educated world went into mourning for Hocol.

I wanted Hocol to have a presence amongst my people, even after his death. I ordered the construction of a statue one hundred feet high and lit by a thousand giant bulbs, but this project was soon overshadowed by the greater issues of the day: the direct threats from Halford and from Atlantis, and the more distant rumblings in Asia.

'Asian food gives me distant rumblings,' whispered Matt. No one reacted.

'A more significant question is our use of the name *Atlantis*,' said the Patient. 'I know we argued at length about whether it was an appropriate interpretation of the word in the scroll, but we have to accept that its use is dependent upon a number of assumptions being correct.'

'I thought we chose it in order to get those hippie types interested in our work,' said Ratty.

'I don't think it matters either way,' sighed Ruby. 'Let's crack on with the next scroll.'

SPHINX SCROLL # 04

The terrible fate of the world is inextricably conjoined with my own story. For that reason I must focus this written account increasingly on myself, not for reasons of personal glory – for I deserve none whatsoever – but because only through my perspective can sense be made of this global catastrophe. And should my body breathe its last during my anecdotage, I have taken the precaution of dictating the final scroll first so that our descendants will at least know the nature of the danger that threatens them.

Hours before the revolution began, I was standing on a

white stone balcony hardly bigger than myself, overlooking the spires and domes and solar panels of Tikal. Leaders were arriving in the chamber below. I gazed upon a mêlée of extravagant hats bobbing about like boats on a pond. The leaders were in a subdued mood, their voices failing to register above the squeaking and clattering of the cables that pulled the public transporters constantly up and down the street.

I stepped inside and opened the chocolate cupboard on the wall. I helped myself to a large chunk and let it melt on my tongue, relaxing as the liquid slid down my throat and the mild intoxicants sped to my brain. I shoved a smaller piece in my shoulder bag for later, put on my gold-trimmed hat and had started to descend the staircase when a muffled explosion threw me down the steps onto the body of my personal assistant.

In all the confusion, the thought occurred that I had always wanted to lie on top of her. As a member of the ruling class, selected in infancy for my intelligence and creativity, I was expected to be and to remain homosexual. Reproduction was left to the lower social classes, a chore deemed unsuitable for 'thinkers'. I was famed, however, for my complete celibacy, and much admired during times of prosperity for judgements unimpaired by the euphoria of sex. However, the truth was that my heterosexual urges were in constant conflict with my expected bias.

The ebullient eyes of a former nuclear scientist looked down upon my terrified face. I knew of this man. Halford had been cast out when I ceased investing in new nuclear technologies. No longer able to pay his taxes, he was forced into exile. His time in the forests was not spent idly – his writings quickly made him famous and earned him free food and simple lodging from his numerous supporters, people who regarded him as their return ticket to the prosperity they had once known.

I didn't know at the time whether Halford had started to train his followers as an army, but it was widely believed that the assassination of Hocol was the result of a lucky pot-shot by a Halford supporter. Now Halford had struck at me directly. Strengthened by the growing unrest following Hocol's death, his supporters had been persuaded to attack.

He sneezed explosively, but I was too scared to move an arm to wipe the spit from my face. I had heard rumours that he had caught a recurrent sickness from living rough, a mild cold that had stayed with him since his initial exile.

'I know you, Jamel. You know me, I take it?' asked Halford, brushing back his hair with one hand while keeping a weapon aimed at me with the other.

I wriggled, uncomfortable on my assistant's body. I nodded in nervous recognition of the notorious rebel leader.

He sneezed again, making no effort to direct his germs anywhere other than at my face.

'I don't want to kill you,' continued Halford with a sickly grin, gazing towards me without looking me in the eye. He picked up the shoulder bag that I had dropped. 'Or do I? Not sure. What's this? Chocolate? Is that what great leaders carry?' He gave it to me, and I ate it gratefully. 'I have a thousand armed men in Tikal today. The majority of the population is with me. One hundred of my best people are in this building. Any one of them would kill you for me. Why should I let them have the honour?'

His tone quickly changed from false joviality to bitterness.

'Perhaps I want the honour. Maybe. I'll see. I'm not yet sure about killing you.'

I squared my lips, about to respond, to try to sway

Halford's apparent indecision in my favour, but he didn't give me the chance to speak.

'Perhaps I should,' continued Halford, pausing to cough. 'Maya could have been great. We could have been the most powerful nation on Earth. We could have conquered lands that possess all the natural resources we need. You have failed your people. I've watched you failing until I could watch no more.'

'Why couldn't you talk to me? You've met leaders of other states, but not me.' I felt betrayed by the rest of the world in my plight.

'I was banned from the city. I couldn't pay the taxes – a victim of the recession you created.' He blew his nose on his sleeve. 'This damn cold is your fault. It's tough living amongst the trees. Anyway, you would have had me locked up the moment I was identified.'

'Do you realise what you're doing?'

'I'm not a maniac. Don't look on this as the destruction of old Maya.'

My bemusement must have been evident.

'This is the birth of a new nation. Maya will again enjoy prosperity. We will become the most powerful nation on Earth. We –'

'You'll lead us into war and deprivation.'

'Hocol's dead. There'll be wars soon. Who can stop them? And we'll be ready. We'll be first. The best form of defence is to attack.'

'You're crazy. How can wars help the world?'

Halford kicked me at the mention of 'crazy'.

'I'm not out to help the world,' explained Halford. 'This is for my people. Your people. This is for Maya.'

'For a traitor you sound quite patriotic. It'll almost be a shame when my soldiers have to execute you,' I said unconvincingly.

'I regret to inform you,' he replied, 'that the execution

will be your own. This is nothing personal, you understand. Well, perhaps it is a little. I cannot let you live, of that I am now sure. Take comfort from the good that will come from it.'

'OK, we get it,' said Matt. 'Jamel gets thrown in jail by Halford. We can skip the next bit – it's just that one-eyed guy getting thrown in jail too. What's his name?'

'Sotay,' said Ruby. 'The leader of the doctors. He just lost an eye in the uprising, remember? I really think it's a bad idea to leave anything out. We need it all in context.' She looked vainly at her companions for a sign of agreement. 'Fine. Whatever. I'll start from the second part of scroll number five.'

SPHINX SCROLL # 05

As they took me away I saw the nearly completed statue of Hocol thunder to the ground in a downpour of rubble, killing a handful of the rebels who had instigated its demolition. Through the settling dust it became clear that the nearby buildings were decorated with flags carrying Halford's symbol of a Sphinx, courtesy of a public relations campaign to convert allegiances to the new leader.

The stained steel door of my new cell had not been long silent when it squeaked open to reveal Halford, flanked by guards.

'What do you want, Halford?'

'All the leaders are now in custody. They can do no more damage. What's left of Sotay will share with you. The other cells are already full. Indicative of inadequate provision of cell space by the state during the last fifteen years, in my opinion.'

'I should have built a cell for you long ago,' I said,

turning resolutely away from such insane arrogance.

Halford produced a lump of chocolate from his pocket and childishly waved it under my nose. 'Yummy,' he murmured, eyes half-closed in mock ecstasy. He stepped back, making way for the guards to shove Sotay towards me. He was bound at the wrists, head bowed submissively, and literally covered in blood.

'What happened to you?' I asked.

'It doesn't matter,' replied Sotay. 'I have no further service to perform. I can't help anyone here. My health is irrelevant.'

'Does it hurt?'

He sighed. A soft sound, but from such a disciplined stoic, it was as if he had howled in agony. I flinched in sympathy.

'Yes, but I'm fine.'

I crouched to look up at his face. The absence of an eye made it seem quite lop-sided.

'My eye has gone completely,' whispered Sotay without raising his head. 'I was attacked with a knife and left for dead. Fortunately, they did not pierce the brain. I have cleaned out the socket.' He spoke bleakly, but more out of sadness for the mentality of his attacker than for his own predicament.

'That's awful, Sotay.'

'It is of no matter.'

I helped Sotay to sit comfortably on the floor, then sat with him. Two of the nation's most powerful men now had no more influence than the cockroaches with which they shared their cell. We had barely moved when a messenger from Halford entered the cell several hours later and handed me a letter.

'Can you get us some water, please?' I asked.

'Sure, it's the least I could do. Not much of a last wish, though, is it?'

I froze. Last wish? I looked at the messenger for clarification, afraid to look at the words on the paper.

'Won't be long,' he said, leaving us alone.

I was in good physical shape, apart from the cuts and bruises to my face and body from the explosion, but they would heal completely given the chance. Now I knew that my wounds would never be given the opportunity to heal. I was holding my own death warrant.

'What is it?' asked Sotay, although he already knew.

'A public execution will take place tomorrow.'

'Who?'

'It doesn't mention you, Sotay.'

'I don't care what happens to me, I only care for Maya.'

'They're going to put me beneath the rolling stone until my body is as flat as a bar of chocolate. Halford will then preserve my flattened remains and paste them to the wall of the city. To deter potential dissidents.'

'Not even mummification? They can't do that to you.'

'They can't stab you in the face either, can they?'

SPHINX SCROLL # 06

The cell walls breathed a dirty moisture into the room. Insects trying to scale the brickwork would slide down as if riding on the drips. Little sound penetrated the room, save for the occasional passing footsteps and the clicking of cockroaches.

'Have you ever felt worse than this?' I asked Sotay.

Sotay looked quizzical.

'Physically or psychologically?'

How could he be so academically detached now, of all times?

'The latter, Sotay,' I explained wearily.

'The country I love is facing destruction. Our people

are growing up. They want to try to run things in a new way. It will fail, of course, and they know that deep inside. This is nothing to do with you, except that you were in power when it happened. No one could have foreseen or prevented it. We know that nothing in life is predictable, except its unpredictability.'

'There's a good chance that Maya's instability will tempt a full Atlantan invasion,' I whispered. 'Or they may simply take the opportunity to wipe us out.'

'Halford knows this, but I doubt he'll do anything,' said Sotay.

'He's the sort to press the button the moment he gets scared.'

'Are you scared, Jamel?'

I squirmed at the question. I had never been more scared, and concentrating on the fact made the terror rise in me.

'If I could only get out of here, I could go to Atlantis and negotiate peace. If only to buy us time.'

'You'd be a new Hocol,' suggested Sotay.

'That's what we need. Halford's leaving us open to attack from all sides.'

'They say the Atlantans will settle for nothing less than full scale usurpation of our lands.'

'They have to find somewhere to live. Everyone accepts that. Atlantis could be uninhabitable in a decade or two. Of course they're going to fight for new lands. It is, however – or rather, it was – my job to ensure they don't come here. I want to protect my people ... but they don't want me to.'

A muffled roar filtered into the cell, dislodging a tiny shower of drips from the ceiling and sending a brick crashing down close to me. There was shouting in the corridor, and running feet that came tantalisingly close to our door, but didn't actually stop.

'Pandemonium,' murmured Sotay with a slight roll of his one good eye.

The noises abated as suddenly as they had started, leaving an unsettling silence that seemed even more penetrating than the recent explosion. I picked up the dislodged brick and held it before me, my fingers gripping its slimy surface.

'Move out of the way,' I ordered. Sotay shuffled sideways.

In all of my adult life I had been taught to use my brain rather than my hands. My pampered frame was far from muscular, looking all of its fifty-one years, but I now summoned all my strength at once and hurled the brick into the centre of the steel door.

The shattered silence reassembled itself as the brick dust settled. I waited some moments to see if the noise had attracted anyone's attention. When no one came, I went over to the door to inspect it closely.

'I'm going to get out,' I announced confidently, running my fingers along the slightly buckled steel cross-bar on the door. 'Someone's got to get out there and work for Maya. If I let them kill me they'll be killing themselves too.'

I tugged at the door, but the brick had caused no structural damage and the frame wasn't even loose. I picked up the largest fragment of brick and banged it against the edge of the door, but it just broke in my hand, grazing my palm.

'It's not going to work, Jamel.'

'It's got to. I have to get out of here.' I walked over to where I had been sitting and studied the hole in the ceiling from where the brick originally fell. The ancient brickwork was damp and decayed, and looked easy to demolish without tools, but only by jumping up was I able to reach it.

'You'll bring the ceiling down on us!' protested Sotay.

'There has to be a way out!' I shouted, dodging a falling brick. I jumped up to grab another, but it held firm.

'Hey – someone's coming,' called Sotay.

I tried again to dislodge the brick.

'I'm under a sentence of death, Sotay,' I stated breathlessly. 'I don't care if they catch me.'

'You don't mean that. Sit down.'

I quickly sat down as the door opened and a young woman peered in, overshadowed by the bulk of a man who was blocking the exit behind her. She pushed back her long, dirty hair to reveal a face that was extensively scratched and bleeding, as if she had been dragged violently through a bush. In her right hand was a large bag.

'I'll have to be quick,' she announced, stepping into the cell and kneeling beside Sotay. 'Things are rough out there, gentlemen.'

'Who are you?' I asked.

'I'm a doctor. I expect Sotay doesn't recognise me.'

Sotay turned his eye to her. Every feature on her face blurred into the next, a mess of blood and localised swelling. She seemed oblivious to the pain, able to smile and breathe normally, totally calm and professional. Just as Sotay would have trained her to be.

'Katia,' he said softly.

'Sotay, you're going to be freed. Halford needs you. There have been horrendous casualties today. This is a spare medicine bag. They told me you were wounded, so take it. You'll be down here for another hour. Patch yourself up.'

'An hour, you say?' verified Sotay.

'That's what they told me.'

'Katia,' I said, 'how long have I got?'

The shadow behind Katia moved. A throat cleared, and

Katia backed out of the cell, avoiding my question.

'Katia! Wait! You don't understand what's at stake.' My voice faded to nothing, shut off by the bang of the slammed door and the retreating footsteps.

Sotay silently checked the contents of the medicine bag. It was equipped with basic surgical tools, dressings and needles, but it also contained a range of medicines and gels. He rummaged carefully, then closed the bag.

A reluctant raising of the eyebrows in the direction of the medicine bag was all I could do to offer my assistance in patching Sotay's eye. There was no response.

Sotay stared into the bag, saying nothing, before standing up abruptly and pacing the floor, as I had done moments before.

'What is it?' I asked.

'I think we're coming up to the gory section,' said Ruby. 'I don't mind fast-forwarding over that scene if everyone is happy to skip it?'

'The bit where they transplant Jamel's living eye into Sotay's socket with no anaesthetic?' asked Matt with a level of enthusiasm that was both surprising and disturbing. 'You can't miss that out. It's the part I've been waiting for. The ultimate identity swap.'

'I could cheerfully miss that and bash on to scroll seven,' said Ratty. 'When he writes about the scalpel heading for his eye it makes me feel acutely queer.'

'To miss this scene would be to the philosophical detriment of us all,' explained the Patient, 'for it reads in the style of a Socratic dialogue, and no finer style of writing exists.'

'Well, I don't care about its Socratic structure,' said Ruby. 'Personally it makes me feel sick so I'm going to skip to the end.'

Sotay withdrew a scalpel from the bag in a smooth movement, trying to avoid making the action appear sinister. He failed. I made a conscious effort to look at the room through two eyes, to see in three dimensions. Then I closed my 'safe' eye and took a look around me using only the condemned one. The room took on a new beauty, its intricacy and detail were suddenly wildly visually pleasing, the angular lines of the bricks flowing like poetry. Colour and light were streaming into my eye, filling it with aesthetic pleasures that it had never noticed before. A veil of moisture started to cloud the view as a tear formed.

'Lie on your back, please, arms by your side. Look at the ceiling.' Sotay knelt on one of my arms and jammed a piece of wood into my mouth. 'I'm going to cover the other eye with a bandage.' He reached over and prised my condemned eye open unnaturally wide. Although he did it swiftly and gently, even that hurt. I bit down on the wood so hard my teeth vibrated.

Through my condemned eye, I just caught the glint of a silver blade before the lightning strike of agony turned it hideously wet and dark.

Ruby put the pile of papers down for a moment and looked at her friends. Matt was wide awake, grinning as if he was viewing his favourite horror movie. And Ratty – well, his eyes were already beginning to open. He had slumped forward on the kitchen table at the first mention of 'scalpel', but the colour was now returning to his cheeks and he seemed to be coming round.

'Welcome back, Ratty,' she whispered in his ear.

He pretended to yawn and stretch.

'How rude of me. So sorry. Do carry on.'

'Wait,' said Matt. 'We're at that part where Jamel feels like crap and Halford rants about his dreams of world domination. We should fast forward to the execution.'

Ruby gave up her hope that this reading session would be sufficiently thorough to provide any real enlightenment. She flicked through some more pages and settled on the first reference to the apparatus of execution towards the end of the seventh scroll.

SPHINX SCROLL # 07

All eyes were drawn to the stone wheel, more than ten feet tall and as wide as the fattest man, in the centre of the arena. Wooden handles protruded from its sides, and the short track in front of it was of polished marble. The sharply defined shadows of the handles looked like sinister teeth waiting to devour Sotay. My ruined eye socket still hurt terribly, but it was nothing compared to the agony in my mind as I looked on the spectacle and knew it should have been me at the centre of attention.

Just a few feet from the stone was a small platform with two wooden chairs. It was close – horribly close – to the stone, and it was to one of these seats that I was led. Halford indicated that I should sit on one, which I did, head bowed low in case someone should recognise me despite the bloody deformity of my face. The arena was soon filled to capacity with a bloodthirsty crowd eager to witness 'my' death. Their enthusiasm was both humbling and depressing. I felt shamed, desolate, unloved and irrelevant. The years I had spent being treated with grovelling respect, almost worshipped, seemed a lifetime away. I recognised now how fickle at heart was the populace.

Halford stood in front of me, sneezed twice into his

hands, blew his nose and addressed the crowd.

'Citizens,' he began, swinging round three hundred and sixty degrees to give an illusion of inclusivity, 'I have called you here today to witness the execution of a traitor to the state of Maya, a man who has robbed you all of your prosperity, a man who has sold out your country and thrown away every chance you had to make it great. As your new ruler, I must make it my first duty to cleanse our country by destroying the old leadership.'

As he spoke, Sotay was being strapped to the rolling stone. His feet were tied to two of the wooden handles near the ground. Next, without the slightest sign of resistance, his hands were tightly bound to the handles near his waist. Then his knees were secured, followed by his thighs. A band was placed around his waist, another around his chest, and a loose one around his neck. He was barely able to move a muscle.

'This day will be remembered and celebrated throughout history. You are all present at the dawn of a new hope, a new opportunity, a new Maya!' Halford paused to allow the cheers to subside. 'Is there anything you would like to say before I push the wheel, Jamel?'

He thrust his face just inches from Sotay's features, staring closely at him for fleeting moments in between facing the crowds. Sotay said nothing, did nothing. In my opinion, the only way he was able to get through the experience was by mentally dying minutes before the actual crushing. He had achieved a level of detachment from his body, already given it up for dead.

'Very well. I shall now fulfil my duty and push the wheel.'

Ruby paused and looked at the assembled faces. To her surprise each one was paying complete attention to her, and no one asked for the next section to be glossed over.

This was mildly disappointing since she knew there were some unpleasantly graphic descriptions of Sotay's expiration coming up. She took a sip of water and cleared her throat, then continued with scroll number eight.

SPHINX SCROLL # 08

I didn't want to look, but I couldn't help myself. Revolting though it was, I couldn't throw up because my stomach was so knotted. In any case, it would have caused suspicion if I had vomited because as a 'doctor' it would be assumed that I was accustomed to such sights. It was true that I had witnessed executions many times, but always on the side of the executioner and with a feeling of satisfaction that justice was being done. Helplessly watching an innocent friend and colleague die – and one who had volunteered his life in place of mine – put a wholly different perspective on it. I prayed that Halford would push the wheel quickly so that Sotay would not have to endure a prolonged demise.

There was an expectant hush from the crowd as Halford rolled up his sleeves and braced his feet against the special notches in the ground. He motioned as if to push the wheel very hard, then gave it just the gentlest of nudges. I winced, as, I believe, did most other people present. The wheel rolled forward by no more than ten or fifteen degrees. Sotay's feet buckled between the bottom of the wheel and the marble floor, crushed to little more than the thickness of paper from his toe to the ankle. His scream still rings in my head today. But then he checked himself and started breathing very quickly.

Halford casually walked around to the front of the rolling stone and faced Sotay.

'That,' he announced, 'is for the humiliation you made me experience when I was cast out from the city.'

There were cheers and applause from the audience as Halford returned to the other side of the stone wheel for another push. Again, he pushed the wheel with minimal effort, crunching Sotay's bones and muscles up to the knee.

A sympathetic pain shot through my own legs. Sotay shouted out something incomprehensible, then resumed controlling his breathing. Again, Halford returned to face Sotay, determined to leave him (or rather, me) to suffer for as long as possible.

'That one's for the hunger, the cold and the desperation of my first nights alone in the forest.'

I couldn't understand how the entire crowd seemed to be on his side rather than on the side of the man who was obviously the victim. They cheered and shouted in approval as Halford returned again. Some women held children up to see the spectacle better.

The next push was a little harder, bringing the wheel up to Sotay's pelvis and destroying enough internal organs to cause eventual death even if the wheel were to be pushed no further. He could contain the pain no longer and emitted long, low cries of despair. Now it was I who needed to control my breathing, to control my loathing for Halford.

Sotay was alive and conscious with only half a body.

'What you are experiencing now, Jamel, is the equivalent of the aggregate of all the suffering of all the people who have been victimised by your régime. It's not pleasant, is it? You have no legs, no manhood, no kidneys, no bowels. Your stomach is squashed tight and will shortly be flattened into a paste. Notice how I never offered you a second chance, just as your government never offered me, or any other of its outcast citizens, a second chance. You may moan all you like, Jamel. It is too late. Your era has ended, and in a few seconds you will be dead, as I am sure you will be relieved to hear. Any final words?'

I watched Sotay's face, confident that he would not reveal the truth now that all hope was lost for him. His facial muscles were twitching violently, his complexion already dulling. The crowd hushed. In short gasps he managed to say a few words.

'Halford, you will be defeated.'

'Something tells me you are misguided, half-man. You are in no position to win. Everyone, I welcome you to the new Maya!'

Sotay grimaced as Halford began the final push of the wheel. There was no need to make this a partial turn, for the slightest movement would be sufficient to asphyxiate what was left of him, and Halford gave it a very hard shove that enabled it to roll completely over Sotay's chest and head. The wheel only came to a halt when his remains appeared, upside-down, on the other side of it.

I could not take my eye off this gruesome sight, and neither could anyone else. A former human, my friend, was displayed in the most demeaning form imaginable, mashed across the surface of the stone, fragments of bone and unidentifiable entrails protruding everywhere.

Halford was strutting around, shaking the hands of virtually everyone in the front rows. He paid no attention to me, and nor, it seemed, did anyone else. Anonymity beckoned. I needed to rebuild my life. There would be no point in trying to fix Maya until I had fixed myself. Within reach, I now realised, was the fulfilment of Sotay's plan to get me free to the forest. My return to power would be a lengthy and difficult struggle that must begin with my own mental and physical recovery, followed by motivating and training enough supporters to raise an army.

I took the first step and walked away from the grisly

remains of the great Sotay, now out of sight behind the throng of ghoulish voyeurs.

'Sotay – is that you?'

I turned to the female voice.

'Sotay, come with me. We need your help.'

It was Katia, the young doctor who had visited us in the cell, and to whom, in a way, I owed my life.

'Katia, I cannot help you. You must forgive me; I have to get away. I'm too traumatised to be an effective surgeon. My hands are shaking, see?'

Before she could reply we were joined by two men whom she greeted as colleagues.

'Ah, I see you have found the great man,' said one of them.

'Come, we have work to do,' said the other.

There was no attempt to introduce themselves to me, no social pleasantries or enquiries after my obviously poor health. I had to assume that they would have been well known to Sotay, and that his no-nonsense attitude had rubbed off on them during the years they would have spent working together.

With one of the male doctors on either side of me and Katia leading the way, we jostled our way out of the square onto the streets and walked in the direction of the medical centre.

'Would someone please give Ratty a nudge?' Ruby asked, placing the papers on the table in order to fill a glass of water to assist in the resuscitation of the delicate Earl. It sounded to her more like a hefty slap than a nudge, but Matt's overly enthusiastic physical contact with Ratty appeared to work.

'Jesus, how do you read all that stuff in your library if you pass out at every mention of blood?' Matt asked. 'Do you have a nurse on standby next to your goddamn desk?'

'Bit of a delicate constitution, I'm afraid,' Ratty replied, sipping the water handed to him sympathetically by Ruby.

'So where are we up to in the scrolls? I think we have that stuff coming up about Jamel at the hospital with those neat descriptions of surgery, severed limbs –' began Matt mischievously before Ruby covered his mouth with her hand.

'Sorry, Ratty, but I need to read the next part. What happens to Halford's wife at the hospital is significant to his mental state.'

SPHINX SCROLL # 08 [CONTINUED]

In the hospital, a doctor was tending to patients from his own wheelchair, his leg freshly amputated below the knee. Another in the next ward had his arm in a sling. It appeared that only the fittest doctors had been despatched to find me.

'We have to get you scrubbed up for surgery. *Now,*' said Katia, her battered face etched with intensity.

Katia led me into the washroom and helped to clean my bloodied face and dusty hands. I resisted her help, concerned that if I were too clean my true identity would be obvious. I didn't know her well enough to trust her with the truth. Perhaps I would have been justified in killing her and making my escape right then. But such an act would have reduced me to Halford's level, and that was a level of degradation to which I was not prepared to sink.

Katia was keen to patch my eye socket in order to prevent infection. I kept moving my head around so that she couldn't get to it or see it clearly.

'What do you want me to do, Katia?'

'What do you mean? I want you to be telling *us* what

to do. Once we get to surgery it's your domain. We're following the major incident plan *you* put in place, Doctor, but we need you to direct it. You have the most experience.'

This was a huge responsibility, but at least it didn't seem to involve any actual surgery. Yet I was being scrubbed up, and I couldn't understand how I could be expected to manage the crisis at the hospital at the same time as patching up its patients.

I finished cleaning my face on my own, and kept my head turned away from her. From that position I was able to put on the surgical mask, and then I felt sufficiently confident to let her come close with her swab and bandage. It felt comforting finally to receive treatment for the eye socket. Then Katia declared me ready for work.

I chose not to ask any questions in case she found me suspiciously stupid. We walked along a wide corridor lined with patients lying on the floor, many in a deplorable condition, only hanging on to life. Nurses attended frantically, trying to keep the worst cases alive until their turn arrived for surgery.

The air was putrid with the stench of disinfectant, excrement and vomit. The faces of those slumped on the floor as I walked by were pitiful. They all looked at me with hope in their eyes, hoping their prognoses were not so poor that mummification would be unavoidable.

As we drew close to the operating theatre, the injuries of the patients became more horrific and urgent. A man sat with his severed arm on his lap. The person next to him, of indeterminable sex and age, was flat on the floor palpitating violently, stained with blood as if it had been sprayed over him or her.

I dreaded to see what horrendous injuries would have befallen the people at the very front of the queue and inside the theatre itself. Katia paid little attention to the long production line of gruesome sights at her side. She was concerned only with getting into the theatre to relieve two of the doctors inside. They had been working for more than fourteen hours without a break, she told me. Surely they didn't expect me to match that? Fourteen seconds would be enough to demonstrate my ineptitude.

The first patient in the queue outside the door of the theatre seemed hardly injured at all. She sat still on a chair, holding her hands over a gash in her leg. That she would be treated next seemed a huge injustice. There was an uninjured Halford soldier nearby in the corridor, though how he was of any help to wounded or dying people was unclear. For this woman to be at the head of the queue she must have had his protection from angry doctors and patients. Either she was a doctor who had to be treated as a priority to get back to work, or she had some seniority in the Halford régime. The idea that a prominent Halford supporter would receive preferential treatment sickened me.

The woman was helped onto a bed and her wound laid bare. I winced at the sight of so much exposed muscle tissue and stepped back to allow Katia to treat her.

'Make sure you do a good job,' barked the woman on the bed. 'I don't want any scars.'

'Madam, that may be impossible. This gash runs deep. It will need stitching,' said Katia.

'Do you know who I am?' asked the woman, curling her lip in distaste at the girl who was trying to help her.

I didn't have a clue. All I knew was that she was getting preferential treatment and didn't deserve it.

'I know,' said Katia. 'You are the new First Lady.'

'That's right. Halford will be here shortly. Don't give me cause to complain about you.'

There was a great deal I wanted to say, but I was feeling queasy about the woman's ripped open leg and didn't want to start any trouble.

'You will get the best treatment currently available, rest assured,' said Katia.

'I'm sure you will soon have better resources than in the old days. Halford assures me that the medical services will get more funding than under Jamel. That is why it was a good thing that he died. Good riddance to the bastard.'

'I need to check on the other departments,' I bluffed. 'You take care of this one and the next few, and I'll be back before you know it.'

Katia looked at me, baffled. She said nothing and commenced treating the patient, while I shuffled off through the door. Once outside I walked briskly past the injured and dying, feeling like a coward, but knowing that these people stood a better chance without my intervention. I ripped off my surgical attire and flung it on the ground. Soon I found myself on the street, my injuries passing unnoticed amid the confused, battle-scarred people.

I took the shortest route out of the city and stopped at the western gate. A glass cabinet, just a couple of inches thick, but taller and wider than a man, was being hoisted up onto a display frame, from where everyone entering or leaving the city could see it. At first it was difficult to make out its contents, but as I drew closer the truth became horribly apparent: it was what was left of Sotay, squashed flat and wide, now undergoing the final indignity of public display. Yet to everyone else, that was me up there. It was vile, but it set me free.

I found a reserve of energy and ran. The city had always seemed large, a place of life and vigour surrounded by insignificant jungle. Now it was the reverse. I was leaving behind a claustrophobic urban island and entering an infinite vibrant forest of real life, and real hope. As I stepped down from the trading plaza onto the grass beyond the city limits, no one paid any attention to me. For the first time in my life I was truly anonymous.

SPHINX SCROLL # 09

'Who are you?'

It was an inevitable question, the answer to which I had yet to resolve. The face of the questioner looked too innocent to pollute with the convoluted story of who I really was, so I parried with an echo of her enquiry.

'I asked first,' she insisted.

Could I use my real identity? Was I ready even to admit who I was and to take on the inevitable responsibility and potential for conflict that could ensue?

I was not ready. I was an exhausted, broken outcast. My head still reeled from the events of the past days. I needed time to find myself and calculate a plan. I gave her a false name.

She walked up to me and stood so close that her bare breasts touched my stomach.

Something inside me was telling me to run away. It was the voice of myself as the noble leader of the nation, the hidden me who would one day return and must remain pure and perfect as a man. My head filled with questions about my reputation while my body filled with adrenaline and wonderful surging feelings. I thought of Sotay's great strength and of my own weakness as I gave into the desires of this stranger.

Thus began many months of animal lustfulness in the untamed and lawless world of the trees. I know the sexual acts were harmless in themselves, but the distraction they provided me from my great cause of liberating Maya was inexcusable.

If I could have that time again, I would be stronger and would resist the many temptations. I would have taken steps much sooner to undermine Halford's régime before he could make his great mistakes and put us in the precarious situation in which we now find ourselves. Halford's grip on the people was growing, and it would get increasingly difficult to mobilise an effective opposition. And this made me even weaker, for it gave me an excuse not to bother.

Occasional passing travellers would bring news from the city, and it was from one such man that I learned the horrific story of the death of the First Lady and its repercussions. Her leg wound had become infected, and she had been mummified shortly before she would have died. In his rage, Halford had ordered the execution of the entire medical team responsible for treating her. This had, in turn, caused a general strike amongst the profession, and thousands had died as a result. He tightened his military grip on his people, with summary execution for any political dissension.

Everyone, it seemed, had stopped regarding Halford as their saviour. They now saw him as the man I'd known him to be all along: a power-hungry madman who would cause great damage to Maya and to the world.

Halford was preparing to do battle with the Atlantans, building Mayan forces and weaponry up to a devastating level. I knew what I had to do, and that was to leave the country and visit Atlantis at statesman level to try to persuade them to negotiate peace with Maya. And yet something inside stopped me. My mind was in turmoil, making it easy prey to the new-found apathy that now controlled me. I would spend hours merely staring up at the trees, flat on my back, justifying my inactivity. I was officially dead, I reminded myself. That would make it difficult for me to be accepted into the company of the

Atlantan leadership. I was no longer the leader of this country; it was someone else's responsibility. Always the arguments were the same, and always the memory of Sotay left me feeling wretched and feeble.

One evening I learned from a traveller that the secretive Atlantan space programme had been wound up. There was a rumour regarding the loss of an entire pioneering crew on Mars. The mission doctor had been unable to cope. They were too weak to wait for their return launch window. They had perished, alone, on an alien world.

Most countries, including Maya, had put satellites and men into space for short periods. Even our own little space programme had run experiments to find ways to conquer the muscle-wasting effects of weightlessness and problems of long-term hardware reliability. We had also made progress on the challenge of how to preserve and reanimate astronauts during automated interstellar journeys. This was the key to the doomed Project Quetzalcoatl.

The science of astronaut preservation evolved directly from our medicine. Sotay invested a great deal of time and resources into developing techniques for preserving those who were dying. His assumption was that, based on historical indications, future medicine would far outshine the current state of knowledge, and that if a body could be preserved indefinitely prior to its decay then that person might at some future date be saved. His ultimate goal was to ensure that no Mayan citizens would ever fear death. He experimented at first with cryonics, but a controlled, chilled environment required either a power supply or regular topping up of liquid coolants, and no one could guarantee such things over centuries and millennia.

That is why he developed his mummification system. It was entirely self-perpetuating, requiring no electricity or other external energy source. The intricacies of the science are beyond my comprehension, but the subject is fed certain fluids intravenously, then wrapped tightly in bandages laced with a chemical substance, then placed in a sealed container full of a chemical compound. The effect of the compound is to halt the biological processes within the body, pausing cellular activity without inducing decay or corruption. A reversal of the process with the appropriate liquid compounds should reanimate the individual. The theoretical limit for the preservation of a body under this system is fifteen thousand years, at which point it would no longer be possible to get their organs to function.

Nine months after my disappearance into the jungle, and desperately hoping that it wasn't too late, I resolved to make my life useful and worthy by beginning the fight against Halford. I left my group of friends and returned to the jungle close to Tikal, from where I could get regular news updates with less of the inevitable distortion of facts caused by long distance travel.

Halford was mentally in a bad way, it seemed. In everything he did, his judgements had become blurred by his unending grief for his wife. He appeared to have lost the ability to assess the mood of the people, or he no longer cared what they thought, which amounted to the same thing. All around the city walls were pinned the flattened bodies of dissenters who had been crushed by the rolling stone. I began to doubt that I would ever see a civilised Mayan society again.

I tried developing relationships with other outcasts, but distrust was so deeply ingrained in everyone's psyche that no one would talk to me about political matters, other than to report the facts as they saw them. No one dared express any opinion or criticism of Halford. With this kind of barrier all around me, I knew I stood no chance of raising a liberating force. It seemed useless even to remain close to the city with its inherent risks of discovery by government troops. I took up a position a few miles back in a hidden cave in the side of the hills. The cave was deep and safe, and there I bided my time.

During my forays for food, I would meet people in passing and hear reports of Mayan invasions of surrounding lands. Nobody would say so explicitly, but I understood that Halford had made a severe error of judgement when he sent troops into the southern states where there were many casualties. The nature of the error was unclear, but I learned that in his madness he was planning to distract his people from the catastrophe by announcing another invasion, this time on a grander scale. It appeared to be a prelude to an attempt at world conquest by attacking Atlantis, India and all of the southern continents.

The evidence from my vantage point on the hillside was clear. Instead of being better off under Halford's rule, ordinary people were becoming bankrupt from sacrifices for the war effort, and hundreds appeared to leave the city every day, never to return.

My information about the planned invasions of all the most powerful states in the world was incomplete, I was subsequently to learn. There was to be no actual invasion, only destruction. All of Maya's nuclear bombs were to be armed and fired at every opposing state on the globe. I learned this when one morning, instead of hundreds of people fleeing the city, there were suddenly tens of thousands of traumatised refugees. There was widespread panic; people were stealing vehicles and aircraft in their desperation to escape.

This, then, was the end. No matter where these people went they wouldn't be able to avoid the retaliatory strikes that would surely come. I grabbed as much food off the trees as I could and ran into my cave. As I stood, looking out for one last time over the city and the surrounding lush greenery, I saw a rocket take off from behind a remote hill. People started screaming as it rose into the air, but I knew it wasn't a nuclear missile – they were located in secure bunkers further from the city. The site of the rocket launch was the centre of Maya's space operations, the heart of Project Quetzalcoatl. Someone was leaving the planet before the bombs arrived.

I picked up my small stores of food and water and continued deep into the cave, where I might have a chance of surviving a direct hit upon Tikal. When the blast came, it knocked me over. A ramrod of air made my ears bleed and caused temporary deafness. It was accompanied by a light that lasted only a fraction of a second, but for that time it was as bright as the sun. I clutched my head and wept for a lost world, distraught that I had survived only to face a post-nuclear nightmare.

I remained deep in the cave, cut off from light and unaware of anything that was happening in the world, if indeed anything at all was left there to happen. My remorse for the neglect of my duty that had led to the destruction of the world nearly drove me to suicide. The only thing that prevented me from taking my life was the thought that if survival was to be as difficult and unpleasant as I suspected, then it was something that I deserved. I imagined a handful of survivors struggling through a nuclear winter, living off ageing stores of food and drinking contaminated water, slowly dying from starvation and radiation poisoning.

I was heavily despondent, feeling as if I had already entered hell and must now face an eternity of torture. I wondered if I was the only man left alive, or whether there might be sufficient humans for the species to survive, or whether the number was irrelevant if we were all destined to die slowly from the effects of the nuclear fallout.

When my food and water ran out, I slowly moved to the mouth of the cave, shielding my eye from the daylight for many minutes until I could see without pain. The sky was thickly overcast, but even the diffused light burned more brightly than was comfortable for a subterranean dweller. When I looked out across the hillside I saw the result of my indulgence, my neglect, my apathy. Tikal was gone, reduced to a few piles of charred remains. The surrounding jungle was gone, scorched down to the brown soil. Nothing moved on the ground. Nothing flew in the sky except the fluttering flakes of fallout, whisked up from the dry land by the wind.

I had inherited an empty and silent world. Even those already dead had suffered, robbed of their chance of resurrection. The cemetery annexe was an immense limestone building based on a quadrilateral foundation with four triangular sides that tapered to a central peak. It was designed to withstand the ravages of time and nature, and had contained every mummified body so carefully preserved by our doctors. And yet it had been built at the heart of the city, and had been vaporised in the nuclear strike.

It seemed futile to attempt to do anything. I could stay in the cave and die quietly, alone and in shame. I could go into the remains of the city to look for food and people, but I knew I would find nothing there. Or I could walk east, towards the nearest coast, where it might be possible to find food in the sea. I would probably end up in a ditch, decaying, becoming part of the earth, every atom of what was once me for ever bound up in this dead planet, but I resolved to undertake the journey to the east. It gave me the illusion of purpose and challenge.

I walked at a slow and steady pace for two days. At the end of the second day, Tikal seemed an immense distance behind me, but the eastern coast was still an even more impossible journey ahead. There was no recognisable road or path that I could follow; my only indication of which direction to take was the rising sun, towards which I pointed myself. The remains of the vegetation were eerie, all leaning in the same direction, where the blast had flattened them, as if bowing to their god.

On the morning of the third day, I found a river that had not been scorched dry. I knew the water would be contaminated, but even radioactive water would help me walk further than no water at all.

For a few hours after that drink I had more energy, but by the time I arrived at a high point from where I could see the beautiful coast I was starting to sicken. I felt as if what little there was inside me wanted to come out. I sat for an hour to nurse my aching insides. I was on high ground, and could see clearly the scorched land that ran all the way to the blackened beach. The sea looked unchanged, as blue as I had remembered it, but the islands that were once so green were charred like the rest of the country.

Something was moving on the water. I wiped my eye to check that I wasn't imagining it. It was a ship, and it seemed to be heading closer to the shore. I was not the only survivor. Feeling strangely elated, I ignored my sickness and walked briskly down the hillside, covering the final few miles to the coast in less than an hour.

The relief and joy at seeing other humans were indescribable. Here, on the singed sand, were humans in varying states of illness, all hoping the ship they had spotted would come and take them away. Some were losing hair, some had lost areas of skin, and many were weakened by hunger and by vomiting blood. I ran my hands tentatively through my hair and realised that I too had lost much of it in the past days. Clumps of hair remained tangled in my fingers, having fallen out without any sensation of pain.

It was a sad scene, we pitiful remnants of a grand civilisation reduced to a helpless state on a hot, shadeless beach without food or water. We were all too weak to speak to one another, and there was nothing really about which to talk. Either this ship would rescue us and some of us might live, or we would all be dead by the following morning. No amount of talking would change that. Already I felt death surround me, but I hoped, when my final moment came, to welcome it with dignity.

SPHINX SCROLL # 10

I woke up in a dark room that was swaying. Tubes were connected to my arm and my stomach, and I could hear hushed voices close by.

'The eye injury predates the radiation,' I heard a woman saying in an Atlantan tongue. It was a language in which I was entirely fluent, having been involved in international political negotiations throughout my time as Leader. 'He's one of the stronger ones. It looks like he avoided the worst of the fallout.'

'Is he worth keeping?'

'We should get a couple of years out of him before he becomes too sick to be useful.'

'Right. That's another one accepted then.'

The woman came into my room alone.

'Are you awake yet?'

I groaned to let her know I was alive.

'Good. The rehydration seems to be doing the trick. Glad to have you on board.'

'Where am I?'

'I'm not sure where we are exactly. You were lucky, you know. Yours was the last batch of survivors we picked up. Unless we decide to dump any more non-viable patients in the sea there won't be any more stops until we find somewhere habitable, if there is anywhere left.'

I wanted to tell her my name, to declare my former importance – my leadership experience would be valuable to any community in a crisis situation – but I succumbed to apathy once again, content to wallow in easy anonymity. My degraded physical appearance and the widespread reporting of my public execution would doubtless have made prohibitively difficult the job of convincing anyone of my identity.

'How did you survive?' I simply enquired.

'We were in the South Atlantic on an expedition to collect living animal and botanical samples. This ship is full of specimens of edible plants, mating pairs of animals, insects, young trees, anything we find. We've got virtually every species you've ever heard of. It's a nightmare keeping them all happy down there. The purpose was to have sufficient variety of plant and animal stock that, whatever land Atlantans decided to colonise, we would have everything we needed to ensure sufficient biodiversity to keep everyone healthy. Of course, it's all irrelevant now. After this war there's no significant population to relocate. There's just us, and possibly other small groups like us, sailing around what remains of our world. We were on our way home. Now we have no home to go back to.'

'Everyone we knew is dead,' I said.

'Yes,' she replied, her eyes suddenly filling with a sadness that we would all come to take for granted. 'Our country was doomed by the shrinking of the polar regions and the melting of the ice, and then the bombs hit. If anyone tried to find any trace of Atlantis under the sea, they would find nothing at all. Our entire culture and history now only resides in the memories of a handful of survivors.' Her voice was becoming dry, but she seemed to benefit from talking. 'Even the people who underwent mummification in order to guarantee that our culture would have an influence thousands of years from now are all gone.'

'Same with Maya,' I remarked.

'Except one,' she said coldly.

'I saw the destruction for myself. Nothing could have survived it. The cemetery annexe was obliterated.'

'I refer to your Project Quetzalcoatl,' she said in a tone that was oddly accusatory. 'Do you know anything of it?'

'The Project Quetzalcoatl rocket contained a ballistic probe designed for deep space exploration,' I told her. 'It was fitted with a mummification tank. We were planning to send an astronaut on an elliptical loop that would return him to Earth in the distant future. The astronaut would be clean of all infections and diseases in order to avoid contaminating future populations with viruses to which they might have no immunity. The capsule was designed to be as basic as possible with no life support systems, no parts that could fail. Just a solid tomb that would follow a course determined by the relative gravitational pulls of the planets, ultimately falling back to Earth. The astronaut had to self-mummify before the oxygen expired. The trajectory was intended to return him to the Earth after twelve and a half thousand years. It was conceived as a cultural gift to our descendants, an opportunity to deliver to them someone who could enlighten them as to our way of life, our beliefs, our knowledge. Another Quetzalcoatl, in other words. We felt we had a duty to continue his example. We believed that a deep space entombment would be safe from earthquake and the other forms of natural and human destruction to which burials on Earth are vulnerable.'

She looked at me suspiciously.

'How come you know so much about Mayan rocketry?'

'I used to work in a governmental position,' I replied. 'Before Halford. I thought Project Quetzalcoatl was abandoned when he took over.'

'Oh no. Far from it,' she told me. 'Halford disappeared before the annihilation. He made a radio transmission before the bombs hit. We traced the source of the signal to a position two hundred miles above the Earth.'

I said nothing for a moment, and then suddenly I sat bolt upright and started hyperventilating. The woman checked my pulse and administered something with a needle, and soon had me calmed again.

'It's nothing physical,' I explained. 'It's just that you've made me realise something terrible. Are you saying Halford hijacked Project Quetzalcoatl?'

I recalled the rocket launch I had witnessed. I felt a deepening sickness at the realisation of who was on board. My former belief that Halford had died in Tikal with everyone else had been a small comfort for me. To learn of his survival was to lose what little hope remained for our dying planet.

'That is what I heard.'

'So precisely twelve and a half thousand years from now Halford is going to return to the Earth, not a day older, not cleared of infection, and still as psychotic and evil as he was in our time. He's going to return to a planet that has healed from the atomic explosions and is ripe for him to exploit and destroy again.'

'Yes, but it's not something we're going to have to worry about, is it?'

'What do you mean? These are our children we're

talking about. These are our descendants. If the species is going to survive at all, it's going to be our genes specifically that will make up the human race of the future. We can't let this man come back and destroy us again.'

'How can we warn our children? It's not as if we can put another mummified person into space to arrive before him. As far as I know, all space technology on Earth has been destroyed. The atomic pulse generator in this ship could be the only advanced engine left on the planet, and there's no way we could build a rocket out of these spare parts.'

I conceded, but I spent the remainder of the voyage mulling over the problem of how to send a message forward in time to those who would benefit from it.

With the enormous ship up above the waves on its hydrofoils, virtually flying, we crossed the Atlantic Ocean, in search of unspoiled lands, in just a few days. The coast of Africa loomed large on the horizon, but gave everyone immense disappointment when they realised that it too showed evidence of the mass destruction that had afflicted the world. The shoreline was scorched and bare, save for occasional unmoving human forms.

The Atlantans decided to move on northwards, following the coastline until they found land that was unaffected by the bombs and the fallout. As we travelled on this leg of the journey, I decided it was time to tell them who I was and to reveal to them the idea I had conceived for sending a warning into the future. The validity of my identity was taken less than seriously by most present, but I made them understand that in our current circumstances my identity was actually irrelevant. All that mattered now was our responsibility to future generations, my idea and its fulfilment.

I told them we must find a location that would support

us all, first and foremost. Supplies aboard the ship were limited, especially with all those animals to feed, and it was essential that we settle somewhere quickly. The animals must not be sacrificed for short-term gains, for they were vital to our future on the planet. When we had settled, our task would be to construct a time machine that would carry our message of warning into the distant future, from the Age of Leo to the Age of Aquarius, more than twelve thousand years from now. Given that there was no prospect of our small group being able to reproduce the achievements of Atlantis at its recent scientific height, our only option was to build a machine that travelled through time at the same rate as us.

I explained what I meant. We had to build something that would last more than twelve millennia. We had to build it with simple tools. We had to find some way of indicating when we had built it and of containing our story within it. Those criteria were accepted by all present, but no ideas came forward as to how it could all be achieved.

I took a tour of the lower decks of the ark. In an atmosphere of atrocious odours and noises, a team of men and women was working hard to care for the animals in captivity. In the small refrigerated deck at the very bottom there were penguins and large birds that I didn't recognise. On the next deck up were seed banks and endless rows of plants growing under artificial light. There were flowers, cereals, vegetables and fruit, and even the weeds seemed to be cherished. The dung from the animals elsewhere in the boat was being used to fertilise these plants. On the next deck I was met with the astonishing sight of hundreds of cages containing wild and domesticated animals of all varieties. The cacophony deafened me as I strolled nervously amongst the snakes, llamas, giraffes, pigs and other species, but it was the lions that caught my attention. Lying in her cage was a lioness, staring with great dignity out through the bars. I looked at her form, marvelling at her majesty. This was Halford's symbol.

The shoreline curved eastwards until we passed through a narrow entrance to the enclosed sea to the north of Africa. Briefly there was land to the north and to the south of us, all of it dead and uninhabitable, and then we passed through into more open waters. The land on our right started to look less damaged now. The colour of the sand became more yellow, and although the land was bereft of life it was not scorched, just natural bedrock. And it was this bedrock and the form of the lioness that provided the answer.

I only hope that, as we build it and as I write these final words, you will have found these scrolls before it is too late. Halford is a dangerous, evil man who has technological knowledge at a level which mankind may not re-attain before his return. He may therefore be able to rule you, control you, subjugate you in the cruellest fashion. And you, my descendants, my children, must do everything in your power to prepare for his return.

I am slowly dying of the radiation sickness. I have no hair and my skin bleeds spontaneously. It is a horrible life – if indeed it can be called a life – and many of us are similarly afflicted, but between us we have found enough strength to build this Sphinx from the bedrock and to place within it our message to the future. Some of our people will now attempt to return to our homeland across the ocean, where they will build an identical Sphinx to contain another set of these writings. I hope for their sakes that the land has healed enough to be able to support them. I hope they will succeed in rebuilding the Mayan culture that was once so great, and I pray that they will be diligent in keeping their vow to measure the days, months, years and millennia until Halford's return.

She put the pages down on the kitchen table amid the four empty breakfast plates and listened. The windows still rattled with every gust of frozen air. The water still gurgled sedately through the antique heating system. The contented snoring continued unashamedly. Ratty gave Matt a jab that seemed sufficiently forceful to be a retaliatory gesture. The American opened his eyes and yawned, expecting to find Ruby staring at him impatiently, but she was looking outside, into the snow.

'Any sign of him?' Matt asked, now stretching his arms into the air.

She returned her attention to her friends, searching for a sign, hoping a spark of inspiration would show in their eyes. There was nothing to give her any hope, however.

'The scrolls simply represent the truth that any civilisation will rise and fall,' said the Patient when it was clear to him that no one else had anything to say. 'It has happened before and will keep happening in the future. Man's capacity for evil and destruction is his Achilles heel. It will always trip him up in the end, and sometimes it will take millennia for him to find his feet again. It does not matter if Halford returns to us. We have enough bad people already. The same weapons that destroyed the ancient world have been reinvented. Sadly, it is merely a matter of time before one of us is forced to write our own scrolls as a warning to our descendants.'

'So you think this Halford guy's a no-show, huh?' said Matt.

Ruby turned to see a desperate snow-covered fist battering the window pane from outside, rattling the glass. She leapt back from the window with a shriek, falling into Ratty's arms. Matt growled, recognising Charlie's chubby frozen features. Another fist was raised to the window, this one clutching a sorry-looking white cardboard box that wilted under the weight of its topping of snow.

'Doughnuts!' came Charlie's muffled voice.

Ratty opened a door just enough to address the portly stranger.

'Much as I appreciate your Shackletonesque perseverance, and whilst I cannot deny a degree of esurience in the gastric department,' he explained, 'I thought I'd made it clear to the master *Boulanger* that he must halt all deliveries of victuals pending the resolution of my fiscal –'

'Rula! Matt!' called Charlie, pushing the door fully open and squeezing past a confused aristocrat. 'Great to see you guys. Hey, what was the French dude trying to say?'

'French?' echoed Ratty in horror. 'Are you not cognisant with our mother tongue?'

Charlie shrugged his shoulders, blinking to prevent his eyes from glazing over.

'Er, Ratty, this is Charlie,' said Matt. 'He kinda helped me out in Guatemala. Charlie, this is Ratty. Lord Ballashiels.'

'A French Lord, huh? Coolsville Shropshire!'

'How do you do?' said Ratty, holding out his hand to Charlie. The lad stuck a sugary doughnut in it. 'Gosh, most kind,' he continued, placing the doughnut immediately on the kitchen table and wiping his hands with a tea towel. 'It appears you already know Doctor Towers and Mister Mountebank, and that just leaves me to introduce to you this fellow, er, gosh, I forgot to ask if you'd chosen a name for yourself yet.'

The Patient shook his head.

'Charles, please allow me the pleasure to introduce a Mister Patient.'

'How's it hanging, dude?'

Years of clandestine study in Otto's extensive personal library had not equipped the Patient with the means to answer such a question. He correctly deduced, however, that Charlie had no desire to listen to a reply.

'I came to show Matt the new love wagon. Bought it in London at the start of my European tour. Wanted to thank him for keeping his word. It's out front. Wanna see?'

Stiff, cold legs shuffled along several corridors and hallways to the front door. Ruby's frustration at this unexpected interruption to their planned discussion of the meaning of the scrolls was tempered by Charlie's infectious cheerfulness. The others all seemed glad of the distraction from the imminent destruction of their planet by a mummified tyrant. They pulled on boots and grabbed heavy winter coats and hats that hung from a rack above an umbrella stand made from the foot of an unfortunate elephant.

'Someone should tell the French guy his doorbell's busted,' Charlie shouted above the icy wind that whipped around them when Ratty pulled open the oak front door. 'I was ringing for, like, ever, and no one came. Same with some delivery dude. He quit and got me to sign for this crate. Anyone order something off eBay lately?'

It was a cube, roughly six feet on each axis, made from unplaned planks of softwood nailed together and reinforced at the corners. Snow was already starting to settle upon its roof, but its contents appeared to be protected by a layer of heavy plastic sheeting that protruded here and there between the planks. Ratty inspected the documentation stapled to it. Country of origin: Guatemala. He grinned.

Behind the crate was parked a long wheelbase high-top Volkswagen campervan. No rusting panels or crudely-painted motifs on this one. No fading echoes of the swinging sixties and free love culture. This was a new van. Immaculate. Sensible. Grown-up.

'You bought this with my money, huh?' asked Matt. 'Sweet. Shame you won't get far before Halford comes and vaporises us.'

Ratty crunched through the snow to a barn at the side of the house, and returned with a hammer and a crowbar. He set to work dismantling the crate while the others were engrossed in inspecting the finer points of the campervan's interior.

'Very posh,' declared Ruby.

'Am I to deduce that you have chosen this device for your habitation, and have done so of your own volition?' asked the Patient. 'I too was once imprisoned in a vehicle such as this. It was the best of times and the worst of times. Do you not find it inconvenient?'

'Bathroom's at the back,' replied Charlie. 'Easy to find.'

As they exited the van at the completion of the tour, they found Ratty engrossed in a struggle to prise open the front of the crate. With grudging assistance from Matt, the final nail slid out with a loud squeak. The panel fell onto the snow. Ratty tore away the plastic sheeting with his hands and stood back in admiration.

He had seen it before. A symphony in stone. A sculpture in white marble with a teasing smile and a sparkle in the eyes. A face from an ancient time, preserved for eternity by the chisel of a long-forgotten mason. But it was a face that was always in his head, guiding him, castigating him, confusing him, yet never loving him even though he loved her.

And it would become the ultimate suitor's gift to his paramour. It would end the uncertainty. This miracle of history, this profound impossibility, this accurate portrayal of the face of Ruby Towers that had been buried beneath a Caracol pyramid for millennia, would finally win Ratty the affection he craved.

Or so his naïve thought processes led him to believe. When he explained the origin of the piece the tirade of bitter fury that subsequently flew from Ruby's mouth almost knocked him backwards. The Patient found himself instinctively protecting his friend by standing between the crazed female and the target of her vitriol.

'An angry woman is again angry with herself when she returns to reason,' the Patient pointed out.

'Well quite,' said Ratty. 'Although I believe Publilius Syrus also remarked that one should make a woman angry if one wishes her to love.'

'Is that what this is about?' screeched Ruby. 'If you wanted to make me angry you could have told me my arse was too big or made one of your stupid remarks about the deficiencies you perceive in the lower social classes. But that would have been too easy. So instead you've raped the cultural heritage of the Maya for a token of love. This isn't the nineteenth century any more. You're not great-great-great Uncle Bilbo.'

'Great-great,' corrected Ratty, almost immediately wishing he hadn't.

'That's no Mayan face,' chipped in Charlie. 'I liberated a few antiquities myself, and they sure never looked like Ruthy.'

'Keep out of this, Charlie,' Ruby hissed.

'It's obviously you,' he persisted. 'Look at it. That's your face. Although you don't have a crack on your cheek.'

Ratty called on the might of his gentlemanly powers in order to resist the temptation of pointing out that such a scar could be arranged if she neglected to calm down.

'This stone is nothing like me,' she continued to rant without actually looking closely at it. 'There is no rational way in which it can be me.'

419

'Perhaps not,' said Matt, jerking his head back and forth between the artefact and Ruby as if watching a tennis match. 'But it sure is you, hun.'

'Rubbish!'

'Sure, maybe it doesn't look like you *now*,' said Charlie, 'but that's because your face is, like, all screwed up in anger.'

'It is not!' she retorted furiously.

'The serenity captured by the stonemason depicts Ruby as she might look when her rage has dissipated,' said Ratty. 'Such a state may be hard to imagine, but perhaps it exists during her periods of somnolence.'

'Let's assume that this priceless artefact that you've looted does resemble me in some way,' grumbled Ruby. 'And if it only looks like me when I'm not cross then you may never really know, because right now you've wound me up enough to last a lifetime, though a lifetime may not be very long in the present circumstances. But there is no significance to it. A one-off chance resemblance means nothing.'

'You are logically correct in your observance, Ruby, whilst being simultaneously incorrect from a factual standpoint,' said the Patient.

'Did you have something to do with this crime?' she sighed.

'If any crime has been committed, it was the fault of my brother who sent his soldiers into Belize without the permission of the Belizean authorities. Those men returned with hundreds of items found within the temples of that land, including this face. And dozens more. All identical.'

'I didn't steal it, Ruby. I found it with my scanning thingy on my way to Tikal, and when I learned that it had subsequently been taken to Guatemala along with a multitude of Ruby Towers clones in stone, I asked Mister

420

Patient chappy if he could persuade his sibling to let me bring one here. In any case, they're not going back into their pyramids, they're going to museums around the world.'

'So, there was, like, an ancient cult of Ruby Towers, huh?' wobbled Charlie. 'What happened? One of your documentary episodes get beamed back in time or something?'

'Don't be stupid, Charlie. Of course not. Some long-forgotten queen or goddess must have looked a bit like me, that's all there is to it.'

'Again, you speak with logic that is indisputable, but with authority that is questionable,' stated the Patient. 'Did you ever truly know the reason why you were so important to my brother?'

'He told me it was because I'm an expert. I have a high profile. He needed my reputation and public persona as a front for his, for his … no, it never really stacked up. He could never make a properly coherent case for needing me close to him. To be honest, I just thought he fancied me.'

'He never told you about the stone face he found before he became President? And he never explained about the legend of the ruby and the towers? Without such knowledge your incarceration must have been as puzzling as was my own.'

'He did let on about the ruby tower. Pretty weak link, in my opinion.'

'What about the ruby tower?' Ratty asked, intrigued.

'It is all in the stelae, the acquisition of which obsessed my father,' explained the Patient. 'There is a carving on them that once contained red pigment, and another showing castle ramparts. A ruby. A tower. Orlando understood its meaning, and when he saw the ancient stone impression of your face he was convinced that he needed you. He didn't know why; he just knew you were a vital part of the puzzle. And on top of all those coincidences, there was the lost Aristotle text. Well, not strictly lost, since it was found by Josef Mengele among hoards of artworks and priceless books looted by the Nazi thugs with whom he used to associate.'

'A lost Aristotle text?' repeated Ruby. 'Now that I'd like to see.'

'I assume you are fluent in classical Greek?'

'Enough to order a glass of ouzo, but that's about it,' she replied.

'The text now resides at the palace with Orlando, but I memorised it during my subterranean years when it was part of Otto's collection. If you will permit me to paraphrase, it is a treatise that concerns the past and the future of the world. It begins with a retelling of Plato's myth of Atlantis, but it has subtle differences in its description. More significantly, Plato's story ended too soon. It failed to mention the return of the most evil man from the antediluvian civilisation. Aristotle told the whole story. He described the prophesied reappearance and what must be done to prepare for and understand the threat posed by Halford. Aristotle laid out the steps that needed to be taken, and wrote that he who controlled the ruby and the towers would control the world. Being in possession of the ruby and the towers enabled a conquest not just of the past, but of the future.'

'None of what you've said answers the very obvious questions. Why me, and if me, how the hell could my presence on this planet and my name and my face have been known thousands of years ago? There is no logical way to resolve that.'

'Piece of cake,' said Charlie. 'It's obvious. Someone's going to invent a time machine and send Ruby back to

Halford's day. Maybe Matt ordered you a DeLorean for Christmas.'

'Backwards linear time travel is impossible,' said Ruby. 'If it existed, we'd surely have seen visitors from the future. Even if traversable wormholes could be constructed, we could only return to the time they were built. If you build a road, you can only travel on it to the points you started and ended it. If I went back in time by any other means, which I couldn't because it's not possible, I'd enter a parallel universe, so it wouldn't affect this reality.'

'By that logic,' wheezed Charlie, 'it's possible that a clone of you from another universe went back in time to this universe, which is why all the ancients worship you and you didn't know a thing about it.'

'Logic follows many paths. Only one leads to the truth,' said the Patient. 'The existence of ancient faces in your likeness is indisputable. The writings of Aristotle using words that are similar to your name is also a fact. The reason for these phenomena is a matter of conjecture. There are logical routes we can explore. There is the possibility of an elaborate coincidence. Some philosophers believe in the circular nature of time. There is a tribe in Papua New Guinea that is convinced the cycle of time is not circular but shaped like a banana. If Aristotle was conscious of an inherited genetic memory that gave him the knowledge to write about the past and the future, perhaps that genetic memory has somehow come full circle – or banana – from now back to the beginnings of life on this planet. Many possibilities, but without more knowledge we cannot conclude any of them is correct.'

'What would life be without a queer mystery or two? We don't know if Halford really will manage to return to Earth. We don't know why Ruby seems to have been a goddess, and I still have no inkling as to why the shadowy new owner of this old house of mine refuses to accept rent.'

'Halford's gonna show. For sure,' chirped Charlie.

'How would you know about that?' asked Ruby.

'Because it would be so coolsville if he did.'

'But he's been mummified,' she said. 'The chances of him emerging alive from all that goo are minimal.'

'Not really,' said Charlie. 'That mummifying stuff works. He looks like shit, and his skin looks like a zombie and he stinks like a rotting raccoon, but he's alive.'

'Halford?' asked Ruby.

'Huh? No, I'm talking about Brad. They thought he was dead, but they got him back. The experiment worked. Kinda. So Halford could show. No mystery there.'

When the relief at the news of Brad's survival started showing in her expression, her features softened and she began more closely to resemble the serenity of the weighty stone head. But then that piece of information slotted into the others whirling around inside her. The legend of Halford really could be true. She had witnessed their technology, so launching a rocket on a twelve thousand year return trajectory was not impossible. And if mummification could be reversed, then the threat was real.

'I know it's not much warmer inside, Ratty, but I think we should get back in before we all turn to stone,' she said, leading the frozen group into the house. Ratty directed everyone to the library where a devilish fire welcomed them into its hypnotic sphere. Ruby jogged to the kitchen and back to retrieve her copy of the scrolls, determined not to let the subject drop. The mystery of Ratty's new landlord, however, had subsumed everyone's attention upon her return.

'I don't get it. What kinda schmuck spends their hard-earned dough on a place like this without looking for a profit?' said Matt.

'Not all money is hard to earn,' said the Patient. 'It could be argued that the royalties which you used to pay for Charlie's vehicle, in return for him smuggling you to Belize, were not hard-earned. They flow like water, above and beyond that which you yourself admitted would have been sufficient remittance for your literary efforts.'

'So what?' asked Matt, unimpressed at being compared to the idiot who paid for Stiperstones Manor.

'An unfair comparison, perhaps,' admitted the Patient. 'The vehicle was a gift, a compensatory gesture. Let us consider another scenario. Could it be that whoever now owns this house cannot legally receive rent?'

'Like if he's a crook? Or a kid? Or a dog?' asked Charlie.

'It may surprise you to know that there are examples in history of rent being paid to all such types as you mention. Try thinking about it from a logical stance.'

'Logically you can't charge rent to yourself if you're the owner,' sighed Ruby. 'Whoever paid for the manor could have registered it in Ratty's name. An extravagant gesture of altruism, which I hardly believe can have been possible. Now perhaps we can talk about the scrolls? If Brad's alive then there's nothing about the Halford story that can't come true. It's far more important than whether Ratty owes rent.'

'Ruby is correct,' said the Patient. 'The rent mystery is solved. Let us continue our deliberations about Halford.'

Ratty's eyes danced excitedly around the room, not knowing where to focus. Impossibly wonderful thoughts were filling his head. The Patient watched him calmly from the leather Chesterfield. Finally, the restless aristocratic eyes settled upon the Patient. Ratty fell forward from his chair onto his knees and crawled across the parquet floor to the feet of the Patient. He knelt there, head bowed as if receiving a knighthood from his monarch. The Patient held out a hand. Ratty kissed it. He understood. He was humbled by gratitude.

Charlie and Matt looked at each other. Matt shrugged. Charlie mimed a limp wrist. Ruby pointed a stern finger at him.

'Right, moving on, does anyone have anything else to say about the scrolls? Any sparks of inspiration?' asked Ruby, ignoring Ratty who was busy kissing his floor, his books and his furniture.

'I thought they said we're all going to die,' said Charlie. 'Brad said that whether or not we see Halford again, we're all doomed unless the world learns the lessons from the past.'

'Brad told you that?' asked Ruby.

'Well, from a distance. I couldn't get too close without a peg on my nose.'

'The lessons from the past are in the scrolls,' sighed Ruby. 'That's what we're trying to understand. So let's work it through. Halford lands on Earth tomorrow, right?'

'After twelve thousand years in space?' asked Matt. 'The capsule's gonna be a block of ice. Nothing will work. No parachutes. No retro-rockets. Bang! He smashes into a million pieces.'

'If you had paid attention,' said the Patient, 'you would know that the spacecraft was designed not to need any active systems. Mathematics and gravity will return it to this planet. Logic suggests it will land in an ocean in order to minimise the stresses on the vehicle.'

'It's still going to break up when it hits the sea,' said Matt.

'Perhaps,' suggested the Patient, 'that is the intention. A body that is essentially dead, sealed in a protective casket, can withstand far greater gravitational loading and impact shock than a live person. The breakup of the capsule would be a failsafe way to release the casket containing the body.'

'So what stops the sticky fellow from drowning?' asked Ratty.

'Sea water,' said Charlie.

Matt laughed as loudly as Ruby growled.

'Everyone, we have to take this seriously,' she said. 'If you can't make a sensible contribution to the discussion, Charlie, keep out of it.'

'I believe he is serious,' said the Patient. 'Sea water contains the dissolved nutrients, gases and salts needed to create life. Our biology began in that environment. Is it therefore unreasonable to consider that sea water might trigger reanimation following the mummification process?'

'I, er, don't know,' said Ruby.

'I mummified my father, just as he mummified his own father, but Otto was obsessed with perfecting the process of reversal. He was preparing to reanimate Josef Mengele now that medical science is capable of treating the illness that killed him, but his attempts to bring back prisoners from mummified stasis were not always successful. The ancient texts from which he took his instructions described a fluid containing sodium, magnesium, sulphur, calcium, potassium, bromine, chloride, hydrogen and oxygen. He spent years trying to perfect the mix. I suspect raw sea water was the answer. And if Halford's casket is designed to float, then there is no impediment to Halford's reanimation, even without external assistance.'

'So the guy lands in the sea,' said Matt. 'Floats in his coffin until the water wakes him up. Paddles ashore. Then what? Starts killing everyone? With what?'

'Alone, only his germs are potentially deadly,' said the

Patient. 'But ours are equally dangerous to him. Without medical supervision he may succumb to a virus and die before he has a chance to harm anyone.'

'Or he may trigger a pandemic,' said Ruby.

'And what if he gets control of an army?' asked Matt.

'If my father had maintained his mind control over my brother, they would have been ready to receive Halford. They would have kept him in isolation, protected from infection, and used his knowledge as the missing link needed to reproduce all of the ancient technologies and create a state with military capability beyond anything the present world has seen. But that won't happen now. If Halford shows up, I don't think he can be a credible threat to the world without Orlando's help.'

'So why the big hullabaloo in the scrolls about preparing for his second coming?' asked Ratty.

'Good question. Let's work it out. The scrolls were written when society had crashed back to the Stone Age,' said Ruby. 'So if Halford returned before civilisation rebuilt its technologies, then he would have had the upper hand, being the only human on the planet with the knowledge to create advanced weaponry.'

'Sure!' said Matt, suddenly realising that there would be a tomorrow. 'That was the danger. It makes sense. But we beat him to it!'

'Exactly,' added Ruby. 'There's nothing he could achieve now without a sympathetic dictator at his side, and with Orlando no longer under Otto's influence, he's going to struggle to find one.' She smiled and exhaled slowly, contentedly. They had cracked it. Halford could be no immediate threat to a civilisation that had already achieved technological advancement.

'So would you say that by shooting Orlando and making the Patient guy take Otto's liver, I kinda saved the world?' asked Matt.

'Matt, I think we all played a part,' said Ruby.

'My friends,' said the Patient, 'it is time I explained to you a little more of what I have recently learned. My brother was fooled by our father. Orlando intended to use the ancient technical knowledge that Halford would provide to make his country powerful, but he did not know of Halford's evil ways. Otto edited his translation of the Sphinx scrolls so that Orlando had no knowledge that he would be entering into a deal with the devil. Otto's blinkered determination to fulfil Josef Mengele's dream of global oppression would have been disastrous for us all, but Otto's absence in the final days before Tikal's destruction weakened his control over Orlando for the first time. Orlando began to think for himself. After I saved his life I told him of the true contents of the scrolls. Halford remains a danger if any other nation is naïve enough to attempt to exploit him, but Orlando is planning to ensure that will not happen.'

'How's he going to stop the rest of the world getting hold of Halford when he lands?' asked Ruby. 'NASA and ESA will be scanning the skies looking for him. A small country like Guatemala won't have the resources to be the first to locate the rocket.'

'Otto and Orlando had this planned for months; they had astronomers and recovery ships on standby. But that was before other nations knew what was happening, so Orlando has established a new contact at the front line. She will inform my brother when the time comes. And my brother has a special reception planned for Halford if he gets to him first.'

'What's he gonna do?' asked Matt.

'There is a small chamber within the Sphinx we found in Temple IV,' said the Patient. 'Before Halford can be reanimated, he will be placed within the Sphinx. It will be sealed. And no one need fear Halford again. The transition from the end of the Mayan calendar to the next era will pass peacefully.'

'I propose a drink, then,' said Ruby. 'Let's toast the end of this *baktun*, and the start of the next.'

Ratty nodded his approval and headed off to the wine cellar.

'Guys, what if the date is wrong?' whispered Charlie, hoping not to be shouted down. 'I mean, what if his capsule has already landed?'

'Huh?' asked Matt.

'Halford might have crashed in Roswell. Nineteen forty-seven. He's already here. Might have teamed up with the President and developed those cold war nuclear weapons. Or maybe he became President. Changed his name to Kennedy or something. When someone found out they had to kill him.'

'That is the daftest conspiracy theory I've ever heard,' said Ruby. 'But it doesn't matter, Charlie. I really don't think there's a threat now, so you can waste time saying whatever rubbish you like.'

'But what about the connection with your name, Rubes?' asked Matt. 'If Halford arrives and Orlando doesn't get to him, he's gonna come looking for you. Halford's gonna think you're the key to controlling the world.'

'You know what, Matt? Perhaps I am the key to ruling the world. Why not? I'm sure I can do a better job of it than some!'

They laughed away the tension of the previous days. Ratty returned from the cellar holding a bottle of expensive wine. He looked at the cheerful faces assembled in his library and suddenly dropped the bottle on the parquet floor, glass fragments and Grand Cru spraying over the legs of his friends. He showed no reaction to the exploding Saint-Émilion, but just spread

430

his lips wide and mouthed several silent words before remembering to speak aloud.

'Scrolls. Warning. One almost forgot. Eggs. Descendants.'

The burbling gibberish extinguished any sign that an intelligent revelation was coming. It was just Ratty being Ratty, Ruby decided.

'Scrolls,' he repeated, pacing crunchily back and forth across the stained parquetry. 'Forgot to mention that I found some. Well, not as such. Not scrolls, I mean. I did find them, but they were pages bound in a book. A notebook. A diary.'

'Another of Bilbo's?' Ruby asked.

'Good Lordy, no. Different chap this time. Actually more of a chappess, if you catch my drift. Lady Doodah. Friends with everyone. Mitfords. Mosley. Dali. Wrote a lot of shopping lists, mainly – eggs and wotnot, don't you know – but she had things to say about this and that. Said she found something queer. Locked it up again and threw away the key. Forbade any of the Ballashiels clan ever to open the door again. Wrote a sort of a warning for the descendants, you see, in amongst the reminders to feed the horses and whip the servants. Probably nothing. Shouldn't have mentioned it, really.'

He looked down at the wine on his floor.

'Tea, anyone?'

SATURDAY 22ND DECEMBER 2012

Monika returned to the desk, placed the steaming coffee down carefully, checked her seat had not been tampered with, looked around for anything that appeared to be out of the ordinary and sat down. It was a routine for her now. A defensive habit. She had learned to live with Rocco's eccentricities. His games no longer possessed the power to aggravate her. She almost felt a kind of fondness for him. Working next to him was like watching a pet dog playing with a toy. Sometimes she even thought she could feel the beginnings of a smile cracking the sides of her face when she thought about him.

She viewed his conspiracy theories with a little more respect these days. The diligent research that had resulted in finding the identity of her father showed that there was some substance to Rocco, even if she hadn't been comfortable with the result he had obtained. Gerhard. He had graduated in 1977 and practised as a doctor in London for two years before relocating to Guatemala. Dr Otto Gerhard had been using the pseudonym that his adoptive father had chosen after the war, but when his father died he had reverted to the true family name: Mengele. Monika felt a chill run through her whenever she thought of it. Despite her misgivings she had wanted to write a letter to her father to introduce herself, but Rocco had discovered that Otto's address no longer existed, his home having sunk into the ground. The trail would have ended there, were it not for the publicity surrounding the new President of Guatemala who was rumoured to have had a close relationship with Otto. Rocco continued to dig for information, and finally presented Monika with the staggering revelation that President Orlando was her half-brother. She was grateful to Rocco, and had even managed to force herself to display her gratitude with a hug.

The shift they'd shared the previous day was unlike any other, however. His playfulness was gone. He barely spoke. An Internet news channel was playing constantly, reporting the events taking place around the globe to mark the end of the Mayan calendar, and he watched it obsessively. Occasionally he would mumble about some or other cover-up, but he appeared genuinely in fear for his life, as if an asteroid were about to come crashing down upon the planet. Which was exactly the kind of thing he need not fear, since he was part of the team tracking the heavens for just such an eventuality. Today his mood had lifted, though, and he was almost back to his normal insufferable self.

Monika sipped her coffee and looked at her screen. As usual, in the five minutes she had spent away from her desk Rocco had programmed the computer to spin the massive radar away from where it was supposed to point in order to check out his latest conspiracy theory.

'What is it this time?' she asked. 'Checking to see if the moon is really a giant potato?'

'I'm trying to get a lock on a Chinese communications satellite. It looks like it's out of alignment.'

'So it's died. Big deal.'

'No, a very, very big deal. There's still power left to re-align it, but no one is doing it. A billion-dollar machine and no one's looking after it. Why? Because there's no one to look after it.'

'You're not still on about the Chinese scientists getting sick?'

'They're keeping things hushed up, and no one knows how bad it is, but if you look in the right places you can see the effects of a community that's in trouble.'

Monika gritted her teeth and punched in the correct co-ordinates for directing the radar. Perhaps Rocco had a point. There was a kind of logic in his theory, but a satellite's misalignment could remain uncorrected for any number of reasons. Slowly her monitor started to fill with the celestial objects she was actually being paid to track. One by one, the computer compared the items it was seeing to a database of what it expected to see. Red blips turned to green as it identified the objects. The algorithms in the software were complex, elegant creations that could predict the orbit of a speck of dust, taking into account the gravitational pull of the Earth, the moon, the sun and the surrounding satellites. To Monika these algorithms were like poetry. The poetry of motion. And they were astonishingly accurate.

There was still a red blip on the screen. She looked closely, waiting for the algorithms to turn it green. It was not on an orbital trajectory according to the tracking data; its path would shortly bring it into the Earth's atmosphere. Five metres in diameter, announced the screen. Someone must have spotted it before. The computer would match it soon enough. The red would turn green.

She waited.

It stayed red.

She picked up the phone and dialled her brother.

Stewart Ferris
THE BALLASHIELS MYSTERIES

Don't miss the exciting continuation of the Ballashiels
Mysteries in ...

Book Two: The Dali Diaries

and

Book Three: The Chaplin Conspiracy

JODI TAYLOR
JUST ONE DAMNED THING AFTER ANOTHER

Behind the seemingly innocuous façade of St Mary's, a different kind of historical research is taking place. They don't do 'time-travel' - they 'investigate major historical events in contemporary time'. Maintaining the appearance of harmless eccentrics is not always within their power - especially given their propensity for causing loud explosions when things get too quiet.

Meet the disaster-magnets of St Mary's Institute of Historical Research as they ricochet around History. Their aim is to observe and document - to try and find the answers to many of History's unanswered questions...and not to die in the process.

But one wrong move and History will fight back - to the death. And, as they soon discover - it's not just History they're fighting.

For more information about **Stewart Ferris**

and other **Accent Press** titles

please visit

www.accentpress.co.uk